ERICA SPINDLER

IN SILENCE

MIRA® BOOKS

MIRA is a registered trademark of Harlequin Enterprises Limited,
used under licence.

First published in Great Britain 2003.
MIRA Books, Eton House, 18-24 Paradise Road,
Richmond, Surrey, TW9 1SR

ISBN 0 7783 2037 5

58-0803

Printed and bound in Spain
by Litografía Rosés S.A., Barcelona

"The cruellest lies are often told in silence."
—Robert Louis Stevenson

Friday 23 April 2004

PROLOGUE

Cypress Springs, Louisiana
Thursday, October 17, 2002
3:30 a.m.

The one called the Gavel *waited* patiently. The woman would come soon, he knew. He had been watching her. Learning her schedule, her habits. Those of her neighbors as well.

Tonight she would learn the price of moral corruption.

He moved his gaze over the woman's darkened bedroom. Garments strewn across the matted carpeting. Dresser top littered with an assortment of cosmetic bottles and jars, empty Diet Coke and Miller Lite cans, gum and candy wrappers. Cigarette butts spilled from an overflowing ashtray.

A pig as well as a whore.

Twin feelings of resignation and disgust flowed over him. Had he expected anything different from a woman like her? An alley cat who bedded a new man nearly every night?

He was neither prude nor saint. Nor was he naive. These days few waited for marriage to consummate their relationship. He could live with that; he understood physical urges.

But excesses such as hers would not be tolerated in Cypress Springs. The Seven had voted. It had been unanimous. As their leader, it was his responsibility to make her understand.

The Gavel glanced at the bedside clock. He had been waiting nearly an hour. It wouldn't be long now. Tonight she had gone to CJ's, a bar on the west side of town, one frequented by the hard-partying crowd. She had left with a man named DuBroc. As was her MO, they had gone to his place. To the Gavel's knowledge, this was a first offense for DuBroc. He would be watched as well. And if necessary, warned.

From the front of the apartment came the sound of the door lock turning over. The door opening, then clicking shut. A shudder moved over him. Of distaste for the inevitable. He wasn't a predator, as some might label him. Predators sought the small and weak, either to sustain themselves or for twisted self-gratification.

Nor was he a bloodthirsty monster or sadist.

He was an honorable man. God-fearing, law-abiding. A patriot.

But as were the other members of The Seven, he was a man driven to desperate measures. To protect and defend all he held dear.

Women like this one soiled the community, they contributed to the moral decay running rampant in the world.

They were not alone, of course. Those who drank to excess, those who lied, cheated, stole; those who broke not only the laws of man but those of God as well.

The Seven had formed to combat such corruptions. For the Gavel and his six generals, it wasn't about punishing the sinful but about maintaining a way of life. A way of life Cypress Springs had enjoyed for over a hundred years. A community where people could still walk the streets at night, where neighbor helped neighbor, where family values were more than a phrase tossed about by political candidates.

Honesty. Integrity. The Golden Rule. All were alive and well in Cypress Springs. The Seven had dedicated themselves to ensuring it stayed that way.

The Gavel likened individual immorality to the flesh-eating bacteria that had been in the news so much a few years back. A fisherman had contracted necrotizing fasciitis through a small cut on his hand. Once introduced to the body, it ate its covering until only a putrid, grotesque patchwork remained. So, too, was the effect of individual immorality on a community. His job was to make certain that didn't happen.

The Gavel listened intently. The woman hummed under her breath as she made her way toward the back of the apartment and the bedroom where he waited. The self-satisfied sound sickened him.

He eased to his feet, moved toward the door. She stepped through. He grabbed her from behind, dragged her to his chest and covered her mouth with one gloved hand to stifle her screams. She smelled of cheap perfume, cigarettes. Sex.

"Elaine St. Claire," he said against her ear, voice muffled by the ski mask he wore. "You have been judged and found guilty. Of contributing to the moral decay of this community. Of attempting to cause the ruination of a way of life that has existed for over a century. You must pay the price."

He forced her to the bed. She struggled against him, her attempts pitiable. A mouse battling a mountain lion.

He knew what she thought—that he meant to rape her. He would sooner castrate himself than to join with a woman such as her. Besides, what kind of punishment would that be? What kind of warning?

No, he had something much more memorable in mind for her.

He stopped a foot from the bed. With the hand covering

her mouth, he forced her gaze down. To the mattress. And the gift he had made just for her.

He had fashioned the instrument out of a baseball bat, one of the miniature, commemorative ones fans bought in stadium gift shops. He had covered the bat with flattened tin cans—choosing Diet Coke, her soft drink of choice—peeling back V-shaped pieces of the metal to form a kind of sharp, scaly skin. The trickiest part had been the double-edged knife blade he had imbedded in the bat's rounded tip.

He was aware of the exact moment she saw it. She stilled. Terror rippled over her—a new fear, one born from the horror of the unimaginable.

"For you, Elaine," he whispered against her ear. "Since you love to fuck so much, your punishment will be to give you what you love."

She recoiled and pressed herself against him. Her response pleased him and he smiled, the black ski mask stretching across his mouth with the movement.

He could almost pity her. Almost but not quite. She had brought this fate upon herself.

"I designed it to open you from cervix to throat," he continued, then lowered his voice. "From the *inside*, Elaine. It will be an excruciating way to die. Organs torn to shreds from within. Massive bleeding will lead to shock. Then coma. And finally, death. Of course, by that point you will pray for death to take you."

She made a sound, high and terrified. Trapped.

"Do you think it would be possible to be fucked to death, Elaine? Is that how you'd like to die?"

She fought as he inched her closer. "Imagine what it will feel like inside you, Elaine. To feel your insides being ripped to shreds, the pain, the helplessness. Knowing you're going to die, wishing for death to come swiftly."

He pressed his mouth closer to her ear. "But it won't. Perhaps, mercifully, you'll lose consciousness. Perhaps not. I could keep you alert, there are ways, you know. You'll beg for mercy, pray for a miracle. No miracle will come. No hero rushing in to save the day. No one to hear your screams."

She trembled so violently he had to hold her erect. Tears streamed down her cheeks.

"This will be your only warning," he continued. "Leave Cypress Springs immediately. Quietly. Tell no one. Not your friends, your employer or landlord. If you speak to anyone, you'll be killed. The police cannot help you, do not contact them. If you do, you'll be killed. If you stay, you'll be killed. Your death will be horrible, I promise you that."

He released her and she crumpled into a heap on the floor. He stared down at her shaking form. "There are many of us and we are always watching. Do you understand, Elaine St. Claire?"

She didn't answer and he bent, grabbed a handful of her hair and yanked her face up toward his. "Do you understand?"

"Y-yes," she whispered. "Anythi...I'll do...anything."

A small smile twisted his lips. *His generals would be pleased.*

He released her. "Smart girl, Elaine. Don't forget this warning. You're now the master of your own fate."

The Gavel retrieved the weapon and walked away. As he let himself out, the sound of her sobs echoed through the apartment.

CHAPTER 1

Cypress Springs, Louisiana
Wednesday, March 5, 2003
2:30 p.m.

Avery Chauvin drew her rented SUV to a stop in front of Rauche's Dry Goods store and stepped out. A humid breeze stirred against her damp neck and ruffled her short dark hair as she surveyed Main Street. Rauche's still occupied this coveted corner of Main and First Streets, the Azalea Café still screamed for a coat of paint, Parish Bank hadn't been swallowed by one of the huge banking conglomerates and the town square these establishments all circled was as shady and lovely as ever, the gazebo at its center a startlingly bright white.

Her absence hadn't changed Cypress Springs at all, she thought. How could that be? It was as if the twelve years between now and when she had headed off to Louisiana State

University in Baton Rouge, returning only for holiday breaks, had been a dream. As if her life in Washington, D.C., was a figment of her imagination.

If they had been, her mother would be alive, the massive, unexpected stroke she had suffered eleven years in the future. And her father—

Pain rushed over her. Her head filled with her father's voice, slightly distorted by the answering machine.

"Avery, sweetheart... It's Dad. I was hoping...I need to talk to you. I was hoping—" Pause. *"There's something... I'll...try later. Goodbye, pumpkin."*

If only she had taken that call. If only she had stopped, just for the time it would have taken to speak with him. Her story could have waited. The congressman who had finally decided to talk could have waited. A couple minutes. A couple minutes that might have changed everything.

Her thoughts raced forward, to the next morning, the call from Buddy Stevens. Family friend. Her dad's lifelong best friend. Cypress Springs' chief of police.

"Avery, it's Buddy. I've got some...some bad news, baby girl. Your dad, he's—"

Dead. Her dad was dead. Between the time her father had called her and the next morning, he had killed himself. Gone into his garage, doused himself with diesel fuel, then lit a match.

How could you do it, Dad? Why did you do it? You didn't even say—

The short scream of a police siren interrupted her thoughts. Avery turned. A West Feliciana Parish sheriff's cruiser rolled up behind her Blazer. An officer stepped out and started toward her.

She recognized the man by his long, lanky frame, the way he moved and held himself. Matt Stevens, childhood friend, high-school sweetheart, the guy she'd left behind to pursue her dream of journalism. She'd seen Matt only a handful of times since then, most recently at her mother's funeral nearly a year ago. Buddy must have told him she was coming.

Avery held up a hand in greeting. Still handsome, she thought, watching him approach. Still the best catch in the parish. Or maybe that title no longer applied; he could be attached now.

He reached her, stopped but didn't smile. "It's good to see you, Avery." She saw herself reflected in his mirrored sunglasses, smaller than any grown woman ought to be, her elfin looks accentuated by her pixie haircut and dark eyes, which were too big for her face.

"It's good to see you, too, Matt."

"Sorry about your dad. I feel real bad about how it all happened. Real bad."

"Thanks, I...I appreciate you and Buddy taking care of Dad's—" Her throat constricted; she pushed on, determined not to fall apart. "Dad's remains," she finished.

"It was the least we could do." Matt looked away, then back, expression somber. "Were you able to reach your cousins in Denver?"

"Yes," she managed, feeling lost. They were all the family she had left—a couple of distant cousins and their families. Everyone else was gone now.

"I loved him, too, Avery. I knew since your mom's death he'd been...struggling, but I still can't believe he did it. I feel like I should have seen how bad off he was. That I should have known."

The tears came then, swamping her. *She'd been his daughter. She was the guilty party. The one who should have known.*

He reached a hand out. "It's okay to cry, Avery."

"No...I've already—" She cleared her throat, fighting for composure. "I need to arrange a...service. Do the Gallaghers still own—"

"Yes. Danny's taken over for his father. He's expecting your call. Pop told him you were getting in sometime today."

She motioned to the cruiser. "You're out of your jurisdiction."

The sheriff's department handled all the unincorporated areas of the parish. The Cypress Springs Police Department policed the city itself.

One corner of his mouth lifted. "Guilty as charged. I was hanging around, hoping to catch you before you went by the house."

"I was heading there now. I just stopped to...because—" She bit the words back; she'd had no real reason for stopping, had simply responded to a whim.

He seemed to understand. "I'll go with you."

"That's really sweet, Matt. But unnecessary."

"I disagree." When she tried to protest more, he cut her off. "It's bad, Avery. I don't think you should see it alone the first time. I'm following you," he finished, voice gruff. "Whether you want me to or not."

Avery held his gaze a moment, then nodded and wordlessly turned and climbed into the rented Blazer. She started up the vehicle and eased back onto Main Street. As she drove the three-quarters of a mile to the old residential section where she had grown up, she took a deep breath.

Her father had chosen the hour of his death well—the middle of the night when his neighbors were less likely to see or smell the fire. He'd used diesel fuel, most probably the arson investigators determined, because unlike gasoline, which burned off vapors, diesel ignited on contact.

A neighbor out for an early morning jog had discovered the still smoldering garage. After trying to rouse her father, who he'd assumed to be in bed, asleep, he had called the fire department. The state arson investigator had been brought in. They in turn had called the coroner, who'd notified the Cypress Springs Police Department. In the end, her dad had been identified by his dental records.

Neither the autopsy nor CSPD investigation had turned up

any indication of foul play. Nor had any known motives for murder materialized: Dr. Phillip Chauvin had been universally liked and respected. The police had officially ruled his death a suicide.

No note. No goodbye.

How could you do it, Dad? Why?

Avery reached her parents' house and turned into the driveway. The lawn of the 1920s era Acadian needed mowing; the beds weeding; bushes trimming. Although early, the azaleas had begun to bloom. Soon the beds around the house would be a riot of pinks, ranging from icy pale to deep rose.

Her dad had loved his yard. Had spent weekends puttering and planting, primping. It all looked forlorn now, she thought. Overgrown and ignored.

Avery frowned. How long had it been since her father had tended his yard? she wondered. Longer than the two days he had been gone. That was obvious.

Further evidence of the emotional depths to which he had sunk. How could she have missed how depressed he had grown? Why hadn't she sensed something was wrong during their frequent phone conversations?

Matt pulled in behind her. She took a deep breath and climbed out of her vehicle.

He met her, expression grim. "You're certain you're ready for this?"

"Do I have a choice?"

They both knew she didn't and they started up the curving driveway, toward the detached garage. A separate structure, the garage nestled behind the main house. A covered walkway connected the two buildings.

As they neared the structure the smell of the fire grew stronger—not just of wood smoke, but of what she imagined was charred flesh and bone. As they turned the corner of the driveway she saw that a large, irregularly shaped black mark marred the doorway.

"The heat from the fire," Matt explained. "It did more damage inside. Actually, it's a wonder the building didn't come down."

A half-dozen years ago, while working for the *Tribune,* Avery had been assigned to cover a rash of fires that had plagued the Chicago area. It turned out the arsonist had been the estranged son of a firefighter, looking to punish his old man for kicking him out of the house. Unfortunately, the police hadn't caught him before he'd been responsible for the deaths of six innocent people—one of them an infant.

Avery and Matt reached the garage. She steeled herself for what would come next. She understood how gruesome death by fire was.

Matt led her to the side door. Opened it. They stepped into the building. The smell crashed over her. As did the stark reality of her father's last minutes. She imagined his screams as the flames engulfed him. As his skin began to melt. Avery brought a hand to her mouth, her gaze going to the large char mark on the concrete floor—the spot where her father had burned alive.

His suicide had been an act of not only despair but self-hatred as well.

She began to tremble. Her head grew light, her knees weak. Turning, she ran outside, to the azalea bushes with their burgeoning blossoms. She doubled over, struggling not to throw up. Not to fall apart.

Matt came up behind her. He laid a hand on her back.

Avery squeezed her eyes shut. "How could he do it, Matt?" She looked over her shoulder at him, vision blurred by tears. "It's bad enough that he took his own life, but to do it like that? The pain...it would have been excruciating."

"I don't know what to say," he murmured, tone gentle. "I don't have any answers for you. I wish I did."

She straightened, mustering anger. Denial. "My father

loved life. He valued it. He was a doctor, for God's sake. He'd devoted his life to preserving it."

At Matt's silence, she lashed out. "He was proud of himself and the choices he'd made. Proud of how he had lived. The man who did that hated himself. That wasn't my dad." She said it again, tone taking on a desperate edge. "It wasn't, Matt."

"Avery, you haven't been—" He bit the words off and shifted his gaze, expression uncomfortable.

"What, Matt? I haven't been what?"

"Around a lot lately." He must have read the effect of his words in her expression and he caught her hands and held them tightly. "Your dad hadn't been himself for a while. He'd withdrawn, from everybody. Stayed in his house for days. When he went out he didn't speak. Would cross to the other side of the street to avoid conversation."

How could she not have known? "When?" she asked, hurting. "When did this start?"

"I suppose about the time he gave up his practice."

Just after her mother's death.

"Why didn't somebody call me? Why didn't—" She bit the words back and pressed her trembling lips together.

He squeezed her fingers. "It wasn't an overnight thing. At first he just seemed preoccupied. Or like he needed time to grieve. On his own. It wasn't until recently that people began to talk."

Avery turned her gaze to her father's overgrown garden. No wonder, she thought.

"I'm sorry, Avery. We all are."

She swung away from her old friend, working to hold on to her anger. Fighting tears.

She lost the battle.

"Aw, Avery. Geez." Matt went to her, drew her into his arms, against his chest. She leaned into him, burying her face in his shoulder, crying like a baby.

He held her awkwardly. Stiffly. Every so often he patted her shoulder and murmured something comforting, though through her sobs she couldn't make out what.

The intensity of her tears lessened, then stopped. She drew away from him, embarrassed. "Sorry about that. It's...I thought I could handle it."

"Cut yourself some slack, Avery. Frankly, if you *could* handle it, I'd be a little worried about you."

Tears flooded her eyes once more and she brought her hand to her nose. "I need a tissue. Excuse me."

She headed toward her car, aware of him following. There, she rummaged in her purse, coming up with a rumpled Kleenex. She blew her nose, dabbed at her eyes, then faced him once more. "How could I not have known how bad off he was? Am I *that* self-involved?"

"None of us knew," he said gently. "And we saw him every day."

"But I was his daughter. I should have been able to tell, should have heard it in his voice. In what he said. Or didn't say."

"It's not your fault, Avery."

"No?" She realized her hands were shaking and slipped them into her pockets. "But I can't help wondering, if I had stayed in Cypress Springs, would he be alive today? If I'd given up my career and stayed after Mom's death, would he have staved off the depression that caused him to do...this? If I had simply picked up the pho—"

She swallowed the words, unable to speak them aloud. She met his gaze. "It hurts so much."

"Don't do this to yourself. You can't go back."

"I can't, can I?" She winced at the bitterness in her voice. "I loved my dad more than anyone in the world, yet I only came home a handful of times in all the years since college. Even after Mom died so suddenly and so horribly, leaving so much unresolved between us. That should have been a wake-up call, but it wasn't."

He didn't respond and she continued. "I've got to live with that, don't I?"

"No," he corrected. "You have to learn from it. It's where you go from here that counts now. Not where you've been."

A group of teenagers barreled by in a pickup truck, their raucous laughter interrupting the charged moment. The pickup was followed by another group of teenagers, these in a bright-yellow convertible, top down.

Avery glanced at her watch. *Three-thirty. The high school let out the same time as it had all those years ago.*

Funny how some things could change so dramatically and others not at all.

"I should get back to work. You going to be okay?"

She nodded. "Thanks for baby-sitting me."

"No thanks necessary." He started for the car, then stopped and looked back at her. "I almost forgot, Mom and Dad are expecting you for dinner tonight."

"Tonight? But I just got in."

"Exactly. No way are Mom and Dad going to let you spend your first night home alone."

"But—"

"You're not in the big city anymore, Avery. Here, people take care of each other. Besides, you're family."

Home. Family. At that moment nothing sounded better than that. "I'll be there. They still live at the ranch?" she asked, using the nickname they had given the Stevenses' sprawling ranch-style home.

"Of course. Status quo is something you can count on in Cypress Springs." He crossed to his vehicle, opened the door and looked back at her. "Is six too early?"

"It'll be perfect."

"Great." He climbed into the cruiser, started it and began backing up. Halfway down the driveway he stopped and lowered his window. "Hunter's back home," he called. "I thought you might want to know."

Avery stood rooted to the spot even after Matt's cruiser disappeared from sight. Hunter? she thought, disbelieving. Matt's fraternal twin brother and the third member of their triumvirate. Back in Cypress Springs? Last she'd heard, he'd been a partner at a prestigious New Orleans law firm.

Avery turned away from the road and toward her childhood home. Something had happened the summer she'd been fifteen, Hunter and Matt sixteen. A rift had grown between the brothers. Hunter had become increasingly aloof, angry. He and Matt had fought often and several times violently. The Stevenses' house, which had always been a haven of warmth, laughter and love, had become a battleground. As if the animosity between the brothers had spilled over into all the family relationships.

At first Avery had been certain the bad feelings between the brothers would pass. They hadn't. Hunter had left for college and never returned—not even for holidays.

Now he, like she, had come home to Cypress Springs. Odd, she thought. A weird coincidence. Perhaps tonight she would discover what had brought him back.

CHAPTER 2

At six sharp, Avery pulled up in front of the Stevenses' house. Buddy Stevens, sitting on the front porch smoking a cigar, caught sight of her and lumbered to his feet. "There's my girl!" he bellowed. "Home safe and sound!"

She hurried up the walk and was enfolded in his arms. A mountain of a man with a barrel chest and booming voice, he had been Cypress Springs's chief of police for as long as she could remember. Although a by-the-books lawman who had as much give as a concrete block when it came to his town and crime, the Buddy Stevens she knew was just a big ol' teddy bear. A hard-ass with a soft, squishy center and a heart of gold.

He hugged her tightly, then held her at arm's length. He

searched her gaze, his own filled with regret. "I'm sorry, baby girl. Damn sorry."

A lump formed in her throat. She cleared it with difficulty. "I know, Buddy. I'm sorry, too."

He hugged her again. "You're too thin. And you look tired."

She drew away, filled with affection for the man who had been nearly as important to her growing up as her own father. "Haven't you heard? A woman can't be too thin."

"Big-city crapola." He put out the stogie and led her inside, arm firmly around her shoulders. "Lilah!" he called. "Cherry! Look who the cat's dragged in."

Cherry, Matt and Hunter's younger sister, appeared at the kitchen door. The awkward-looking twelve-year-old girl had grown into an uncommonly beautiful woman. Tall, with dark hair and eyes like her brothers, she had inherited her mother's elegant features and pretty skin.

When she saw Avery she burst into a huge smile. "You made it. We've been worried sick." She crossed to Avery and hugged her. "That's no kind of a trip for a woman to make alone."

Such an unenlightened comment coming from a woman in her twenties took Avery aback. But as Matt had said earlier, she wasn't in the city anymore.

She hugged her back. "It wasn't so bad. Cab to Dullas, non-stop flight to New Orleans, a rental car here. The most harrowing part was retrieving my luggage."

"Big, tough career girl," Buddy murmured, sounding anything but pleased. "I hope you had a cell phone."

"Of course. Fully charged at all times." She grinned up at him. "And, you'll be happy to know, pepper spray in my purse."

"Pepper spray? Whatever for?" This came from Lilah Stevens.

"Self-protection, Mama," Cherry supplied, glancing over her shoulder at the older woman.

Lilah, still as trim and attractive as Avery remembered, crossed from the kitchen and caught Avery's hands. "Self-protection? Well, you won't be needing *that* here." She searched Avery's gaze. "Avery, sweetheart. Welcome home. How are you?"

Avery squeezed the other woman's hands, tears pricking her eyes. "I've been better, thanks."

"I'm so sorry, sweetheart. Sorrier than I can express."

"I know. And that means a lot."

From the other room came the sound of a timer going off. Lilah released Avery's hands. "That's the pie."

The smells emanating from the kitchen were heavenly. Lilah Stevens had been the best cook in the parish and had consistently won baking prizes at the parish fair. Growing up, Avery had angled for a dinner invitation at every opportunity.

"What kind of pie?" she asked.

"Strawberry. I know peach is your favorite but it's impossible to find a decent peach this time of year. And the first Louisiana berries are in. And delicious, I might add."

"Silly woman," Buddy interrupted. "The poor child is exhausted. Stop your yapping about produce and let the girl sit down."

"Yapping?" She wagged a finger at him. "If you want pie, Mr. Stevens, you'll have to get yourself down to the Azalea Café."

He immediately looked contrite. "Sorry, sugar-sweet, you know I was just teasing."

"Now I'm sugar-sweet, am I?" She rolled her eyes and turned back to Avery. "You see what I've put up with all these years?"

Avery laughed. She used to wish her parents could be more like Lilah and Buddy, openly affectionate and teasing. In all the years she had known the couple, all the time she had spent around their home, she had never heard them raise their voices at one another. And when they'd teased each other, like just now, their love and respect had always shown through.

In truth, Avery had often wished her mother could be more like Lilah. Good-natured, outgoing. A traditional woman comfortable in her own skin. One who had enjoyed her children, making a home for them and her husband.

It had seemed to Avery that her mother had enjoyed neither, though she had never said so aloud. Avery had sensed her mother's frustration, her dissatisfaction with her place in the world.

No, Avery thought, that wasn't quite right. She had been frustrated by her only child's tomboyish ways and defiant streak. She had been disappointed in her daughter's likes and dislikes, the choices she made.

In her mother's eyes, Avery hadn't measured up.

Lilah Stevens had never made Avery feel she lacked anything. To the contrary, Lilah had made her feel not only worthy but special as well.

"I do see," Avery agreed, playing along. "It's outrageous."

"That it is." Lilah waved them toward the living room. "Matt should be here any moment. All I have left to do is whip the potatoes and heat the French bread. Then we can eat."

"Can I help?" Avery asked.

As she had known it would be, the woman's answer was a definitive no. Buddy and Cherry led her to the living room. Avery sank onto the overstuffed couch, acknowledging exhaustion. She wished she could lean her head back, close her eyes and sleep for a week.

"You've barely changed," Buddy said softly, tone wistful. "Same pretty, bright-eyed girl you were the day you left Cypress Springs."

She'd been so damn young back then. So ridiculously naive. She had yearned for something bigger than Cypress Springs, something better. Had sensed something important waited for her outside this small town. She supposed she had found it: a prestigious job; writing awards and professional respect; an enviable salary.

What was it all worth now? If those twelve years hadn't been, if all her choices still lay before her, what would she do differently?

Everything. Anything to have him with her.

She met Buddy's eyes. "You'd be surprised how much I've changed." She lightened her words with a smile. "What about you? Besides being as devastatingly handsome as ever, still the most feared and respected lawman in the parish?"

"I don't know about that," he murmured. "Seems to me, these days that honor belongs to Matt."

"West Feliciana Parish's sheriff is retiring next year," Cherry chimed in. "Matt's planning to run for the job." There was no mistaking the pride in her voice. "Those in the know expect him to win the election by a landslide."

Buddy nodded, looking as pleased as punch. "My son, the parish's top cop. Imagine that."

"A regular crime-fighting family dynasty," Avery murmured.

"Not for long." Buddy settled into his easy chair. "Retirement's right around the corner. Probably should have retired already. If I'd had a grandchild to spoil, I—"

"Dad," Cherry warned, "don't go there."

"Three children," he groused, "all disappointments. Friends of mine have a half-dozen of the little critters already. I don't think that's right." He looked at Avery. "Do you?"

Avery held up her hands, laughing. "Oh, no, I'm not getting involved in this one."

Cherry mouthed a "Thank you," Buddy pouted and Avery changed the subject. "I can't imagine you not being the chief of police. Cypress Springs won't be the same."

"Comes a time one generation needs to make room for the next. Much as I hate the thought, my time has come and gone."

With a derisive snort, Cherry started toward the kitchen. "I'm having a glass of wine. Want one, Avery?"

"Love one."

"Red or white?"

"Whatever you're having." Avery let out a long breath and leaned her head against the sofa back, tension easing from her. She closed her eyes. Images played on the backs of her eyelids, ones from her past: her, Matt and Hunter playing while their parents barbecued in the backyard. Buddy and Lilah snapping pictures as she and Matt headed off to the prom. The two families caroling at Christmastime.

Sweet memories. Comforting ones.

"Good to be back, isn't it?" Buddy murmured as if reading her thoughts.

She opened her eyes and looked at him. "Despite everything, yes." She glanced away a moment, then back. "I wish I'd come home sooner. After Mom... I should have stayed. If I had—"

The unfinished thought hung heavily between them anyway. *If she had, maybe her dad would be alive today.*

Cherry returned with the wine. She crossed to Avery; handed her a glass of the pale gold liquid. "What are your plans?"

"First order of business is a service for Dad. I called Danny Gallagher this afternoon. We're meeting tomorrow after lunch."

"How long are you staying?" Cherry sat on the other end of the couch, curling her legs under her.

"I took a leave of absence from the *Post,* because I just don't know," she answered honestly. "I haven't a clue how long it will take to go through Dad's things, get the house ready to sell."

"Sorry I'm late."

At Matt's voice, Avery looked up. He stood in the doorway to the living room, head cocked as he gazed at her, expression amused. He'd exchanged his uniform for blue jeans and a soft chambray shirt. He held a bouquet of fresh flowers.

"Brought Mom some posies," he said. "She in the kitchen?"

"You know Mom." Cherry crossed to him and kissed his cheek. "Dad's already complained about the dearth of grandchildren around here. Remind me to be late next time."

Matt met Avery's eyes and grinned. "Glad I missed it. Though I'll no doubt catch the rerun later."

Buddy scowled at his two children. "No grandbabies *and* no respect." He looked toward the kitchen. "Lilah," he bellowed, "where did we go wrong with these kids?"

Lilah poked her head out of the kitchen. "For heaven's sake, Buddy, leave the children alone." She turned her attention to her son. "Hello, Matt. Are those for the table?"

"Yes, ma'am." He ambled across to her, kissed her cheek and handed her the flowers. "Something smells awfully good."

"Come, help me with the roast." She turned to her daughter. "Cherry, could you put these in a vase for me?"

Avery watched the exchange. She could have been a part of this family. Officially a part. Everyone had expected her and Matt to marry.

Buddy interrupted her thoughts. "Have you considered staying?" he asked. "This is your home, Avery. You belong here."

She dragged her gaze back to his, uncertain how to answer. Yes, she had come home to take care of specific family business, but less specifically, she had come for answers. For peace of mind—not only about her father's death, but about her own life.

Truth was, she had been drifting for a while now, neither happy nor unhappy. Vaguely dissatisfied but uncertain why.

"Do I, Buddy? Always felt like the one marching to a different drummer."

"Your daddy thought so."

Tears swamped her. "I miss him so much."

"I know, baby girl." A momentary, awkward silence fell between them. Buddy broke it first. "He never got over your mother's death. The way she died. He loved her completely."

She'd been behind the wheel when she suffered a stroke, on her way to meet her cousin who'd flown into New Orleans. For a week of girl time—shopping and dining and shows. She had careened across the highway, into a brick wall.

A sound from the doorway drew her gaze. Lilah stood there, expression stricken. Matt and Cherry stood behind her. "It was so...awful. She called me the night before she left. She hadn't been feeling well, she said. She had run her symptoms by Phillip, had wondered if she shouldn't cancel her trip. He had urged her to go. Nothing was wrong with her that a week away wouldn't cure. I don't think he ever forgave himself for that."

"He thought he should have known," Buddy murmured. "Thought that if he hadn't been paying closer attention to his patients' health than to his own wife's, he could have saved her."

Avery clasped her shaky hands together. "I didn't know. I...he mentioned feeling responsible, but I—"

She had chosen to pacify him. To assure him none of it was his fault.

Then go on her merry way.

Matt moved around his mother and came to stand behind her chair. He laid a comforting hand on her shoulder. "It's not your fault, Avery," he said softly. "It's not."

She reached up and curled her fingers around his, grateful for the support. "Matt said Dad had been acting strangely. That he had withdrawn from everyone and everything. But still I...how could he have done what he did?"

"When I heard how he did it," Cherry said quietly, "I wasn't surprised. I think you can love someone so much you do something...unbelievable because of it. Something tragic."

An uncomfortable silence settled over the group. Avery tried to speak but found she couldn't for the knot of tears in her throat.

Buddy, bless him, took over. He turned to Lilah. "Dinner ready, sugar-sweet?"

"It is." Lilah all but jumped at the opportunity to turn their attention to the mundane. "And getting cold."

"Let's get to it, then," Buddy directed.

They made their way to the dining room and sat. Buddy said the blessing, then the procession of bowls and platters began, passed as they always had been at the Stevenses' supper table from right to left.

Avery went through the motions. She ate, commented on the food, joined in story swapping. But her heart wasn't in it. Nor was anyone else's, that was obvious to her. As was how hard they were trying to make it like it used to be. How hard they were wanting to comfort with normalcy.

But how could anything be normal ever again? In years gone by, her parents had sat with her at this table. She, Matt and Hunter would have been clustered together, whispering or joking.

She missed Hunter, Avery realized. She felt the lack of his presence keenly.

Hunter had been the most intellectual of the group. Not the most intelligent, because both he and Matt had sailed through school, neither having to crack a book to maintain an A average, both scoring near-perfect marks on their SATs.

But Hunter had possessed a sharp, sarcastic wit. He'd been incapable of the silliness the rest of them had sometimes wallowed in. He had often been the voice of wry reason in whatever storm was brewing.

She hadn't been surprised to hear he had become a successful lawyer. Between his keen mind and razor-sharp tongue, he'd no doubt consistently decimated the opposition.

She brought him up as Lilah served the pie. "Matt tells me that Hunter's moved back to Cypress Springs. I'd hoped he would be here tonight."

Silence fell around the table. Avery shifted her gaze from one face to the next. "I'm sorry, did I say something wrong?"

Buddy cleared his throat. "Of course not, baby girl. It's just that Hunter's had some troubles lately. Lost his partnership in the New Orleans law firm. Was nearly disbarred, from what I hear. Moved back here about ten months ago."

"I don't know why he bothered," Matt added. "For all the time he spends with his family."

Cherry frowned. "I wish he hadn't come home. He only did it to hurt us."

"Now, Cherry," Buddy murmured, "you don't know that."

"The hell I don't. If he was any kind of brother, any kind of son, he would be here for us. Instead, he—"

Lilah launched to her feet. Avery saw she was near tears. "I'll get the coffee."

"I'll help." Cherry tossed her napkin on the table and got to her feet, expression disgusted. She looked at Avery. "Tell you the truth, all Hunter's ever done is break our hearts."

CHAPTER 3

Talk of Hunter drained the joy from the gathering, and the remainder of the evening passed at a snail's pace. Lilah's smile looked artificial; Cherry's mood darkened with each passing moment and Buddy's jubilance bordered on manic.

Finally, pie consumed, coffee cups drained, Avery said her thanks and made her excuses. Cherry and Lilah said their goodbyes in the dining room; Buddy accompanied her and Matt to the door.

Buddy hugged her. "You broke all our hearts when you left. But no one's more than mine. I'd had mine set on you being my daughter."

Avery returned his embrace. "I love you, too, Buddy."

Matt walked her to her car. "Pretty night," she murmured,

lifting her face to the night sky. "So many stars. I'd forgotten how many."

"I enjoyed tonight, Avery. It was like old times."

Avery met his eyes; her pulse fluttered.

"I've missed you," he said. "I'm glad you're back."

She swallowed hard, acknowledging that she'd missed him, too. Or more accurately, that she'd missed standing with him this way, in his folks' driveway, under a star-sprinkled sky. Had missed the familiarity of it. The sense of belonging.

Matt put words to her thoughts. "Why'd you leave, Avery? My dad was right, you know. You belong here. *You're* one of us."

"Why didn't you go with me?" she countered. "I asked. Begged, if I remember correctly."

Matt lifted a hand as if to touch her, then dropped it. "You always wanted something else, something more than Cypress Springs could offer. Something more than I could offer. I never understood it. But I had to accept it."

She shifted her gaze slightly, uncomfortable with the truth. That he could speak it so plainly. She changed the direction of their conversation. "Your dad and Cherry said you're the front-runner in next year's election for parish sheriff. I'm not surprised. You always said you were destined for great things."

"But our definitions of great things always differed, didn't they, Avery?"

"That's not fair, Matt."

"Fair or not, it's true." He paused. "You broke my heart."

She held his gaze. "You broke mine, too."

"Then we're even, aren't we? A broken heart apiece."

She winced at the bitter edge in his voice. "Matt, it...wasn't you. It was me. I never felt—"

She had been about to say how she had never felt she belonged in Cypress Springs. That once she'd become a teenager, she had always felt slightly out of step, different in subtle but monumental ways from the other girls she knew.

Those feelings seemed silly now. The thoughts of a self-absorbed young girl.

"What about now, Avery?" he asked. "What do you want now? What do you need?"

Discomfited by the intensity of his gaze, she looked away. "I don't know. I don't want to return to where I was, I'm certain of that. And I don't mean the geographical location."

"Sounds like you have some thinking to do."

A giant understatement. She turned to the Blazer, unlocked the door, then faced him once more. "I should go. I'm asleep on my feet and tomorrow's going to be difficult."

"You could stay here, you know. Mom and Dad have plenty of room. They'd love to have you."

A part of her longed to jump at the offer. The idea of sleeping in her parents' house now, after her father...she didn't think she would sleep a wink.

But taking the easy way would be taking the coward's way. She had to face her father's suicide. She'd begin tonight, by sleeping in her childhood home.

He reached around her and opened her car door. "Still fiercely independent, I see. Still stubborn as a mule."

She slid behind the wheel, started the vehicle, then looked back up at him "Some would consider those qualities an asset."

"Sure they would. In mules." He bent his face to hers. "If you need anything, call me."

"I will. Thanks." He slammed the door. She backed the Blazer down the steep driveway, then headed out of the subdivision, pointing the vehicle toward the old downtown neighborhood where she had grown up.

Avery shook her head, remembering how she had begged her parents to follow the Stevenses to Spring Water, the then new subdivision where Matt and his family had bought a house. She had been enamored with the sprawling ranch homes and neighborhood club facilities: pool, tennis court and clubhouse for parties.

What had then looked so new and cool to her, she saw now as cheaply built, cookie-cutter homes on small plots of ground that had been cleared to make room for as many houses per acre as possible.

Luckily, her parents had refused to move from their location within walking distance of the square, downtown and her father's office. Solidly built in the 1920s, their house boasted high ceilings, cypress millwork and the kind of charm available only at a premium today. The neighborhood, too, was vintage—a wide, tree-lined boulevard lit by gas lamps, each home set back on large, shady lots. Unlike many cities whose downtown neighborhoods had fallen victim to the urban decay caused by crime and white flight, Cypress Springs's inner-city neighborhood remained as well maintained and safe as when originally built.

Despite the fact that most of Louisiana was flat, West Feliciana Parish was home to gently rolling hills. Cypress Springs nestled amongst those hills—the historic river town of St. Francisville, with its beautiful antebellum homes, lay twenty minutes southwest, Baton Rouge, forty-five minutes south and the New Orleans's French Quarter a mere two hours forty-five minutes southeast.

Besides being a good place to raise a family, Cypress Springs had no claim to fame. A small Southern town that relied on agriculture, mostly cattle and light industry, it was too far from the beaten path to ever grow into more.

The city fathers liked it that way, Avery knew. She had grown up listening to her dad, Buddy and their friends talk about keeping industry and all her ills out. About keeping Cypress Springs clean. She remembered the furor caused when Charlie Weiner had sold his farm to the Old Dixie Foods corporation and then the company's decision to build a canning factory on the site.

Avery made her way down the deserted streets. Although not even ten o'clock, the town had already rolled up its sidewalks for the night. She shook her head. Nothing could be more different from the places she had called home for the past twelve years—places where a traffic jam could occur almost anytime during a twenty-four-hour period; where walking alone at night was to take your life in your hands; places where people lived on top of each other but never acknowledged the other's existence.

As beautiful and green a city as Washington, D.C., was, it couldn't compare to the lush beauty of West Feliciana Parish. The heat and humidity provided the perfect environment for all manner of vegetation. Azaleas. Gardenias. Sweet olive. Camellias. Palmettos. Live oaks, their massive gnarled branches so heavy they dipped to the ground, hundred-year-old magnolia trees that in May would hold so many of the large white blossoms the air would be redolent of their sweet, lemony scent.

Once upon a time she had thought this place ugly. No, that wasn't quite fair, she admitted. Shabby and painfully small town.

Why hadn't she seen it then as she did now?

Avery turned onto her street, then a moment later into her parents' driveway. She parked at the edge of the walk and climbed out, locking the vehicle out of habit not necessity. Her thoughts drifted to the events of the evening, particularly to those final moments with Matt.

What *did* she want now? she wondered. Where did she belong?

The porch swing creaked. A figure separated from the silhouette of the overgrown sweet olive at the end of the porch. Her steps faltered.

"Hello, Avery."

Hunter, she realized, bringing a hand to her chest. She let

out a shaky breath. "I've lived in the city too long. You scared the hell out of me."

"I have that effect on people."

Although she smiled, she could see why that might be true. Half his face lay in shadow, the other half in the light from the porch fixture. His features looked hard in the weak light, his face craggy, the lines around his mouth and eyes deeply etched. A few days' accumulation of beard darkened his jaw.

She would have crossed the street to avoid him in D.C.

How could the two brothers have grown so physically dissimilar? she wondered. Growing up, though fraternal not identical twins, the resemblance between them had been uncanny. She would never have thought they could be other than near mirror images of one another.

"I'd heard you were back," he said. "Obviously."

"News travels fast around here."

"This is a small town. They've got to have something to talk about."

He had changed in a way that had less to do with the passage of years than with the accumulated events of those years. The school of hard knocks, she thought. The great equalizer.

"And I'm one of their own," she said.

"It's true, then? You're back to stay?"

"I didn't say that."

"That's the buzz. I thought it was wrong." He shrugged. "But you never know."

"Meaning what?" she asked, folding her arms across her chest.

"Am I making you uncomfortable?"

"No, of course not." Annoyed with herself, she dropped her arms. "I had dinner with your parents tonight."

"And Matt. Heard that, too."

"I thought you might have been there."

"So they told you I was living in Cypress Springs?"

"Matt did."

"And did he tell you why?"

"Only that you'd had some troubles."

"Nice euphemism." He swept his gaze over the facade of her parents' house. "Sorry about your dad. He was a great man."

"I think so, too." She jiggled her car keys, suddenly on edge, anxious to be inside.

"Aren't you going to ask me?"

"What?"

"If I talked to him before he died."

The question off-balanced her. "What do you mean?"

"It seemed a pretty straightforward question to me."

"Okay. Did you?"

"Yes. He was worried about you."

"About me?" She frowned. "Why?"

"Because your mother died before the two of you worked out your issues."

Issues, she thought. Is that how one summed up a lifetime of hurt feelings, a lifetime of longing for her mother's unconditional love and approval and being disappointed time and again? Her head filled with a litany of advice her mother had offered her over the years.

"Avery, little girls don't climb trees and build forts or play cowboys and Indians with boys. They wear bows and dresses with ruffles, not blue-jean cutoffs and T-shirts. Good girls make ladylike choices. They don't run off to the city to become newspapermen. They don't throw away a good man to chase a dream."

"He thought you might be sad about that," Hunter continued. "She was. He hated that she died without your making peace."

"He said that?" she managed to get out, voice tight.

He nodded and she looked away, memory flooding with the words she had flung at her mother just before she had left for college.

"Drop the loving concern, Mother! You've never approved of me or my choices. I've never been the daughter you wanted. Why don't you just admit it?"

Her mother hadn't admitted it and Avery had headed off to college with the accusation between them. They had never spoken of it again, though it had been a wedge between them forever more.

"He figured that's why you hardly ever came home." Hunter shrugged. "Interesting, you couldn't come to terms with your mother's life, he her death."

She jumped on the last. "What does that mean, he couldn't come to terms with her death?"

"I would think it's obvious, Avery. It's called grieving."

He was toying with her, she realized. It pissed her off. "And when did all these conversations take place?"

Hunter paused. "We had many conversations, he and I."

The past two days, her shock and grief, the grueling hours of travel, the onslaught of so much that was both foreign and familiar, came crashing down on her. "I don't have the energy to deal with your shit, even if I wanted to. If you decide you want to be a decent human being, look me up."

One corner of his mouth lifted in a sardonic smile. "I didn't answer your question before, the one about my opinion of the local buzz. Personally, I figured you'd pop your old man in a box and go. Fast as you could."

She took a step back, stung. Shocked that he would say that to her. That he would be so cruel. After the closeness they had shared. She pushed past him, unlocked her front door and stepped inside. She caught a glimpse of his face, of the stark pain that etched his features as she slammed the door.

Hunter Stevens was a man pursued by demons.

To hell with his, she thought, twisting the dead-bolt lock. She had her own to deal with.

CHAPTER 4

Hunter gazed at the row of unopened bottles: beer, wine, whisky, vodka. All sins from his past. Each a nail in the coffin of his life.

He kept them around to prove that he could. Such a strategy went counter to traditional AA teaching, but he was a masochistic son of a bitch.

Hunter thought of Avery and anger rose up in him in a white-hot, suffocating wave. Once upon a time they'd been the best of friends: him, Matt and Avery. Before everything had begun spinning crazily out of control. Before his life had turned to shit.

He pictured her sitting next to Matt at his family's dinner

table. All of them laughing, swapping memories. Reveling in the good old days.

What part had he played in those memories? Had they shared stories that hadn't included him? Or had they simply plucked him out as if he had never existed?

Shut out again. Always the one on the outside, looking in. The one who didn't belong.

"What's wrong with you, Hunter? What went wrong with you?"

Good question, he thought, gazing at the bottles, squeezing his fists against the urge that swelled inside him. The urge to open a bottle and get stinking, fall-down drunk.

He'd been down that path; he knew the only place it would lead him was straight to hell.

A hell of his own making. One populated by children screaming in terror. One in which he was helpless to stop the inevitable. Helpless to do more than look on in horror and self-loathing. In despair.

Hunter swung away from the bottles. He sucked in a deep breath and moved deliberately away from the kitchen and toward the makeshift desk he had set up in the corner of his small living room. On the desk sat a computer, monitor glowing in the dimly lit room, fan humming softly. Beside it the pages of a novel. His novel. A story about a lawyer's spiral to the depths.

If only he knew the story's end. Some days, he thought his protagonist would manage to claw his way up from those depths. Other days, hopelessness held him so tightly in its grip he couldn't breathe let alone imagine a happy ending.

He pulled out the chair and sat, intent on channeling his energy and anger into his novel. Instead, he found his thoughts turning to Avery once more.

What caused a man to douse himself with a flammable substance and strike a match?

He knew. He understood.

He had been there, too.

The blinking cursor drew his attention. He focused on the words he had written:

Jack fought the forces that threatened to devour him. To his right lay the laws of man, to his left the greatness of God. One wrong step and he would be lost.

Lost. And found. He had come home to set things right. To start over. He had already begun.

And now, here was Avery.

All together again, he thought. He, Matt and Avery. The same as when his life had begun to implode. How would this affect his plans? The timetable of events he had carefully constructed?

It wouldn't, he decided. Things would be set right. His life would be set right. No matter how much it hurt.

CHAPTER 5

Avery bolted upright in bed, heart pounding, her father's name a scream on her lips. She darted her gaze to the bedroom door, for a split second a kid again, expecting her parents to charge through, all concerned hugs and comforting arms.

They didn't, of course, and she sagged back against the headboard. She hadn't slept well, no surprise there. She'd tossed and turned, each creak and moan of the old house unfamiliar and jarring. She had been up a half dozen times. Checking the doors. Peering out the windows. Pacing the floor.

In truth, she suspected it hadn't been the noises that had

kept her awake. It had been the quiet. The reason for the quiet.

Finally, she'd taken the couple of Tylenol PM caplets she'd dug out of her travel bag. Sleep had come.

But not rest. For sleep had brought nightmares. In them, she had been enfolded in a womb, warm and contented. Protected. Suddenly, she had been torn from her safe haven and thrust into a bright, white place. The light had burned. She had been naked. And cold.

In the next instant flames had engulfed her.

And she had awakened, calling out her father's name.

Not too tough figuring that one out.

Avery glanced at the bedside clock. Just after 9:00 a.m., she noted. Throwing back the blanket, she climbed out of bed. The temperature had dropped during the night and the house was cold. Shivering, she crossed to her suitcase, rummaged through it for a pair of leggings and a sweatshirt. She slipped them on, not bothering to take off her sleep shirt.

That done, she headed to the kitchen, making a quick side trip out front for the newspaper. It wasn't until she was staring at the naked driveway that two things occurred to her: the first was that Cypress Springs's only newspaper, the *Gazette,* was a biweekly, published each Wednesday and Saturday, and second, that Sal Mandina, the *Gazette*'s owner and editor-in-chief had surely halted her father's subscription. There would be no uncollected papers piling up on a Cypress Springs stoop.

No newspaper? The very idea made her twitch.

With a shake of her head, she stepped inside, relocked the door and headed to the kitchen. She would pick up the New Orleans *Times-Picayune* or *The Advocate* from Baton Rouge when she went into town this morning.

That trip might come sooner than planned, Avery realized moments later, standing at the refrigerator. Yesterday she hadn't thought to check the kitchen for provisions. She wished she had.

No bread, milk or eggs. No coffee.

Not good.

Avery dragged her fingers through her short hair. After the huge meal she'd consumed the night before, she could probably forgo breakfast. Maybe. But she couldn't face this morning without coffee.

A walk downtown, it seemed, would be the first order of the day.

After changing, brushing her teeth and washing her face, she found her Reeboks, slipped them on then headed out the front door.

And ran smack into Cherry. The other woman smiled brightly. "Morning, Avery. And here I was afraid I was going to wake you."

"No such luck." Avery eyed the picnic basket tucked against Cherry's side. "I was just heading to the grocery for a newspaper and some coffee. You wouldn't happen to have either of those, would you?"

"A thermos of French roast. No newspaper, though. Sorry."

"You're a lifesaver. Come on in."

Cherry stepped inside. "I remembered that your dad didn't drink coffee. Figured you'd need it this morning, strong."

Her mother had been a coffee drinker. But not her dad. Cherry had remembered that. But she hadn't. What was wrong with her?

"Figured, too, that you hadn't had time to get to the market." She held up the basket. "Mom's homemade biscuits and peach jam."

Just the thought had Avery's mouth watering. "Do you have any idea how long it's been since I had a real biscuit?"

"Since your last visit, I suspect," Cherry answered, following Avery. They reached the kitchen and she set the basket on the counter. "Yankees flat can't make a decent biscuit. There, I've said it."

Avery laughed. She supposed the other woman was right. Learning how to make things like the perfect baking powder biscuit was a rite of passage for Southern girls.

And like many of those womanly rites of passage, she had failed miserably at it.

Cherry had come prepared: from the basket she took two blue-and-white-checked place mats, matching napkins, flatware, a miniature vase and carefully wrapped yellow rose. She filled the vase with water and dropped in the flower. "There," she said. "A proper breakfast table."

Avery poured the coffees and the two women took a seat at the table. Curling her fingers around the warm mug, Avery made a sound of appreciation as she sipped the hot liquid.

"Bad night?" Cherry asked sympathetically, bringing her own cup to her lips.

"The worst. Couldn't sleep. Then when I did, had nightmares."

"That's to be expected, I imagine. Considering."

Considering. Avery looked away. She cleared her throat. "This was so sweet of you."

"My pleasure." Cherry smoothed the napkin in her lap. "I meant what I said last night, I've missed you. We all have." She met Avery's eyes. "You're one of us, you know. Always will be."

"Are you trying to tell me something, Cherry?" Avery asked, smiling. "Like, you can take the girl out of the small town, but you can't take the small town out of the girl?"

"Something like that." She returned Avery's smile; leaned toward her. "But you know what? There's nothing wrong with that, in my humble, country opinion. So there."

Avery laughed and helped herself to one of the biscuits. She broke off a piece. It was moist, dense and still warm. She spread on jam, popped it in her mouth and made a sound of pure contentment. Too many meals like this and the one last night, and she wouldn't be able to snap her blue jeans.

She broke off another piece. "So, what's going on with you, Cherry? Didn't you graduate from Nicholls State a couple years ago?"

"Harvard on the bayou to us grads. And it was last year. Got a degree in nutrition. Not much call for nutritionists in Cypress Springs," she finished with a shrug. "I guess I didn't think *that* through."

"You might try Baton Rouge or—"

"I'm not leaving Cypress Springs."

"But you'd be close enough to—"

"No," she said flatly. "This is my home."

Awkward silence fell between them. Avery broke it first. "So what are you doing now?"

"I help Peg out down at the Azalea Café. And I sit on the boards of a couple charities. Teach Sunday school. Make Mom's life easier whenever I can."

"Has she been ill?"

She hesitated, then smiled. "Not at all. It's just...she's getting older. I don't like to see her working herself to a frazzle."

Avery took another sip of her coffee. "You live at home?"

"Mmm." She set down her cup. "It seemed silly not to. They have so much room." She paused a moment. "Mama and I talked about opening our own catering business. Not party or special-events catering, but one of those caterers who specialize in nutritious meals for busy families. We were going to call it Gourmet-To-Go or Gourmet Express."

"I've read a number of articles about those caterers. Apparently, it's the new big thing. I think you two would be great at that."

Cherry smiled, expression pleased. "You really think so?"

"With the way you both cook? Are you kidding? I'd be your first customer."

Her smile faltered. "We couldn't seem to pull it together.

Besides, I'm not like you, Avery. I don't want some big, fancy career. I want to be a wife and mother. It's all I ever wanted."

Avery wished she could be as certain of what she wanted. Of what would make her happy. Once upon a time she had been. Once upon a time, it seemed, she had known everything.

Avery leaned toward the other woman. "So, who is he? There must be a guy in the picture. Someone special."

The pleasure faded from Cherry's face. "There was. He— Do you remember Karl Wright?"

Avery nodded. "I remember him well. He and Matt were good friends."

"Best friends," Cherry corrected. "After Matt and Hunter...fell out. Anyway, we had something special...at least I thought we did. It didn't work out."

Avery reached across the table and squeezed her hand. "I'm sorry."

"He just up and...left. Went to California. We'd begun talking marriage and—"

She let out a sharp breath and stood. She crossed to the window and for a long moment simply stared out at the bright morning. Finally she glanced back at Avery. "I was pushing. Too hard, obviously. He called Matt and said goodbye. But not me."

"I'm really sorry, Cherry."

She continued as if Avery hadn't spoken. "Matt urged him to call me. Talk it out. Compromise, but..." Her voice trailed helplessly off.

"But he didn't."

"No. He'd talked about moving to California. I always resisted. I didn't want to leave my family. Or Cypress Springs. Now I wish..."

Her voice trailed off again. Avery stood and crossed to her. She laid a hand on her shoulder. "Someone else will come along, Cherry. The right one."

Cherry covered her hand. She met Avery's eyes, hers filled

with tears. "In this town? Do you know how few eligible bachelors there are here? How few guys my age? They all leave. I wish I wanted a career, like you. Because I could do that on my own. But what I want more than anything takes two. It's just not fai—"

Her voice cracked. She swallowed hard; cleared her throat. "I sound the bitter old spinster I am."

Avery smiled at that. "You're twenty-four, Cherry. Hardly a spinster."

"But that's not the way I... It hurts, Avery."

"I know." Avery thought of what Cherry had said the night before, about loving someone to the point of tragedy. In light of this conversation, her comment concerned Avery. She told her so.

Cherry wiped her eyes. "Don't worry, I'm not going to do anything crazy. Besides," she added, visibly brightening, "maybe Karl will come back? You did."

Avery didn't have the heart to correct her. To tell her she wasn't certain what her future held. "Have you spoken with him since he left?"

Fresh tears flooded Cherry's eyes. Avery wished she could take the question back. "His dad's gotten a few letters. He's over in Baton Rouge, at a home there. I go see him once a week."

"And Matt?"

"They spoke once. And fought. Matt chewed him out pretty good. For the way he treated me. He hasn't heard from him since."

Avery could bet he had chewed him out. Matt had always returned Cherry's hero worship with a kind of fierce protectiveness.

"He's missed you, you know."

Avery met Cherry's gaze, surprised. "Excuse me?"

"Matt. He never stopped hoping you'd come back to him."

Avery shook her head, startled by the rush of emotion she

felt at Cherry's words. "A lot of time's passed, Cherry. What we had was wonderful, but we were very young. I'm sure there have been other women since—"

"No. He's never loved anyone but you. No one ever measured up."

Avery didn't know what to say. She told Cherry so.

The younger woman's expression altered slightly. "It's still there between you two. I saw it last night. So did Mom and Dad."

When she didn't reply, Cherry narrowed her eyes. "What are you so afraid of, Avery?"

She started to argue that she wasn't, then bit the words back. "A lot of time's passed. Who knows if Matt and I even have anything in common anymore."

"You do." Cherry caught her hand. "Some things never change. And some people are meant to be together."

"If that's so," Avery said, forcing lightness into her tone, "we'll know."

Instead of releasing her hand, Cherry tightened her grip. "I can't allow you to hurt him again. Do you understand?"

Uncomfortable, Avery tugged on her hand. "I have no plans of hurting your brother, believe me."

"I'm sure you mean that, but if you're not serious, just stay away, Avery. Just...stay...away."

"Let go of my hand, Cherry. You're hurting me."

She released Avery's hand, looking embarrassed. "Sorry. I get a little intense when it comes to my brothers."

Without waiting for Avery to respond, she made a show of glancing at her watch, exclaiming over the time and how she would be late for a meeting at the Women's Guild. She quickly packed up the picnic basket, insisting on leaving the thermos of coffee and remaining biscuits for Avery.

"Just bring the thermos by the house," she said, hurrying toward the door.

It wasn't until Cherry had backed her Mustang down the

driveway and disappeared from sight that Avery realized how unsettled she was by the way their conversation had turned from friendly to adversarial. How unnerved by the woman's threatening tone and the way she had seemed to transform, becoming someone Avery hadn't recognized.

Avery shut the door, working to shake off the uncomfortable sensations. Cherry had always looked up to Matt. Even as a squirt, she had been fiercely protective of him. Plus, still smarting from her own broken heart made her hypersensitive to the idea of her brother's being broken.

No, Avery realized. Cherry had referred to her brothers, plural. She got a little intense when it came to her *brothers*.

Odd, Avery thought. Especially in light of the things she had said about Hunter the night before. If Cherry felt as strongly about Hunter as she did about Matt, perhaps she'd had more interaction with Hunter than she'd claimed. And perhaps her anger was more show than reality.

But why hide the truth? Why make her feelings out to be different than they were?

Avery shook her head. Always looking for the story, she thought. Always looking for the angle, the hidden motive, the elusive piece of the puzzle, the one that broke the story wide open.

Geez, Avery. Give it a rest. Stop worrying about other people's issues and get busy on your own.

She certainly had enough of them, she acknowledged, shifting her gaze to the stairs. After all, if she got herself wrapped up in others' lives and problems, she didn't have to face her own. If she was busy analyzing other people's lives, she wouldn't have time to analyze her own.

She wouldn't have to face her father's suicide. Or her part in it.

Avery glanced up the stairway to the second floor. She visualized climbing it. Reaching the top. Turning right. Walking to the end of the hall. Her parents' bedroom door was closed. She had noticed that the night before. Growing up, it had always been open. It being shut felt wrong, final.

Do it, Avery. Face it.

Squaring her shoulders, she started toward the stairs, climbed them slowly, resolutely. She propelled herself forward with sheer determination.

She reached her parents' bedroom door and stopped. Taking a deep breath, she reached out, grasped the knob and twisted. The door eased open. The bed, she saw, was unmade. The top of her mother's dressing table was bare. Avery remembered it adorned with an assortment of bottles, jars and tubes, with her mother's hairbrush and comb, with a small velveteen box where she had kept her favorite pieces of jewelry.

It looked so naked. So empty.

She moved her gaze. Her father had removed all traces of his wife. With them had gone the feeling of warmth, of being a family.

Avery pressed her lips together, realizing how it must have hurt, removing her things. Facing this empty room night after night. She'd asked him if he needed help. She had offered to come and help him clean out her mother's things. Looking back, she wondered if he had sensed how halfhearted that offer had been. If he had sensed how much she hadn't wanted to come home.

"I've got it taken care of, sweetheart. Don't you worry about a thing."

So, she hadn't. That hurt. It made her feel small and selfish. She should have been here. Avery shifted her gaze to the double dresser. Would her mother's side be empty? Had he been able to do what she was attempting to do now?

She hung back a moment more, then forced herself through the doorway, into the bedroom. There she stopped, took a deep breath. The room smelled like him, she thought. Like the spicy aftershave he had always favored. She remembered being a little girl, snuggled on his lap, and pressing her face into his sweater. And being inundated with that smell—and the knowledge that she was loved.

The womb from her nightmare. Warm, content and protected.

Sometimes, while snuggled there, he had rubbed his stubbly cheek against hers. She would squeal and squirm—then beg for more when he stopped.

Whisker kisses, Daddy. More whisker kisses.

She shook her head, working to dispel the memory. To clear her mind. Remembering would make this more difficult than it already was. She crossed to the closet, opened it. Few garments hung there. Two suits, three sports coats. A half-dozen dress shirts. Knit golf shirts. A tie and belt rack graced the back of the door; a shoe rack the floor. She stood on tiptoe to take inventory of the shelf above. Two hats—summer and winter. A cardboard storage box, taped shut.

Her mom's clothes were gone.

Avery removed the box, set it on the floor, then turned and crossed to the dresser. On the dresser top sat her dad's coin tray. On it rested his wedding ring. And her mother's. Side by side.

The implications of that swept over her in a breath-stealing wave. He had wanted them to be together. He had placed his band beside hers before he—

Blinded by tears, Avery swung away from the image of those two gold bands. She scooped up the cardboard box and hurried from the room. She made the stairs, ran down them. She reached the foyer, dropped the box and darted to the front door. She yanked it open and stepped out into the fresh air.

Avery breathed deeply through her nose, using the pull of oxygen to steady herself. She had known this wouldn't be easy.

But she hadn't realized it would be so hard. Or hurt so much.

The toot of a horn interrupted her thoughts. She glanced toward the road. Mary Dupre, she saw. Another longtime neighbor. The woman waved, pulled her car over and climbed out. She hurried up the driveway, short gray curls bouncing.

She reached Avery and hugged her. "I'm so sorry, sweetie."

Avery hugged her back. "Thank you, Mary."

"I wish I'd gone to Buddy or Pastor Dastugue, but I...didn't. And then it was too late."

"Go to Buddy or Pastor about what?"

"How odd your daddy was acting. Not leaving the house, letting his yard go. I tried to pay a visit, bring him some of my chicken and andouille gumbo, but he wouldn't come to the door. I knew he was home, too. I thought maybe he was sleeping, but I glanced back on my way down the driveway and saw him peeking out the window."

Avery swallowed hard at the bizarre image. It didn't fit the father she had known. "I don't know what to say, Mary. I had no...idea. We spoke often, but he didn't...he never said...anything."

"Poor baby." The woman hugged her again. "I'm bringing some food by later."

"There's no need—"

"There is," she said firmly. "You'll need to eat and I'll not have you worrying about preparing anything."

Avery acquiesced, grateful. "I appreciate your thoughtfulness."

"I see I'm not the first."

"Pardon?"

The woman pointed. Avery glanced in that direction. A basket sat on the stoop by the door.

Avery retrieved it. It contained homemade raisin bread and a note of condolence. She read the brief, warmly worded note, tears stinging her eyes.

"Laura Jenkins, I'll bet," Mary Dupre said, referring to the woman who lived next door. "She makes the best raisin bread in the parish."

Avery nodded and returned the note to its envelope.

"You're planning a service?"

"I'm meeting with Danny Gallagher this afternoon."

"He does good work. You need help with anything, anything at all, you call me."

Avery promised she would, knowing that the woman meant it. Finding comfort in her generosity. And the kindness she seemed to encounter at every turn.

She watched the woman scurry down the driveway, a bright bird in her purple and orange warm-up suit, waved goodbye, then collected Laura Jenkins's basket and carried it to the kitchen.

The last thing she needed was more food, but she sliced off a piece of the bread anyway, set it on a napkin and placed it on the kitchen table. While she reheated the last of the coffee, she retrieved the cardboard box from the foyer.

She had figured the box would contain photos, cards or other family mementos. Instead, she found it filled with newspaper clippings.

Curious, Avery began sifting through them. They all concerned the same event, one that had occurred the summer of 1988, her fifteenth summer.

She vaguely remembered the story: a Cypress Springs woman named Sallie Waguespack had been stabbed to death in her apartment. The perpetrators had turned out to be a couple of local teenagers, high on drugs. The crime had caused a citizen uproar and sent the town on a crusade to clean up its act.

Avery drew her eyebrows together, confused. Why had her father collected these? she wondered. She picked up one of the clippings and gazed at the grainy, yellowed image of Sallie Waguespack. She'd been a pretty woman. And young. Only twenty-two when she died.

So, why had her father collected the clippings, keeping them all these years? Had he been friends with the woman? She didn't recall having ever met her or heard her name, before the murder anyway. Perhaps he had been her physician?

Perhaps, she thought, the articles themselves would provide the answer.

Avery dug all the clippings out of the box, arranging them by date, oldest to most recent. They spanned, she saw, four months—June through September 1988.

Bread and coffee forgotten, she began to read.

As she did, fuzzy memories became sharp. On June 18, 1988, Sallie Waguespack, a twenty-two-year-old waitress, had been brutally murdered in her apartment. Stabbed to death by a couple of doped-up teenagers.

The Pruitt brothers, she remembered. They had been older, but she had seen them around the high school, before they'd dropped out to work at the canning factory.

They'd been killed that same night in a shoot-out with the police.

How could she have forgotten? It had been the talk of the school for months after. She remembered being shocked, horrified. Then...saddened. The Pruitt brothers had come from the wrong side of the tracks— actually the wrong side of what the locals called The Creek. Truth was, The Creek was nothing more than a two-mile-long drainage ditch that had been created to keep low areas along the stretch from flooding but ultimately had served as the dividing line between the good side of town and the bad.

They'd been wild boys. They'd gone with fast girls. They'd drunk beer and smoked pot. She'd stayed as far away from them as possible.

Even so, the tragedy of it all hadn't been lost on her, a sheltered fifteen-year-old. All involved had been so young. How had the boys' lives gone so terribly askew? How could such a thing happen in the safe haven of Cypress Springs?

Which was the question the rest of the citizenry had wondered as well, Avery realized as she shuffled through the articles. They fell into two categories: ones detailing the actual crime and investigation, and the lion's share, editorials written by the outraged citizens of Cypress Springs. They'd demanded change. Accountability. A return to the traditional values that had made Cypress Springs a good place to raise a family.

Then, it seemed, things had quieted down. The articles became less heated, then stopped. Or, Avery wondered, had her father simply stopped collecting them?

Avery sat back. She reached for the cup of coffee and sipped. Cold and bitter. She grimaced and set the cup down. Nothing in the articles answered the question why her father had collected them.

She had lived through these times. Yes, her parents had discussed the crime. Everyone had. But not to excess. She had never sensed her father being unduly interested in it.

But he had been. Obviously.

She glanced at her watch, saw that it was nearly noon already. Perhaps Buddy would know the why, she thought. If she hurried, she should have plenty of time to stop by the CSPD before her two o'clock appointment with Danny Gallagher.

CHAPTER 6

Cypress Springs's police headquarters hadn't changed in the years she had been gone. Located in an old storefront downtown, a block off Main in back of the courthouse, it resembled a hardware store or feed and seed more than a modern law enforcement center.

Avery entered the building. The whirling ceiling fans kicked up fifty years of dust. The sun streaming through the front window illuminated the millions of particles. The officer on desk duty looked up. He was so young, he still sported a severe case of adolescent acne.

She stopped at the desk and smiled. "Is Buddy in?"

"Sure is. You here to see him?"

"Nope, just wanted to see if he was here."

The kid's face went slack for a moment, then he laughed. "You're teasing me, right?"

"Yes. Sorry."

"That's okay. Are you Avery Chauvin?"

She nodded. "Do I know you?"

"You used to baby-sit me. I'm Sammy Martin. Del and Marge's boy."

She thought a moment, then smiled. As a kid, he had been an absolute terror. Interesting that he had decided to go into law enforcement. "I never would have known it was you, Sammy. Last time I saw you, you were what? Eight or nine?"

"Eight." His smile slipped. "Sorry about your dad. None of us could believe it."

"Thanks." She cleared her throat, furious with herself for the tears that sprang to her eyes. "You said Buddy was in?"

"Oh, yeah. I'll tell him you're here." He turned. "Buddy! Got a visitor!"

Buddy shouted he'd be out in a "jiffy" and Avery grinned. "Fancy intercom system, Sammy."

He laughed. "Isn't it, though. But we make do."

His phone rang and she wandered away from the desk. She crossed to the community bulletin board, located to the right of the front door. Another one just like it was located in the library, the post office and the Piggly Wiggly. Cypress Springs's communications center, she thought. That hadn't changed, either.

She scanned the items tacked to the board, a conglomeration of community information flyers, Most Wanted and Missing posters and For-Sale-by-Owner ads.

"Baby girl," Buddy boomed. She turned. He came around Sammy's desk, striding toward her, boots thundering against the scuffed wooden floors.

"I was afraid you'd be at lunch."

"Just got back." He hugged her. "This is a nice surprise."

She returned the hug. "Do you have a minute to talk?"

"Sure." He searched her expression. "Is everything okay?"

"Fine. I wanted to ask you about something I found in my dad's closet."

"I'll try. Come on." He led her to his office. Cluttered shelves, battered furniture and walls covered with honorary plaques and awards spoke of a lifetime of service to the community.

Avery sat in one of the two chairs facing his desk. She dug out the couple of clipped articles she had stuffed into her purse and handed them to him. "I found a box of clippings like these in Dad's bedroom closet. I hoped you'd be able to tell me why he'd kept them."

He scanned the two clippings, eyebrows drawing together. He met her eyes. "Are you certain your dad collected them and not your mom?"

She hesitated, then shook her head. "Not one hundred percent. But Dad had removed everything else of Mom's from the closet, so why keep these?"

"Gotcha." He handed the two back. "To answer your question, I don't know why he saved them. Even considering the nature of the case, it seems an odd thing for him to do."

"That's what I thought. So, he wasn't involved with the investigation in any way?"

"Nope."

"Was he Sallie's physician?"

"Could have been, though I don't know for sure. I'd guess yes, just because for a number of years he was Cypress Springs's only general practitioner. And even after Bobby Townesend opened his practice, then Leon White, your daddy remained the town's primary doctor. People around here are loyal and they certainly don't like change."

She pursed her lips. "Do you remember this event?"

"Like it was yesterday." He paused, passed a hand over his forehead. "In my entire career, I've only investigated a handful of murders. Sallie Waguespack's was the first. And the worst."

He hesitated a moment, as if gathering his thoughts. "But the trouble started before her murder. From the moment we learned that Old Dixie Foods was considering opening a factory just south of here. The community divided over the issue. Some called it progress. A chance to financially prosper. A chance for businesses that had always fought just to survive to finally have the opportunity to grow, maybe even turn a profit.

"Others predicted doom. They predicted the ruination of a way of life that had stood for a century. A way of life disappearing all over the South. They cited other Southern communities that had been changed for the worse by the influx of big business."

He laid his hands flat on the desk. She noticed their enormous size. "The topic became a hot button. Friendships were strained. Working relationships, too. Some families were divided on the issue.

"I admit I was one of those blinded by the idea of progress, financial growth. I didn't buy the downside."

"Which was?"

"The influx of five hundred minimum-wage workers, many of them unmarried males. The housing and commercial support system that would have to be created to accommodate them. How they would alter the social and moral structure of the community."

"I'm not certain I understand what you mean."

"This is a community devoted to God and family. We're a bit of an anachronism in this modern world. Family comes first. Sunday is for worship. We live by the Lord's commandments and the Golden Rule. Put a couple hundred single guys on the street on a Friday night, money in their pockets and what do you think is going to happen?"

She had a pretty good idea—and none of it had to do with

the Golden Rule. "And my father?" she asked. "Where did he stand on the issue?"

Buddy met her eyes. His brow furrowed. "I don't remember for sure. I'm thinking he saw the downside all along. He was a smart man. Smarter than me, that's for certain."

After a moment, he continued. "In the end, of course, the town had little recourse. The factory was built. Money began pouring into Cypress Springs. The town grew. And people's worst predictions came true."

He stood and turned toward the window behind his desk. He gazed out, though Avery knew there was little to see—just a dead-end alley and the shadow of the courthouse.

"I love this town," he said without looking at her. "Grew up here, raised my family here. I'll die here, I suspect. Those four months in 1988 were the only time I considered leaving."

He turned and met her eyes. "The crime rate began to climb. We're talking the serious stuff, the kind of crimes we'd never seen in Cypress Springs. Rape. Armed robbery. Prostitution, for God's sake."

He released a weary-sounding breath. "It didn't happen overnight, of course. It sneaked up on us. An isolated crime here, another there. I called them flukes. Pretty soon, I couldn't call them that anymore. Same with some of the other changes occurring in the community. Teenage pregnancies began to rise. As did the divorce rate. Suddenly, we were having the kind of trouble at the high school they had at big-city schools—alcohol, drugs, fighting."

She vaguely recalled fights, and somebody getting caught smoking pot in the bathroom of the high school. She had been insulated from it all, she realized. In her warm, protected womb.

"It must have been difficult for you," she said.

"Folks were scared. And angry. Real angry. The town was turning into a place they didn't like. Naturally they turned their anger on me."

"They felt you weren't doing enough."

It wasn't a question but he nodded anyway. "I was in over my head, no doubt about it. Didn't have the manpower or the experience to deal with the increased crime rate. Hell, our specialty had been traffic violations, the occasional barroom brawl and sticky-fingered kids shoplifting bubble gum from the five-and-dime. Then Sallie Waguespack was killed."

He returned to his chair and sank heavily onto it. "This town went ballistic. The murder was grisly. She was young, pretty and had her whole life ahead of her. Her killers were high on drugs. There's just nothing easy about that scenario."

"Why'd they kill her, Buddy?"

"We don't know. We suspect the motive was robbery but—"

"But," she prodded.

"Like I said, she was young and pretty. And wild. They ran in the same crowd, frequented the same kinds of places. The Pruitt boys knew her. Could have been that one—or both—of them were romantically involved with her. Maybe they fought. Maybe she tried to break it off. Won't know any of that for sure, but what I do know is, the evidence against them was rock solid."

He fell silent. She thought a moment, going over the things he had told her, trying to find where her father fit in. *If* he fit in. "What happened then, Buddy?"

He blinked. "We closed the case."

"Not that, I mean with the community. The crime rate."

"Things quieted down, they always do. Some good came of Sallie's death. People stopped taking the community, their quality of life, for granted. They realized that safety and a community spirit were worth working for. People started watching out for each other. Caring more. Service groups formed to help those in need. Drug awareness began being taught in the schools. As did sex education. Counseling was provided for those in need. Instead of condemning people in crisis, we began to offer help. The citizens voted to increase my budget and I put more officers on the street. The crime rate began to fall."

"My first thought upon driving into town was how unchanged Cypress Springs seemed."

"A lot of effort has gone into maintaining that." He smiled. "Would you believe, tourism has become our number one industry? Lots of day-trippers, people on their way to and from St. Francisville. They come to see our pretty, old-time town."

She wondered if that was a hint of cynicism she heard in his voice.

"What about the canning plant?"

"Burned a couple years back. Old Dixie was in financial difficulty and didn't rebuild. Without job opportunities, those without other ties to Cypress Springs moved. If you're looking for an apartment, there're plenty of vacancies."

Avery smiled. "I'll keep that in mind."

"Old Dixie went belly-up last year. The burned-out hulk's for sale. Myself, I can't see anyone buying it. It's a stinking eyesore on the countryside. And I mean that literally."

She arched an eyebrow in question and he laughed without humor. "Just wait. You haven't been here long enough to know what I'm talking about. When conditions are just right—the humidity's high, the temperature's warm and the wind's blowing briskly from the south, the sour smell of the plant inundates Cypress Springs. Folks close their windows and stay inside. Even so, it's damn hard to ignore."

"Makes it hard to forget, too, I'll bet." Avery wrinkled her nose. "Does the town have any recourse?"

"Nope, company's Chapter 7." He leaned toward her. "Can't squeeze blood out of a turnip. Waste of time to try."

Avery fell silent a moment, then looked at Buddy, returning to the original reason for her visit. "Why did Dad clip and save all these articles, all these years, Buddy?"

"Don't know, baby girl. I just don't know."

"Am I interrupting?" Matt asked from behind her.

Avery turned. Matt stood in the doorway, looking official in his sheriff's department uniform.

"What're you doing here, son?"

"Do I need a reason to pop in to see my old man?"

"'Course not." Buddy glanced at his watch. "But it's past lunch and the middle of a workday."

Matt shifted his gaze to hers. "You see why I chose the sheriff's department over the CSPD? He'd have been all over me, all day."

Buddy snorted. "Right. Nobody needs to sit on top of you and you know it. You practically breathe that job." He wagged a finger at his son. "Truth be told, I wouldn't have had you work for me—I'd never have gotten a moment's peace."

"Slacker." Matt strode into the room, stopping behind Avery's chair. "You have a woman call in a missing person last week?" he asked his dad.

Buddy's expression tensed. "Yeah. What about it?"

"Just got off the phone with her. She thinks you're not doing anything on the case, asked the sheriff's department to check it out."

The older man leaned back in his chair. "I don't know what she expects. I've done everything I can do."

"Figured as much. Had to ask anyway."

Avery moved her gaze between the two men. "Do I need to go?"

"You're okay." Matt laid a hand on her shoulder. "In fact, you're an investigative reporter, you give us your take on this. Dad?"

Buddy nodded and took over. "I got a call last week from a woman who said her boyfriend contacted her by cell phone from just outside Cypress Springs. He told her he broke down and was going to call a service station for a tow. She never heard from him again."

"Where was he heading?" she asked.

"To St. Francisville. Coming from a meeting in Clinton."

"Why?"

"Business. Meeting with a client. He was in advertising."

"Go on."

"I spoke with every service station within twenty miles. Nobody got a call. I asked around town, put up flyers, haven't gotten a nibble. I told her that."

Matt moved around her chair and perched on the edge of the desk, facing her. "So, what do you think? She's screaming foul play."

"So where's the body?" Avery asked. "Where's the car?"

"And not any car. A Mercedes. Tough to lose one of those around here." Matt pursed his lips. "But why would this woman lie?"

"We see a lot of that in journalism. Everybody wants their fifteen minutes of fame. To feel important. Or in this woman's case, maybe to rationalize why her boyfriend hasn't called."

She glanced at her watch and saw that it was nearly time for her meeting at Gallagher's. She stood. "I've got to go. Danny Gallagher is expecting me in at two." She looked at Buddy. "Thanks for taking all this time to talk to me, I appreciate it."

"If something comes to mind, I'll let you know." He came around the desk and kissed her cheek. "Are you going to be okay?"

"I always am."

"Good girl."

Matt touched her arm. "I'll walk you out."

They exited the station and stepped into the bright midday sun. Avery dug her sunglasses out of her handbag. She slipped them on and looked up to find him gazing at her.

"What were you and Dad talking about?"

"A box of newspaper clippings I found in Dad's closet. They were all concerning the same event, the Sallie Waguespack murder."

"That doesn't surprise me."

"It doesn't?"

"That's the story that blew this little burg wide open."

"I hardly remembered it until I read those clippings today."

"Because of Dad, I lived it." He grimaced. "The night of the murder, I heard him with Mom. He was...crying. It's the only time I ever heard him cry."

She swallowed past the lump in her throat. "I feel like such an ostrich. First Dad, now learning this. I wonder—" She bit the words back and shook her head. "I need to go. Danny's expecting—"

"You wonder what?" he asked, touching her arm.

She let out a constricted-sounding breath. "I'm starting to wonder just what kind of person I am."

"You were young. It wasn't your tragedy."

"And what of now? What about my dad? Was that my tragedy?"

"Avery, you can't keep beating yourself up about this. You didn't light that match. He did."

But if she had been here for him, would he still have done it?

"I've got to go, Matt. Danny's waiting."

She started off. He called her name, stopping her. She turned.

"Next Sunday? Spring Fest?"

"With you?"

He shot her his cocky smile. The one that had always had her saying yes when she should have been saying no. "If you think you could take an entire day of my company?"

She returned the smile. "I think I could manage it."

"Great. I'll give you a call about the time."

Pleased, she watched him head back to his cruiser. In that moment, he looked sixteen. Full of the machismo of youth, buoyed by a yes from the opposite sex.

"If you're not serious, just stay away. Just....stay...away."

Her smile slipped as she remembered Cherry's warning.

Avery shook off the ripple of unease that moved over her. She was being ridiculous. Cherry was a sweet girl who was worried about her brother. Matt was lucky to have someone who cared so much about him.

CHAPTER 7

The Gavel called the meeting to order. All six of his generals were in attendance. Ready to do battle. To lay down their lives for their beliefs and their community.

Each believed himself a patriot at war.

He surveyed the group, proud of them, of his selections. They represented both the old and new guard of Cypress Springs. Wisdom invigorated by youth. Youth tempered by the wisdom of experience. A difficult combination to beat.

"Good evening," he said. "As always, I appreciate the sacrifice each of you made to be here tonight."

Because of the nature of the group, because some would not understand their motives—even those who stood to benefit most from their efforts, indeed, their sacrifice—they met in secret and under cover of late night. Even their families didn't know the location or true nature of these meetings.

"I have bad news," he told the group. "I have reason to believe Elaine St. Claire has contacted a Cypress Springs citizen."

A murmur went around the table. One of his generals spoke. "How certain are you of this?"

"Quite. I saw the letter myself."

"This is bad," another said. "If she's brazen enough to contact someone in Cypress Springs, she very well might contact the authorities."

"I plan to take care of it."

"How? Isn't she living in New Orleans?"

"She can destroy us," another interjected. "To leave Cypress Springs is to lose the safety of our number."

The Gavel shook his head, saddened. New Orleans had been the perfect place for her. Sin city. Anything went.

But, it seemed, she hadn't been able to help herself. No doubt, the passing months had dimmed her fear, had lessened the immediacy of the danger. It was human nature, he acknowledged. He hadn't been surprised.

He was beginning to doubt the effectiveness of the warning system they had devised. Warnings rarely worked. Or only proved a short-term deterrent.

"She's in St. Francisville now," he said.

"Better," a general murmured. "We have friends there."

"We won't need them," the Gavel said. "I've planned a trap. A carefully executed trap."

"Lure her back to Cypress Springs," General Blue said. "Once here, she's ours."

"Exactly." He gazed from one face to another around the table. "Are we in agreement, shall I set the trap?"

The generals didn't hesitate. They had learned nothing good came with lack of conviction. Weakness opened the door to destruction.

The Gavel nodded. "Consider it done. Next? Any concerns?"

Blue spoke again. "A newcomer to Cypress Springs. An outsider. She's asking questions about The Seven. About our history."

The Gavel frowned. He'd heard, too. Outsiders always posed serious threats. They didn't understand what The Seven were fighting for. How seriously they took their convictions. Invariably, they had to be dealt with quickly and mercilessly.

Outsiders with knowledge of The Seven posed an even more significant danger.

Damn the original group, he thought. They'd been weak. They hadn't concealed their actions well. They hadn't been willing to take whatever measures were required, no matter the consequences to life or limb.

Too touchy-feely, the Gavel thought, lips twisting into a sneer. They'd bowed to internal fighting and the squeamishness of a few members. Bowed to a member who threatened to go to the American Civil Liberties Union and the Feds. And to any and all of those prissy-assed whiners who were sending this country to hell in a handbasket.

It made him sick to think about it. What about the rights of decent, law-abiding folks to have a safe, morally clean place to live?

That's where he and his generals differed from the original group. The Gavel had chosen his men carefully. Had chosen men as strong-willed as he. Men whose commitment to the cause mirrored his own in steadfastness and zeal.

He was willing to die for the cause.

He was willing to kill for it.

"The outsider," the Gavel asked, "anyone have a name yet?"

No one did. A general called Wings offered that she had just moved into The Guesthouse.

The Gavel nodded. Her name would be easy to secure. One call and they would have it.

"Let's keep an eye on this one," he advised. "She doesn't make a move we don't know about. If she becomes more of a risk, we take the next step."

He turned to Hawk, his most trusted general. The man inclined his head in the barest of a nod. The Gavel smiled. Hawk understood; he agreed. If necessary, they would take care of this outsider the way they'd taken care of the last.

Determination flowing through him, he adjourned the meeting.

CHAPTER 8

The Azalea Café served the best buttermilk pancakes in the whole world. Fat, fluffy and slightly sweet even without syrup, Avery had never stopped craving them—even after twelve years away from Cypress Springs. And after a weekend spent preparing her childhood home for sale, Avery had decided a short stack at the Azalea wasn't just a treat—it was a necessity.

She stepped into the café. "Morning, Peg," she called to the gray-haired woman behind the counter. Peg was the third-generation Becnal to run the Azalea. Her grandmother had opened the diner when her husband had been killed in the Second World War and she'd needed to support her five kids.

"Avery, sweetheart." She came around the counter and

gave Avery a big hug. She smelled of syrup and bacon from the griddle. "I'm so sorry about your daddy. If I can do anything, anything at all, you just let me know."

Avery hugged her back. "Thanks, Peg. That means a lot to me."

When the woman released her, Avery saw that her eyes were bright with tears. "Bet you came in for some of my world-famous pancakes."

Avery grinned. "Am I that transparent?"

"You ate your first short stack at two years old. I remember your daddy and mama like to have died of shock, you ate the whole thing. Every last bite." She smoothed her apron. "Have yourself a seat anywhere. I'll send Marcie over with coffee."

The nine-to-fivers had come and gone, leaving Avery her choice of tables. Avery slipped into one of the front window booths. She looked out the window, toward the town square. They had begun setting up for Spring Fest, she saw. City workers were stringing lights in the trees and on the gazebo. Friday night it would look like a fairyland.

A smile tipped the corners of her mouth. Louisianians loved to celebrate and used any opportunity to do so: the Blessing of the Fleet on Little Caillou Bayou, the harvest of the strawberries in Pontchatoula, Louisiana's musical heritage in New Orleans at the Jazz Fest, to name only a few. Spring Fest was Cypress Springs's offering, a traditional Louisiana weekend festival, complete with food booths, arts and crafts, music and carnival rides for the kids. People from all over the state would come and every available room in Cypress Springs would be booked. She had gone every year she'd lived at home.

"Coffee, hon?"

Avery turned. "Yes, thanks."

The girl filled her cup, then plunked down a pitcher of cream. Avery thanked her, added cream and sugar to her coffee, then returned her gaze to the window and the square beyond.

The weekend had passed in an unsettling mix of despair and gratitude, tears and laughter. Neighbors and friends had stopped by to check on her, bringing food, baked goods and flowers. The last time she'd seen most of them had been at her mother's funeral and then only briefly. The majority had stayed to chat, reliving times past—sharing their sweet, funny, outrageous and precious memories of her father. Some, too, shared their regret at not having acted on his bizarre behavior before it had been too late. The outpouring of concern and affection had made her task less painful.

But more, it had made her feel less alone.

Avery had forgotten what it was like to live among friends, to be a part of a community. Not just a name or a P.O. box number, but a real person. Someone who was important for no other reason than that they shared ownership of a community.

Avery sipped her coffee, turning her attention to her dad's funeral. Danny Gallagher had recommended Avery wake her father Wednesday evening, with a funeral to follow the next morning. He had chosen that day so the *Gazette* could run an announcement in both the Saturday and Wednesday editions. The whole town would want to pay their respects, he felt certain. This would offer them the opportunity to do so.

Lilah had insisted on opening her home for mourners after the service on Thursday. Avery had accepted, relieved.

Two days and counting.

Would burying him enable her to say goodbye? she wondered, curving her hands around the warm mug. Would the funeral give her a sense of closure? Or would she still feel this great, gaping hole in her life?

The waitress brought the pancakes and refilled her coffee. Avery thanked her and not bothering with syrup, dug in, making a sound of pleasure as the confection made contact with her taste buds.

In an embarrassingly short period of time, she had plowed through half the stack. She laid down her fork and sighed, contented.

"Are they as good as you remember?" Peg called from behind the counter.

"Better," she answered, pushing her plate away. "But if I eat any more I'll burst."

The woman shook her head. "No wonder you're so scrawny. I'll have Marcie bring your check."

Avery thanked her and turned back toward the square. She began to look away, then stopped as she realized that Hunter and his mother were standing across the street, partially hidden by an oak tree, deep in conversation.

Not a conversation, Avery saw. An argument. As she watched, Lilah lifted a hand as if to slap her son but he knocked her hand away. He was furious; Avery could all but feel his anger. And Lilah's despair.

She told herself to look away. That she was intruding. But she found her gaze riveted to the two. They exchanged more words but as Hunter turned to walk away, Lilah grabbed at him. He shook her hand off, his expression disgusted.

Lilah was begging, Avery realized with a sense of shock. But for what? Her son's love? His attention? In the next moment, Hunter had strode off.

Lilah stared after him a moment, then seemed to crumble. She sagged against the tree and dropped her head into her hands.

Alarmed, Avery scooted out of the booth, hooking her handbag over her shoulder. "Peg," she called, hurrying toward the door, "could you hold my check? I'll be back later."

She didn't wait for the woman's answer but darted through the door and across the street.

"Lilah," she said gently when she reached the other woman. "Are you all right?"

"Go away, Avery. Please."

"I can't do that. Not when you're so upset."

"You can't help me. No one can."

She dropped her hands, turned her face toward Avery's. Ravaged by tears, stripped of makeup, she looked a dozen years older than the genteel hostess of the other night.

Avery held out a hand. "At least let me help you to your car. Or let me drive you home."

"I don't deserve your kindness. I've made so many mistakes in my life. With my children, my—" She wrung her hands. "God help me! It's all my fault! Everything's my fault!"

"Is that what Hunter told you?"

"I've got to go."

"Is that what Hunter told you? I saw you arguing."

"Let me go." She fumbled in her handbag for her car keys. Her hands shook so badly she couldn't hold on to them and they slipped to the ground.

Avery bent and snatched them up. "I don't know what he said to you, but it's not true. Whatever's wrong with Hunter is not your fault. He's responsible for the mess of his life, not you."

Lilah shook her head. "You don't know... I've been a terrible mother. I've done everything wrong. Everything!"

Lilah attempted to push past; Avery caught her by the shoulders. She forced the woman to meet her eyes. "That's not true! Think about Matt. And Cherry. Look how well they're doing, how happy they are."

The older woman stilled. She met Avery's eyes. "I don't feel well, Avery. Could you take me home?"

Avery said she could and led Lilah to her sedan, parked on the other side of the square. After helping the woman into the front passenger seat, Avery went around to the driver's side, climbed in and started the vehicle up.

The drive out to the ranch passed in silence. Lilah, Avery felt certain, possessed neither the want nor emotional wherewithal to converse. Avery pulled the sedan into the driveway and cut the engine. She went around the car, helped Lilah out, up the walk and into the house.

At the sound of the door opening, Cherry appeared at the top of the stairs. She looked from her mother to Avery. "What happened?"

"I'm all right," Lilah answered, an unmistakable edge in her voice. "Just tired."

Cherry hurried down the stairs. She took her mother's arm. "Let me help you."

"Please, don't fuss."

"Mother— —"

"I don't want to talk about it." She eased her arm from her daughter's grasp. "I have a headache and..." She turned toward Avery. "You're an angel for bringing me home. I hope I didn't interfere with your plans."

"Not at all, Lilah. I hope you feel better."

"I need to lie down now. Excuse me."

Cherry watched her mother make her way slowly up the stairs. When she had disappeared from view, she swung to face Avery, obviously distressed. "What happened?"

"I don't know." Avery passed a hand over her face. "I was at the Azalea, in one of the window booths. I looked out and there was your mother and Hunter—"

"Hunter!"

"They were arguing."

Her expression tightened. "Son of a... Why won't he leave her alone? Why won't he just go away?"

Avery didn't know what to say, so she said nothing. Cherry shook with fury. She strode to the entryway table, yanked up the top right drawer and dug out a pack of cigarettes and a lighter. Her hands shook as she lit the smoke. She crossed to the front door, opened it and stood in the doorway, smoking in silence.

After several drags, she turned back to Avery. "What were they arguing about?"

"That I don't know. She wouldn't say."

Cherry blew out a long stream of smoke. "What *did* she say?"

"That she had made a mess of her life. Of her children's lives. That everything was her fault."

Cherry squeezed her eyes shut.

"I told her it wasn't true," Avery continued. "I told her Hunter's problems were his own."

"But she didn't believe it."

"Actually, it seemed to calm her."

"Hallelujah." Cherry moved out onto the porch, stubbed out her cigarette in an ashtray hidden under a step, then returned to the foyer. "There's a first."

"I take it this has happened before."

"Oh, yeah. He hadn't been back in Cypress Springs twenty-four hours before he started shoveling his shit her way. All of our way, actually. You wouldn't believe some of the things he said. The things he accused us of."

Cherry sighed. "It doesn't matter how well Matt and I are doing, all she can focus on is Hunter and his troubles. And somehow it's all her fault."

"What happened to him, Cherry? Hunter used to be so...kind. And funny."

She lifted a shoulder. "I don't know. None of us do."

"It began that summer, didn't it? That summer Sallie Waguespack was killed."

Cherry looked sharply at her. "Why do you say that?"

"Because it was that summer he and Matt started fighting. Just after they'd gotten their driver's licenses." She paused. "It's when Hunter seemed to...change."

Cherry didn't comment; Avery filled the silence. "I wouldn't have thought of it except for all the clippings I found in Dad's closet." She quickly explained how she had found the box, sorted through it then questioned Buddy about the contents. "Truthfully, I'd forgotten the incident."

"Why do you think one had anything to do with the other?"

"Excuse me?"

"Why do you think that murder has anything to do with Hunter?"

Avery blinked, surprised by the other woman's assumption. "I didn't. I was just placing it in a time frame."

Cherry rubbed the spot between her eyes with her thumb, in obvious discomfort. "I was just a kid, I hardly remember it all. But it was...a time of upheaval. Everybody was upset. All the time, it seemed."

She dropped her hand and met Avery's eyes. "For whatever reason, Hunter's changed. He's not one of us anymore. As much as it hurts me to admit, I can't imagine what it does to Matt. They're twins, for God's sake. Once they were as close as two people could be."

Cherry shivered slightly and closed the door. "To his credit, Matt's gone on. So have Daddy and I. But Mother can't seem to...let go." She paused. "It's been much worse since Hunter came back to Cypress Springs. Before, we could forget, you know? Out of sight, out of mind. Even Mom. I think she consoled herself with his professional success."

Out of sight, out of mind. Avery understood. In a way, she had done that with her father. She had told herself he was happy, that he had a nice comfortable life. Now she had to live with just how wrong she'd been.

"Then home he came," Cherry continued, "with a shitload of bad attitude and so many chips on his shoulder it's amazing he can walk upright."

"Why, Cherry? The other night your dad said Hunter almost lost his license to practice law. Do you know what happened?"

"Yeah, I know. He had it all and he blew it. That's what happened. Professional success. Money, brains. A family who loved him. And he's blown it all to hell.

"You know what he's doing?" she asked. "The man's gone from practicing corporate law at one of the top firms in the South to taking the odd divorce and bankruptcy case in Cypress Springs. I don't get it. He's working and living down in what used to be Barker's Flower Shop, one block off the square. At the corner of Walton and Johnson. Remember it?"

Avery indicated she did.

"You already know what I really think about why he came back to Cypress Springs." She didn't wait for Avery to reply. "He's come back to hurt us. To punish us for some imagined sin or slight against him."

Cherry glanced toward the stairway thinking, Avery knew, of her mother. "And what's really sad is, he's succeeding."

CHAPTER 9

Avery left the ranch a short time later. Cherry told her to go ahead and take her mother's car—after one of these spells her mother didn't go out for days anyway.

As she drove through town, Avery couldn't stop thinking about what Cherry had said. About Hunter coming back to punish them. She'd dismissed Cherry's earlier claim, but now Avery couldn't put the image of Lilah's devastation out of her mind.

And the more she thought about it, the angrier she became. How could Hunter treat his family that way? All they had ever done was love and support him.

She didn't care if she had been gone for twelve years, she wasn't going to let him get away with it. The Stevenses were the closest thing to a family she had left, and she wasn't about to stand back and let Hunter hurt them.

She reached Walton Street, took a left, heading back toward Johnson. She found a parking spot a couple doors down from what had been Barker's Flower Shop. She angled into the spot and climbed out.

Barker's had been Cypress Springs's preferred florist during Avery's high-school years. Every corsage she'd worn had come from this shop.

And they'd all been from Matt, she realized. Every last one of them.

She reached the shop and felt a moment of loss at the empty front window. She used to love peering through at the buckets of cut flowers.

She tried the door. And found it locked. A cardboard clock face propped in the window proclaimed *Will Return At—*

Problem was the clock's hour hand was missing.

Cherry had said that Hunter used the front of the shop as his law office and lived in the back. If she remembered correctly, the Barkers had done the same. No doubt, the residence was accessed from the rear.

She went around back, to the service alley. Sure enough, the rear had been set up as a residential entrance.

She crossed to it and found the outer door stood open to allow fresh air in through the screen. She knocked on the door frame. "Hunter?" she called out. "It's Avery."

From inside came a scuffling, followed by a whimper. She frowned and knocked again. "Hunter? Is that you?"

The whimpering came again. She leaned closer and peered through the dirty screen. The room immediately beyond the door was a kitchen. It appeared empty.

From inside came a thud. Like something hitting the floor. Something? Or someone?

Reacting, she tried the screen door, found it unlocked and

pushed it open. She stepped through. Save for a handful of dishes in the sink, the kitchen was as neat as a pin.

Heart pounding, she made her way through the room. "Hunter?" she called again, softly. "It's Avery. Are you all right?"

This time, silence answered. No whimper, whine or scuffle.

Not good.

She rushed through the doorway to the next room and stopped short. The biggest, mangiest dog she had ever seen blocked her way, teeth barred. The beast growled low in its throat and Avery's stomach dropped to her toes.

She took a step back.

Whimpering from behind the dog drew her gaze. On a blanket shoved into the corner lay a half-dozen squirming pups, so young their eyes weren't open yet.

"It's okay, girl," Avery said gently, returning her gaze to the mama. "I won't hurt your pups."

The dog cocked its head as if deciding if Avery could be trusted, then turned and loped back to her babies. She flopped onto her side on the floor and the pups began rooting for a teat. With a heavy sigh, she thumped her tail—which was as thick as a broom handle—once against the wooden floor.

Avery shook her head, feeling more than a little ridiculous. What an imagination she had. Big bad Avery, rushing in to save the day.

She turned away from the nursing dog to take in the room. Neat but spartan, she thought. A shabby but comfortable mishmash of furniture and styles. An ancient-looking couch in a shade that had probably once been a bright gold, but could now only be described as vomit colored. A beat-up coffee table. And a beautiful, butter-colored leather easy chair.

Left over from the good old days, she would bet. The piece he hadn't been able to get rid of.

She turned. A makeshift desk and file cabinet had been set

up in the corner behind her. A computer rested atop the desk, screen dark. Beside the PC sat a stack of printer paper, a couple inches thick.

Curious, she crossed to the desk. A manuscript, she saw. She tipped her head to read. *Breaking Point*. A novel by Hunter Stevens.

Hunter was writing a novel? Why hadn't Matt or Cherry mentioned it?

Maybe they didn't—

"Come right in," Hunter said from behind her. "Make yourself at home."

Avery whirled around, hand to her throat. "Hunter!"

"You sound so surprised to see me. Were you expecting someone else?"

"This isn't how it looks. I didn't mean to—"

"To what?" he asked. "Break and enter?"

Cheeks burning, she tilted up her chin. "It wasn't like that. I can explain."

"Sure you can." He stalked past her, retrieved the manuscript and placed it in a file drawer. Avery noticed the way he handled the pages—carefully, with something akin to reverence.

"I didn't read anything but the title," she said softly. "And I didn't break in. The door was open."

He locked the drawer, pocketed the key then turned and faced her, arms folded across his chest. "How careless of me."

"I stopped by. And I heard a sound from inside. A...cry, then a thud. Like someone...falling. I thought you—"

At his disbelieving expression, she made a sound of frustration. "It was the dog and her pups I heard. I thought, you know, that something was wrong."

"Sarah?" He glanced over at the dog. At the sound of her name, the canine looked up and slapped her tail against the floor.

"See?" Avery said. "That's what I heard."

He smiled then, taking her by surprise. "You're right, that is a scary noise. Did you think the boogeyman had gotten me? Was big bad Avery going to rush in and save the day?"

The curving of his lips changed him into the young man she remembered from all those years ago and she returned his smile. "Why not? It could happen. I carry pepper spray. Besides, if you recall, I'm not one of those prissy, sissy girls like you dated in high school. Hunter," she mocked in an exaggerated drawl, "you're so big and strong. I don't know what I would do without you to protect me."

He laughed. "True, I would never call you prissy."

"Thank you for that."

"I'm sorry," he said. "For the other night. I acted like an ass."

"A bastard *and* an ass, actually. Apology accepted anyway."

The dog stood, shook off a last greedy pup and ambled over to Hunter. She looked adoringly up at him. He squatted beside her and scratched behind her ears. She practically swooned with delight.

Avery watched the two, thinking Hunter couldn't be quite as heartless as he acted. "She seems devoted to you."

"It's mutual. I found her when she was as down and out on her luck as I was. Figured we made a good pair."

Silence fell between them. Avery longed to ask about the circumstances that had brought him to this place, but didn't want to spoil the moment of camaraderie.

She chose a safer topic instead, motioning the computer. "Your family didn't mention that you were writing a novel."

"They don't know. No one does. Unless like you, they make a habit of breaking and entering." He straightened. Sarah remained by his feet. "And I'd appreciate it if you didn't tell them."

"If that's what you want. But I'm sure if they knew they'd be nothing but supporti—"

"It is what I want."

"All right." She tilted her head. "The book, what's it about?"

"It's a thriller." He didn't blink. "About a lawyer who goes off the deep end."

"It's autobiographical then?"

"What are you doing here, Avery?"

She decided that beating around the bush would be a waste of time. "I want to talk to you about your mother."

"There's a shock."

She stiffened at his sarcasm. "I saw the two of you this morning. Arguing. She was really upset, Hunter. Hysterical, actually."

He didn't respond. Not with surprise or remorse. Not with concern or guilt. His impassive expression made her blood boil. "You don't have a comment about that?"

"No."

"She couldn't even drive, Hunter. I had to take her home."

"What do you want me to say? That I'm sorry?"

"For starters."

"That's not happening. Anything else?"

She stared at him, stunned. That he could be so unfeeling toward his mother. So careless toward those who loved him.

She told him so and he laughed. "That's rich. The pot calling the kettle black."

"What's that supposed to mean?"

"You know damn well what it means. Where have you been the last few years, Avery?"

She saw what he was doing and backed off, not about to let him divert the conversation. "We're not talking about me here, Hunter. We're talking about you. About you blaming everyone but yourself for your problems. Why don't you grow up?"

"Why don't you butt out, Ms. Big-City Reporter? Head back to your important job. Your life isn't here. It never was."

Stung, she struck back. "You're lucky you have such a great family. A family who loves you. One willing to stick by you even when you're such a colossal jackass. Why don't you show a little gratitude?"

"Gratitude?" He laughed, the sound hard. "Great family? For an investigative reporter you're pretty damn obtuse."

She shook her head, disbelieving. "No family is perfect. But at least they've stayed committed to one another. They've tried to be there for one another, through thick and thin."

"When did you become such an expert on my family? You've only been here, what? A week? Wait!" He brought his fingertips to his forehead. "I've got it! You're psychic?"

"It's senseless to even try to have a conversation with you." She started toward the door. "I'm out of here."

"Of course you are. That's your MO, isn't it, Avery?"

She froze, then turned slowly to face him. "Excuse me?"

"Where have you been the past twelve years?"

"In case you haven't noticed, Cypress Springs isn't exactly the place to have a career in journalism."

He took a step toward her. "You're a fine one to scold me about how I treat my mother. Look at how you treated yours. How many times did you visit her after you moved away?"

"I called. I visited when I could. I couldn't just take off whenever the mood struck."

"How long did you stay after her funeral, Avery? Twenty-four hours? Or was it thirty-six?"

She swung toward the door; he followed her, grabbing her arm when she reached it. "And where were you, Avery, when your dad was so depressed he set himself on fire?"

A cry spilled past her lips. She tugged against his hand. He tightened his grip. "Your dad needed you. And you weren't here."

"What do you know about my father! About how he felt or what he needed!"

"I know more than you could imagine." He released her

and she stumbled backward. "I bet you didn't know that your dad and mine weren't even on speaking terms. That it had gotten so bad between them that if one saw the other coming on the street, he would cross to the other side to avoid making eye contact. I bet neither Matt nor Buddy told you that."

"Stop it, Hunter." She backed toward the door.

"I bet they didn't tell you that my parents haven't shared a bed in over a decade. Or that Mom's addicted to painkillers and booze." He laughed bitterly. "Dad's played the part of the jovial, small-town cop so long, he wouldn't recognize an authentic thought or feeling if it shouted his name. Matt's trying his damnedest to follow in the old man's footsteps and is so deeply in denial it's frightening. And Cherry, poor girl, has sacrificed her life to holding the dysfunctional lot together.

"Great family," he finished. "As American as apple pie and Prozac."

She stared at him, shaking with the force of her anger. "You're right. I wasn't here. And I hate myself for it. I would do anything, give anything, to change that. To bring them back. But I can't. I've lost them."

She grasped the door handle, fighting not to cry. Determined not to let him know he had won. "I didn't believe what Cherry told me. That you'd come back just to punish them. I believe it now."

He held out a hand. "Avery, I—"

"When did you become so cruel, Hunter?" she asked, cutting him off. "What happened to make you so hateful and small?"

Without waiting for an answer, she let herself out and walked away.

CHAPTER 10

Gwen Lancaster stood at the window of her rented room and peered through the blinds at the gathering darkness. Lights in the buildings around the square began popping on. Gwen kept her own lights off; she preferred the dark. Preferred to watch in anonymity.

Did they know she was here? she wondered. Did they know who she was? That Tom had been her brother?

Had they realized yet that she would stop at nothing to find his killer?

As always, thoughts of her brother brought a lump to her throat. She swung away from the window, crossed to the desk and the Cypress Springs *Gazette* she had been reading. It lay open to the upcoming calendar of events. She had marked off those she planned to attend. First on the list was tonight's wake.

She shifted her gaze to the paper and the black-and-white image of a kindly-looking older man. The caption identified him as Dr. Phillip Chauvin. Survived by his only child, a daughter, Avery Chauvin.

The entire town would be in attendance tonight. She had heard people talking about it. Had learned that the man had committed suicide. And that he had been one of Cypress Springs's most beloved brothers.

Suicide. Her lips twisted. Cypress Springs, it seemed, was just that kind of town.

Fury rose up in her. *They* would most probably be there. The bastards who had taken her brother from her.

Tom had been working toward his doctorate in social psychology from Tulane University. He'd been writing his dissertation on vigilantism in small-town America. A story he'd uncovered in the course of his research had brought him to Cypress Springs.

A story about a group called The Seven. A group that had operated from the late 1980s to the early 1990s, systematically denying the civil rights of their fellow citizens in the name of law and order.

After only a matter of weeks in Cypress Springs, Tom had disappeared without a trace.

Gwen swallowed hard. That wasn't quite true. His body had disappeared. His car had been found on the side of a deserted stretch of highway in the next parish. It had been in running order. There'd been no sign of a struggle or an accident. The keys had been gone.

Both the Cypress Springs police and sheriff's department had investigated. They'd combed her brother's car and the surrounding area for evidence. They'd searched his rented room, interviewed his fellow boarders, worked to reconstruct the last days of his life. Neither suspect nor motive had emerged.

They told her they believed he had been the victim of a random act of violence—that Tom had simply been in the wrong place at the wrong time. They had promised not to close the case until they uncovered what happened to him.

Gwen had a different theory about his disappearance. She believed his research into The Seven had gotten him killed. That he had gotten too close to someone or something. She had talked to him only days before he disappeared. He'd found so much more than he'd expected, he had told her. He believed that The Seven was not a thing of the past, but operating still. He had made an important contact; they were meeting the following night.

Gwen had begged him to be careful.

That had been the last time she'd heard his voice. The last time, she feared, she would ever hear his voice.

Although his research notes revealed nothing sinister, she hadn't a doubt his contact had either set him up or killed him.

Gwen brought the heels of her hands to her eyes. What if she was wrong? What if she simply needed someone —or something—she could point to and say they did it, that her brother was gone because of them. The therapist she had been seeing thought so. Hers was a common reaction, he'd said. The need to make sense out of a senseless act of violence. To create order out of chaos.

She dropped her hands, weary from her own thoughts. Chaos. That's what her life had become after Tom's disappearance.

She crossed back to the window. For several days city workers had been stringing lights in the trees. Tonight, it seemed, was the payoff. The thousands of twinkling lights snapped on, turning the town square into a fairyland.

It was so beautiful. Charming. A postcard-perfect community populated by the nicest people she had ever encountered.

It was a lie. An illusion. This place was not the idyllic paradise it seemed. People here were not the paragons they seemed.

And she would prove it. No matter what it cost her.

CHAPTER 11

Gallagher's funeral home was housed in a big old Victorian on Prospect Street. The Gallagher family had been in the funeral game for as long as Avery could remember. She and Danny had gone to school together, and she remembered a report he had given in the seventh grade on embalming. The girls had been horrified, the boys fascinated.

Being the biggest tomboy in Cypress Springs, she had fallen in line with the boys.

Danny Gallagher met her at the front door of the funeral home. He'd been a lady-killer in school and although time had somewhat softened his chin and middle, he was still incredibly handsome.

He caught her hands and kissed her cheeks. "Are you all right?"

"As well as can be expected, I guess."

He looked past her, a frown wrinkling his forehead. "You drove yourself?"

She had. Truth was, half a dozen people had offered to drive her tonight, including Buddy and Matt. She had refused them, even when they had begged her to reconsider. She had wanted to be alone.

"I'm a city girl," she murmured. "I'm used to taking care of myself."

He ushered her inside, clearly disapproving. "If you need anything, let me or one of the staff know. I'm expecting a big crowd."

Within twenty minutes he was proved correct—nearly the entire town was turning out to pay their respects. One after another, old friends, neighbors and acquaintances hugged her and offered their condolences. Some she recognized right off, others had to remind her who they were. Again and again, each expressed their shock and dismay over father's death.

Nobody actually said the word. But it hung in the air anyway. It was written on their faces, in the carefully chosen words and softly modulated tones. It was there in the things they didn't say.

Suicide.

And with that word, their unspoken accusation. Their condemnation. She hadn't been there for him. He had needed her and she had been off taking care of herself.

"Where were you, Avery, when your dad was so depressed he set himself on fire?"

Hunter's taunt from two days before was burned into her brain. She told herself he had meant to hurt her. That he was angry, hurting, just plain mean. She told herself he wouldn't win unless she let him.

But she couldn't tell herself the one thing she longed to: that the things he'd said weren't true. Because they were.

And in that lay their power.

Minutes ticked by at an agonizing pace. The walls began to close in on her. Her head became light; her knees weak. She felt as if she were suffocating on the smell of colognes and flowers, cloying, too sweet. Each vying for dominance over the other.

She had to get some air.

The patio.

She inched in that direction, fighting her mounting panic. She reached the doors, slipped through them and out into the unseasonably cool night air. She hurried to the patio's edge; grasped the railing for support.

"Keep it together, Avery. You can't fall apart yet."

From the other side of the patio came an embarrassed-sounding cough. She swung in that direction, realizing she wasn't alone. That she had been talking to herself.

A man she didn't recognize stood on the other side of the patio, smoking. She scolded herself for the spear of irritation she felt. It was she who was intruding. Not he.

He met her eyes. "Sorry about your dad, Ms. Chauvin. He was a fine man."

"Thank you," she said, fighting past the emotion that rose in her throat and crossing to him. "I'm sorry, but do I know you?"

He looked embarrassed. "We've never met." He extinguished the cigarette and held out a hand. "John Price. Cypress Springs Volunteer Fire Department."

She shook his hand. "Good to meet you."

He looked away, then back, expression pure misery. "I was on call that morning. I was the first to...see your dad."

He had seen her father.

He had been the first.

A half-dozen questions popped into her head. She uttered the first to her tongue. "What did you do then?"

He looked surprised. "Pardon?"

"After you found him, what happened next?"

"Called my captain. He called the state fire marshal. They sent the arson investigator assigned to our region. He's a good guy. Name's Ben Mitchell."

"And he called the coroner."

"Yup." He nodded. "Parish coroner. Coroner called Buddy."

"That's how it works?"

He shuffled slightly. "Yeah. Our job's elimination and containment of the fire itself, as well as search and rescue. Once our job's done, we call the state fire marshal. He determines how the fire started."

"And calls the coroner?"

"Yes. If there are victims. He calls the PD. Chain of command."

She felt herself emotionally disengaging, slipping into the role of journalist. It was an automatic thing, like breathing. She found it comforting. "And my father was dead when you got there?"

"No doubt about that. He—" The man bit back what he was about to say.

"What?"

"He was dead, Ms. Chauvin. Absolutely."

She shut her eyes, working to recall what she knew of death by burning. The arson piece she'd done. Those two little victims; she had seen a picture. Charred cadavers. Entirely black. Generic fea—

"Avery? Are you okay?"

At Matt's voice, she opened her eyes. He stood in the doorway, Cherry hovering just behind him.

"Fine." As she said the word, she realized she felt a hundred percent better than when she'd stepped outside.

"People are looking for you."

She nodded and turned back to the fireman. "John, I'd like to talk to you more about this. Could I give you a call, set up something?"

He shifted his gaze, obviously uncomfortable. "Sure, but I don't know what I could tell you that would—"

"Just for me," she said quickly. "For closure."

"I guess. You can reach me through the dispatcher."

She thanked him, turned and crossed to where Matt and Cherry waited.

"Ms. Chauvin?" She stopped and glanced back at the fireman. "You might want to call Ben Mitchell, at the state fire marshal's office in Baton Rouge. He could tell you a lot more than I can."

"Thanks, John. I'll do that."

"What was that all about?" Cherry asked.

"Nothing. I needed some air."

Cherry frowned slightly and glanced over her shoulder, obviously annoyed with her answer. "Jill Landry married him. You remember Jill? Met him through her sister, in Jackson."

"He seems like a nice guy."

"I guess."

Avery stopped and looked at the other woman. "Are you trying to tell me something, Cherry?"

"No. I just thought you should know...he's not from around here, Avery."

"He found Dad," she said sharply. "I was asking him about it. Is that okay with you?"

"I didn't mean anything—" She glanced from Avery to her brother, expression wounded. "I just...I'm worried about you, that's all."

"I'm a big girl, Cherry. I don't need protecting."

"I see that." Color flooded her cheeks. "I won't make that mistake again. Excuse me."

"She was only trying to be your friend," Matt said softly, tone reproachful. "She cares about you. We all do."

Avery swore softly. "I know. I just reacted."

Matt laid a hand on her arm. "I understand. Just don't—" He paused.

"What?"

"You're hurting. I'm sympathetic to that. We all are. But don't push us away, Avery. We love you."

She swallowed hard, eyes burning. He was right. Alienating the people who cared about her would do nothing but leave her more alone than she already was.

She caught his hand, squeezed his fingers. "Thank you," she whispered. "Your friendship means more to me than I can say."

He curled his fingers around hers. "I'm here for you, Avery. I've always been here for you."

The moment was broken by three older women. Members of her mother's quilting group, she learned.

Matt greeted the women, then excused himself. She watched as he made his way through the crowded room, heading in the direction Cherry had gone. He meant to find and comfort his sister.

She would apologize later, Avery promised herself, turning back to the three, accepting their condolences. The Quilting Bees, as they called themselves, exited, leaving Avery momentarily alone.

She swept her gaze over the gathering, stopping on a group of men who stood at the far end of the room. They spoke to one another quietly, expressions intent. She recognized several of them; though by face not name. None had spoken to her tonight. As she watched, one of them nodded toward someone outside their circle. The others glanced in the direction he indicated.

She turned. They seemed to be discussing a woman she didn't recognize. Tall, slim and sandy-haired, she wore a simple black skirt and white, button-front blouse. She was alone, standing by a tall, potted fern. Something about her expression looked lost.

Avery frowned and shifted her gaze back to the men. They were definitely looking at the woman. One of them laughed. She didn't know why that struck her as wrong, but it did.

She darted another glance at the woman. Who was she? A friend of one of the men?

"Avery, honey, I'm so sorry."

She dragged her gaze from the group, meeting the eyes of the woman who had been Avery's first-grade teacher. She accepted the woman's condolences, hug and promised to call if she needed anything.

Avery turned back toward the group of men. They had dispersed. The woman they'd been talking about was gone as well. She checked out the thinning crowd, searching for her without luck. She wondered if she had imagined the whole thing.

It wouldn't surprise her, she acknowledged, glancing toward her father's closed casket and experiencing a moment of pure panic. Nothing would surprise her anymore.

CHAPTER 12

Hunter stared at his computer screen, the things he'd written swimming before his eyes. Mocking him. With a sound of disgust he hit the delete button and watched as the cursor ate one letter after another until nothing was left but the blank page.

How could he write when the words filling his head were ones he had flung at Avery? How could he envision his characters when her image crowded his mind? Her hurt expression. The accusation in her eyes.

She had looked at him as if he were some sort of monster. *Dammit!* Hunter pushed away from the desk and stood. At the kitchen door, Sarah whined to go out. The dog had been antsy and agitated all evening—much as he himself had been.

He ignored her and made his way through the apartment and to the office in front. Empty, dark save for the blinking message light on his answer machine, he recalled the space as it had been: filled with the scent and color of flowers. Now it smelled as colorless as it looked. Like blank paper and law books.

He crossed to the front window and peered out at the dark street. From this vantage point he could see Gallagher's roof, one block over. They were all at Phillip's wake, he thought. His mother and father. Cherry. Matt. Most likely the entire town.

That's the kind of town this was.

He had figured Avery wouldn't care to see him. And he sure as hell hadn't wanted to see the Stevens clan. He wasn't certain he would have been able to hold his tongue.

And the last thing Avery needed was a confrontation.

He pressed the heels of his hands to his eyes. *Phillip. What a mess. Dammit.*

Hunter dropped his hands, acknowledging grief. Frustration. Truth was, he longed to be there. Longed to pay his respects to a man he had always admired. One who had become his friend. And who he now missed.

Some might have considered their friendship unusual, he supposed. After all, their ages had been separated by thirty years. But they'd had loneliness in common. Feelings of alienation. And a tremendous amount of history.

History that had included Avery.

Yeah, great. Avery. Some send-off for his friend. Flinging accusations at her. Hitting her where she was most vulnerable. Where she was already hurting.

She had called him hateful. And cruel.

Maybe she was right, he thought. Most probably she was.

What was it about him? Why was everything always black or white? Why couldn't he swallow his thoughts? Blur his personal line just a little? And who the hell was he to think he owned the high moral ground?

Everything he touched turned to shit.

Hunter glanced over his shoulder, toward the apartment. He longed for a drink. He needed one. The need clawed at him. He pictured himself walking to the kitchen, selecting the immediate poison of choice and drinking until he no longer possessed the ability to question the course of his life.

Drink to the point where he felt little but cynical amusement when someone he cared about called him hateful and cruel.

He swallowed hard against the urge. Wallowing instead in the pain. His anger and frustration. His feelings of loss. For they were real. Authentic. As much a part of life as breathing.

Never again, he promised himself, fisting his fingers. Never again would he anesthetize himself to life's highs and lows.

Sarah pawed at the kitchen door, then woofed softly. Hunter turned in that direction. She hadn't been out that long ago. Or had she? When he worked, he lost track of both time and the mundane details of life.

He exited the office and made his way to the kitchen. The dog whined. "Okay, girl." He grabbed the leash from the hook, snapped it to her collar and opened the door. She leaped forward, dragging him through the door and into the alley before he got a firm grip on the lead.

When he did, he yanked hard on it. Sarah heeled.

"What's up with you?" Hunter bent and scratched behind her ears. Instead of sinking on her haunches and sagging against him in grateful ecstasy, she stayed at attention, muscles taut. Quivering.

He frowned and turned his gaze in the direction of hers—the narrow, dark alley. "What is it, Sarah? What's wrong?"

She growled, low in her throat. The fur along the ridge of her back stood up.

"Anyone there?" he called.

Silence answered. He squinted at the darkness ahead, working to make out details, differentiate shape from shadow. Wishing for Sarah's acute sense of smell and hearing. He called out once more. Again, without answer.

Wondering at the wisdom of what he was about to do, he eased his grip slightly. The dog charged forward. Or tried to. He held her back, forcing her to proceed slowly, giving his eyes time to adjust to the dark.

As they reached the middle point of the alley, she angled right. Her growl deepened. Hunter drew back on the leash, struggling to hold her. The dog's muscles bunched and rippled as she fought him, digging in with each step.

Produce crates, he saw. A stack of them sent askew. From the Piggly Wiggly around front. And tipped trash barrels, discarded bakery and deli items spewing out into the alleyway. Sarah began to bark. Not a high, shrill bark of excitement, but a fierce one. Deep, threatening.

"Sarah," he chided, "all this over a little spoiled chow?" He bent and thumped her side. "Or is the possum or coon that made this mess still hanging around?"

The sound of his voice did little to comfort her. As he moved to straighten, something peeking out from under the pile of crates and boxes caught his eye.

An animal's tail. No wonder Sarah was going bonkers. The creature that caused this mess had gotten itself trapped under one of the tipped crates. It could be hurt, maybe dead.

He glanced around, looking for something he could use to move the crates. No way was he about to use his hand. Cornered creatures defended themselves ferociously. Especially when hurt.

He spotted a broom propped in the opposite doorway. He retrieved it, then wedged its handle through the crate's wooden slats and tipped it up. His stomach rose to his throat.

He took a step backward, Sarah's frenzied barking ringing in his ears.

Not an animal's tail. Human hair.

The woman it belonged to stared up at him, face screwed into a death howl.

CHAPTER 13

Hunter stumbled backward, dragging Sarah with him. Bending, he propped his hands on his knees and dragged in deep breaths. *Steady, Stevens. Don't throw up. Dear God, don't—*

The image of the woman filled his head. He squeezed his eyes shut and sucked in another lungful of oxygen. *A woman....Jesus... What to do? What—*

Make certain she's dead. Call the cops.

Hunter expelled a long breath and straightened slowly. He turned his gaze toward the woman. She hadn't moved. She stared fixedly at him, mouth stretched into that horrible scream.

He hadn't a doubt she was dead. And that her death had been excruciating. But still, he should check her pulse.

Shouldn't he? Wasn't that what they always did in the movies and on TV? That or fall completely apart.

Not an option, Stevens. He shortened his hold on Sarah's lead and inched closer. Carefully, he moved a couple of the toppled crates, revealing the woman's arm.

Sometime before she'd died, she'd polished her fingernails a bright, bloody red. Now, the contrast between the red polish and the fish-belly white of her skin affected him like a shouted obscenity.

Hunter moved closer. He circled his fingers around the woman's wrist. She was cold. Her skin spongy to the touch.

No pulse. Not even a flutter.

He yanked his hand back, instinctively wiping it against his blue jeans, and straightened.

Get the cops. His dad. Or Matt.

They were all around the corner. At Phillip's wake.

He considered his choices and decided he could notify them as quickly on foot as he could by calling the department. Decision made, he started forward at a run. As if sensing his urgency, Sarah stayed by his side. They cleared the alley, making the block to Gallagher's in less than three minutes.

He took the front steps two at a time, ordered Sarah to stay and burst through Gallagher's front door. Danny Gallagher stood just inside the door. His eyes widened. "Hunter, what—"

"Where are they?"

Danny pointed. "Number one, but—"

Hunter darted forward, not waiting for him to finish. He spotted his family the moment he entered the room. They stood in a tight clutch.

Stevens clan against the world. Minus one, of course.

He strode forward; the crowd parted silently for him. Conversations ceased. Expressions registered surprise. Then excitement. They expected a scene. They wanted one.

He could liven things up, all right. Just not for the reason they thought.

Hunter saw the moment his family became aware of his presence. They turned. Their gazes settled on him. Matt frowned; Buddy's eyebrows shot up even as his stance altered subtly, becoming defensive. Preparing for battle. His mother looked particularly pale, her eyes wide, alarmed. Cherry averted her gaze when he looked at her.

As American as apple pie and Prozac.

Damn them all.

"Dad," he said, not bothering with a greeting, "we need to talk."

Matt stepped forward, fists clenched. "You picked a hell of a time for one of your confrontations. Get out of here before Avery—"

"Back off," Hunter snapped. "This is an emergency, Dad. We need to speak privately."

"It'll have to keep, son. Tonight I'm honoring my best friend."

Hunter leaned toward him. He lowered his voice. "There's been a murder. Think that'll keep?"

From behind him came the sound of a sharply drawn breath. He turned. Avery had come up behind them, that she'd heard was obvious by her distraught expression.

She shifted her gaze from him to his dad, then Matt. "What's going on?"

Hunter held out a hand. "I'm sorry, Avery. I didn't mean to involve you in this."

Matt stepped between them. "Let's take this outside."

Hunter was happy to oblige. He followed his father and brother out front. Sarah thumped her tail against the porch when she saw him.

The two men faced him. Matt spoke first. "This better not be your idea of a sick—"

"Joke? I wish it was."

Quickly, Hunter explained, starting with Sarah pawing at the door and finishing with checking the woman's pulse.

Buddy and Matt exchanged glances, then met his eyes once more. Buddy took the lead. "Are you certain the woman was murdered?"

Hunter hesitated. He wasn't, he realized. She could have been a street person. Or someone who worked at one of the businesses on the alley. She could have had a heart attack, fallen into the crates, causing them to topple.

He pictured those ruby-colored nails and his relief died. Street people didn't get manicures. The businesses lining the alley all closed at five; if the woman worked in one of those businesses, wouldn't a loved one be looking for her by now? Wouldn't they think to check the alley?

Still, the woman could have died of natural causes.

"Hunter?"

He blinked, refocusing on his father. "I just assumed...because she was dead, in the alley..."

"Show us where she is."

Hunter did, leading the men to the spot. As he passed his door he could hear the puppies crying and stopped to put Sarah in. His dad and brother continued without him.

"Son of a bitch. Shit."

"Oh, goddamn."

They'd found her. Their brief responses expressed volumes.

Hunter made his way up the alley. He hung back a few feet, keeping his gaze averted as the other two men carefully shifted the crates to get a better look at the victim. He listened to their dialogue.

"This woman did not die of natural causes."

"No shit."

"Oh man, she's torn up bad."

That had come from Matt; he sounded weird, more than shaken. As if someone had a hold on his vocal cords and was squeezing. Hard.

"Slow down," his father warned. "We don't know what happened. We have to be careful not to destroy any evidence."

Hunter glanced at his brother. He saw him nod at his father's advice. Saw him trying to pull himself together. Saw the moment he got a grip on himself.

"Look, she's propped up on the right—" Matt squatted and peered closely at the corpse. "But no lividity on her left side."

"So she's been moved."

"Bingo."

It was human nature, Hunter supposed, that made him look her way. He immediately regretted it, but couldn't tear his gaze away. The woman's lower half was naked, her legs spread. It looked as if her panties had been ripped away, her mini skirt shoved up over her hips, bunching at her waist.

Blood...everywhere. Smeared over her thighs, belly.

Bile rose in his throat. He averted his gaze, struggling to breathe. Not to throw up.

"I've got to call this in," Buddy said, voice thick. "Get a crew here, ASAP."

"You need the sheriff's department's help on this one, Dad?" Matt sounded just as shaky. Hunter realized that for all their years in law enforcement, they had little experience with this kind of thing.

This kind of thing? He was already dehumanizing it. Making it palpable.

Call it what it was. Murder. The violent extinguishing of a human life.

"Hell yes," his father answered. "We're not equipped...this... It's Sallie Waguespack all over again."

Buddy and Matt made their calls. Within twenty minutes a crew consisting of both the Cypress Springs Police Department and the West Feliciana Parish Sheriff's Department had assembled at the scene.

Hunter stood back as a CSPD officer secured the scene with yellow tape. Another stood at each end of the alley to keep the curious away. The sheriff's department's crime scene guys had begun to do their thing: they'd set up portable spotlights to illuminate the alley so they could begin the painstaking job of collecting evidence. The police photographer was shooting the scene from every imaginable angle.

Except from the perspective of the victim, Hunter thought. Her eyes would never see anything again.

He turned his back on the scene and pressed the heels of his hands to his eyes. Still he pictured her, as if her image had been stamped on the inside of his eyelids. How long would it take to fade? he wondered. Would it ever?

"Need to ask you a few questions, Hunter."

The request came from Matt. Hunter dropped his hands and looked over his shoulder at his brother, realizing then how tired he was. Bone tired. "Figured. What do you want to know?"

"Tell us again the sequence of events that led to your finding the victim. As exactly as you can recall. Every detail."

The victim. Hunter angled a glance her way. "She have a name?"

"Yeah," Buddy answered. "Elaine St. Claire. Keep it to yourself for a couple hours until we notify her next of kin."

He wasn't surprised his father knew her name—he knew everybody in his town. "Who was she?"

"A local barfly. Party girl." Buddy glanced over his shoulder at her, grimaced and looked back. "Last I heard, she'd left town."

She hadn't gotten far. Poor woman. He sometimes thought of Cypress Springs as a spiderweb. Once tangled in its threads, there was no escape.

If the town was the web, who was the spider?

Matt made a sound of irritation. "Can we get on with it?"

"Sure." Hunter narrowed his eyes on his brother. "What do you want to know?"

His brother repeated his question and for the second time Hunter detailed how he had come upon Elaine St. Claire.

"And that's it? You're certain?" Buddy asked.

"Yes."

Matt frowned. "And you heard nothing, no commotion from the alley?"

"No. Nothing. I was working."

"Working?"

"At my computer."

"The dog, did she bark anytime during the evening?"

Hunter searched his memory. "Not that I noticed."

"A big dog like her must have a pretty big bark."

"I get preoccupied when I'm working. Tune out the world."

"What were you working on?"

Hunter hesitated. He didn't want his family to know about the novel. So he lied. "A divorce settlement."

Matt arched an eyebrow. "You don't seem so certain."

"No, I'm certain."

"Whose divorce?"

Hunter shook his head, disgusted. "That, as I'm sure you know, is confidential. And has nothing to do with why we're standing here."

Matt turned toward Buddy. "Could she have been here a while?"

"No way. The alley is busy during business hours. Employees out for a smoke, deliveries, kids skateboarding."

"That means she was dumped here sometime after the close of business today."

Buddy nodded. "I'll get one of my guys to talk to Jean about the crates, when they were put out." Jean, Hunter knew, was the owner of the grocery. "Make certain they were neatly stacked when she locked up."

"What about the trash barrels?" Matt asked. "Why aren't they depositing this stuff in the Dumpster?"

"I know the answer to that," Hunter offered. "If she's short staffed at the end of the day, she'll leave them in the barrels until morning." The two men looked at him. Hunter shrugged. "I ran into her one morning while walking Sarah."

"It seems this alley *is* a busy place."

Hunter frowned at Matt's tone. "Are we finished here? Can I go?"

"How much traffic does the alley see at night?"

"It's dead. Pardon the word choice."

"No traffic at all?" Matt questioned.

"Kids making out sometimes. Somebody turning in by mistake, realizing it and backing out. Me and Sarah, out for a walk. That's about it."

"You hear the kids, the cars, from your apartment?"

"Yeah. Most of the time."

"But tonight you didn't see or hear anything?"

Hunter stiffened at the sarcasm in his brother's voice. At his smirk. "If that's it, I'd like to go. It's been a rough night."

"Go on," Buddy said. "When we know more, we might need to speak with you again."

Hunter walked away, aware of his father's and brother's speculative gazes on his back. He longed to look back at them, to read their expressions. His every instinct shouted for him to do it.

He wouldn't give them the satisfaction. Wouldn't let them know just how weird this encounter had made him feel.

They'd treated him like a stranger.

A stranger whose sincerity they doubted.

"Hey, Hunter?"

He stopped, turned. Met his brother's gaze. "You remember anything else, it'd help. Give one of us a call."

CHAPTER 14

The morning of her father's funeral dawned bright and warm. Turnout proved much smaller than the wake, mostly close family friends and neighbors. But Avery had expected that.

Lilah stood on her right, Buddy on her left. Each held her arm in a gesture of comfort and support. Lilah seemed much stronger than the night before, though she cried softly throughout the service. Matt stood behind his mother, Cherry beside him. Directly across from her stood Hunter. Alone. Expression resolute.

Avery's gaze went to his. She saw no grief there. No pity or sympathy. Only anger. Only the chip he carried on his shoulder. A shudder moved over her. Without compassion, what would a man become? What would such a man be capable of?

He would be capable of anything.

He would be a monster.

The pastor who had baptized her spoke warmly of the person her father had been, of the difference he had made in the community and to so many individuals' lives.

"He was a light in a sometimes dark world," the pastor finished. "That light will surely be missed."

She shifted her gaze to the casket, acknowledging dizziness. Conscious of rubberiness in her legs. A feeling of being disconnected from the earth.

"Ashes to ashes—"

"He doused himself with diesel fuel and lit a match."

"Dust to dust—"

"Where were you, Avery, when your dad was so depressed he set himself on fire?"

Avery couldn't breathe. She swayed slightly. Buddy tightened his grip on her arm, steadying her.

This wasn't right, she thought, a thread of panic winding through her. Her father couldn't have taken his own life. He couldn't be gone.

She hadn't said goodbye.

It was her fault.

Avery stared at the casket. Scenes of grief she had witnessed over the years played in her head: weeping widows; too-solemn children; despairing family, friends, neighbors, colleagues, all of humanity.

Death. The ultimate loss. The universal gut shot.

She fought the urge to throw herself on the casket. To scream and flail her fists and sob. She closed her eyes, fighting for calm. He would rest beside her mother, she told herself. His partner in this life and the next.

Or would he? Tears choked her. Would his sin separate them for eternity? Who would absolve him of it?

Who would absolve her?

"Avery, honey, it's over."

Over. The end.

Ashes to ashes...doused himself in diesel fuel and lit a...where were you, Avery? Where were you when he...

Dust to dust.

"Avery? Sweetheart, it's time."

She looked blankly at Buddy and nodded. He led her away from the grave. She shifted her gaze, vision swimming. It landed on the group of men from the wake. All in black. Standing together. Again.

Seven of them. They were staring at her. One of them laughed.

A sound passed her lips. She stumbled and Buddy caught her. "Avery, are you all right?"

She looked up at him, pinpricks of light dancing before her eyes. "Those men, that group over there. Who are they?"

"Where?"

"Over th—"

They were gone.

She shook her head. "They were just— " She swayed again. A roaring sound filled her ears. Blood, she realized. Rushing. Plummeting.

"Matt, quick! Give me a—"

When Avery came to, she lay on the ground looking up at the cloudless blue sky. A half-dozen people had gathered around her and were gazing down at her in concern.

"You fainted," someone said softly.

Buddy, she realized, blinking. She shifted her gaze. Matt. Cherry. Lilah. Pastor Dastugue. The world came into clear focus. The moments before she fainted filled her head.

Making a sound of dismay, she struggled to get up.

Matt laid a hand gently on her shoulder, holding her down. "Don't rush it. Take a deep breath, make certain you're steady."

She complied. A moment later, they allowed her to come carefully to a sitting position, then ease to her feet. Matt kept his arm around her, even though she assured him she was fine.

"I'm so embarrassed," she said. "I feel like an idiot."

"Nonsense." Lilah brushed leaves and other debris from her black jacket. "When's the last time you ate?"

She didn't know; she couldn't remember, couldn't seem to gather her thoughts. She wet her lips. "I don't know...lunch yesterday, I guess."

"No wonder you passed out," she said, distressed. "I should have brought you a meal."

Avery looked at Matt. "Did you see them?"

"Who?"

"That group of men. Standing together. There were seven of them."

Matt and Buddy exchanged glances. "Where?"

She pointed to the spot where the group had been standing. "Over there."

They looked in that direction, then back at her. "I don't recall seeing a group," Matt said. He looked at Cherry and Lilah. "Did either of you?"

The two women shook their heads no. Matt met her eyes. "Are you certain of what you saw?"

"Yes, I...yes. They were at the wake, too."

"Who were they?"

She rubbed her head, confused. At the wake, she had thought she recognized several of them. Now she couldn't recall who they had been.

She was losing her mind.

"I don't know. I..." Her words trailed off. She moved her gaze from one face to another, reading the concern in their expressions.

They thought she was losing it, too.

Lilah slipped an arm around her shoulders. "Poor baby,

you've been through so much. Come now, I have finger sandwiches and cookies back at the house. We'll fix you right up."

Lilah did fix her up—as best as was possible anyway, considering the circumstances. She and the rest of the Stevens clan hovered around her, making certain she had plenty to eat, insisting she stay off her feet, shooing people off when she began to fade.

When the last mourner left, Matt drove her home. She laid her head against the rest and closed her eyes. After a moment, she opened them and looked at him. "Can I ask you something?"

He glanced at her, then back at the road. "Shoot."

"You really didn't see a group of men huddled together? Not at the wake or funeral?"

"I really didn't."

"I was afraid you were going to say that."

He reached across the seat, caught her hand and squeezed. "Stress and grief play havoc with the mind."

"I'd heard that."

He frowned slightly, looked at her again. "I'm worried about you, Avery."

She laughed without humor. "Funny you should say that, I'm worried about me, too."

He squeezed her fingers again, then returned his hand to the wheel. "It'll get better."

"Promise?"

"Sure."

They fell silent. She studied him, his profile, as he drove. Strong nose and chin. Nice mouth, full without being feminine. Kissable. She remembered that.

Damn handsome. Better-looking than he'd been all those years ago.

"Matt?" He cut another glance her way. "What was that about, with Hunter last night?"

"I don't think now's the time—"

"People were whispering about it at your mother's."

He turned onto her parents' street. "A woman was found murdered last night."

"Hunter found her?"

"Yes, in the alley behind his place."

In the places she had lived since leaving Cypress Springs, murders were commonplace. But here...

Things like that weren't supposed to happen in Cypress Springs.

But neither were beloved physicians supposed to set themselves on fire.

"How was she murdered?"

He reached her parents' house and eased up the driveway. At the top, Matt stopped, cut the engine. He angled in his seat to face her. "Avery, you don't need to know this. You have enough to deal with right now."

"How?" she persisted.

"I can't tell you. And I won't. I'm sorry."

"Are you?"

He caught her hand. "Don't be angry."

"I'm tired of everyone around here trying to protect me."

"Really? Beats the alternative, don't you think? I'm sure Elaine St. Claire would think so. If she were alive."

The murdered woman. Obviously. Heat stung Avery's cheeks. She sounded like a petulant child.

She curled her fingers around his. "I'm sorry, Matt. I'm not myself."

"It's okay. I understand." He brought their joined hands to his mouth, pressed a kiss to her knuckles, then released hers. "Are you sure you're going to be okay here alone?"

"There you go," she teased, "taking care of me again."

He returned her smile. "Guilty as charged."

"I'll be fine." She grabbed the door handle. Popped open the door. "I'm thinking nap. A long one."

He reached across the seat and caught her hand once more.

She turned and met his eyes. His were filled with regret. "I really am sorry, Avery."

"I know, Matt. And that helps. A lot."

She climbed out of the vehicle, slammed the door and started toward the front walk. When she reached the door she glanced back. Matt hadn't made a move to leave.

She lifted her hand and waved. He returned the gesture, started up the vehicle and backed down the driveway. She watched as he disappeared from sight, then unlocked her door and stepped inside.

The phone was ringing. She hurried to answer it. "Hello?"

"Is this Dr. Phillip Chauvin's daughter?"

The voice was a woman's. Deep. Coarse-sounding. The voice of a lifelong chain-smoker.

"This is Avery Chauvin," she answered. "Can I help—"

"To hell with you," the woman spat. "And to hell with your father. He got what he deserved. You will, too."

In the next instant, the line went dead.

CHAPTER 15

For the next twelve hours, Avery thought of little else but the woman's call. The things she'd said had played over in her head, a disturbing chant.

He got what he deserved.

You will, too.

At first she had been stunned. Shocked that someone could say such a thing about her father. Those emotions had given way to anger. She had tried dialing *69 only to discover her dad hadn't subscribed to the callback service. She had considered calling Buddy or Matt, then had discarded the thought. What could they do? Assure her the woman was just a crank? Advise her to get an unlisted number?

The woman could be a crank, that was true.

But what if she wasn't? What if the woman's call represented a legitimate threat?

Avery paced, thoughts whirling. Her father had been both a Christian and physician. He'd believed in the sanctity of life. Had devoted his own life to preserving it.

What if her first reaction to his suicide had been the correct one? What if he hadn't killed himself?

Avery stopped pacing, working to recall word for word that last message he'd left her.

"I need to talk to you. I was hoping—There's something... I'll...try later. Goodbye, pumpkin."

When news of his suicide had reached her, she'd assumed that call had been a desperate plea for help. She'd assumed he'd called to give her a chance to talk him out of it. Or to say goodbye. She'd agonized over not taking that call ever since. She'd told herself that even if he hadn't spoken directly of suicide, she would have known. Would have picked up something in his voice. In her *if onlys* she would have been able to save his life.

He got what he deserved.

You will, too.

Those words, that threat, changed everything. Perhaps her dad had realized he was in danger. That he had an enemy. Maybe he had wanted to discuss it with her. Maybe he'd needed to bounce something by her.

He had done that a lot.

Avery acknowledged that what she was contemplating flew in the face of what everyone else believed to be true. People she trusted and cared about. Matt. Buddy. Lilah. The entire town.

Avery breathed deeply, battling her conflicting emotions: loyalty to people she loved, distrust of her own emotional state, suspicion for a criminal justice system that made mistakes, that often went with what looked obvious rather than digging for the truth.

But if he hadn't killed himself, that meant he'd been—
Murdered.

The word, its repercussions, ricocheted through her. A murderer in Cypress Springs? Two, she realized, thinking of the woman Hunter had found in the alley. Could they have been killed by the same person?

That hardly seemed likely, she acknowledged, becoming aware of the fast, heavy beat of her heart. Just as unlikely, however, was the idea of two murderers in Cypress Springs.

Avery returned her thoughts to her father, his death. Who would have wanted to hurt her father? He'd been loved and respected by everyone.

Not everyone. He'd had an enemy. The woman's call proved that. Obviously, she herself had an enemy now as well.

He got what he deserved.

You will, too.

She crossed to the front window, inched aside the drape and peered out at the dark street. A few cars parked along the curbs, all appeared empty.

From what she could see. Which frankly, wasn't a hell of a lot.

Avery drew her eyebrows together. Had the woman called before, when Avery was out? She could have. Her father had neither caller ID nor an answering machine. Had she been watching Avery? Following her? Laying in wait? She could be anywhere. As close as a cell phone.

Don't get paranoid, Chauvin. This is a story. Get the pieces. Figure it out.

Avery released the drape, turned and headed for the kitchen. She glanced at the wall clock, registering the time: 1:27 a.m. She dug a message tablet and pen out of the drawer by the phone, laid it on the counter, then crossed to her newly purchased Mr. Coffee coffeemaker. She filled the glass carafe with water, measured coffee into the basket, then flipped on the machine.

While the coffee brewed, she searched her memory for what she knew of the act of murder. She had never worked the crime beat, but had managed to absorb a bit from sharing a cubicle with someone who did. He had been the zealous, self-important sort, had loved to hear the sound of his own voice and for some quirky reason, had thought crime scene details served as a sort of aphrodisiac for women.

Who would have thought she would ever be grateful for those four, long months of cubicle cohabitation?

The coffeepot burbled its last filtered drop and she filled a mug. She carried it, the tablet and pen to the big oak dining table and sat down. Obviously, if her father had been murdered, it hadn't been a random act of violence. That left a crime of passion or premeditated murder. Zealous Pete, her cubicle mate, had called love, hate and greed the Holy Trinity of murder. Meaning, most killers were motivated by one of those three.

She brought the mug to her mouth and sipped. Her hand shook slightly, whether from exhaustion or nerves she didn't know. She had a hard time imagining her gentle, kindhearted father being involved with anyone or anything that would lead to murder.

She squeezed her eyes shut. *Get outside the box, Avery. Let go of what you think you know.*

Get the pieces. Then place them in the puzzle.

She opened her eyes; picked up the pen. Her next step was to find out as much as she could about her dad's death. Talk to Ben Mitchell. The coroner. Buddy about his investigation.

And while she was at it, she would see what she could discover about Elaine St. Claire's murder to ascertain whether there was a connection between the two.

Later that morning, Avery paid a visit to Ben Mitchell at the state fire marshal's office in Baton Rouge. She had discovered that arson investigators were assigned by region, for the entire parish. Cypress Springs fell into region eight. She had also learned arson investigators had the authority to arrest those suspected of arson and to carry firearms.

Ben Mitchell, a middle-aged man with dark brown hair sprinkled with gray, was that investigator.

He greeted her warmly. "Have a seat, Ms. Chauvin."

She took the one directly across from his, laid her reporter's notebook on her lap and smiled. "Please, call me Avery."

He inclined his head. "Your dad was a good man."

"You knew him?"

"I think everybody in the parish did, in one capacity or another. He helped my sister through a tough time." He lowered his voice. "Cervical cancer. Even after she switched to an oncologist, he stood by her every step of the way."

He'd been that kind of a doctor. It had always been about the patients as people, about their health. Never about money.

"Thank you," she said. "I think he was a good man, too."

His gaze dropped to the tablet, then returned to hers. "How can I help you?"

She laced her fingers. "As I mentioned, I spoke with John Price at my father's wake. He suggested I contact you. I'm curious about...about my father's death."

"I don't understand."

She met his gaze evenly. "May I be completely honest with you?"

"Of course."

"Thank you." She took a deep breath, preparing her words, intending to be anything but completely honest. "I'm having some difficulty dealing with my father's death. With...understanding it. I thought if you could...share what you found at the scene...I might be able to...that it would help me."

His expression softened with sympathy. "What do you want to know."

"What you saw at the scene. The path your investigation took. Your official findings."

"Are you certain you want to hear this?" he asked.

She tightened her fingers. "Yes."

"Arson investigators study what caused a fire. Where it started and how long it burned. We can tell what kind of fuel was used by the fire's path, how hot and how long it burned."

"And what did my father's fire tell you?"

"Your father used diesel fuel, which, unlike gasoline, ignites on contact rather than on vapors. To do what he did, the diesel fuel was a better choice."

"Any other fuel do the same thing?"

"Jet fuel. JP-5 to the trade. Burns hotter, too. Harder to get." He paused as if to collect his thoughts. Or carefully choose his words. "Are you at all familiar with death by burning?"

"Refamiliarize me." He hesitated and she leaned forward. "I'm a journalist. Give me the facts. I can handle them."

"All right. First off, the human body doesn't actually burn to ash, the way it would if cremated. A house fire, for example, burns at about one thousand degrees. To completely incinerate, a body requires heat of around seventeen hundred degrees. The body maintains its form. The skin basically melts but doesn't disintegrate. It's not uncommon for areas of soft tissue to survive the fire.

"There's a shrinking that occurs," he continued. "For example, a two-hundred-pound man will weigh one hundred fifty pounds burned. The clothes, flesh and hair burn. The features, including the lips, remain. All solid black. Generic. Meaning the person no longer resembles themselves."

Her father couldn't have done this. Could he?

"How often do you see suicide committed this way?"

"Almost never."

"Why not?" she asked, though she had her own idea why. Through her profession she had learned the importance of not putting words in other people's mouths.

"Understand, I'm not a psychologist. I'm an expert on fire.

Anything I offer would be my opinion, one not necessarily based on fact."

"I'd like to hear it anyway."

"Most people who choose to take their own life, want to get the job done. They want to go fast and as painlessly as possible."

"And burning to death is the antithesis of that."

"In my opinion."

"Yes." Avery glanced at her tablet, then back at the man. "Do you believe my father knew the difference in the way diesel fuel and gasoline burns?"

"Don't know. Could have been he chose the diesel fuel because he had it on hand."

"He siphoned the gas from his Mercedes."

"Yes."

"You ruled out arson? No question in your mind?"

He nodded. "As I mentioned earlier, following a fire's path tells us its story. With arson, the source of the fire is typically an outside perimeter. In addition, we find the gas can, rags, whatever the arsonist used to set the fire. People are funny, they think we won't find them or something. 'Course, some don't care."

"But my dad's case wasn't like that?"

"No. The fire started with your father and moved out from there. The remnants of the syphoning hose were found with him."

"Was there anything unusual about the scene? Anything that gave you pause?"

He drew his eyebrows together, as if carefully sifting through his memory. "Found one of your dad's bedroom slippers on the path between the house and the garage."

"And the other one?"

"There was no sign of it. I suspect he was wearing it."

"Where on the path?"

He thought a moment. "A few feet from the kitchen door."

Her dad had always worn slip-on-style slippers. He'd lost one just outside the door. Why hadn't he stopped for it? That didn't make sense. She wasn't an expert in human behavior, but it seemed to her that stopping for it would be an automatic response.

"You don't find that odd?" she asked.

"Odd?"

"Have you ever tried to walk in one shoe, Ben? It feels wrong. A kind of sensory disruption."

"But I imagine a man in your father's emotional state would be totally focused on what he intended to do. Although never in that position myself, I suspect it would be all consuming."

Avery wasn't convinced but dropped the subject anyway. "Anything else?"

He shifted his gaze slightly. "It appeared as if he crawled a couple feet toward the door. After he was aflame."

He'd changed his mind. He tried to crawl for help.

It had been too late.

She struggled to keep her despair from showing. Failing miserably, she knew.

"I'm sorry. I shouldn't have said—"

"No." She held up a hand. It trembled. "I appreciate your candor. It may be hard for you to understand, but knowing the facts will help me deal with this. I *have* to know exactly what happened."

"I do understand, being that kind of person myself." He glanced at his watch. "Have you talked to Buddy about his investigation? Or to the coroner about his findings?"

"Buddy, though not in great detail. I haven't spoken to the coroner yet. But I plan to."

He stood and held out his hand. "Good luck, Avery."

She followed him up. Took his hand. "Thanks, Ben. I appreciate the time." She started for the door, then stopped and looked back at him. "Ben, one last question. Do you have any doubt he committed suicide?"

From his expression she saw that the question surprised him. He hesitated, as if choosing his words carefully. "My job is to determine how and where a fire starts. Cause and circumstance of death fall to the coroner and police."

"Of course," she said, turning toward the door once more.

"Avery?" She looked back. "Buddy did a good job on this. I've never seen him so...shaken. He didn't want it to be true either."

But even the most conscientious cop made mistakes. It happened, things went unnoticed, slipped through the cracks.

But she didn't say those things to him. Instead, she thanked him again, turned and walked away.

CHAPTER 16

Hunter hadn't set foot in the Cypress Springs Police Department in thirteen years. It hadn't changed, he saw. But then, in Cypress Springs nothing seemed to change, no matter how many years passed.

He had come today because he had remembered something about the other night that might prove useful to the St. Claire murder investigation.

And because since finding the dead woman thirty-six hours ago, he had been unable to think of much else. He couldn't put the image of the dead woman out of his head.

The front desk stood empty. Not for long, Hunter surmised by the steaming mug of coffee and half-eaten doughnut sitting on a napkin on its top. Hunter didn't wait, instead he strolled past as if he still had every right to do so.

He found the door to his father's office open, the room empty. Hunter stepped inside. It smelled like his dad, he realized. And like his childhood.

Hunter scowled at the thought, at the rush of memories that flooded his mind. Of playing under the big, old oak desk, of him and Matt staring openmouthed as their dad chewed out a couple underlings, of his last visit to the office, on his way to college.

Hunter had attempted, one last time, to broach his feelings of exclusion and alienation from his family.

"Dad, just tell me what I've done. Tell me why you've shut me out. You and Mom, Matt and Cherry. It's like I'm not one of you anymore. Talk to me, Dad. I'll do whatever it takes to make it better."

But his father hadn't had time for him. He had brushed him off, insisting Hunter was imagining it. That the fault lay with Hunter's perceptions, not reality.

Angry, hurt, he had left, promising that he would show them all, someday, somehow he would show them.

Hunter's gaze landed on the desk. A file folder stamped *Photos* lay on its top.

From the murder scene? he wondered, inching toward the desk. He saw immediately that they were; the file's tab bore the name St. Claire, Elaine.

"Hello, son."

Son. Hunter turned, feeling that one, quietly spoken word like a punch to his gut. He met his father's gaze. "Dad."

His father's shifted to the desk, then back to his. "What brings you in this morning?"

"The St. Claire murder."

The man nodded and ambled across to his desk. He motioned to the chair directly in front of it. "Have a seat."

Hunter would have preferred to stand, but he sat anyway. "Place hasn't changed a bit."

Buddy settled into his own chair. It creaked under his weight. "It's been a while."

"Thirteen years."

Hunter moved his gaze over the room. His Little League championship trophy was gone, as was the picture that had sat front and center on his dad's desk, of the two of them with the prizewinning fish at the Tarpon Rodeo. He scanned the shelves and walls, taking a quick, mental inventory.

He returned his gaze to the other man. "You've done some redecorating. Looks like you removed every trace of my existence."

"You left us, Hunter."

"Did I? Maybe I don't see it that way."

"Don't you ever get tired of the same old story, bro?"

Hunter twisted in his seat. The way Matt stood in the doorway, as if he owned the place, raised Hunter's hackles. "You're just in time for our little family reunion."

"Lucky me," Matt murmured.

"Hunter says he's here about the St. Claire investigation."

"That so?" Matt ambled in, stopping in front of the desk. He folded his arms across his chest and leaned against its edge.

"I walked Sarah around five forty-five, we took our usual route. Saw nothing out of the ordinary."

"And what's your usual route?"

"Walton to Main, around the square and back." He paused, then continued. "I was thinking, she...the victim, couldn't have been there yet. Because Sarah would have gone nuts. The way she did later."

"Why didn't you tell us this last night?" Matt asked.

"You didn't ask. And I didn't think of it until today."

Matt inclined his head. "Actually, it's fortuitous you dropped by. We had a couple more questions for you."

"Questions for me?" He shifted his gaze between the two men. "All right. Shoot."

"Did you know the victim?"

"No."

"Never heard the name Elaine St. Claire before?"

"Before last night, never."

"Where were you yesterday, between four in the afternoon and when you came to find us at Gallagher's?"

"Is that when she died?"

"Answer the question, please."

"You're kidding." He could tell by their expressions that they weren't. "Am I a suspect?"

"Standard investigative procedure. You found the body, that automatically makes you a suspect."

He got to his feet. "This is bullshit."

"Sit down, son," Buddy murmured, sending an irritated glance at Matt. "Answer the question. Where were you yesterday between the hours of four and eight?"

"I was working. Alone. Sarah was with me. Seems to me she should make a great alibi. She's certainly more loyal than most humans. Present company included."

"Other than taking Sarah for a walk, did you go out at all?"

"No."

"On the walk, did you speak with anyone?"

Hunter thought a moment. "No."

"Did anyone call during that time, someone who could substantiate your being home."

Again Hunter replied in the negative. "But that doesn't make me a killer, now, does it?"

"But it doesn't rule you out either."

Hunter longed to wipe the smug expression off his brother's face. "Can I go now?"

"Not quite yet." Matt glanced at his father, then back at Hunter. "You know how she died, Hunter?"

"Obviously not."

"A sharp or jagged instrument was repeatedly inserted—jammed really—into her vaginal canal."

Hunter went cold. "Oh, Christ."

"She bled to death from internal wounds. It was an excruciating, punishing death."

Buddy stepped in. "Do you have any idea who might have been capable of such a crime?"

"A psychopath."

"You got a name to go with that personality, bro?"

Hunter stiffened. "I wish I did."

"Why's that?" Buddy asked.

Hunter glanced at his father. "Obviously, so you could catch him before he hurts anyone else."

"Noble," Matt murmured. "What a guy."

Hunter stood and met his brother's gaze evenly. "You got a problem with me, Matt? This town too small for the two of us?"

"And here I thought I was the cowboy in the family."

"You didn't answer my question."

"I have a problem with disloyalty. And with cowards."

Hunter laughed without humor, throat tight. "And you see me as both."

"I do."

At times like this, he saw his brother so clearly. He'd always had to be right. Have the last word, have it his way. He had demanded the lion's share of their parents' attention. Adoration from the girls. He couldn't be simply part of the team, he'd had to be the *star.*

Hunter hadn't required adulation. He had been happy to let his twin have it.

But he had drawn the line when his brother had wanted him to stop thinking for himself. Matt had expected his brother to like who and what he did, to think like him. No, Hunter corrected, not expected. Required it of him. Of anyone who remained in his circle.

"You're not engaging me in this, Matt. There's no point in it."

"Like I said, bro, a disloyal coward."

"Because I won't fight with you?" Hunter demanded. "Or because I left, went on with my life? Because I didn't give one hundred percent loyalty to the great Matt Stevens? Is that it?"

"Boys—"

That one deeply uttered word shattered Hunter's veneer of control; anger burst through, white hot, blinding. Memories with it. His father had intoned that warning a million times growing up, from as early as Hunter could remember.

Only then, he had been one of them.

"You hate that I can think for myself, don't you, Matt? I'm not your dutiful little soldier and that makes you crazy."

"Whatever you need to tell yourself, bro."

"If you tried leaving your personal oyster shell, you would have realized you're not the be all and end all, Sheriff Stevens. But then, maybe that's why you never did."

Angry color flooded Matt's face. "You were always jealous of me. You still are. Because I got the girl."

"Leave Avery out of this."

"She's always been a part of it. You couldn't handle that it was me she wanted, not you."

Hunter met his eyes. "Wanted you? If that's so, where's she been all these years? Seems to me she left you behind."

Matt took a step toward him. Hunter curled his hands into fists, ready to throw the first punch. Eager.

Buddy stepped between them before he could. "Thanks for coming in, Hunter. We'll be in touch."

CHAPTER 17

The West Feliciana Parish Coroner's office was located in St. Francisville. An elected official, Dr. Harris served all the parish, one of the smallest in Louisiana. The coroner examined the circumstances of death, performed toxicology tests, called time and manner of death and signed the certificate of death.

Avery had learned all this from the man's wife when she'd called to make an appointment. She had also learned that Dr. Harris had served for almost twenty-eight years. His office employed two deputy coroners, both physicians, and handled an average of eighty deaths a year. If he determined an autopsy was required to establish cause of death, the body was transported to Earl K. Long Hospital in Baton Rouge. There, a forensic pathologist would perform an autopsy. Unlike big parishes in the state, West Feliciana Parish didn't have the funding to employ its own forensic pathologist. That had surprised Avery.

Dr. Harris was a charming sprite of a man, with a wreath of thinning gray hair and a twinkle in his eye. Not what one expected from a parish coroner.

"Thank you for seeing me, Dr. Harris. I appreciate it." He smiled and she went on. "Your wife told me you've been the parish coroner for twenty-eight years."

"On and off. Took a hiatus to tend to my own practice, can't do it all, you know. Or so the wife tells me."

"But you came back."

"Being a perfectionist is a devil of a thing to be. Can't let go. Couldn't stand to see the job not being done right."

He leaned toward her, eyes twinkling with amusement. "They got a joker in here who called cause of every death cardiac arrest. Didn't look at medical records or any other circumstances surrounding the death. Several times the man had a nurse sign the certificates of death. Couldn't stand it. Agreed to come back. Twice."

He sat back, then forward again. "The thing is, ultimately we all have cardiac arrest, but that's not always what sends us off."

"Do things like that happen often?" she asked, thinking of her father. "Cause of death being miscalled because facts slip through the cracks?"

"Not when I'm in charge." He searched her gaze, then smiled gently. "How can I help you, Ms. Chauvin?"

"As I said on the phone, I'm looking into my father's death."

His expression puckered with sympathy. "I'm sorry for your loss."

"Thank you." She hesitated, searching for the right direction to proceed. "I learned from your wife that you handle about eighty deaths a year. And that you or one of your deputies go to the scene of every one."

"That's correct."

"She also told me that neither you nor your deputies perform autopsies, that those are done in Baton Rouge."

"Yes. By the forensic pathologist. Dr. Kim Sands."

"And you requested an autopsy on my father."

"I request one for every suicide. I have her report here."

"And she classified my dad's death a suicide?"

He nodded. "Her findings were consistent with mine."

Avery folded her hands in her lap to hide that they shook. "What did Dr. Sands call Dad's official cause of death?"

"Asphyxiation."

"Asphyxiation?" she repeated, surprised. "I don't understand."

"There's no reason you should," he said gently. "It's a little known fact that most victims of fire die of asphyxiation. In your father's case, with his first breath his airways would have filled with fuel vapors and flames. Death came quickly."

He crawled a couple feet toward the door. "Are you saying he died instantly?"

"Death is never instant. In forensics they speak of death coming in terms of seconds to minutes, minutes to hours, hours to days and so on. In your father's case we're looking at seconds to minutes."

She struggled to separate herself from her father's pain and focus on the medicolegal facts. "Go on."

"The presence of smoke and soot in the throat and lungs is one of the ways the pathologist determines the victim actually died in the fire."

"Or if he was dead before he was set on fire."

"Exactly."

"And Dr. Sands found both in his throat and lungs?"

"Yes." He reached for her father's file, flipped it open and read. "Yes," he repeated,

She cleared her throat. "What else would the pathologist look for in a case like my father's?"

"To confirm cause and manner of death?" She nodded. "Hemorrhages in the remaining soft tissue. Evidence of drugs or alcohol in the toxicology tests. We test blood, urine, bile and vitreous fluid. Each serves as a check for the other."

"And in my father—"

"We found trace amounts of the drug Halcion in his system. It's a sleep medication."

She straightened. "Sleeping pills? Are you certain?"

He looked surprised by her response. "You didn't know? I spoke with Earl, the pharmacist at Friendly Drugs in Cypress Springs. Your dad had been taking sleeping pills for some time."

"Who prescribed them?"

He thought a moment, then held up a finger, indicating she should wait. He referred to the file again. "There it is. Prescribed them for himself."

Avery didn't know what to say.

"Inability to sleep is not uncommon in people who are depressed."

She struggled to find her voice. *He hadn't been sleeping. Another thing she hadn't known about her father, his state of mind.*

What kind of daughter was she?

"Why would he do that?" she managed to say finally. "If he planned to kill himself the way he did, why take sleeping pills before?"

"Pill," he corrected. "The level of the drug in his bloodstream was consistent with having taking a .25-milligram tablet at bedtime. Which, by the way, was the dose he'd prescribed himself."

"I still don't understand, then—"

"Why?" he finished for her. "We can't be certain, of course.

Could be he wanted to take the edge off, dull his senses. Or that he decided to act after he'd taken it."

It appeared as if he crawled a couple feet toward the door.
"Ms. Chauvin?"

She looked up. He held out a box of tissues. She hadn't realized she was crying. She plucked a tissue from the box and dried her eyes and cheeks, working to pull herself together. "Was there anything...suspicious about his death?"

"Suspicious?" He drew his eyebrows together. "I'm not certain I understand."

"Anything that suggested his death wasn't a suicide?"

When he spoke, his tone was patient. "If you discount leaving a death unclassified, there are only four classifications of death. Natural causes. Accident. Suicide or homicide. We can eliminate the first two. That leaves suicide. Or homicide."

"I realize that."

He frowned slightly. "What are you getting at, Ms. Chauvin?"

"I'm just—" She crumpled the tissue. "Frankly, I can't believe he did this. He didn't leave a note. In our conversations, and we spoke often, he gave no indication of being so depressed that he might take his own life."

Another man might have been offended, might have thought she was questioning his skill or professionalism; Dr. Harris was sympathetic. She suspected he dealt with grieving family members a lot.

"The Cypress Springs police did a thorough investigation. As did I. Dr. Sands is a top-notch forensic pathologist. Toxicology revealed nothing but the Halcion. I found nothing about the body to suggest homicide. Neither did Dr. Sands. Friends and neighbors described him as acting strangely for some time before his death. Reclusive. Depressed. That behavior seemed consistent with suicide. I understand, too, that your mother had died recently."

"A year ago," she murmured, shaken.

He got what he deserved.

You will, too.

Avery pressed her lips together.

He sat forward. "Is there something you think I should know? Something you're not saying?"

She met his eyes. What would he think if she shared her anonymous caller's message? Would he call it a sick joke— or a serious threat?

She shook her head. "No. Nothing."

"You're certain?"

"Absolutely." She stood and held out her hand. "You've been very helpful, Dr. Harris. Thank you for your time."

He followed her to her feet, took her hand. "If you need anything further, just call. I'm mostly here."

She started for the door. He called her name, stopping her. She looked back.

"I hope you'll forgive an old man for meddling, but I've done this job for a lot of years. Talked with a lot of grieving family members. I understand how difficult it is to accept when a loved one takes their own life. The guilt you feel. You tell yourself you should have seen it coming, that if you had, your loved one would be alive.

"The ones who do the best get on with living. They accept that the act wasn't about them, that it wasn't about anything they did or didn't do." He paused. "Time, Ms. Chauvin. Give yourself some time. Talk to someone. A counselor. Clergyman. Then get on with living."

If only it were that easy. If only it all didn't feel so wrong.

She forced a small smile. "You're very kind, Dr. Harris."

"Just so you know, I intend to tell your sister the same thing."

She stopped. Turned. "Excuse me?"

"Your sister. She called after you did. She's coming at

three." At her expression, he frowned. "Is something wrong, Ms. Chauvin?"

"I don't have a sister, Dr. Harris."

CHAPTER 18

Avery waited in the parking lot beside Dr. Harris's office, the SUV's windows lowered to let in the mild March breeze. She'd positioned the Blazer at the edge of the lot, alongside a dilapidated Cadillac Seville.

At two fifty-five, another vehicle pulled into the lot, a woman at the wheel. Avery slid low in her seat, not wanting the woman to spot her—yet. Not until she couldn't avoid coming face-to-face with Avery.

The woman parked her Camry, never even glancing Avery's way. She flipped down her sun visor, checked her appearance in the lighted mirror, then snapped it shut and got out of the vehicle.

Only then did Avery get a clear view of her. A small sound of surprise slid past her lips.

The woman from her father's wake. The one the group of men had been staring at.

Avery threw open her door and jumped out, slamming it behind her. The woman stopped. Turned toward her. Her face registered shock. Then dismay.

Avery closed the distance between them. "We need to talk."

"Excuse me?"

"Don't be coy. You were at my father's wake. And now you're here. Claiming to be my sister. I think you'd better tell me why."

She opened her mouth as if to deny the allegations, then shut it. She motioned to the picnic table at the rear of the building, set up under a sprawling old oak tree. "Over there."

They sat. The woman met her eyes. Tall and slender with short, curly blond hair, Avery judged her to be about the same age as she was.

"My name's Gwen Lancaster. I'm sorry if I've upset you. I know this is a difficult time. I...I lost my brother not long ago."

Avery gazed at her, unmoved. "Did you know my father?"

"No, I didn't."

"May I ask then, why you attended his wake and why you're here today?"

She paused a moment before answering. "I'm new to Cypress Springs. Pretty town."

"Yeah, it is." Avery narrowed her eyes. "Friendly, too."

Her lips twisted slightly. "Doesn't look so friendly from where I'm sitting."

"Do you blame me?"

She laughed, the sound short. Tight. "Actually, I don't." She glanced away, then back at Avery. "I've come to Cypress Springs to do some research. I'm working on my Ph.D. in social psychology. From Tulane University."

"Good for you," she said flatly. "So, what does that have to do with my father's death?"

"If I tell you, will you promise to keep an open mind?"

Avery leaned toward her. "I'm not promising you anything. I don't think I should have to."

Gwen held her gaze, then nodded. "At least allow me to begin at the beginning."

"Fair enough."

The woman folded her hands and laid them on the table's top, over a set of initials someone had carved in the wood. "I'm writing a thesis titled 'Crime, Punishment and the Rise of Vigilantism in Small-Town America.'"

She paused. Avery wondered if she used the time to collect her thoughts—or to manufacture her answer. Avery had earned her right to suspicion, earned it through years of interviewing people with agendas that ran counter to the truth, people who manipulated and manufactured. People, she had learned, lied for a variety of reasons. Because it was easier than telling the truth. Or to shield themselves from punishment or incrimination. They lied to protect their reputations. Or as a way to keep from revealing who they really were.

"In my undergraduate studies, I became fascinated with the psychology of groups and group dynamics. What motivates a seemingly average, law-abiding citizen to take on the role of crusader? To take the law into their own hands or act outside the law?"

She lowered her eyes a moment, then returned them to Avery's, her blue gaze unblinking. "Vigilantes are strong believers in law and order. They're usually patriots and highly moral. It's a form of extremism, of course. And like all extremists, they turn their beliefs inside out and upside down."

Avery acknowledged being intrigued despite herself. "Like Timothy McVeigh, the Oklahoma City bomber."

"Exactly. He fit the profile to a T, although he acted alone. Remember, the thing that makes these people so dangerous is that they absolutely believe in their cause and are willing to die for it. Their beliefs aren't a way to justify their acts, in their minds those acts *are* justified by their beliefs."

Avery nodded, understanding. "So, you'd lump all extremists in this same category? Religious groups like Afghanistan's Taliban, political extremists like Al-Qaeda?"

"And white supremacists, survivalists or any other group that pushes its ideology to the extreme. No country, religion or race is immune. History is riddled with the bodies of those killed in the name of a cause."

"Why are you here?"

"A bartender told me a story about this picture-perfect Louisiana town. The town began to suffer an increase in crime. Instead of combating it through traditional law enforcement, they took the law into their own hands. They organized a group that policed the behavior of its citizens. They nipped in the bud behavior they considered aberrant. The crime rate fell, further justifying their actions in their own minds. I did some digging and found information that seemed to corroborate the story."

She was talking about Cypress Springs. Avery stared at her, waiting for the punch line. When it didn't come, she laughed. "A vigilante group? In Cypress Springs? You can't be serious."

"These types of groups are more likely to arise in communities like Cypress Springs. Insular communities, resistant to change, reluctant to welcome outsiders."

"This is ridiculous."

Avery made a move to stand; the woman reached out, caught her hand. "Hear me out. The group formed in the late 1980s as a reaction to the rapid increase in crime. They disbanded sometime later, beset by internal fighting and threats of exposure from within their own ranks."

The 1980s? During the time before and after Sallie Waguespack's murder.

The hair on the back of her neck stood up. If it weren't for the fact that she had just relived that time through her father's clippings and Buddy's recollections, she would have totally discounted the woman's assertions. She had learned during her years in investigative journalism that when one element of a story rang true, often others would, too.

But vigilantism? Could the people of Cypress Springs have been so concerned, desperate really, that they'd taken the law into their own hands? Could her father have been that desperate? Or Buddy? Their friends and fellow community leaders? She couldn't imagine them in the role of Big Brother.

"The core group was small, but they had an intricate network of others who monitored the activities of the citizens and reported to the group."

Avery frowned. "Spies? You're saying Cypress Springs citizens spied on each other?"

"Yes. The citizens were watched. Their mail read. What they ate, drank, read and watched was monitored. Where they went. If they worshiped. If need be, they were warned."

"Warned? You mean threatened?"

She nodded. "If the warnings went unheeded, the group took action. Businesses were boycotted. Individuals shunned. Property vandalized. To varying degrees, everyone was in on it."

"Everyone?" Avery made a sound of disbelief. "I have a hard time believing that."

"In groups such as these, responsibility for acts are disbursed throughout the group. What that means is, no one person carries the burden of responsibility for an act against another. It's the *group's* responsibility. By lessening the burden, the act becomes much easier to carry out. In addition, the individual's sense of responsibility shifts from the self to the group and its ideology."

Avery shook her head again. "I grew up here, I've never heard of any of this."

"It's not as outlandish as it sounds. It began as little more than a Neighborhood Watch-type program. A way to help combat crime. As unchecked good intentions sometimes do," the woman continued, "theirs spun out of control. Anyone who's actions fell outside what was considered right, moral or neighborly was singled out and warned. Before it was all over, they'd broken the civil rights of their fellow citizens in the name of righteousness, law and order."

"And nobody went to jail?"

"Nobody talked. The community closed ranks. Not untypical for this type of group." Gwen leaned toward Avery. Lowered her voice. "They called themselves The Seven."

At her father's wake, the group of men. Watching Gwen. Seven of them.

A coincidence, she told herself, struggling to keep her thoughts from showing. To deny them. "And what exactly does all this have to do with my father? And you posing as my nonexistent sister?"

Gwen Lancaster didn't blink. "I'm trying to locate sources to verify the information I've gotten so far. Your dad fits the profile."

"My father's dead, Ms. Lancaster."

"Fit the profile," she corrected, flushing. "White. Male. Lifelong Cypress Springs resident. A respected community leader during that time."

Her meaning sank in and Avery stiffened. "You're saying you believe my father might have been a part of this Seven?"

"Yes."

Avery stood. She realized she was shaking. "He wasn't," she said flatly. "He would never have been a part of something like that. Never!"

"Wait, please!" She followed Avery to her feet. "Hear me out. There's—"

"I've heard enough." Avery snatched her purse off the picnic bench. "There's a difference between thinking you're honorable and being honorable. And you know that, Ms.

Lancaster. My father was a highly principled, moral man. A man others looked up to. A man who dedicated his life to helping others. To doing right, not to self-righteousness. It's an insult to his memory, to all he was, to suggest he would be party to this extremist garbage."

"You don't understand. If you would just—"

"I do understand, Ms. Lancaster. And I've listened quite enough." Avery backed away. "Stay away from me. If I find out you're prying into my father's life or death again, I'll go to the police. If I hear you're spreading these lies, I'll go to a lawyer."

Without waiting for the woman's reply, Avery turned and walked away.

CHAPTER 19

Avery sat at the kitchen table, laptop open in front of her, hands curled around a mug of freshly brewed coffee. Early-morning sun streamed through the window. The screen glowed softly; the text blurred before her eyes.

She set the mug on the table and rubbed her eyes. Her head ached. She'd slept little. She'd left St. Francisville and driven blindly home, thoughts whirling. She'd been angry. Furious. That Gwen Lancaster could accuse her father of such despicable acts toward his fellow citizens. That she could suggest the people of Cypress Springs capable of spying on one another, punishing them for behavior that fell outside what a few had decided was acceptable.

Cypress Springs was a nice place to live. People cared about one another. They helped one another.

Gwen Lancaster, she had decided was either a liar or an academic hack. She had dealt with journalists like that. They started with a story someone told them, something juicy, outrageous or shocking. Like the one the bartender told Gwen Lancaster about a picture-perfect small town that turns to vigilantism to combat crime.

Great hook. A real grabber. They proceeded on the premise that it was true and began collecting the "facts" to prove it. Tabloid journalism cloaked in the guise of authentic journalism. Or in Gwen Lancaster's case, academia.

The group of seven men at the wake. Watching Gwen Lancaster. The one laughing.

Avery shook her head. A coincidence. A group of men, friends, standing together. Admiring an attractive woman. One making a sexual comment, then laughing. It happened all the time.

She turned her attention to the computer screen. She had realized she knew little more about vigilantism and extremism than what Gwen had told her and had spent the night researching both via the Internet.

She'd done searches on vigilantism. Crowd mentality and social psychology. Fanaticism. She had read about the Ku Klux Klan. Nazism. Experiments in group behavior.

Extremist groups had been much in the news since the September 11, 2001, attacks on the United States by the al-Qaeda terrorist organization. Her search had led her there and to pieces written in the aftermath of Timothy McVeigh's bombing of the Alfred P. Murrah Building in Oklahoma City in 1995. And others concerning the 1993 FBI shootout with the Branch Davidians in Waco, Texas.

What she'd found disturbed her. Any idea or belief, it seemed, could be taken to an extreme. The amount of blood spilled for God and country staggered. A chief motivator, she'd learned, was fear of change. The intense desire to keep the world, the order of things, the way it was.

Folks were scared. And angry. Real angry. The town was turning into a place they didn't like.

People stopped taking their community, their quality of life for granted. They realized that safety and a community spirit were worth working for. People started watching out for each other.

Avery stood and crossed to the sink. She flipped on the cold water, bent and splashed her face. How frightened had the people of Cypress Springs been? Enough to take the law into their own hands?

Could this be why her father had clipped and kept all those articles?

Avery ripped off a paper towel, dried her face, then tossed the towel into the trash. As much as she wanted to discount everything Gwen Lancaster had told her, she couldn't. Because of that damn box.

Gwen Lancaster knew something about her father that she wasn't telling. Why else would she have wanted to talk to the coroner about Phillip's death? Avery couldn't imagine he would have been able to shed any light on The Seven or her father's involvement in the group.

The coroner could answer questions about her father's death, not life.

That was it, Avery realized. Gwen Lancaster doubted the official explanation of Dr. Phillip Chauvin's death.

And Avery was going to find out why. First, she needed to locate the woman.

She crossed to the phone and dialed the ranch. Buddy knew everybody in this town, even outsiders. He answered.

"Hi, Buddy, it's Avery. Good morning."

"Baby girl. Good morning to you, too." Pleasure radiated from his voice. "How are you? We've been so worried, but wanted to give you some space."

"I'm hanging in there, Buddy. Thanks for your concern. How's Lilah?"

"She's good. Come by for dinner. Anytime."

"I will. Got a question. You know everyone around here, right?"

"Pretty much. Figure it's my job."

"I'm trying to find a woman named Gwen Lancaster. She's only been here a couple of weeks, tops."

"Pretty blonde? Writing some sort of paper?"

"That's her."

"You might check The Guesthouse. Why're you looking for her?"

Avery hesitated. She didn't want to lie. But she didn't want to let on what she was thinking. Not yet. She settled on a partial truth. "She was asking some questions about Dad, I want to find out why."

"That's odd. What kind of questions?"

"I thought it odd, too."

If he noticed her evasiveness, he didn't let on. "Good luck then. Let me know if you need anything else."

Avery thanked him and after promising to stop out for dinner in the next night or two, hung up. She started upstairs to dress. As far as she was concerned, there was no time like the present to call on Gwen Lancaster, ungodly hour or not.

A mere twenty minutes later, Avery crossed The Guest-house's wide, shady front porch. The Landry family had owned The Guesthouse for as long as she could remember. They had converted the huge old Victorian, located right across from the square, into a guesthouse in the 1960s when they neither needed nor could afford to maintain the structure as a single-family residence.

The family occupied two-thirds of the first floor; the up-stairs had been converted into four units consisting of a bed-room/sitting room combination, a kitchenette and bath. The remaining third of the main floor housed the same as the rooms above, with the addition of a small, separate parlor.

She stepped inside. The small registration area occupied the far end of the foyer. The young woman behind the desk looked up and smiled. The next-generation Landry, Avery thought. She was a mirror image of both Laurie, one of Avery's friends, and her older brother, Daniel.

"Hi," Avery said, crossing to the desk. "I bet you're Danny's daughter."

"I am." The teenager popped her gum. "How did you know?"

"I grew up here. Was a friend of your aunt Laurie's. You look just like your dad."

The girl pouted. "Everybody says that."

"I'm looking for Gwen Lancaster. I think she's staying here."

"She is. She's in 2C."

"Thanks." Avery said goodbye, then climbed the stairs. Room 2C was located on the left side of the hall, at the end. She reached the door and knocked, hoping it was still early enough to catch her in.

It was. Gwen opened the door, still bleary-eyed with sleep. She had awakened her, Avery realized without apology.

She laid a hand on the door, just in case the other woman tried to slam it on her. "Why are you so interested in my father's death? I want to know the truth. The whole truth."

The woman gazed unblinkingly at her a moment, then opened the door wider and stepped aside. "Come on in."

Avery did. Gwen shut the door behind her, then yawned. "Coffee?"

"No, thanks. I'm full up."

"Sorry, but I need a cup." She motioned toward the small seating area. "I'll be back in a jif."

True to her word, in less than five minutes Gwen sat across from her, cup clutched in her hands. Avery didn't even give her time to sip. "What you told me yesterday was bullshit. Talking to the coroner about my father's death would tell you nothing about his supposed role in The Seven. Obviously, you're interested in his death. Why?"

Gwen met her gaze. "Okay, the straight shit. I wonder if your dad's death was a suicide."

An involuntary sound slipped past Avery's lips. She brought a hand to her mouth and stood, turning her back to the other woman, struggling to compose herself.

"I'm sorry," Gwen murmured.

Avery shook her head but didn't turn. "Why?" she asked. "What makes you think—"

"For such a small town, Cypress Springs suffers a disproportionate number of suicides."

Avery turned. Met the woman's eyes. "Excuse me?"

"The population of Cypress Springs is around nine hundred. Correct?" Avery agreed it was. "In the last eight months, six of her citizens have taken their own lives. A rather large number, particularly for a community that purports to be such a great place to live. To give you an idea how huge that is, the annual total for Louisiana is 1.2 per thousand, per year. To stay within the state average, Cypress Springs should have about 1.2 suicides annually."

"Your figure can't be right."

"But it is. In addition," the woman continued, "there've been a number of strange disappearances."

"Disappearances?" Avery repeated.

"People picking up and moving in the night. No word to anyone. Not to family or friends." She took a sip of coffee. "The accidental death rate is also high. Hunting accidents. Car wrecks. Drownings. Most of them in the last year."

"And before that?"

"Much lower. All categories."

Avery struggled to assimilate the information. To place it

in the framework of what she believed to be true. "I'll have to check this out myself."

"Be my guest."

She fell silent a moment. Craziness. What she was thinking was insanity. "Why would someone want to kill my father?"

"I don't know. I'm thinking he knew too much."

"About The Seven?"

"Yes."

"Then what about you?"

Gwen seemed startled by the question. "What do you mean?"

"It seems to me that *you* might know too much about this group. If it actually exists, that is."

"It exists," Gwen said, following her to her feet. Avery saw that she shook. "And they're getting bolder. Not even trying to cover up their work with an accident."

"What are you talking about?"

"The murder. Elaine St. Claire. I believe The Seven is responsible."

CHAPTER 20

Avery left The Guesthouse. She angled across the square, making her way through the already thick throng of Spring Fest attendees. Though the festival ran from Friday evening through Sunday, Saturday's crowds were always the thickest. The smell of deep-fried crawfish pies and spicy shrimp étouffé floated on the morning air. Vendors preparing for the day laughed and called to one another.

Avery paid them little attention, instead reviewing the things she *knew* to be true. Her father was dead of an apparent suicide. An anonymous caller had threatened her, claiming her father had gotten what he deserved. That she would, too. A woman named Elaine St. Claire had been found murdered in the alley behind Walton Street. None of the official agencies that had investigated her father's death had found anything to suggest it had been other than a suicide.

And she was no longer alone in her belief that her father had been murdered. Gwen Lancaster believed it, too.

Great. A conspiracy-theorist nutcase fell in line with her. Reassuring.

She would start with the facts, the place every good journalist began. Those facts would lead to others, which would either confirm or allay her suspicions. Hunter and the Elaine St. Claire murder seemed a good first step.

Avery stepped off the square onto Main Street, heading toward Johnson Avenue. It would be fruitless to approach Matt or Buddy; they were lawmen, they'd tell her nothing more than what was reported in the most recent issue of the *Gazette*.

But Hunter had been there. He'd discovered the body. Had been privy to Matt's and Buddy's reactions, he'd no doubt overheard some of their conversation at the scene.

She acknowledged excitement. A quickening of the blood that told her she was onto something, a high she experienced whenever she hit on the real thing— a powerhouse story with the ability to affect real change.

What change would this story precipitate if true?

Avery reached Johnson and turned down it. Moments later, she reached Hunter's law office. Peering through the window she saw the room was empty, so she went around to the alley entrance.

Hunter appeared at the door before she could knock. Sarah stood at his side. From inside she heard the whimpering of puppies.

He pushed open the screen door. She saw he was dressed in a T-shirt and running shorts.

"I was hoping we could talk," she said.

"About?" he asked, not looking at her. He clipped the lead onto Sarah's collar.

"About...stuff."

He met her eyes. "Stuff? Big-city journalists always use such technical words?"

"Smart-ass."

"Sarah and I are going for a run."

"I'll join you."

He skimmed his gaze over her. Unlike him, she had dressed for comfort—not exercise. She had, however, worn her athletic shoes. "Sorry. But this is our time."

"Our time? You and the dog's?"

"That's right. Haven't you heard the one about dog being man's best friend?"

"If you want an apology," she said, frustrated, "you've got it."

"For what?"

"Our argument."

One corner of his mouth lifted. "Seems to me that was a two-way street." He looked down at Sarah. "What do you think, girl? Can she keep up with us?"

As if she understood her master's question, the dog looked up at her. Avery returned the dog's baleful stare. "Come on, Sarah, give me a little credit. We girls have to stick together."

She seemed to nod, then swung her gaze to Hunter. He laughed. "No fair, you pulled the girl-solidarity thing on me."

Avery laughed. "Why not? It worked, didn't it?"

He stepped through the door, turned and locked it, then began to stretch.

"Where are we going?"

"Tiller's farm."

Tiller's farm was a forty-acre spread just east of Cypress Springs. Now used to raise mostly feeder cattle, the land had been in the Tiller family forever and old Sam Tiller refused to sell even an acre. Cypress Springs had built up around him. In retrospect, Tiller's refusal to budge had been one of the factors that had helped keep Cypress Springs small and pastoral.

Three miles. There. And back.

Not good.

Hunter glanced over at her. His lips lifted in amusement. "Want to back out now?"

"Not at all," she lied. "Just worried about that shotgun of his." Sam Tiller had not been happy when he'd discovered the shady, spring-fed pond on his property had become an oasis for Cypress Springs teenagers.

Buddy had dragged him in on a number of occasions for firing at the kids. Never mind that it'd only been buckshot and that the kids had been trespassing—shooting at teenagers was against the law.

"No worries, doll. I handled a legal problem for him, he gave Sarah and I carte blanche to visit anytime. Could even skinny-dip if we wanted."

She ignored the reference to a mercilessly hot August night when they had done just that. Hunter had promised not to look. She had believed him.

Then caught him staring.

"Ready?"

As she would ever be. "You bet."

They set off, the three of them, the pace relaxed. Warming up. Avery managed to keep up easily at first. Soon, however, she had to press to keep up, even though Hunter paced himself to accommodate her shorter legs.

After three-quarters of a mile, Avery was sweating. Out of breath. Her blue jeans and cotton blouse clung uncomfortably to her damp skin, twisting slightly, restricting her movement.

She'd give her kingdom for a pair of shorts and a sports bra, she decided, yanking her shirt from the waistband of her jeans as she ran. She unbuttoned the cuffs and rolled up the sleeves.

He glanced back. "You okay?"

"Fine," she managed to say, furious at herself. For her own pigheadedness. And for allowing herself to get so out of shape. In the past few months she had gone from a daily run to managing to fit one in once a week. Between that and the difference in their strides, she was hurting.

By the halfway point, however, her endorphins kicked in and the discomfort eased. Hunter drew ahead; she didn't try to keep up. Instead, she luxuriated in the pure pleasure of being outdoors, lungs, heart and muscles working in tandem.

"Meet me at the pond," he called over his shoulder.

She indicated she would, then watched as he pulled away.

When she arrived, Hunter was waiting for her, Sarah panting at his side. The way Avery figured it, she'd been about six minutes behind him.

He passed her a water bottle. "I'd forgotten that about you."

"What?" She accepted the bottle and took a long swallow.

"How determined you are."

She took another swallow, then handed the bottle back. "You mean pigheaded."

"Sometimes." His mouth twitched. "Personally, I believe determination is an admirable trait."

Sarah stood and wandered down to the pond. Avery watched longingly as she waded in for a drink. The water looked delicious.

"Go ahead," he said. "Take a dip. It's spring fed."

"In your dreams, Stevens."

"I didn't say skinny-dip. You, Ms. Chauvin, have a dirty mind."

"Actually, I don't think I'm the one with the dirty mind." She stood and crossed to the water's edge. Kneeling, she splashed water on her face, soaking her shirt in the process.

She glanced down at the now-transparent fabric. So much for modesty. Hell with it, she decided, unbuttoning the clinging fabric.

"Don't look," she ordered, glancing at him over her shoulder.

He rested back on an elbow. "Depends on what I'm going to miss."

"Hunter," she warned, narrowing her eyes at his cheesy smile.

"All right. No peeking, scout's honor."

She waited until he had dutifully turned his head, then peeled off her blouse.

"Very pretty."

She whirled around, wet blouse to her chest. "You looked."

"Of course I did." He laughed. "Can't stop a bird dog from hunting."

"Or a snake from striking."

He laid back, hands folded behind his head and gazed up at the blue sky. "Your honor's safe, doll. Most bathing suits reveal more than that bra, pretty as it is."

He had a point. She soaked her blouse in the chilly water, then draped the dripping fabric across her shoulders. The water sluiced over her shoulders and breasts, leaving trails of goose bumps in their wake.

She made her way back to where he rested. To his credit, he didn't look at her.

"What did you want to talk to me about?"

She hesitated, reluctant to ruin the warm, relaxed mood with talk of murder, then asked anyway. "Wondered if you could tell me anything about the St. Claire murder."

He didn't act surprised by her question. "What do you want to know?"

"The *Gazette* didn't say how she died."

"It's pretty grim."

"I think I can take it."

He tilted his face toward hers. "A sharp object was repeatedly inserted into her vaginal canal. Tore her insides to shreds. She bled to death."

Avery hugged herself, suddenly cold. "Who was she?"

"Dad knew her. Party girl. Heavy drinker. Spent a little time in jail."

Anyone whose actions fell outside what was considered right, moral or neighborly was singled out.

A woman like Elaine St. Claire fit that description. But she was also the kind who put herself in dangerous situations.

"They have any suspects?"

"Just me."

"Funny."

"I'm not laughing." He lay back again, draping an arm across his eyes. "Dad and Matt, in their infinite wisdom, are looking no further than the first to the scene."

"I find that difficult to believe."

He shrugged. "Could just be me, still chafing under Matt's interrogation. Wondered where I'd been that day between the hours of four in the afternoon and eight that night."

"And where were you?"

"Working on the novel. Nobody but Sarah for an alibi."

She didn't know what to say so she said nothing.

"Why so interested?" he asked.

Good question. How did she answer it? She decided on bluntness. "You have any doubt my dad killed himself?"

He sat up at that one. Looked at her. "Where did *that* come from?"

Ignoring the question, she tipped her face to the sky, then returned her gaze to his. "You'd become friends. Spent some time with him. Do you have any doubt he took his own life?"

For a long moment, he said nothing. When he spoke, his tone was heavy with regret. "No, Avery. I'm sorry."

A knot of tears clogged her throat. She pressed on. "Why?"

He looked at her. "Talking about this isn't going to change anyth—"

"Why, Hunter? Tell me."

"All right." He sat up. "I hadn't been back in Cypress Springs a week when your dad looked me up. I appreciated it. A lot. He didn't ask too many questions, didn't make me explain why or justify my actions. He did it for me, but I think, for himself, too. He needed somebody to talk to.

"Anyway, it worked for both of us and we started meeting every Friday morning for coffee. Then, one Friday, he didn't show. So I went by the house, found him still in his pajamas. All the blinds drawn. He insisted he had simply overslept, but he was acting...strange. Different."

"Different? What do you mean?"

"Jumpy, I guess. He didn't look me in the eye. After that, our meetings became sporadic. Our conversations...less comfortable. He began talking a lot about the old days. When your mom was alive and you were home. Never about the future, rarely about the here and now."

Hunter let out a long breath. "It should have rung a warning bell, but it didn't. I'm sorry," he said again.

She shook her head, as much in denial of his words as of the tears burning her eyes. "He lost a bedroom slipper that night, on his way out to the garage. The arson investigator told me that."

He didn't comment and her cheeks heated. "I think that's significant, Hunter. Walking in one shoe isn't natural. The path between the house and garage would have been cold, the stepping stones rough. He would have stopped and slid it back on."

"Avery," he said gently, "I hate that he did this, too. I know it hurts. I know—"

"No, you don't know. You *can't* know what I feel." Tears choked her; she fought them. "On fire, he crawled toward the door. He didn't want to do it, Hunter. He didn't."

"Avery, hon—" He made a move to take her into his arms and she jumped to her feet. "No," she said, more to herself than him. "No, I will not cry. No more."

She hugged herself, staring at the shimmering surface of the pond. In the tree behind her a couple of squirrels played tag. Sarah growled, low in her throat.

"Who would want your dad dead, Avery?" Hunter asked quietly. "Everyone loved him."

She couldn't take her gaze from the diamond-faceted surface of the water. "Not everyone. I got a call, this woman...she said Dad had gotten what he deserved. That I would, too."

"Who, Avery? What woman?"

"Don't know." Cocking her head, she moved toward the water. The surface was broken by a large, odd shadow. "She wouldn't identify herself and I didn't recognize her voice."

"Has she called again?"

"No." Avery reached the pond's edge, stopped and frowned.

"Most probably a crank," he said. "Someone with an ax to grind. Or someone in desperate need of attention. Even Cypress Springs is home to mentally unstable people."

"What's that?" She glanced over her shoulder at him. He was staring with unabashed admiration at her butt. Her cheeks warmed even as she motioned him to come. "Look."

He stood and ambled over, Sarah at his heels. She pointed. "A shape just beneath the water. See? Its edges are silvery."

He bent closer, then looked at her. "I think it's a car."

"A car?" She turned back to the pond. Made a sound of surprise as the shape that had caught her eye suddenly became clear to her. "I think you're right."

"One way to find out." He stripped down to his jogging shorts, then waded in. She watched as he took a deep breath, then dived under.

A moment later, he surfaced. "It is. And a fine car at that. A Mercedes coupe."

She frowned, something plucking at her memory.

"I'm going to take another look."

Hunter went under again. Sarah began to bark. This time when he reappeared he swam back, then climbed out. "I think we better call Dad."

CHAPTER 21

Neither Avery nor Hunter had a cell phone. They decided the quickest route to a phone would be through the woods and across a pasture to Sam Tiller's place. The man caught sight of Hunter and broke into a broad smile, his weathered face creasing up like a Shar-Pei's hide.

He pushed open the screen door, smile faltering when he saw the condition they were in. "A bit early in the year to be swimming. Water'd be real cold." He shifted his gaze to her. "You're the doc's girl."

"Yes, sir. Good to see you."

"Damn shame about the doc. He was a good man." He turned to Hunter. "What's this all about?"

"We need to use a phone, Sam. To call Buddy." Hunter explained about jogging to the pond, Avery seeing the shadowy form of something under the water, then realizing it was an automobile.

The man scratched his head. "A car, you say? A Mercedes? Damned if I can figure how it got there. Come on in, phone's this way."

They followed him inside. Sam's wife had died back when they were in high school and as far as Avery knew, the couple hadn't had children. The old farmhouse's interior begged for a little TLC. Fabrics were frayed, curtains dingy and any feminine touches had long since gone the way of the dinosaurs.

It reminded her of how her dad's house had begun to look.

Hunter dialed. Avery could tell by Hunter's side of the conversation that his father was surprised to be hearing from his son.

"You want me to call or— Fine. We'll meet you there."

Hunter hung up the phone. He turned to her and Sam. "Dad's calling Matt. The farm's outside the city limits and falls under the sheriff department's jurisdiction."

"Seeing it's in my pond," Sam said, "I think I'd better get a look at this thing. I'll drive us."

They all three crowded onto the bench seat of his battered old pickup truck; Sarah rode in back. The sky had begun to turn dark, fat black clouds forming to the south.

Within minutes they reached the turn for the pond. Hunter hopped out and unhooked the chain barricade; Sam eased the truck through. Avery wasn't surprised to see they had beaten both Buddy and Matt there.

Sam stopped the pickup; they climbed out. The farmer crossed to the water, squinted down at the cloudy surface. After a moment, he looked at Hunter. "Damned if it isn't a car. I'll be."

Just then, Matt pulled up, followed by Buddy. The younger

Stevens climbed out, waited for his father, then crossed to the trio.

"What's the deal?" Matt asked.

Sam stepped forward. "A car," he said. "In my pond. Damned if I know where it came from."

Matt shifted his gaze briefly to her, then turned to Hunter. "You seem to be in the thick of everything these days."

"What can I say? Trouble finds me."

"How about you give me the sequence of events."

Hunter did. Matt shifted his gaze to hers. "You want to add anything to that?"

Dark clouds drifted over the sun; she shivered and shook her head. "I can't think of anything."

"How you goin' to get it out of there?" Sam asked.

"Call Bubba, get one of his wreckers over here, haul it out," Matt answered.

"You're certain it was a Mercedes?" Buddy asked.

"One hundred percent. Silver. A CLK 350."

The two lawmen exchanged glances. "But you say it was empty?"

"It appeared so," Hunter confirmed.

"But you're not certain?"

"No."

"If we need anything else, we'll be in touch." Matt looked at her. Something in his gaze had her folding her arms across her chest. "Storm's moving in," he said softly. "I suggest you take cover."

CHAPTER 22

At the same moment the storm hit, Avery remembered what had cluded her before: the guy whose Mercedes had supposedly broken down outside of Cypress Springs, the one whose girlfriend had claimed he'd gone missing. She'd cried foul play, but without any evidence of a homicide, Buddy and Matt could only assume the story a fabrication or that the guy had wanted to disappear.

They had their evidence now. Though a submerged vehicle did not a murder make.

That's why Matt had asked twice about the vehicle being empty. He was looking for a body to go with the car.

"Here you are," Sam said, interrupting her thoughts. His

pickup rattled as it crept up her driveway, then creaked to a stop.

She turned to him. "Thanks for the ride. I really appreciate it."

He peered out at the rain. A boom of thunder shook the truck. "I don't mind waitin' a minute, till it eases up out there."

"I appreciate that, Sam. But I'm already wet. A little more water's not going to hurt me." She grabbed the door handle. "Thanks again for the—"

"It's not true," he said, cutting her off. "What they all say about him."

She stopped, looked back at him. "Pardon?"

"Hunter's a good man. Rock solid. Your father liked him."

Her mouth dropped. He motioned to the door. "Go on now. Before it gets any worse."

She did as she was told, hopping out into the downpour. Instantly soaked, she hurried to the front porch. There, she watched the old truck rumble off.

What who said about Hunter? His family? Others in the community?

Your father liked him.

She sank onto the porch swing and stared out at the rain. Her lips lifted with a curious kind of pleasure. The old farmer's comment shouldn't matter to her, but it did. It warmed her. She had always considered her father an excellent judge of character. Had turned to him for advice about people often, during both her adolescence and adulthood.

She liked Hunter, too, despite their recent clashes. She always had. As a young person, she had admired his intelligence and wit. His fine, dry sense of humor. She thought back, recalling the times he had helped her with math, the subject that had given her never-ending fits. She recalled how he'd had the ability to make her smile, even when she had not been in the mood to. She remembered the time, after a particularly upsetting disagreement with her mother, when he had held her and talked her through it. Quietly supporting her while getting her to see her mother's point of view as well.

Where had Matt been that day? she wondered. Busy? Or had she sought Hunter out because she'd known that he would be the one able to calm her?

And now, as an adult, she sensed a deep, abiding honesty in him—about himself and his shortcomings and about others. That made him difficult for some to take, she supposed. It made him confrontational.

Cypress Springs didn't embrace diversity. Round peg, round hole. PLUs—People Like Us. That made them feel safe. Secure.

She had always been the square peg. She hadn't realized it until now, but Hunter had been, too.

Lightning flashed, thunder shook the sky and the rain came down in blinding sheets. Avery turned her thoughts to Matt and Buddy at Tiller's Pond, arranging to have the vehicle hauled out. Standing in the rain, drenched and chilled. And she wondered if Hunter had made it home before the rain had come. He had eschewed Sam's offer of a ride in favor of completing his run.

She recalled Matt's comment to Hunter about being in the thick of everything of late. He'd been making reference to Hunter's having found Elaine St. Claire, now this car. His tone had been adversarial. Confrontational. To Hunter's credit, he hadn't taken the bait.

Matt had hardly looked at her, she realized. Neither had Buddy. Matt hadn't directed but one of the questions her way. His only comment to her had been about the approaching storm.

She glanced down at herself. The wet, white cotton was nearly transparent, her lilac-colored bra clearly visible. Her cheeks warmed. *Great, Chauvin. Very classy.*

She stood, took one last look at the rain and headed inside to change. The phone was ringing; she grabbed it.

She knew a split second before the woman spoke that it was her—the one who had called before. The heavy moment of silence when she picked up the phone tipped her off. She didn't give the woman a chance to speak. "Who are you? What do you want?"

"Damn you to hell," the woman said, laughing thickly, the sound mean. "Your father's already there."

"My father was a good man. He—"

"Was a liar and murderer. He got what he deserved."

"How dare you," Avery snapped, so angry she shook. "My father was a saint. He—"

The woman began to laugh, a witch's cackle. Pure evil.

With a cry, Avery slammed down the receiver. Without missing a beat, she picked it back up and punched in the Stevenses home phone. Cherry answered.

"Cherry," she said, "is Buddy there?"

"Avery? Are you all right?"

"Yes...I—" She sucked in a deep, calming breath, the woman's awful laugh, her words, still ringing in her ears. "Is he there?"

"No. He and Matt are out at Tiller's Pond. Do you need me to beep him?"

"No, it's not urgent. It's just...could you have him ring me when he gets in? It's important."

Cherry called Matt instead, Avery realized several hours later. He stood at her door, expression concerned. "What's wrong?"

"Cherry told you I called."

"She said you were upset."

Avery made a sound of embarrassment. In the hours that had passed, she'd put the incident into perspective. "I over-reacted about something." She pushed open the door. "Come in."

He stepped inside. He'd changed out of his uniform and

wore a pair of old, soft blue jeans and a white golf shirt. His arms and neck looked tan against the startling white.

He met her eyes. "What's up?"

"Did my father have any enemies?"

The question surprised him, she saw. "Enemies? Not that I know of. Why?"

"I've gotten a couple of unsettling anonymous calls. I got one this afternoon and it...I got upset. I called Buddy."

"The calls, were they from a woman or a man?"

"A woman."

"The nature of the calls?"

"Ugly." She folded her arms across her chest, then dropped them to her sides again. "The first time she called, she said that Dad had...gotten what he deserved. And that I would, too. This time she called him a—" she had to force the words out "—a murderer. And a liar."

"And you have no idea who the woman is?"

"No. None."

"You try *69?"

"Tried it. Dad didn't subscribe."

"You might want to add it or caller ID. Just in case she calls again."

Avery nodded. "I will."

He searched her expression. "She's just a crank, Avery. You know that, right?" When she hesitated, he shook his head. "We're talking about the doc here. Nobody had a higher moral character than your dad. I believe that. Black and white, no moral gray area."

"I know. But—" She clasped her hands in front of her. "I keep coming back to what she said, that he got what he deserved. Like maybe, he didn't kill himself. Like maybe somebody helped him out."

For a long moment, he said nothing. "You mean, somebody killed him?"

She met his gaze evenly. "Yes."

"Who would hurt your dad?" he asked.

"Someone who thought him a liar and murderer."

He caught her hands, rubbed them between his. She hadn't realized until that moment how cold they had been. "The CSPD did a thorough job. Dr. Harris is a crackerjack coroner who doesn't let anything slip by him. I reviewed everything as well, Avery." He gentled his tone. "I didn't want to believe it either."

Avery couldn't bring herself to look at him. He squeezed her fingers. "This caller is a mentally disturbed person. Or someone with an ax to grind, maybe with Buddy. Maybe someone trying to cause trouble through you. Why don't you take a look at Dad's report. It'll put your mind at rest."

"You don't think Buddy would mind?"

"No way." He smiled. "When it comes to you, Avery, Dad'll do anything."

She changed the subject. "How'd it go at the pond?"

He slid his hands into his front pockets. "Figured you might want an update."

"Car belonged to that guy who went missing, didn't it? The one you and Buddy were talking about the other day? The one reported missing by his girlfriend."

"Yup, sure did. His name was Luke McDougal."

"Was? He's dead?"

"Don't know. The vehicle's been hauled out. It's empty. Cell phone's in the car. Evidence team has it." He glanced at his watch. "The property's being searched, the pond dredged."

Avery shivered and rubbed her arms. "When will that be done?"

"The rain's slowed us down. Not until tomorrow, I suspect." He met her eyes, expression grim. "I need to ask you something, Avery. What were you and Hunter doing at Tiller's Pond?"

"I went to see him. He was going for a run. I joined him." She lifted a shoulder. "Ended up there."

He looked away, dragging a hand through his hair, swearing softly.

"What is it, Matt?"

He returned his gaze to hers. "I'm wondering why you went to see him in the first place."

"He and I were friends, I guess I still think of him that way. Does it matter?"

She saw by his expression that it did matter to him. It mattered a lot. She let out a pent-up breath. "I wanted to find out more about the St. Claire murder. Since he had been at the scene, I figured he could tell me what I needed to know."

"You could have come to me. I would have answered your questions."

"Matt," she chided, "I'm a journalist. I'm experienced enough to know what the police will, or will not, share."

He tipped his face toward the ceiling, the picture of frustration. "Help me out here, Avery. I feel like a jerk."

She smiled. "You're jealous?"

"Don't laugh." He glowered good-naturedly at her. "Hell, yes, I'm jealous. I know the kind of things that went on at Tiller's Pond."

Flattered, she closed the distance between them, stopping inches from him. She tilted her face to his, shamelessly flirting. "Yeah, but all those things happened with you."

Something flickered in his eyes, some strong emotion. One that stirred her blood. "Dammit, your shirt was wet."

"I was hot. The water was cool."

He cupped her cheeks in his palms, grip just short of painful. "Be careful, okay? Hunter's not...he's not the boy you knew."

It's not true what they say about him. Hunter's a good man.

"I'm a big girl, not a teenager, Matt." He didn't smile. Hers wavered. "Is there something you're not telling me?"

He bent, pressed his mouth to hers in a quick, hard kiss. "I'll pick you up for Spring Fest tomorrow at three."

Without another word, he left. She watched as he crossed to his cruiser, climbed in and backed down the driveway. She brought a hand to her mouth, to the imprint of his lips against hers. Their date, she realized. Spring Fest, she had forgotten all about it.

A date with Matt Stevens. After all these years. She eased the door shut, locked it, but didn't move from the foyer. What was she getting herself into? What did he want from her?

More than friendship, more than a stroll down memory lane. That was obvious. But what of her feelings? What did she want?

She enjoyed his company, reliving the past. When with him she became the girl she had been back then.

She thought of Hunter, his image slipping into her head, filling it. There was something between her and Hunter as well, she realized. Something strong. Something that caused her to think of him when she shouldn't.

But what? Concerned friendship? Attraction? Sexual awareness?

Or suspicion?

What had Matt meant when he'd said she didn't know Hunter as well as she thought? When he had warned her to be careful?

Moody and aggravating as Hunter could be, she hadn't felt threatened around him. Even when they had clashed. The only thing that had seemed in any imminent danger had been her reputation.

So why his real, nearly palpable concern?

CHAPTER 23

Spring Fest was much as Avery remembered it. The atmosphere of celebration, the sound of children laughing mingling with the smells of good Louisiana food and the warmth of the sun on the back of her neck.

She and Matt did it all: rode the Ferris wheel and Tilt-A-Whirl; sampled foods from all the vendors, so much that she longed to unsnap the top button of her shorts; wandered through the arts and crafts booths; and from the blanket they'd spread under the canopy of the square's biggest oak tree, listened to the various bands scheduled throughout the day.

The day should have been perfect, Avery told herself. She should be relaxed, totally content. Hard to be either, however, when news of Luke McDougal's car being found in Tiller's

Pond and the St. Claire murder was on everyone's lips. Hard to feel carefree when she couldn't shake her suspicions about her father's death. When she couldn't discount what Gwen Lancaster had told her about The Seven and the disproportionate number of suicides in Cypress Springs. Or that she believed her dad had been killed because he had known too much about The Seven.

Avery found herself trying to read people's expressions, trying to see beyond what they were saying to what they weren't. Every glance from one person to another became a signal of some sort. She found herself listening to the conversations around her, hoping to recognize the voice of her anonymous caller.

She hated feeling this way, suspicious and on edge. Distrustful to the point of paranoia.

"Thirsty?"

Avery turned and found Matt's gaze on her. They sat on the blanket; the sun had set and the final band of the day had just finished their first song. "What did you have in mind?"

"Beer?"

"Why not?"

He frowned slightly. "Are you all right?"

"Fine. A little tired."

He opened his mouth as if to say something further, then seemed to change his mind and stood. "Don't disappear on me."

"I won't." As he walked away, her smile faded. Luke McDougal had disappeared. According to Gwen Lancaster, so had a number of Cypress Springs citizens, picking up and moving in the night. No word to anyone.

"Where'd that no-good kid of mine go?"

Avery looked up at Buddy and smiled. Dressed in his uniform, complete with service weapon and nightstick, there was no doubt he was on duty. "Beer run."

"A cold one sure would hit the spot right now."

She made a sound of sympathy. "No rest for the wicked, I see."

"Love Spring Fest. And hate it. With so many visitors in town and so much drinking going on, there's always some sort of commotion." He looked in the direction Matt had gone.

Avery patted the blanket. "Have a seat."

"I'd rather dance. Care to cut a rug with an old man like me?"

She smiled affectionately and stood. "I'd love to."

He led her toward the makeshift dance floor, in front of the bandstand. He held out his arms. She took his hand and they began to move in time to the music, a Cajun two-step. "I've been waiting for a chance to get you alone. Matt's not left your side all day."

"Matt's grown into a good man," she said. "You must be proud."

He shifted his gaze, a sadness crossing his features. Sensing he was thinking of his other son, she murmured, "Hunter's going to be okay. He will, I'm certain of it."

He met her eyes once more, the expression in his gentle. "Thank you, Avery. That means the world to me."

The music's pace shifted, Buddy adjusted smoothly. For such a big man, he was light on his feet, graceful. She told him so.

"Lilah made it clear when we were dating, if I wanted to win her hand, I had to know how to dance. So I learned. It wasn't easy, let me tell you." He chuckled. "Two left feet is my natural inclination."

She smiled at the story. "Where is Lilah tonight? I haven't seen her or Cherry."

"Lilah's home. Under the weather. Cherry elected to stay with her."

"I'm sorry to hear she's not feeling well."

"She suffers horribly this time of year with her allergies."

"Is there anything I can do?"

"Pay her a visit." He smiled, the picture of fatherly affection. "I'm so pleased you're home, Avery."

She kissed his cheek. "I am, too, Buddy. I didn't realize how much I missed this place. The people."

"It's a good place. Good people."

Anyone whose actions fell outside what was considered right, moral or neighborly was singled out.

Her smile faded. "What's wrong?" he asked.

"Buddy, can I ask you something?"

"Sure, baby girl."

"You ever heard of a group called The Seven?"

His steps faltered; he drew his eyebrows together. "When you asked about her, I was afraid this might happen."

"Who?"

"That Gwen Lancaster."

"You know her?"

"Of her," he corrected, expression tight. "She's been going around Cypress Springs spreading lies. Starting rumors."

"So the group never existed?"

"They existed, all right. Just not the way she's portraying them. To hear her talk, they were a bunch of hatemongers and murderers."

He let out a heavy-sounding breath. "They called themselves Seven Citizens Who Care. The group organized in an attempt to stem the tide of social ills that had beset our town. Their feeling was, stop crime before it happened. They began a drug and alcohol awareness program in the schools. They organized a chapter of Planned Parenthood. They arranged counseling for families in crisis. They began a campaign to get families back to church."

Avery remembered suddenly being required to take sex education in the tenth grade, remembered the addition of films about the dangers of alcohol and drugs in health class—subjects that had never been broached in school before.

"They weren't high-profile. They weren't in it for acclaim

or notoriety. They were simply citizens willing to take a stand for this community. Lilah belonged. So did Pastor Dastugue."

"I feel like an idiot. I didn't know."

"I wish they had been more public. Then people like Gwen Lancaster couldn't spread their lies."

"What's going on here, Dad? You trying to steal my girl?"

Buddy's expression cleared. "I think your mother would have something to say about that, son."

A commotion by the bandstand interrupted their banter. Buddy glanced in that direction, then swore softly. "Excuse me, kids. Duty calls."

They watched him go. The band struck up another tune. "Dance with me?"

Matt held out his arms; Avery stepped into them. Her talk with Buddy had changed everything, she realized. She felt as if a thousand-pound weight had been lifted from her shoulders. How could she have trusted a stranger over people she knew and loved?

"You and Dad have a nice talk?" he asked.

"Really nice."

"He loves you a lot, you know. As much as me or Cherry."

But not Hunter. Never Hunter.

"You're thinking of my brother, aren't you?"

How did he so easily read her mind? Did he know her so well, still, after all these years?

"Yes," she said.

"He did this to himself, Avery. He removed himself from our lives."

"But why? I guess I just...don't understand. We were all so close."

"I wish to God I knew what went wrong. You can't imagine—" He looked away, then back, expression in his eyes anguished. "I've never been closer to anybody than I was my brother. He's my other half, Avery. When we were kids...I couldn't have imagined this. That we wouldn't be best friends anymore. That we wouldn't even speak to one another, for God's sake."

"Have you tried to reconcile?"

He laughed, the sound tight. "Are you kidding? We all have. Tried and been rebuffed. Time and again."

"Hunter said something about Dad and Buddy's relationship. That they didn't even speak anymore. That it had become so bad between them, Dad would cross the street to avoid their coming face-to-face. Is that true?"

"Son of a bitch," he muttered, expression tightening. "That prick."

"So, it's not true?"

"Only partially. In the last months before his suicide. I believe he avoided Dad because he knew Dad would realize how bad off he was and stop him."

"Oh," she murmured, feeling small and gullible.

"Did he say anything else about us?"

Nothing she was about to repeat. She shook her head. "He seems so serious now. As if he's facing—"

"I don't want to talk about my brother, Avery. Not tonight." Matt drew her closer against him. "Did today bring back memories?"

She tilted her face up to his. "Good ones."

"Remember the Spring Fest we sneaked off to make out? We were all of thirteen."

"Your dad caught on. Followed us. Made you apologize to me."

"Lectured me about how to treat a lady."

She laughed. "Little did he know, it was the lady's idea."

And three years later, sneaking off to Tiller's Pond had also been her idea. And there, under the star-sprinkled sky they had consummated their passion for one another.

"We were so bad," she said.

"We were in love." His gaze held hers. Her mouth went dry.

"I couldn't get enough of you, Avery. Of touching you. Of being with you."

The blood rushed to her head. He dropped a hand to the small of her back, began moving his fingers in slow, rhythmic circles.

She melted against him. Memories swamped her. Of past moments like this. Of hot, urgent hands and mouths. Of the dizzying rush of their newfound sexuality.

He brought his mouth to her ear. "Seeing you with Hunter yesterday like that, it made me crazy. I couldn't look at you. I was afraid of what I might do. To you. To him."

What would it be like to make love with Matt? Avery wondered. Without the potency of young love, without the heady rush of their burgeoning sexuality? They weren't kids anymore but consenting adults. They'd had other lovers, they had hurt and been hurt. They wouldn't have to hurry, wouldn't need to worry about getting home before curfew or being caught. She knew how to please a man; he to please a woman.

With Matt she could have what she had lost. She could be the girl who was otherwise gone forever.

Cherry's warning to stay away from her brother unless she was serious ran through her mind, as did the assertion that Matt had never loved anyone but her.

Until she knew what she wanted, they couldn't go there. Much as she longed to.

"What are you thinking?" he asked.

"About the past. The way it was between us."

"I'm glad." He dropped his face close to hers. "Because it was good. And it could be good again. Very good."

"I wish I could be as certain. So much has changed, Matt. We've cha—"

He brought a finger to her lips. "I'm a patient man. I've waited this long, I can wait a little longer."

CHAPTER 24

Gwen stared at the front page of the *Gazette*'s Wednesday edition, her morning cup of coffee cooling on the bedstand. Not the headline story about Peggy Trumble's winning entry in the annual Spring Fest bake-off, but the one at the bottom, tucked into a corner, almost an afterthought: Car Hauled Out of Tiller's Pond.

She skimmed the piece for the third time. The story—hardly more than a blurb—went on to report how Avery Chauvin and Hunter Stevens had discovered a car abandoned in Tiller's Pond. The vehicle had been hauled out and found to be empty.

It was the last line of the piece that shook her to the core. The owner of the vehicle, New Orleanian Luke McDougal, who had been heading from nearby Clinton to St. Francisville, had been reported missing by his girlfriend three weeks before. Anyone with information should call the West Feliciana Parish Sheriff's Department.

No body. Just like her brother.

Gwen's legs shook so badly she had to sit. She sank onto the edge of the bed and brought a hand to her mouth. A suicide. A murder. And two disappearances. The Seven were responsible for all three, she hadn't a doubt. Dr. Phillip Chauvin had been killed because he'd known too much about The Seven. Elaine St. Claire had been killed because of her lifestyle. Her brother had gotten too close to the group.

What about Luke McDougal? She shifted her gaze to the *Gazette*. According to the article, he had been passing through town. So what was his connection to the group? Was there a connection?

There had to be. McDougal's disappearance was too similar to her brother's. Car found, seemingly abandoned. No sign of its owner or of foul play.

Avery Chauvin had been at the scene. So had Hunter Stevens. Gwen drew her eyebrows together, curious. She had seen the man's name in connection with another news piece recently. She searched her memory a moment.

He had found Elaine St. Claire's body.

That was odd, even for a community as small as Cypress Springs. It seemed to her that the coincidental and unexplainable were piling up. As were the bodies—even if no one but she saw it.

She could be next.

Avery Chauvin had told her the same thing, though at the time it hadn't frightened her. Now she wondered if the woman meant the words as a warning. Or a threat.

Gwen fought the urge to flee. Fought to come to grips with the overwhelming sensation of being trapped. She had trusted Avery, even though she had known nothing about her. She had automatically assumed she could because Avery had only recently returned to Cypress Springs. And because of her father's suicide.

That hadn't been smart. Avery Chauvin could be sympathetic to The Seven. Their cause. Her father very well may have taken his own life, she had no physical evidence proving otherwise, just a gut feeling.

Gwen recalled Avery's surprise and denial to her assertions about The Seven. Her obvious, nearly palpable relief when Gwen had suggested her father's death might have been other than suicide. As if relieved to have an ally.

Avery could be in cahoots with The Seven, but she thought not.

Gwen stood and crossed to the window, lifted one of the blind's slats and peered out at the brilliant morning. People moved about—on their way to school, work, on errands. City workers were still cleaning up from the weekend festival, removing lights, combing the square for the last remnants of trash.

Though no one as much as glanced her way, she felt as if she was being watched. Her comings and goings recorded. Who she spoke with noted.

Action against her was being planned.

Shuddering, she stepped away from the window. She brought the heels of her hands to her eyes. She had been too vocal about The Seven. Had asked too many questions of too many people. She hadn't used caution.

In her zeal to uncover her brother's fate, she had put herself in harm's way. Just as her brother, in his zeal to prove his thesis, had. Would she, like Tom, simply disappear? Who would come looking for her if she did? Or would her end come via suicide? She could see the headline now: Sister, Despondent Over Disappearance of Brother, Takes Own Life.

Who would doubt she'd done it? Not her mother, who had slid so deeply into depression herself that she could hardly get out of bed in the morning. Not the shrink she had seen, who had prescribed antidepressants, then lectured her for not taking them.

Don't get paranoid. Just be careful.

She needed an ally. She needed someone she could trust. Someone who belonged here, in this community. Someone the citizens of Cypress Springs trusted. Who could poke around and ask questions. Someone skilled at ferreting out facts. A person who had a compelling, personal reason for wanting to help her.

Only one such person came to mind.

Avery Chauvin.

CHAPTER 25

Gwen quickly showered and dressed. She towel-dried her hair, grateful for her no-fuss cap of curls, slapped on a touch of makeup, grabbed her handbag and darted out. Avery, she'd noted, had taken to jogging early then stopping for breakfast at the Azalea Café.

It was a bit late, but if she was lucky she would catch Avery as she was leaving the café.

She was better than lucky, Gwen saw, spotting Avery through the café's picture window—it looked as if the other woman had just gotten her pancakes. She was deep in an animated conversation with Peg, the Azalea's owner.

Gwen stepped into the restaurant. At the jingle of the door

opening, both the café's owner and Avery looked her way. Avery's smile faded.

Gwen pasted on a friendly smile and crossed to the booth. "Morning, Avery."

"Morning." She returned her attention to the other woman in an obvious rebuff.

They'd ended their last conversation if not on a friendly note, then one of growing respect. Avery had begun to believe in The Seven.

What had changed since then?

"Sit anywhere, hon," Peg interjected. "I'll be right with you."

Gwen hesitated, then nodded, choosing the table across the aisle from Avery. When the woman finished, she turned and took Gwen's order.

She asked for an English muffin and coffee, then watched Peg make her way back to the counter. When she reached it, she glanced back at Gwen, frown marring her forehead. Finding Gwen watching her, she smiled cheerfully and headed for the kitchen.

When the woman disappeared through the swinging doors, Gwen turned to Avery. "I was hoping I'd find you here."

Avery dug into her pancakes, not glancing her way.

"I really need to talk to you. It's important."

Avery looked at her then. "I don't want to talk to you. Please leave me alone."

"Did you have the chance to check out the facts I gave you when we spoke last?"

"I didn't realize you gave me any facts. I seem to remember unsubstantiated opinion and half-truths."

"If you would check—"

"I don't care to discuss this."

"Did they get to you? Is that what's happened? Did they threaten you with—"

Avery cut her off. "I don't know if you're delusional or just mean-spirited, but I've had enough."

"I'm neither, I promise you that. As a journalist—"

"I'm a good journalist. I test premise against facts. I don't twist the facts to make them sensational. I don't bend them to fit my own personal needs."

"If you would just listen."

"I listened too much already." Avery leaned toward her. "What you told me about The Seven were untruths. Yes, The Seven existed, but not as you described them. Yes, they were a group of civic-minded residents. But not a secret tribunal that spied and passed judgment on their fellow citizens. They called themselves Seven Citizens Who Care. They started a drug and alcohol awareness program in the schools and tried to get families back to church. My pastor was a member, for heaven's sake. So was Lilah Stevens. I suggest *you* check your facts, Ms. Lancaster."

"That's not true! Who told you this? Who—"

"It doesn't matter." Avery tossed her napkin on the table and slid out of the booth, pancakes hardly touched. "Put it on my tab, Peg," she called. "I need some fresh air."

Gwen stifled a sound of distress, jumped up and started after her, nearly colliding with Peg. The woman jumped back. The coffee she carried sloshed over the cup's side. With a cry of pain, she dropped the cup; it hit the floor and shattered.

Gwen apologized, but didn't stop. She made it out of the restaurant and onto the street moments after Avery.

"Wait!" she shouted. "I haven't told you everything."

Avery stopped and turned slowly. She met Gwen's gaze, the expression in hers resigned. "Don't you get it? I don't want to hear anything else you have to say. I love this town and the people who live here."

"Even if they killed your father? Would you love them then?"

For the space of a heartbeat, the other woman didn't move,

didn't seem to breathe. Then she shook her head. "I see now how desperate you are. To stoop that low. Be so...cruel. I feel sorry for you, Gwen Lancaster."

"I can ask that question," Gwen went on, knowing her time was limited, that the other woman would bolt any moment, "because they killed my brother."

"Nice try, but—"

"It was the same as with Luke McDougal. His car was found. No sign of violence. He was just...gone."

Gwen became aware of the volume of her voice, of the number of people around. Of who might be watching...and listening. She closed the distance between them.

"Tom Lancaster," she continued softly. "The *Gazette* ran a piece about his disappearance. It was about the size of the one they ran about McDougal's. Wednesday, February 6, this year. I have my own copy but you'd probably think I found some way to manufacture it."

Gwen glanced at the café's front window and found Peg there, peering out at them. She shifted her gaze. A CSPD patrolman seemed to be paying more attention to them than to the driver he was ticketing; she glanced toward the square. The old man on the bench across the street was openly watching them over the top of his newspaper.

She lowered her voice even more. "That's how I know about The Seven, from Tom. The thesis was his. He was here researching. He got too close."

"I think you're unstable," Avery said, voice shaking. "I think you should get some help."

"Check it out. Come see me when you believe."

CHAPTER 26

Just past dawn the next morning, Avery lay awake, staring at the ceiling. Fatigue pulled at her. A headache from lack of sleep pounded at the base of her skull. Gwen Lancaster's baldly stated question had played over and over in her head, making rest impossible.

"Even if they killed your father? Would you love them then?"

Avery rolled onto her side, curling into a tight ball. She wished she had never met the woman. She wished she could find a way to find and hold on to the peace of mind she had felt the other night after speaking with Buddy.

Why couldn't she simply believe in Buddy and Matt and the other people she loved and trusted? Why couldn't she put her faith in the various agencies that had investigated her father's death and determined it to be a suicide?

"I can ask that question, because they killed my brother."

"Dammit!" Avery sat up. She balled her hands into fists. Desperate people resorted to desperate measures to get their way. Gwen Lancaster was desperate, that had been obvious. So why should she believe her? Why not write her off as either a nut or a liar?

That very desperation. It rang true. Gwen Lancaster believed what she was saying. She was frightened.

Avery flopped onto her back, staring up at the ceiling once more. Gwen could be suffering from a psychotic disorder. Schizophrenics believed the voices they heard in their heads; their visions, the people who populated them, were as real to them as Matt and Buddy were to her. Paranoid schizophrenics believed that others plotted against them. Some functioned for years without detection.

But that didn't explain her anonymous caller. It didn't explain Luke McDougal's disappearance or Elaine St. Claire's murder.

And it certainly didn't assuage her feeling that her father could take his own life.

She threw back the covers and climbed out of bed. She crossed to the window and nudged aside the curtain. Cypress Springs had not yet awakened. She saw not a single light shining.

Headlights cut across the road, slicing through the dim light, bouncing off the trees and morning mist. A police cruiser, she saw. It slowed as it reached her property line, inching past at a snail's pace. Instinctively, she eased away from the window, out of sight.

Silly. Without a light inside, they wouldn't be able to see her. Besides, the cruiser was no doubt Buddy's doing.

Playing daddy. Watching out for her.

She rubbed her face, acknowledging exhaustion. She *was*

being silly. Losing sleep over this. Letting it tear her apart. She should be able to go on faith. Should be able to, but couldn't. She wasn't built that way. As an investigative reporter, she tested premise against facts, day in and day out.

If she wanted to regain her peace of mind, she would have to disprove Gwen Lancaster's claims.

Avery turned away from the window and began to pace, mind working, the skills she used on her job kicking in. If this were a story she was considering, what would she do?

Begin with a premise. One she thought had merit, that would not only make a good story but also make a difference. Remedy a problem.

Like the story she had done about the flaws in the foster care system. She had exposed the problems. By doing so, she'd helped future children caught in the system. Hopefully. That had been her aim; it was the aim of all good investigative reporting.

She stopped. So what was her premise? A group of small town citizens, frightened over the growing moral decay of their community, take the job of law and order into their own hands. Their actions begin benignly enough but unchecked, become extremist. Anyone who's actions fall outside what is considered right, moral or neighborly is singled out. They break the civil rights of their fellow citizens in the name of righteousness, law and order. Before it's all over, they resort to murder, the cure becoming worse than the illness, the judges more corrupt than the judged.

It was the kind of premise she loved to sink her teeth into. One that would make a startling, eye-opening story. It spoke to her on many levels. She loved her country and believed in the principles on which it had been founded. The freedoms that had made it great. Yet, she also bemoaned the loss of personal safety, the ever-decaying American value system, the inability of law enforcement and the courts to adequately deal with crime.

But this wasn't some anonymous story she was following up, Avery reminded herself. Her role wasn't that of uninvolved, cool-headed journalist. This was her hometown. The people involved her friends and neighbors. People she called family. One of the dead was her father.

She was emotionally involved, all right. Up to her eyeballs.

Premise against facts, she thought, determination flowing through her. She wouldn't let her emotions keep her from being objective. She would stay on her guard, wouldn't be blinded by personal involvement.

And same as always, she would uncover the truth.

CHAPTER 27

A very decided her first stop of the morning would be at the office of the Cypress Springs *Gazette,* located in a renovated storefront a block and a half off the square. Founded in June 1963, just months before the assassination of President John F. Kennedy, a picture of the former president still hung in the front waiting area.

She stepped through the door and a bell tinkled, announcing her presence. The front counter stood empty.

A tall, sandy-haired man appeared in the doorway to the newsroom. Behind his Harry Potter spectacles, his eyes widened. "Avery Chauvin? I was wondering if you were going to stop by for a visit."

"Rickey? Rickey Plaquamine? It's so good to see you."

He came around the counter and they hugged. She and Rickey had been in the same grade and had gone to school together all their lives. They had worked together on the high-school newspaper, had both pursued journalism and attended Louisiana State University in Baton Rouge. He, however, had opted to return to Cypress Springs after graduation, to report for the local paper.

"You haven't changed a bit," she said.

He patted his stomach. "Not if you ignore the thirty pounds I've gained. Ten with each one of Jeanette's pregnancies."

"Three? Last I heard—"

"We just had our third. Another boy."

"Three boys." She laughed. "Jeanette's got her hands full."

"You don't know the half of it." His smile faded. "Damn sorry about your dad. Sorry we didn't make the service. The new one's got colic and the entire household's been turned upside down."

"It's okay." She shifted her gaze toward the newsroom. "Where's Sal?"

He looked surprised. "You didn't know? Sal passed away about six months ago."

"Passed away," she repeated, crestfallen. Sal had been a big supporter of hers and had encouraged her to go into journalism. With each advancement of her career, he'd written her a note of congratulations. In each, his pride in her accomplishments had come shining through. "I didn't know."

His mouth thinned. "Hunting accident."

Avery froze. Goose bumps crawled up her arms. "Hunting accident?"

"Opening day of deer season. Shot dead. In fact, the bullet took half Sal's head off."

Her stomach turned. "My God. Who was the shooter?"

"Don't know, never found the guy."

"Sounds like it could have been a homicide."

"That's not the way Buddy called it. Besides, who'd want Sal dead?"

Her father. Sal Mandina. Two men who had been pillars of the community, men the entire town had looked up to. Both dead in the past six months. Neither from natural causes.

Rickey cleared his throat. She shifted her attention to the task at hand. "I was doing a little research and wondered if I could take a look at the archived issues of the *Gazette*."

"Sure. What're you looking for?"

"The Waguespack murder."

"No kidding? How come?"

She debated a moment about her answer then decided on incomplete honesty, as she called partial truth. "Dad saved a bunch of clippings... I'd forgotten the entire incident and wanted to fill in the blanks." She smiled brightly. "You mind?"

"Not at all. Come on." He led her back into the newsroom. From there they headed up to the second floor. "Biggest local news story we ever carried. I'm not surprised your dad kept clippings."

"Really? Why?"

"Because of the furor the murder caused in the community. Nobody escaped unchanged."

"That's what Buddy said."

"You talked to Buddy about it?"

Was that relief she heard in his voice? Or was she imagining it? "Sure. After all, he and Dad were best friends."

He unlocked the storage-room door, opened it and switched on the light. She stepped inside. It smelled of old newspapers. The room was lined with shelves stacked with bound volumes of the *Gazette*. At the center of the room sat a long folding table, two chairs on either side. Her throat began to tickle, no doubt from the dust.

"Call me if you need me. I'm working on Saturday's edition. The spring Peewee soccer league is kicking into high gear. Pardon the pun." He pointed toward the far wall. "The 1980s are over there. They're arranged by date."

Avery thanked him, and when she was certain she was alone, she crossed to issues from the past eight months. She carried a stack to the table and sat. From her purse she took a steno pad and pen and laid them on the table.

She opened the volume for Wednesday, February 6, of this year. And found the story just where Gwen had said she would.

Young Man Missing

Tom Lancaster, visiting grad student from Tulane University, went missing Sunday night. Sheriff's department fears foul play. Deputy Sheriff Matt Stevens suspects Lancaster a victim of a random act of violence. The investigation continues.

Avery sucked in a shaky breath. One truth did not fact make, she reminded herself. The best lies—or most insidious delusions—contained elements of truth. That element of believability sucked people in, made them open their wallets or ignore warning signs indicating something was amiss.

She found a number of stories about Sal's death. Since he'd been the *Gazette*'s editor-in-chief, the biweekly had followed it closely. As Rickey had told her, he had been shot on the opening day of deer season. The guilty party had never been found, though every citizen who'd applied for a hunting license had been questioned.

Buddy had determined Sal had been shot from a distance with a Browning .270-caliber A-bolt rifle. Both it and the Nosler Ballistic Tip bullet were local hunters' favorites. Closed-casket services had been held at Gallagher's.

Rickey had been wrong about one thing: Buddy had classified the death as a homicide.

For the next two hours she picked her way through the archived issues. What she found shook her to the core.

Gwen Lancaster hadn't been fabricating.

Avery picked up her notepad, scanning her notes. She had listed every death not attributed to natural causes. Kevin Gallagher had died this year, she saw. Danny Gallagher's dad. A car wreck on Highway 421, just outside of town. His Lexus had careened off the road and smashed into a tree. He hadn't been wearing a seat belt and had gone through the windshield.

Deputy Chief of Police Pat Greene had drowned. A woman named Dolly Farmer had hung herself. There'd been a couple more car wrecks, young people involved—both in the same area Sal had died. The city, she saw, had commissioned the state to reduce the speed limit along that stretch of highway.

She frowned. Another hanging—this one deemed accidental. The kid, it seemed, had been into autoeroticism. Another young person had OD'd. Pete Trimble had fallen off his tractor and been run over.

Avery laid the notepad on the table and brought a trembling hand to her mouth. Eight months, all this death. Ten of them. Thirteen if she tossed in Luke McDougal, Tom Lancaster and Elaine St. Claire.

She struggled for impartiality. Even so, Gwen had not presented the facts accurately: she had claimed there'd been six suicides—including her father's—in the past eight months. She saw two.

"You okay up here?"

Avery took a second to compose herself and glanced over her shoulder at Rickey. She forced a smile. "Great." She hopped to her feet. "Just finished now."

She tucked the notebook into her purse, then grabbed up the volume she had been studying. She carried it to the section that housed the 1980s, hoping he wouldn't notice she was shelving it incorrectly.

She wasn't that lucky.

"That doesn't go there." He crossed the room. "Wrong color code."

He slid the volume out, checked the date, frowning. "Thought you wanted to look at stuff from 1988."

"Caught me." She hiked her purse strap higher on her shoulder. "I did, I just—" She looked away then back, working to capture just the right note of sincerity. "It's so maudlin, really. But Dad's...his death...I—"

He glanced down at the volume as the date registered. "Geez, Avery, I'm sorry."

"It's okay." She manufactured a trembling smile. "Want to walk me out?"

He did just that, stopping at the front door. "Avery, can I ask you something?"

"Sure."

"Rumor on the street is you're staying. Is that so?"

She opened her mouth to deny the rumor, then shut it as she realized she didn't know for certain what she was doing. "I haven't decided yet," she admitted. "But don't tell my editor."

He smiled at that. "If you stay, I'd love to have you on the *Gazette* staff. A big step down, I know. But at the *Post* you've got to put up with the city."

"You're right about that." She smiled, pleased by the offer. "If I stay, there's no one I'd rather work with."

"Stop by and see Jeanette. Meet the kids. She'd love it."

"I would, too." She crossed to the door. There she glanced back. "Rickey? You ever hear of a group called The Seven?"

His expression altered subtly. He drew his eyebrows together, as if thinking. "What kind of group? Religious? Civic?"

"Civic."

"Nope. Sorry."

"It's okay. It's something Buddy mentioned. Have a great day."

She stepped out onto the sidewalk. Squinting against the sun, she dug her sunglasses out of her purse, then glanced back at the *Gazette*'s front window.

Rickey was on the phone, she saw. In what appeared to be a heated discussion. He looked upset.

Rickey glanced up then. His gaze met hers. The hair on the back of her neck prickling, she lifted a hand in goodbye, turned and walked quickly away.

CHAPTER 28

Avery went home to regroup and decide on her next step. She sat at her kitchen table, much as she had for the past hour, untouched tuna sandwich on a plate beside her. She stared at her notebook, at the names of the dead.

Such damning evidence. Didn't anyone in Cypress Springs find this rash of deaths odd? Hadn't anyone expressed concern to Buddy or Matt? Was the whole town in on this conspiracy?

Slow down, Chauvin. Assess the facts. Be objective.

Avery pushed away from the table, stood and crossed to the window. She peered out at the lush backyard, a profusion of greens accented by splashes of red and pink. What did she actually have? Gwen Lancaster, a woman who claimed that a vigilante-style group was operating in Cypress Springs. A number of accidental deaths, suspicious because of their number. Two missing persons. A murder. A suicide. And a box of newspaper clippings about a fifteen-year-old murder.

Accidents took lives. People went missing. Murders happened, as tragic a fact as that was. Yes, the suicide rate was slightly higher than the state average, but statistics were based on averages not absolutes. It might be two years before another Cypress Springs resident took his own life.

And the clippings? she wondered. A clue to state of mind or nothing more than saved memorabilia?

If the clippings were evidence to a state of mind, wouldn't her dad have saved something else as well? She thought yes. But where would he have stored them? She had emptied his bedroom closet and dresser drawers, the kitchen cabinets and pantry and the front hall closet. But she hadn't even set foot in his study or the attic.

Now, she decided, was the time.

Two and a half hours later, Avery found herself back in the kitchen, no closer to an answer than before. She crossed to the sink to wash her hands, frustrated. She had gone through her father's desk and bookshelves, his stored files in the attic. She had done a spot check of every box in the attic. And found nothing suspicious or out of the ordinary.

She dried her hands. What next? In Washington, she'd had colleagues to brainstorm with, editors to turn to for opinions and insights, sources she trusted. Here she had nothing but her own gut instinct to guide her.

She let it guide her now. She picked up the phone and dialed her editor at the *Post*. "Brandon, it's Avery."

"Is it really you?" He laughed. "And here I thought you might be hiding from me."

He appreciated bluntness. He always preferred his writers get to the point—both in their work and their pitches. The high-stress business of getting a newspaper on the stands afforded no time for meandering or coy word games.

"I'm onto a story," she said.

"Glad to hear your brain's still working. Though I'm a bit surprised, considering. Tell me about it."

"Small town turns to policing its citizens Big Brother-style as a way to stop the ills of the modern world from encroaching on their way of life. It began when a group of citizens, alarmed by the dramatic increase in crime, formed an organization to counter the tide. At first it was little more than a Neighborhood Watch-type program. A way to help combat crime."

"Then they ran amok," he offered.

"Yes. According to my source, the core group was small, but they had an intricate network of others who reported to the group. Citizens were followed. Their mail read. What they ate, drank and watched was monitored. Where they went. If they worshiped. If the group determined it necessary, they were warned that their behavior would not be tolerated."

"Goodbye civil rights," Brandon muttered.

"That's not the half of it. If their warnings went unheeded, the group took action. Businesses were boycotted. Individuals shunned. Property vandalized. To varying degrees, everyone was in on it."

He was silent a moment. "You talking about your hometown?"

"Yup."

"You have proof?"

"Nope." She pulled in a deep breath. "There's more. They may even have begun resorting to murder."

"Go on."

"The deaths are masked as suicides or accidents. A drowning during a fishing trip, a farmer falling under his tractor, a hanging, a—"

"—doctor setting himself on fire."

"Yes," she said evenly. "Things like that."

"Avery, you're not up to this. You're not thinking clearly right now."

"I can handle it. I haven't lost my objectivity."

"Bullshit and you know it."

She did, but she wasn't about to admit that. "I just want to find out the truth."

"And what is the truth, Avery?"

"I'm not certain. The story could be a work of fiction. My source is—"

"Less than credible? Unreliable? His motivations questionable?"

"Yes."

"They always are, Avery. You know that. And you know what to do."

Follow leads. Find another source. Prove information accurate.

"Not as easy as it sounds," she said. "This is a small community. They've closed ranks. Others, I suspect, are frightened."

"I think you should come back to Washington."

"I can't do that. Not yet. I have to pursue this."

"Why's that, Avery?"

Because of her dad. "It'd make a good story," she hedged. "And if it's true, somebody's getting away with murder."

"It would make a good piece, but that has nothing to do with why you want to go after it. We both know that."

In her editor's vernacular, admitting the story had potential equaled a green light. "It's the stuff Pulitzers are made from," she teased.

"If what you're telling me is true, it's the stuff that fills morgues. I want you back at your desk, Avery. Not laid out on a slab."

"You worry too much. Got any suggestions?"

"Look closely at the facts. Double-check your own motivations. Then go to people you trust." He paused. "But be careful, Avery. I wasn't kidding when I said I wanted you back alive."

CHAPTER 29

Avery took her editor's advice to go to people she trusted. She decided to start with Lilah, who she had been meaning to pay a visit to anyway.

She parked her rental in the Stevenses' driveway and climbed out. Their garage door was open; Avery saw that both Lilah's and Cherry's cars were parked inside.

Avery made her way up the walk, across the porch to the door. She rang the bell. Cherry answered.

"Hey," Avery said.

The other woman didn't smile. "Hey."

"I stopped by to see how Lilah was feeling."

Cherry didn't move from the doorway. "She's better, thanks."

Avery had been meaning to call Cherry and apologize for the way she'd snapped at her at her father's wake, but hadn't. Until that moment, Avery hadn't realized just how badly she had hurt the other woman. Or how angry she was. Her reaction seemed extreme to Avery, but some people were more sensitive than others.

"Cherry, can we talk a moment?"

"If you want."

"I'm sorry about the other night. At the wake. I was upset. I shouldn't have snapped at you. I've been kicking myself for it ever since."

Cherry's expression softened. In fact, for the space of a heartbeat, Avery thought the other woman might cry. Then her lips curved into a smile. "Apology accepted," she said, then pushed open the screen door.

Avery stepped inside and turned to the younger woman who motioned toward the back of the house. "Mother's on the sunporch. She'll be delighted to see you."

She was. "Avery!" the older woman exclaimed, setting aside her novel. "What a pleasure."

Lilah sat on the white wicker couch, back to the yard and its profusion of color. Sun spilled through the window, bathing her in soft, white light—painting her the picture of Southern femininity.

Avery crossed, bent and kissed the woman's cheek, then sat in the wicker queen's chair across from her. "I've been worried about you."

She waved aside her concern. "Blasted allergies. This time of year is such a trial. The headaches are the worst."

"Well, you look wonderful."

"Thank you, dear." Lilah shifted her gaze to her daughter. "Cherry, could you bring Avery an iced tea?"

Avery started to her feet. "I can get it."

"Nonsense," Lilah interrupted. "Cherry's here. Would you

mind, sweetheart? And some of those little ginger cookies from the church bake sale."

"No problem," Cherry muttered. "Got to earn my keep, after all."

Avery glanced at the girl. Her features looked pinched. Avery cleared her throat. "Really, Lilah, I can get my own dri—"

Cherry cut her off. "Don't worry about it, Avery. I'm used to this."

After Cherry left the room, Lilah made a sound of frustration. "Some days that girl is so testy. Just miserable to live with."

"We all have bad days," Avery said gently.

"I suppose so." Lilah looked down at her hands, clasped in her lap. When she lifted her eyes, Avery saw that they sparkled with tears. "It's been...difficult for Cherry. She shouldn't be taking care of us. She should have a family of her own. Children to care for."

"She will, Lilah. She's young yet."

The woman continued as if Avery hadn't spoken. "After Karl left, she changed. She's not happy. None of my children—"

Lilah had been about to say that none of her children were happy, Avery realized. Hunter she understood. And to a degree, Cherry. But what of Matt?

Avery reached across the coffee table and caught Lilah's hand. She squeezed. "Happiness is like the ocean, Lilah. Sometimes swelling, sometimes retreating. Constantly shifting." She smiled. "Sudden swells are what make it all so much fun."

Lilah returned the pressure on her fingers. "You're such a dear child, Avery. Thank you."

"Here you go," Cherry said, entering the room with a tray laden with two glasses of tea, sugar bowl and plate of cookies. Each glass sported a circle of lemon and sprig of mint.

She set the tray on the coffee table. The cookies, Avery saw, were arranged in an artful fan, atop a heart-shaped doily. "How lovely," Avery exclaimed. "Cherry, you have such a gift."

She flushed with pleasure. "It was nothing."

"To you, maybe. I could no sooner put this tray together than run a marathon in world record time."

"You're too sweet."

"Just honest. Join us?"

"I'd love to but there are some things I wanted to do this afternoon. And if I don't get to them, it'll be dinnertime and too late." Cherry turned to her mother. "If you don't need anything else, I'll get busy?"

Lilah waved her off, and for the next few minutes Avery and the older woman chatted about nothing more weighty than the weather. When the conversation lulled, Avery brought up the subject most on her mind. "Buddy told me that back in the eighties you were part of a civic action group called Seven Citizens Who Care."

She drew her eyebrows together. "Why in the world did he do that?"

"We were talking about Cypress Springs. How it's such a great place to live." Avery reached for a cookie, laid it on her napkin without tasting. "Said you enacted real change in the community."

"Those were difficult times." She smoothed the napkin over her lap. "But that's ancient history."

Avery ignored her obvious bid to change the subject. "He said Pastor Dastugue was part of the group. Who else was a member of The Seven?"

"What did you say?"

"The Seven, who else—"

"We didn't call ourselves that," she corrected sharply. "We were the CWC."

She had struck a nerve, no doubt about it. Ignoring the

prickle of guilt, she pressed on. "I'm sorry, Lilah. I didn't mean to upset you."

"You didn't." She smoothed the napkin. Once. Then again. "Of course you didn't."

"Was there another group called The Seven?"

"No. Why would you think that?"

"Your response...it seemed like The Seven might be something you didn't want to be associated with."

She went to work on the napkin. "Silly, Avery. Of course not."

"I stopped by the *Gazette* this morning," Avery said. "Rickey Plaquamine offered me a job."

"Outstanding." Lilah leaned forward, expression eager. "And? Did you take it?"

"Told him I'd think about it."

She pretended to pout, though Avery could see she was delighted she hadn't outright declined the offer.

"We'd all be thrilled if you decided to make Cypress Springs your home, Avery. But no one more than Matt." She brought her tea to her lips, sipped then patted her mouth with her napkin. "Buddy told me you and Matt seemed to be enjoying yourselves at Spring Fest."

Avery thought of the other night, of dancing with Matt under the stars. Of how comfortable she had felt, how relaxed. Although she hadn't seen him since, he had called every day to check on her.

She smiled. "We did. Very much."

Avery offered nothing further, though she could tell the woman was eager for details. And assurances, Avery supposed. About her and Matt's future. Ones that she was unable to make.

"Rickey looked great. He said he and Jeanette just had their third."

"A handsome boy. Fat. All their babies have been fat." Lilah leaned toward Avery, twinkle in her eyes. "It's all the ice cream Jeanette eats during her last trimester. Belle from the Dairy Barn told me Jeanette came every day, sometimes twice a day, for a double-swirl hot-fudge sundae."

A smile tugged at Avery's mouth. Poor Jeanette. Small-town living—life in a fishbowl.

Avery refocused their conversation. "Until today, I hadn't known Sal was gone. I was so shocked. Dad knew how I felt about Sal, I'm surprised he didn't tell me."

Lilah opened her mouth, then shut it. "This year," she began, struggling to speak, "it's been difficult. Our friends...so many of them...passed away."

Avery stood and crossed to the woman. She bent and hugged her. She felt frail, too thin. "I'm sorry, Lilah. I wish I could do something to help."

"You already have, sweetheart. By being here."

They chatted a couple moments more, then Lilah indicated she needed to rest. They stood. Avery noticed the woman wasn't quite steady on her feet. It alarmed her to see her this way. Just over two weeks ago, she had seemed the picture of health.

They reached the foyer. Lilah kissed Avery's cheek. "Stop by again soon."

"I will. Feel better, Lilah."

Avery watched as the woman made her way up the stairs, noticing how tightly she gripped the handrail, how she seemed to lean on it for support. She found it hard to believe that seasonal allergies would cause this dramatic change in the woman, though she had no real frame of reference for that belief since she had been one of the lucky ones who had been spared them.

Hunter had claimed his mother was addicted to painkillers and booze. Substance abuse took a terrible toll on health and emotional stability. Could that be what she was seeing?

Cherry appeared in the study doorway, to Avery's left. "Mother's going up to nap?" she asked.

"Mmm." Frowning, Avery shifted her gaze to Cherry. "Is she all right?"

"She's fine. The allergy medicine takes it out of her."

"You're certain? She's not having any other problems, is she?"

"Of course not. Why do you ask?"

"I'm concerned. She was so strong just two weeks ago."

"Her bouts are like this." Cherry shrugged. "Mom just doesn't bounce back like she used to."

Avery lowered her gaze. Cherry held a gun, some sort of revolver. She returned her gaze to the other woman's. "Not to be too nosy, but why the—"

"Gun? I'm heading out to the practice range."

"The practice range?" Avery repeated, surprised. Girls in rural Louisiana grew up around hunting and guns, though they were less likely to know how to use one than to bake a peach pie from scratch. "You shoot?"

"Are you kidding? With Matt and Dad as role models? How about you?"

"I'm a bunny-hugging pacifist."

"You want to come along anyway?"

"Why not?"

Avery followed Cherry into her father's study. His gun closet stood open. It held no less than a dozen guns and rifles. Cherry helped herself to a box of bullets, closed and locked the closet. She slipped the key into her pocket, fitted her revolver in its case and snapped it shut.

"Ready?"

She nodded and they headed out, Avery following in her own car. The gun range was actually a cleared field ten miles outside of town, not far from the road to the canning factory. On the edge of the field sat a dilapidated chicken coop and three bales of straw, each set a dozen feet apart, standing on end. The land looked what it was: abandoned and overgrown.

They climbed out of their cars. "This was part of the Weiners' farm, wasn't it?" Avery asked.

"Yup. Sold the whole thing to Old Dixie Foods. Moved up to Jackson."

Avery wrinkled her nose. "What's that smell?"

"The canning factory. Wind's just right for it today." Cherry opened the gun case, took out the gun and began to load it. "Give it a minute, you get accustomed to the smell."

Avery had a hard time believing that. "What kind of gun is it?"

"Ruger .357 Magnum with a six-inch barrel."

"The Dirty Harry gun, right? From the films?"

"Close. Detective Harry Callahan carried the .44 Magnum." She laughed. "Even *I* don't need that much firepower."

Avery watched as Cherry slid six bullets into the chamber, then snapped it shut. "What do you shoot at?" she asked.

"Whatever. The chicken coop, tin cans, bottles. Dad has a hand-operated skeet thrower, sometimes we shoot skeet. For that we use a hunting rifle or shotgun."

To that end she popped open her trunk and took out a cardboard box filled with tin cans. While Avery watched, she crossed the field and set the cans on top of the straw bales and along the chicken coop's window ledges and roof.

She jogged back. She checked her gun, aimed and fired, repeating the process six times. The cans flew. She missed the last and swore.

She glanced at Avery. "I heard what you asked Mom about. That old group, the CWC."

"Do you remember it?"

"Sure. I remember everything about that time."

Avery frowned. "It's so weird, because I don't."

Cherry reloaded the revolver's chamber. "That's not so weird. My family's the reason I remember so clearly."

"It was a rough time, your dad said."

"Rough would be an understatement."

She fell silent a moment, as if lost in her own thoughts. In memories of that time.

"Can I ask you a question?"

"Shoot." Cherry grinned. "Sorry, I couldn't help myself."

"Did you know Elaine St. Claire?"

"Who?"

"The woman who was murdered."

Cherry sighted her mark. She pulled the trigger. The bullet exploded from the gun. She repeated the process five more times, then looked at Avery. "Only by reputation."

"What do you mean?"

Cherry cocked an eyebrow. "Come on, Avery. *By reputation.* She'd seen more mattresses than the guy down at the Sealy Bedding Barn."

Avery made a sound of shock. "The woman's dead, Cherry. It seems so callous to talk about her that way."

"I'm being honest. Should I lie just because she's dead? That would make me a hypocrite."

"Ever hear the saying 'Live and let live'?"

"That's big-city crapola, propagated by those intent on maintaining status quo and contentment of the masses. You have to live with the bottom-feeders."

"And you don't?"

She looked at Avery, expression perplexed. "No, we don't. This is Cypress Springs not New Orleans."

"You're saying Elaine St. Claire got what she deserved? That you're glad she's dead?"

"Of course not." She flipped open the .357's chamber, reloaded, then snapped it shut. "Nobody deserves that. But am I sorry she's not spreading her legs for every dick in town, no I'm not."

Avery gasped; Cherry's smile turned sly. "I've shocked you."

"I didn't think Matt's little sister could talk that way."

"There's a lot you don't know about me, Avery."

"Sounds ominous."

She laughed. "Not at all. You've been gone a long time, that's all." Without waiting for a response, she sighted her tin prey and fired. One shot after another, ripping off six. Hitting her target each time.

Avery watched her, both surprised and awed by her ability. Unnerved by it as well. Particularly in light of their conversation. She shifted her gaze to Cherry's arms, noticing how cut they were. The way her biceps bulged as she gripped the gun, how she hardly recoiled when it discharged.

She'd never noticed what good shape the other woman was in. How strong she was. How strongly built. Avery supposed that was because compared to her, everybody looked big.

Truth was, she'd always thought of Cherry as a girlie-girl, like Lilah. And like her own mother had been. Avery had been the tomboy. The one who hadn't quite fit the mold of Southern womanhood. And now here was Cherry, all buff and macho, blasting the crap out of tin cans.

Cherry reloaded, turned and offered the gun to Avery, grip out. "Want to give it a try?"

Avery hesitated. She disliked guns. Was one of those folks who thought the world would be a better place if every weapon on the planet was collected and destroyed and people were forced to sit across a table from one another and work out their differences. Maybe over a latte or caffe mocha.

Cherry's smug grin had her reaching for the gun. "Okay," she said grimly, "walk me through this."

"It helps to plant your feet. Like this." Cherry demonstrated. "Wrap both hands around the grip. That's right," she said as Avery followed her directions.

"I feel like an idiot," Avery said. "Like an Arnold Schwarzenegger wannabe."

"I felt that way at first. You'll grow to like it."

When pigs fly. "What now?"

"Point and shoot. But be careful, it's got some kick."

Avery aimed at the can that looked closest to her and pulled the trigger. The force of the explosion sent her stumbling backward. She peeked at the target. "Did I hit it?"

"Nope. You might try keeping your eyes open next time."

"Shit."

"Try again."

Avery did. And missed cleanly. After her sixth attempt, she handed the gun back. "My career as a shooter is officially over."

"You might change your mind. If you stay in Cypress Springs."

"Don't hold your breath." She watched Cherry handle the weapon with a sort of reverence completely foreign to Avery. "What's the allure? I don't get it."

Cherry thought a moment. "It makes me feel powerful. In control."

"That's an odd answer."

"Really? Isn't that what weapons are all about? Power and control. Winning."

"And here I always thought they were about killing."

"There are always going to be bad guys, Avery. People determined to take away what you hold dear. People without morals or conscience. Guns, the ability—and willingness— to use them are a necessary deterrent."

Avery had argued this one before and knew she couldn't win. And a part of her knew Cherry spoke the truth. The current truth. But she was idealist enough to believe there was another way. "The only way to fight violence is with violence, that's what you're saying? React to force with greater force until we've blown the entire planet to hell?"

"The one with the biggest *boom* wins."

Moments later, Avery drove off. She glanced in her rearview mirror. The sun was setting behind her, the sky a palette of bloody reds and oranges. Cherry stood where she had left her, standing beside her car, staring after Avery.

Her outing with the younger woman had left her feeling uncomfortable, as if she had been party to something unclean. As if she had witnessed something ugly and had done nothing to stop it.

The things Gwen Lancaster had told her about The Seven played through her head.

Anyone whose actions fell outside what was considered right, moral or neighborly was singled out and warned. Before it was all over, they'd broken the civil rights of their fellow citizens in the name of righteousness, law and order.

Could the woman she had just spent the past hour with be party to that?

Absolutely. Avery didn't have a doubt about it. What she was less certain of, however, was how to reconcile the Cherry Stevens she had been witness to today with the one who had brought her breakfast her first morning in Cypress Springs. The one who had been caring, sweet-natured and sensitive.

Today, nothing about Cherry had rung true to her, from the things she had said about Elaine St. Claire to the subtly sly tone she had assumed with Avery.

But why would she have affected such an attitude with her? It didn't make sense. Why either alienate her or, if part of The Seven, be so open about her beliefs? Surely those involved hadn't maintained their anonymity with such transparency.

Avery drew to a stop at the crossroads, stunned with the course of her own thoughts. She was thinking as if The Seven was a given. As if they had and did exist, as if anyone could be a part of their numbers.

An ill feeling settling in the pit of her stomach, she dug through her purse, found the card with Gwen's phone number on it. She punched the number into her cell phone; on the third ring the woman's recorder answered.

"It's Avery Chauvin," she said. "You've got my attention

now. Call me." She left the number for both her cell and parents' home phone, then hung up.

Through the open window came the sound of a gun discharging. Avery jerked at the sound. She closed the window against it and the sour-smelling breeze.

CHAPTER 30

The Gavel entered the war room. It had been difficult to get away this Friday evening—he was late. His generals were all in place, assembled around the table. Two held the rapt attention of the others as they complained about the Gavel's leadership and the way he had handled Elaine St. Claire.

One by one they became aware of his presence. Nervous silence fell over them. Guilty silence.

He crossed to his place at the table's head, working to control his anger. He shifted his gaze from one of his detractors to the other. Their discomfort became palpable. "You have a problem, Blue? Hawk?"

Blue faced him boldly. "The situation with the outsider is worsening. We must take action."

"Agreed." He turned his gaze to the other. "Hawk?"

"The handling of St. Claire was a mistake."

Shock rippled through the group. Hawk was the Gavel's biggest supporter. His ally from the beginning. His friend.

Fury took the Gavel's breath. A sense of betrayal. He kept a grip on his emotions. "What should we have done, Hawk? Allowed her to continue to sully the character of this town? To tear at its moral fiber thread by thread? Or allowed her to go to the authorities? Have you forgotten our pledge to one another and this community?"

The other man squirmed under his gaze. "Of course not. But if we'd...taken care of her as we have the others, no one would be the wiser. To have so openly disposed of her—"

"Has sent a message to others like her. We will not be discovered, I promise you that."

Hawk opened his mouth as if to argue, then shut it and sat back, obviously dissatisfied. The Gavel narrowed his eyes. He would speak with him privately; if he determined Hawk a risk, he would be removed from the high council.

"What of the reporter?" Blue asked.

"Avery Chauvin? What of her?"

"She's been talking to the other one. The outsider."

"And asking questions," another supplied. "A lot of questions."

He hesitated, surprised. "She's one of us."

"Was one of us," Blue corrected. "She's been away too long to be trusted. She's become a part of the liberal media."

"That's right," Hawk supplied. "She doesn't understand what we cherish. What we're fighting to save. If she did, she would never have left."

A murmur of agreement—and concern—went around the table. Voices rose.

The Gavel struggled to control his mounting rage. Although he didn't let on, he had begun to have doubts about Avery Chauvin's loyalty as well. He, too, had become aware of her snooping. Nosing around things she didn't—and couldn't—understand.

But he was the leader of this group and he would not be questioned. He had earned that right. If he determined Avery Chauvin represented minimal risk, he expected his generals to fall in line.

He held up a hand. His generals turned their gazes to his. "Must I remind you we are only as strong as our belief in our cause? As our willingness to do whatever is necessary to further that cause? Or that dissension among our number will be our undoing? Just as it was the undoing of our fellows who came before?"

He paused a moment to let his words sink in. "We are the elite, gentlemen. The best, the most committed. We will not allow—I will not allow—anyone to derail us. Even one of our own sisters."

The generals nodded. The Gavel continued. "Leave everything to me," he said. "Including the reporter."

CHAPTER 31

Avery had expected Gwen to return her message Thursday evening, within hours of her leaving it. Instead, the next day came and went without word from her, and Avery began to worry. She tried her again. And left another message.

Just as she decided to pay a visit to The Guesthouse, her doorbell rang. Certain it was Gwen, she hurried to answer it. Instead of the other woman on her doorstep, she found Buddy.

He smiled as she opened the door. She worked to hide her dismay even as she scolded herself for it. "Hello, Buddy. What a nice surprise."

"Hello, baby girl." He held up a napkin-covered basket. "Lilah asked me to run these by."

She took the basket, guilt swamping her. "What are they?"

"Lilah's award-winning blueberry muffins."

Even as he answered, their identifying smell reached her nose. Her mouth began to water. "How is she?"

"Better. Back in the kitchen." He mopped the back of his neck with his handkerchief. "Hot out there today. They say it's going to break records."

"Come on in, Buddy. I'll get you a cold drink."

"I'm not going to lie, some ice water would be great."

He stepped inside; she motioned for him to follow her. The air conditioner kicked on. He looked around as they made their way to the kitchen, obviously taking in the disarray, the half-emptied shelves, the stacks of boxes. "Looks like you're making some headway," he said.

"Some." She reached into the freezer for ice, then dropped a couple cubes into a glass. She filled it with water and handed it to him. "I'm not spending as much time on it as I should be. The Realtor is champing at the bit. She has a client looking for a house like this one."

He took a long swallow of water. "It's a great house. Great location. I hate to see—"

He bit the words back, then shifted the glass from one hand to the other, the nervous gesture unlike him. "Have you given any thought to keeping it? To staying in Cypress Springs? I'm growing accustomed to having you around. We all are."

She met his eyes, touched by the naked yearning she saw in them. Torn. How could she on the one hand feel such affection for these people and this community, and on the other suspect them of being party to something as despicable as murder? What was wrong with her?

"I've been thinking about it a lot," she said. "I haven't made a decision yet."

"Anything I can do to sway you?"

"Just being you sways me, Buddy." She stood on tiptoe and kissed his cheek.

He flushed with pleasure. "Lilah told me you stopped by."

"I did." Avery poured herself a glass of water. "We had a nice visit."

"And you spent some time with Cherry as well."

She felt her smile slip. He saw it and frowned.

"What's wrong?"

"Nothing. She's turned into a damn good shot. I was awed."

"She has at that. Personally, I think she would have made a good lawman."

That surprised her. "You encouraged her?"

"I did." He sighed. "But you know how it is down here, sexual stereotypes run deep. Women are supposed to get married and have babies. And if they work, they choose a womanly profession."

Like catering. Not law enforcement. Or journalism. Her own mother had done her damnedest to convince her of that very thing.

"I do know, Buddy."

His expression softened. "You look tired."

She averted her gaze. "I'm not sleeping well." That at least was true. It was *why* she wasn't sleeping that ate at her.

"That's to be expected. Give yourself some time, it'll get better."

Silence fell between them, broken only by the click of the ice against the glass as Buddy took another swallow of his water. "Rickey told me you stopped by the *Gazette*."

She looked at him. He lowered his eyes to his hat, then returned them to her. In his she saw sympathy. "Did you get the answers you were searching for?"

Rickey had called Buddy, she realized. He knew what she had been looking at. That she had asked about The Seven.

He probably knew she had spoken with Ben Mitchell and Dr. Harris as well. Small towns kept no secrets.

Except if what she suspected was true, this town had kept a secret. A big one.

"Talk to me, Avery," he urged. "What's going on with you? I can't help if I don't know what's wrong."

She thought of what her editor had said, that she should go to the people she trusted.

She trusted Buddy. He would never hurt her, she believed that with every fiber of her being.

"Buddy, can I...ask you something?"

"You can ask me anything, baby girl. Anytime."

"I spoke with Ben Mitchell, the arson investigator from the fire marshal's office. Something he said has been bothering me."

"Go on."

She took a deep breath. "He found one of Dad's slippers on the path between the house and the garage. He speculated he was wearing the other one and that it burned in the fire. Do you recall that to be true?"

Buddy drew his eyebrows together in thought. "I do. If you want the specifics, we can check my report."

"That's not—" She thought a moment, searching for the right words. "Does anything about that seem wrong to you?" At his blank expression, she made a sound of frustration. "Obviously not."

"I don't understand." He searched her gaze. "What are you thinking?"

"I don't know. I—"

That was a lie. She did know.

Say it, Avery. Get it out there.

"I don't think Dad killed himself."

The words, the ramifications of them, landed heavily between them. For a long moment Buddy said nothing. When he met her eyes, the expression in his was troubled. "Because of this slipper thing?"

"Yes, and...and because I knew my dad. He couldn't have done it."

"Avery—"

She heard the pity in his voice and steeled herself against it. "You knew him, too, Buddy. He loved life. He valued it. He couldn't have done this, not in a million years."

"You realize," he said carefully, "if you believe this, you're saying he was murdered?"

Heat flooded her cheeks. Standing with him, looking into his eyes, she felt like a fool. She couldn't find her voice, so she nodded.

"Do you doubt I did a thorough investigation?"

"No. But you could have missed something. Dr. Harris could have missed something."

"I could make my report available to you, if that would help."

Gratitude washed over her. "It really would. Thank you, Buddy."

He was silent a moment, then as if coming to a decision, sighed deeply. "Why are you doing this, baby girl?"

"Pardon?"

"Your dad's dead. He killed himself. Nothing's going to bring him back."

"I know, I just—"

"We love you. You belong here, with us. You are one of us. Don't you feel it? Don't you feel like you belong?"

Tears swamped her. The people of Cypress Springs were her friends. They had been nothing but kind to her, welcoming her back unconditionally. The Stevenses were her second family. Now, her only family.

Being back had been good. For the first time in a long time she had felt as if she belonged. She didn't want to lose that.

She told him so, then swallowed hard. "If only I could accept...if only I didn't feel so—" She bit the last back, uncertain how she felt—or rather, which she felt most. Confused? Conflicted? Guilty?

She felt as if the last might eat her alive.

Buddy set his glass on the counter and crossed to her, laid his hands on her shoulders. She lifted her eyes to his, vision swimming. "You are not responsible for your father's death. It's not your fault."

"Then why...how could he have done it?"

He tightened his fingers. "Avery," he said gently, "you may never know exactly what happened. Because he's gone and we can't be party to his thoughts. You have to accept it and go on."

"I don't know if I can," she answered helplessly. "I want to. Lord knows—"

"Give yourself some time. Be good to yourself. Stay away from people like Gwen Lancaster. She doesn't have your best interests at heart. She's unstable."

Avery thought of the other woman. Of her accusations. Her desperation. Their very public discussion outside the Azalea Café.

"Matt's worried about you, too," Buddy continued. "He's working around the clock on the McDougal disappearance. McDougal wasn't the first. A couple months back, another man disappeared."

"Tom Lancaster."

"Yes." He dropped his hands, stepped away from her. "The cases are too similar for them not to be related. And the St. Claire murder coming so close on their heels...it seems a stretch to connect that as well, but we're looking at every possibility. After all, these sorts of things don't happen in Cypress Springs."

"But other sorts of things do."

He frowned. "Excuse me?"

"Haven't you noticed the high number of unexpected

deaths around here in the past eight months? The accidents and suicides?"

His frown deepened. "Every town has its share of accidental deaths. Every town has—"

"What about Pete Trimble's death? He was a farmer all his life. How could he fall under his tractor?"

"We found a nearly empty fifth of Jack Daniel's in the tractor's cab. His blood alcohol level was sky high."

"What about Dolly Farmer? The *Gazette* reported she hung herself? From what I read, she seemed to have everything to live for."

"Her husband had run off with his young secretary. The *Gazette* didn't print that."

"What about Sal?"

"Somebody who had no business with a rifle shot him. In their inexperience, they mistook him for a deer. When they discovered their mistake, they ran off."

"So many deaths, Buddy," she said, hearing the edge of hysteria in her own voice. "How can there be so many...deaths?"

"That's life, baby girl," he said gently. "People die."

"But so many? So close, so tragically?"

He caught her hands, squeezed her fingers. "If not for your father, would any of this seem out of the ordinary to you? If not for the imaginings of a woman in the throes of grief, would any of those deaths have seemed suspicious?"

Was that woman Gwen Lancaster? Or her?

Dear God, how far gone was she?

Her eyes welled with tears. She fought them from spilling. One slipped past her guard and rolled down her cheek.

Buddy eased her against his chest and wrapped his big, bearlike arms around her. "Gwen Lancaster is in a lot of pain. Her brother disappeared and is more than likely dead. I feel for her, I do. Lord knows how much losing my best friend hurt, I can only imagine how she must feel."

He drew slightly away, looked into her eyes. "People in

pain do things, believe in things...that just aren't true. As a way to lessen the pain. To justify their own actions or ease their own guilt. Trust the people you love. The people who love you. Not some woman you don't even know."

He brushed a tear from her cheek with his thumb. "This is a small town, Avery. People around here get their backs up easily. Stop playing the big-city investigative reporter or they'll forget you're one of them and start treating you like an outsider. You wouldn't like that, would you?"

Avery swallowed hard, confused. His words, gently spoken though they had been, smacked of a threat. A warning to cease and desist. "I don't understand. Are you saying—"

"A bit of friendly advice, baby girl. That's all. A reminder what small-town folks are like." He dropped a kiss on her forehead, then stepped away from her. "You're family, Avery, and I just want you to be happy."

CHAPTER 32

Avery stood at her front door for a long time after Buddy left. She felt numb, disconnected. She gazed out at nothing, the things Buddy had said playing over in her head.

Would anything Gwen said to her have made her suspicious if she hadn't been in the throes of grief? Sal's death would have been a terrible tragedy, one of those freak occurrences that made one ask, "Why?" Dolly Farmer another victim of the breakdown of the family, Pete Trimble a drunk-driving statistic.

What did *she* believe? She rubbed her throbbing temples. How could she be so easily swayed? One moment believing the people of Cypress Springs were involved in a conspiracy of discrimination and murder, the next sucked in by an emotionally unstable woman with a questionable agenda. She had always been so firm in her beliefs, so self-confident. She had been able to access the facts, make a decision and move on.

Avery dropped her hands. Is this how a breakdown began? One small confusion at a time? A bout of tears, mounting indecision, a feeling of drowning that passed only to return without a moment's notice?

Becoming aware that the air-conditioning was being wasted, she closed the door, turned and wandered back to the kitchen. Her gaze landed on Buddy's nearly empty water glass.

What did she want to believe?

In the people she loved and trusted. In those who loved her. And that her father hadn't taken his own life.

Therein lay the source of her conflict.

The phone rang. She turned toward it but made no move to pick it up. The caller let it ring nine times before hanging up. A moment later it rang again. Someone needed her. To speak to her.

Her father had needed to speak to her.

She hadn't taken his call.

She leaped for the phone, snatching the receiver off the base. "Hello?"

"Avery? It's Gwen."

Not now. Not her. She fought the urge to slam down the phone.

"I just got your message," the woman continued. "I drove to New Orleans to see my mother." She paused. "Avery? Are you there?"

"Yes, I'm here."

"I'd like to get together as soon as possible. When can you—"

"I'm sorry, Gwen, I can't talk about this just now."

"Are you all right?"

If she could call falling apart at the seams all right. "Yes, fine. I just...this isn't a good time."

"Are you alone?"

Avery heard the concern in the other woman's voice. She could imagine what she was thinking. "Yes."

"You sound strange."

"I think I made a mistake."

"A mistake? I don't understand."

"I can't do this. I feel for you, Gwen, I do. I understand loss, I'm swimming in it myself. But I can't be party to your far-fetched notions. Not anymore."

"Far-fetched? But—"

"Yes, I'm sorry."

"I'm all alone, Avery. I need your help." The other woman's voice rose. "Please help me find my brother's killer."

Avery squeezed her eyes shut. Against the desperation in the other woman's voice. The pain.

Trust the people you love. The people who love you.

"I wish I could, Gwen. My heart breaks for you, but—"

"Please. I don't have anyone else."

She felt herself wavering; she steeled herself against sympathy. "I really can't talk right now. I'm sorry."

Avery hung up. She realized she was shaking and drew in a deep breath. She had done the right thing. Pain shaped reality—her pain, Gwen's. The woman had focused her energy on this conspiracy theory as a way to lessen her pain. To turn her attention away from grief.

Avery had been drawn in for the same reason.

The phone rang again. *Gwen. To plead her case.* As much as she preferred to avoid the woman, she needed to face this. This was part of getting her act together.

She answered without greeting. "Look, Gwen, I don't know how to make it more plain—"

"How does it feel to be the daughter of a liar and murderer?"

The breath hissed past Avery's lips, she took an involuntary step backward. "Who is this?" she demanded, voice quaking.

"I'm someone who knows the truth," the woman said, then laughed, the sound unpleasant. "And there aren't many of us left. We're dropping like flies."

"You're the liar," Avery shot back. Outrage took her breath, fury on its heels. "My father was an honorable man. The most honest man I've ever known. Not a coward who's too afraid to show her face."

"I'm no coward. You're the—"

"You are. Hiding behind lies. Hiding behind the phone, making accusations against a man who can't defend himself."

"What about my boys!" she cried. "They couldn't defend themselves! Nobody cared about them!"

"I don't know who your boys are, so I can't comment—"

"Were," she hissed. "They're dead. Both my boys...dead. And your father's one of the ones to blame!"

Avery struggled not to take the defensive. To remain unemotional, challenge the woman in a way that would draw her out, get her to reveal her identity. "If you had any proof my dad was a murderer, you wouldn't be hiding behind this phone call. Maybe if I knew your sons' names I'd be more likely to think you were more than a pathetic crank."

"Donny and Dylan Pruitt," she spat. "They didn't kill Sallie Waguespack. They didn't even know her."

The Waguespack murder.

Dear God, the box of clippings.

Avery's hands began to shake. She tightened her grip on the receiver. "What did my father have to do with this?"

"Your daddy helped cover up for the real killer." The woman cackled. "So much for the most honest man you've ever known."

"It's not true," Avery said. "You're a liar."

"Why do you think my boys never stood trial?" she demanded. "'Cause they didn't do it. They was framed. None of it would have stood up to judge and jury. And all of them, those hypocrite do-gooders, would have gone to jail!"

"If you had any proof, you'd show it to me."

"I have proof, all right. Plenty of proof."

"Sure you do."

At the sarcasm, the woman became enraged. "To hell with you and your dead daddy. You're like the rest of 'em. Lying hypocrites. I tell you what I got and you'll bring the authorities down on me like white on rice."

Avery tried a different tack. "Why do you think I left Cypress Springs? I'm not one of them. I never was." She let that sink in. "If what you're telling me is true, I'll make it right."

"What's in it for you?"

"I clear my father's name."

The woman said nothing. Avery pressed on. "You want justice for your boys?"

"In this town? Ain't no justice for a Pruitt in this town. Hell, ain't no real justice to be had in Cypress Springs."

"Show me what you've got," Avery urged. "You've got proof, I'll make it right. I promise you that."

She was quiet a moment. "Not over the phone," she said finally. "Meet me. Tonight." She quickly gave an address, then hung up.

CHAPTER 33

Magnolia Acres trailer park was located on the southern boundary of Cypress Springs, just outside the incorporated area. Avery turned into the park, noting that the safety light at its entrance was burned out.

Or had been shot out by kids with BB guns, she thought, seeing that all the park's safety lights were dark.

She made her way slowly down the street, straining to make out the numbers. Even the dark couldn't soften the forlorn, abandoned look of the area. The only thing the neighborhood had going for it, Avery thought, was the large lot given each residence. But even those had a quality of runaway disrepair about them. The weeds were winning.

She found number 12 and parked in front. Avery climbed

out. Music came from several directions: rap, rock and country. From an adjacent trailer came the sound of a couple fighting. A child crying.

Avery slammed the car door and started toward the trailer, scanning the area as she did, noting details. Dead flowers in the single window box. A pitiable attempt at a garden: a few shrubs that badly need trimming, weeds, a rock border, half overgrown. Three steps led up to the front door. A concrete frog sat on the top step.

She neared the door, saw that it stood slightly ajar. Light spilled from inside. As did the smell of fried food.

She climbed the steps, knocked on the door and it swung open. "Mrs. Pruitt," she called. "It's Avery Chauvin."

No answer. She knocked and called out again, this time more loudly.

Again, only silence answered.

She stepped inside. The place was in a shambles. Furniture overturned, newspapers and take-out boxes strewn about, lamp on its side on the floor, light flickering. Her gaze landed on a dark smear across the back wall.

Avery frowned and started toward it. A radio in the other room played the classic "Strangers in the Night." Avery laughed nervously at how weirdly appropriate that was.

She reached the back wall. She squinted at the stain, touched it. It was wet. She turned her hand over. And red.

With a growing sense of horror, Avery turned slowly to her left. Through the doorway to the kitchen she saw a woman stretched out on the floor, back to Avery.

"Mrs. Pruitt?"

Swallowing hard, she crept forward. She reached the woman. Squatted beside her. Stretched out a hand. Touched her shoulder.

The woman rolled onto her back. The woman's eyes were open but it was her mouth that drew Avery's gaze—blood-soaked, grotesquely stretched.

With a cry, Avery scrambled backward. She slipped on the wet floor, lost her balance, landing on her behind. Blood, she realized, gazing down at herself. She had slipped in it, splattering herself, smearing it across the floor.

A sound drew her gaze. The woman blinked. Her mouth moved.

She was alive, Avery realized. She was trying to speak.

Avery righted herself and crept closer. Heart thundering, she knelt beside her, bent her head toward the woman's. A small sound escaped her—little more than a gurgle of air.

"What?" Avery asked, searching her gaze. "What are you trying to tell me?"

Her mouth moved again. She inched her hand to Avery's, fingers clawing.

From the front room came the sound of footsteps. Avery froze. She swung her gaze to the doorway, heart thundering. *The person who had done this could still be in the house.*

The sound came again. Terrified, she jumped to her feet. She looked wildly around her. *No back door. Small window above the sink.*

No way out.

Her gaze landed on the phone. She lunged for it.

"Police!"

Avery whirled around and found herself staring down the barrel of a gun. Her cry of relief stuck on her tongue.

"Get your hands up," the sheriff's deputy said, voice steely. She obeyed the order. Keeping his weapon trained on her, he bent and checked the woman's pulse.

"She's alive," Avery said, fighting hysteria. "She was trying to tell me something. When I heard you, I thought you were the one....the one who did this."

He unhooked his radio, called the incident in and requested an ambulance, never taking his gaze or aim off her.

"Turn around. Hands on the wall."

She did as he ordered, the scream of sirens in the distance.

Her bloody hands would leave marks on the wall, she thought, a cry rising in her throat.

The officer came up behind her. "Feet apart."

"You have the wrong idea. I found her this way." When she twisted to plead her case to his face, she found herself shoved flat against the wall, his hand between her shoulder blades. Gun to her head.

"Back off, Jones! Now!"

At the sound of Matt's voice, the deputy reacted instantly, dropping his hands, stepping back.

"Matt!" Avery cried. She ran to him, and he folded her in his arms.

"Sweetheart, are you all right?"

Avery clung to him, shaking. She managed a nod, eyes welling with tears. "The woman...is she...I thought...I heard a noise and—" She buried her face in his shoulder. "I thought whoever had done this, that he was still here."

He tightened his arms around her. "Deputy Jones?"

"Received a call from a neighbor. They heard a commotion. What sounded like a gunshot. When I arrived, I found the door open and interior ransacked. I called for assistance and made my way in here. I found the suspect kneeling over the victim."

"I found her this way!" Avery looked up at Matt. "The door was open...I called her name. She didn't answer, so I made my way in. I—"

The paramedics arrived then, interrupting her, shouting orders, pushing her and Matt toward the door. Behind them waited several more deputies, ready to process the scene the moment the paramedics gave the okay.

Holding her close to his side, Matt led her from the kitchen through the living room and outside. As they made their way out, her toe caught on the frog and it toppled into the garden. They descended the steps and crossed to two rickety lawn chairs set up around a kid's inflatable wading pool. Yellow crime scene tape had already been stretched around the perimeter of the trailer; a deputy stood sentinel, watching the group of neighbors who had come out to gawk.

"Sit," Matt said. "I have to go now. I need you to wait here. We're going to need to question you." He searched her expression. "Will you be all right?"

She nodded. "I'll be okay."

He squeezed her hands, then turned toward the deputy. "Make sure nobody bothers her. If she has any problems, come get me."

Avery watched him go, an intense sense of loss settling over her. She bit her bottom lip to keep from calling him back and sank onto the chair, the woven seat sagging dangerously.

"You all right?"

She glanced at the deputy, a baby-faced young man who hardly looked old enough to be out past ten, let alone to carry a weapon. She nodded. "The woman...is she Trudy Pruitt?"

The kid looked surprised by her question. And rightly so, she supposed, considering the circumstances. He answered anyway. "Uh-huh. Waitresses over at the Hard Eight."

The pool hall.

Avery hugged herself, the woman's image filling her head. Her vacant stare. Her slack mouth. The feel of her fingers clawing at Avery's.

She squeezed her eyes shut tightly, attempting to block out the images. They played on anyway. The woman's bloody mouth moving, the tiny puff of breath against her cheek. Blood, everywhere.

The paramedics came out. Avery opened her eyes at the sound. One looked her way. Their eyes met. In his she saw regret. Apology.

Her breath caught. She shifted her gaze. *No stretcher.*

They passed her. Climbed into the ambulance. Slammed the doors shut, the sound heavy. Final.

"Avery?"

She turned. Matt stood in the trailer doorway. She got to her feet; he started toward her.

"She didn't make it," she said when he reached her.

"No."

He caught her hands. "What are you doing here, Avery?"

She blinked, confused. "Pardon?"

"Tonight, what brought you here?"

"The woman, Trudy Pruitt. She said she had proof...about my father. And Sallie Waguespack."

His forehead creased. "Avery, sweetheart, you're not making any sense. Start at the beginning."

She drew in a deep breath, working to collect her jumbled thoughts. To fight past twin feelings of panic and confusion. "I need to sit."

He nodded and she did. He swung the second chair to face hers, then sat. He took out a small notepad. "Ready?"

She nodded. "The day of Dad's funeral I got an anonymous call. From a woman. She said that Dad had...gotten what he deserved. That I would, too. Then she hung up."

His expression tightened. "The caller you told me about the day McDougal's car was discovered in Tiller's pond?"

She nodded. "Go on."

"She called again just this afternoon. She said Dad had helped cover up a crime, a murder."

"Sallie Waguespack's."

"Yes. She called him a liar. And a murderer."

"And that woman was Trudy Pruitt."

"She said she had proof. She was...going to show it to me tonight."

"Did she tell you that her sons—"

"She said they didn't do it. That they were framed."

He passed a hand over his face. "Dammit, Avery...I wish you'd called me. Trudy Pruitt has been proclaiming her sons' innocence for fifteen years, to anyone and everyone who'd listen. Twice she hired investigators to review the evidence, neither investigator found anything to suggest killers other than Donny and Dylan.

"Trudy Pruitt was an alcoholic and drug abuser. Before and after her sons' deaths. She's spent her life between jail and rehab, a bitter and desperately unhappy woman."

Avery clasped her hands together. "Why my dad, Matt? Why me? Why did she choose...us?"

"Why does someone like Trudy Pruitt do anything? My guess is, your dad's wake and funeral stirred up memories. The overwhelming love and community support for you fed her bitterness. Unfortunately, we'll never know for sure what her motivations were, not now."

Because she was dead.

Murdered.

The full impact of that hit her with the force of a wrecking ball. Elaine St. Claire. Luke McDougal. Tom Lancaster. Now Trudy Pruitt.

"Who did this, Matt?"

"I don't know," he said grimly. "Not yet. I need your help, Avery."

"How? What can I do?"

"I need you to tell me exactly what happened tonight. What you saw and heard. Every detail, no matter how insignificant it might seem to you."

"All right." She paused a moment, collecting her thoughts, then began with arriving at the trailer park right around 10:00 p.m. "I noticed how dark the park was, that all the safety lights were out."

He made a note. "Did you pass another car on your way in?"

She shook her head. "I found Mrs. Pruitt's trailer and climbed out. I could hear music coming from a number of directions."

"Where?"

"I don't know. I assumed other trailers. I heard the couple next door fighting, a child crying."

"Next door? You're certain?"

Avery glanced in the direction of the nearest trailer. A man, woman and child stood in the doorway, staring her way. "Fairly certain."

Again he made a notation on the pad. "What about inside Trudy Pruitt's?"

"I found the door partially open. I knocked and called out. When she didn't answer, I poked my head inside. Called out again." She closed her eyes, remembering. "The living room was a mess. At first I...I thought she was a slob. I didn't...until I saw the blood...on the back wall, I didn't realize anything was wrong." She pulled in a shaky breath. "And then I saw her. Lying there."

"Did you touch anything?"

She thought a moment. "The blood on the wall. That's when I realized what it was."

"Go on."

"I went to her, reached out and touched her shoulder. She rolled onto her back."

"She was on her side?"

"Yes. She tried to speak to me."

He straightened slightly. "What did she say?"

Avery's eyes welled with tears. "She never...I couldn't make anything out. I heard a noise...and got frightened. I thought maybe the killer was still in the house and now—" She struggled past the emotion welling up in her. "Her hand...she—"

Avery glanced down at her hands. Blood stained the tops of the fingers of her right hand. "Touched mine. Like she needed my attention. Like she needed to tell me something important."

"It might have been nothing more than the need for human contact," he said gently. "She was dying, Avery."

"Now we'll never know."

"Other than Deputy Jones, did you hear anything?"

"The radio playing."

"And that's it?"

She couldn't tear her gaze from her bloodstained fingers. "Yes."

"If you think of anything else, call me. No matter how insignificant you might believe it is." He closed the notepad. "Promise?"

"I will."

"Avery?" She looked up. "Call me if you need anything else. Even just to talk. I'm here for you."

She swallowed hard. "Thank you, Matt."

"I'll have one of my deputies follow you home. Are you up to driving?"

She said she was and Matt called one of his deputies over, gave him directions, then accompanied her to her vehicle.

"I was by your house earlier. Dropped something off."

"For me?"

"In light of this, I wish to hell I..." He swore. "My timing stinks." He opened her car door. "I'll call you tomorrow."

She found what Matt had referred to on her front porch. Flowers. A beautiful spring bouquet. The card read:

Thinking of you and me. Dancing under the stars. Matt.

A hysterical-sounding laugh slipped past her lips. She laughed until she cried.

CHAPTER 34

Avery slept little that night. Every time she'd closed her eyes, she'd seen Trudy Pruitt lying in a pool of red, eyes wide and pleading, blood-soaked mouth working. Finally, Avery had given up and climbed out of bed. After brewing a pot of coffee, she'd dragged out the box of newspaper clippings and had begun poring over them, looking for anything that didn't fit, anything that might suggest a cover-up.

Nothing in the news stories jumped out at her.

What had Trudy Pruitt been trying to tell her? What proof of her father's involvement in the Sallie Waguespack murder did she have? Had she been the bitter, unstable drunk Matt purported her to be? One who had simply chosen Avery as a vehicle for venting her unhappiness?

Avery shifted her gaze to the box of clippings. *Dammit.* If not for these she might be able to believe that. *Why, Dad? Why did you save these?*

Only one person could answer that question.

Buddy.

Twenty-five minutes later Avery found herself at the ranch. She rang the bell, praying she had caught him before he left for church. If she remembered correctly, the Stevenses had most often chosen to attend the late service. They had today as well, she saw as Lilah opened the door.

"Avery," the woman exclaimed, "I heard about what happened. Are you all right?"

She nodded. "Just shaken. Is Buddy here?"

"And Matt. We're having breakfast."

"I'm sorry, I should have called—"

"Nonsense." She caught her hands and drew her inside. The house smelled of bacon and biscuits. "Come on in. I'll set you a place."

Before Avery could tell her not to bother, she was calling out for Cherry to do just that.

The men stood when she entered the kitchen. Matt took one look at her and came around the table. He caught her hands. "Are you okay?"

She forced a weak smile. "Hanging in there. Barely."

He led her to the chair next to his. Cherry set a plate, napkin and utensils on the blue-and-white-checked place mat in front of her. "Coffee?"

"Thanks."

The younger woman filled a mug and handed it to her. "Matt told us about last night. How horrible for you."

Lilah passed her the tray of biscuits. "I can't imagine. I'm quite sure I would have fainted."

Avery took a biscuit, though the thought of eating made her

queasy. She swallowed hard, shifting her gaze to Matt. "How's the investigation coming?"

"We canvassed the trailer park for witnesses. The kid next door says she saw a car pull up with its lights off. Then her folks began fighting."

"So she never saw who got out," Avery said, disappointed.

"Or when it drove off. The crime scene techs have done their thing, but it's too soon for the evidence report. As soon as I'm done here, I've got to get back."

"If you need any assistance from our department, son, we're ready."

"Thanks, Dad. I appreciate that."

Cherry spread strawberry jam on her biscuit. "What were you doing at that awful woman's house, Avery? Why were you there?"

The table went silent. All eyes turned to her. Uncomfortable, Avery opened her mouth then shut it as Matt squeezed her knee under the table.

"I've asked Avery not to talk about that just now," he said quietly. "As difficult as that request is, she's agreed."

Avery silently thanked him.

Cherry pouted. She lifted her right shoulder in a disinterested shrug. "I didn't mean anything by it, I just couldn't imagine, that's all."

Aware of the minutes ticking past, Avery looked at Buddy. "I need your help with something, Buddy. Could we talk privately?"

His forehead creased with concern. "Sure, baby girl. I was done here. Let's go to my office."

She turned to Matt, finding the moment awkward. Feeling Cherry's and Lilah's curiosity. "If you'd like to join us—"

"You guys go on. I'll check in on my way out."

She sent him a grateful glance, for the second time that morning touched by his understanding. By the way he seemed to know what she needed without her having to ask. He made her feel safe. Cared for.

She stood and followed Buddy to his office. He closed the door behind them and motioned to the love seat. She sat and looked up at him. "Matt told you why I was at Trudy Pruitt's last night? He told you about the calls?"

"Yes." His frown deepened. "Why didn't you tell me this was going on?"

"What could you have done? Someone was making crank calls to me. I figured you would tell me to ignore them or change to an unlisted number."

"When you found out who the anonymous caller was, you should have contacted me immediately." He leaned toward her, expression grave. "Avery, if you had shown up fifteen minutes earlier, you might be lying beside Trudy Pruitt in the morgue."

A chill washed over her. She shuddered. She had never considered that fact.

"Trudy Pruitt ran with a rough crowd. Always did. Don't know yet who killed her, but I'll bet money it was one of them."

Matt tapped on the office door, then poked his head in. "I'm leaving."

Buddy waved him inside. "Come in, son."

Matt did, shutting the door behind him and sat down.

"She said her boys didn't kill Sallie Waguespack," Avery continued. "Said my dad was involved in a cover-up. She said she had proof."

"And you believed her?" Buddy said.

"Frankly, I didn't want to, but I...don't you think it's weird that the same night she was going to show me proof her sons were innocent of Sallie Waguespack's murder, she was killed?"

Matt's mouth thinned. "Trudy Pruitt was involved with some dangerous characters. That involvement got her killed."

"But—"

Matt stood. "Look, Avery, there are things you don't know. Things we've uncovered that I can't share with you. I wish I could. I hate to see you tearing yourself up over this, but I can't. I'm sorry."

He bent and brushed his lips against hers. "I've got to go."

Avery stared after him, surprised. Disoriented by the intimacy of the move. Disoriented, she admitted, but not displeased.

Buddy broke the silence, tone soft. "If Trudy Pruitt had this supposed proof, why did she wait until now, until you, to bring it forward?"

Avery turned back to him. She didn't have an answer for that. "She never...came to you with—"

"Of course she did. And the district attorney. And the sheriff's department. And anyone else who would listen. She had nothing, not one scrap of evidence, to support her claim of her sons' innocence."

"I have a favor to ask, Buddy. For my own peace of mind, may I look at your files of the Waguespack murder investigation?"

"Avery—"

"She called Dad a liar, Buddy. And a murderer. Why would she do that?"

"Your daddy was the most honest, upright man I've ever known. I was proud to call him my friend."

"Then you must understand. I feel like I have to uphold his honor. Prove him innocent."

Buddy leaned forward. "Innocent to who, Avery?"

Not liking the answer, she curled her hands into fists. "Why did he keep that box of newspaper clippings, Buddy? Why did he kill himself?"

Buddy sighed heavily and stood. He crossed to her and laid

a hand on her shoulder. "If it'll help you, baby girl, of course you can look at the files. Just let me tell Lilah to go on to the service without me."

CHAPTER 35

Three hours later, Avery thanked Buddy for his help. "I'm sorry I messed up your Sunday," she said.

"You couldn't, baby girl." He kissed her cheek. "Do you feel better now?"

She didn't. She lied.

The information in the file should have reassured her. Everything appeared to be in order. At 10:30 p.m. on the night of June 18th, 1988, Pat Greene, one of Buddy's deputies, called in, requesting assistance. Making rounds, he had seen a couple of young men fleeing Sallie Waguespack's home. He'd investigated and found the woman murdered.

From the deputy's description of them, Buddy had suspected the Pruitt boys. Donny and Dylan, who had been in trouble since they were old enough to steal their first candy bar, had been brought in on suspicion of dealing just the week before. The evidence hadn't supported charges, but it had only been a matter of time.

When Buddy and Pat had found the two young men, Donny and Dylan were high. When confronted, the boys had initiated a shoot-out and were killed. After the fact, the murder weapon was found in the drainage ditch behind their trailer, Donny's prints on it.

The CSPD had launched a full investigation, discovering that Donny and Dylan had been frequenting the bar where Sallie was a cocktail waitress. Drugs had been found in Sallie's house and the Pruitt boys' apartment.

It had been determined that the boys had been dealing; Sallie Waguespack had been buying. A drug deal gone bad, they'd figured. The woman had owed them money or threatened them with the cops. One witness had claimed the three had been sleeping together, further complicating the scenario. Jealousy may have been a motive. Certainly, from the way she had been killed—hacked at with a kitchen knife—it had been a crime of passion.

Avery stopped at Buddy's office door and looked back at him. "Did you ever doubt Donny and Dylan Pruitt's guilt?" she asked. "Even for a moment?"

"Never." He ran a hand over his face, looking every one of his sixty-six years. "The murder weapon was found behind their trailer, Donny's prints on it. Sallie Waguespack's blood was found on the bottom of Dylan's shoe. Drugs were involved. We had Pat Greene, who placed them at the scene. Physical and circumstantial evidence. Can't get a much cleaner case than that."

He was right about that. She knew enough about police work to understand the process, from arrest to prosecution.

She started through the door, then stopped and turned back once more. "I didn't see an autopsy report."

His face puckered with confusion. "It should be there."

"It wasn't."

He shuffled through the folder, then returned his gaze to hers. "It's misfiled. I'll look around, give you a call when I locate it."

"Thanks, Buddy." She forced a smile. "Enjoy the rest of your day off."

Avery left the CSPD and minutes later found herself at Hunter's door. Without pausing to question her own motivation, she rapped on the frame.

Sarah began to bark, the puppies to yip. Hunter appeared at the door. He looked tired. Disheveled. Irritated at having been disturbed.

"You were working," she said. "I'm sorry."

"What do you want, Avery?"

She hesitated, put off by his surliness. "May I come in?"

He pushed opened the screen, moved aside. She stepped into the kitchen—and was immediately surrounded by squirming puppies. Sarah stood by her master's side, eyes pinned on Avery.

"They're getting big," Avery murmured. She squatted and the puppies charged her, licking her hands, butting each other out of the way. "They're so cute."

"If there's a point to your visit I'd appreciate your getting to it."

Her cheeks heated. She straightened. Met his eyes. "Did you hear what happened?"

"You mean Trudy Pruitt's murder?"

"Yes. And that I was there."

"I heard." His mouth thinned. "Even those of us who reside outside the chosen circle are part of the gossip chain."

"Never mind. You're such an asshole." She swung around to go. "I'm sorry I came here."

He caught her arm. "Why did you, Avery? Why do you keep coming around?"

"Let go of me."

He tightened his grip. "You came for something. What do you want from me?"

She didn't know, dammit. She tilted up her chin, furious. At herself. At him. "I don't want anything from you, Hunter. Maybe I'm here because unlike everyone else, I'm not willing to give up on you. Maybe I still see something in you that everyone else has forgotten."

"Bullshit."

"Believe what you want." She yanked her arm free, took a step toward the door.

He blocked her path. "I'd pegged you for being more honest than this, Avery. You want something from me. Spit it out."

"Stop it, Hunter. Let me go."

He moved closer, crowding her. "Why not run to Matt? Isn't he your *boyfriend?*"

He put a nasty emphasis on the last. She wanted to slap him. "Shut up."

He took another step forward; she back. She met the wall. "What would you give to have your father back, Avery?"

His question took her by surprise. Disarmed, she met his eyes. "Anything. I'd give anything."

"What do you want, Avery?" he asked again. He cupped her face in his palms. "Do you want me to tell you he loved you? Do you want me to tell you it's not your fault? Absolve you of guilt? Is that why you're— "

"Yes!" she cried. "I want to wake up to discover this has all been a nightmare. I want to have taken my father's call that last day...I want to stop hating...myself for...I want—"

The words stuck in her throat; she brought her hands to his chest. Curled her trembling fingers into his soft T-shirt. "I want what I can't have. I want my father back."

For long seconds, he gazed at her, expression dark with some strong emotion. Finally, he swore and dragged in a shaky breath. "He loved you, Avery. More than anything.

Every time we were together, he talked about you. How proud he was of you. Proud that you'd had the guts to follow your dreams. That you'd done so well. He took pride in your courage. Your strength of will."

A cry slipped past her lips. One of relief. Of an immeasurably sweet release from pain. Tears flooded her eyes.

"His suicide, it wasn't about you, Avery," he went on. "He was at peace with where you were in your life."

He dropped his hands, stepped back. "Go on. Get out of here. You got what you wanted. I can't give you anything else."

She hesitated, reached a hand out. Laid it on his forearm. "Hunter?" He met her eyes. "Thank you."

He didn't reply. She dragged her hand down to his, laced their fingers. Slowly, deliberately, she brought his hand to her mouth, opened it and pressed a kiss to his palm.

He trembled. Ever so slightly. Revealing himself. What he wanted.

He wanted her.

And in that moment, she realized she wanted him as well. Without thoughts of consequences or tomorrows, she drew him closer, against her. She tilted her face up to his.

She saw the desire in his dark gaze. And the vulnerability. The combination took her breath.

She brought his hand to her chest, just above the swell of her left breast.

"Avery, I don't—"

"Yes, you do." She leaned closer. "And I do, too."

She kissed him then. Deeply. Without hesitation. She wanted him, he wanted her. Simple.

He kissed her back. In a way that left no question who would lead. Not breaking their kiss, he lifted her. She wrapped her legs around his waist, her arms around his neck. He carried her to his bed, laid her on it. For a moment, he stood above her. Holding her gaze.

Her lips tipped into a small, contented smile. She reached up, caught his hands and drew him down to her.

That moment proved the calm before the storm. Passion exploded between them. They tugged at one another's clothes, zippers and buttons, clinging panties. Greedy. Impatient to feel the other's naked body against their own.

They made love, she on top of him. She orgasmed with a cry she worried might be heard at the Piggly Wiggly next door.

She collapsed against his chest. Beneath her cheek his heart thundered. She had always wondered, all those years ago, what kissing Hunter would be like. What being with him would be like.

Now she knew. And she wondered why she had waited so long to find out.

"I hated that."

She lifted her head and met his eyes. "Me, too."

His eyes crinkled at the corners with amusement. "I could tell."

She rubbed her forehead against his bristly chin. "You have anything to eat in this place?"

"A loaded question."

"Funny. Got any homemade chocolate cake?"

"Sure. Baked it this morning."

She grinned, feeling young, randy and totally irresponsible. "How about a PB&J?"

"Got something even better."

He rolled them both out of bed. He gave her one of his T-shirts to wear. The soft white fabric swallowed her. She glanced at its front. "Party hard on Bourbon Street?"

"From the old days."

She followed him to the kitchen, Sarah at their heels, the puppies on hers. Avery leaned against the counter while he made them both PB&M—peanut butter and marshmallow cream—sandwiches, then poured two big glasses of cold milk.

Whole milk, she saw. *Talk about irresponsible.*

They sat at the tiny dinette and dug in. "My God, this is good," she said, mouth full. She washed it down with a long swallow of the creamy milk.

"Awesome, isn't it? Worth shouting about."

He wasn't talking about the milk. Or the sandwiches. She flushed and shifted her gaze. He laughed softly, stood and went to make himself another sandwich.

"Want another?" he asked.

"Not if I want to be able to snap my pants tomorrow. But thanks."

He fixed his and sat back down. "Earlier, you said something about wishing you had taken a call from your dad. What did you mean?"

She laid the last of her sandwich carefully on the plate. "That last day, before Dad...died, he called. I was on my way out. Meeting a source, one who'd finally agreed to talk to me."

Her voice thickened; she cleared it. "I heard Dad's voice on the recorder and I...I thought, I'd call him later. My source couldn't wait, but my father...he'd always be there."

Hunter reached across the table and touched her hand. "I'm sorry, Avery."

"If only I could go back, take that call."

"But you can't."

Silence fell between them. Hunter broke it. "Why were you at Trudy Pruitt's last night?"

"Remember the caller I told you about? The woman who said Dad got what he deserved?" He nodded. "She called again. A couple of times. She said Dad was a liar. And a murderer."

"Your dad? Avery, you can't honestly belie—"

She stopped him. "That woman was Trudy Pruitt. Donny and Dylan Pruitt's mother."

"They're the ones who killed that woman."

"Sallie Waguespack." Sarah whined and laid her head on

Avery's lap. Avery scratched her behind the ears. "She claimed they didn't do it. That they were framed."

"Of course she did. She was their mother."

"She said Dad was part of the cover-up. That she had proof."

"And?"

"She was killed before she could give it to me."

"And you think she was murdered because of that proof?"

"It's crossed my mind. It's an awfully big coincidence, she lives all these years, contacts me and gets herself killed."

He was silent a moment. "And you believe whoever was involved with your dad in this frame-up killed him then Trudy Pruitt?"

She leaned forward. "You ever heard of a group called The Seven?"

He frowned. "My mother was part of a civic organization called The Seven something or other."

"How about a woman named Gwen Lancaster? Ever heard of her?" He shook his head. "Her brother, Tom Lancaster?"

His expression altered subtly. "That name's familiar but I can't place from where."

"He disappeared in February this year. Similar situation to McDougal. A Cypress Springs outsider. No sign of violence, but the police suspected foul play. The *Gazette* ran the story on the sixth."

"That's right." He paused as if remembering. "The big difference between the two, of course, was the car. Lancaster's was left out in the open. McDougal's had been hidden. Which to me suggests the two are unrelated."

"Unrelated? Two young men disappear from the same small community, barely eight weeks apart and you don't think those disappearances are related?"

"Modus operandi, Avery. Criminals tend to repeat their crimes, how they carry out those crimes. If a murderer leaves a body out in the open the first time, they'll do it the second, then the third. Basic investigative technique."

She shook her head. "Trudy Pruitt, Elaine St. Claire, Tom Lancaster, Luke McDougal. If I accept your definition, we're dealing with four different killers."

"McDougal may very well have chosen to go missing. People do it all the time. Coming on the heels of Lancaster is a coincidence. Or clever planning from a man intent on disappearing."

"For heaven's sake." She made a sound of frustration. "Three killers then. In a town that has had only a couple of murders in a decade?"

He pushed his plate away. Sat back. "Okay, you're obviously up to your elbows in this. You tell me."

She began at the beginning, with Gwen Lancaster. She told him about how they'd met, the things she had told Avery about a group called The Seven. And about her brother Tom, who had disappeared while researching the group.

"At first I didn't believe her. The idea of a vigilante-style group operating in Cypress Springs seemed ludicrous. According to Gwen, the original group disbanded after only a few years, but are operating again. Willing to murder to achieve their goals."

"You'll forgive me if I chuckle under my breath."

"I felt the same way." She leaned toward him. "She dared me to check out her facts. I did, Hunter. What I found stunned me. In the past eight months there have been ten unexpected deaths. Not counting Elaine St. Claire, Trudy Pruitt or McDougal and Lancaster. Cypress Springs is a community of about nine hundred, Hunter. That's a lot of deaths."

"Accidents happen."

"Not like that they don't." She paused, then drew a deep breath. "Gwen claims The Seven are responsible for her brother's death. He got too close and they killed him."

"And she hooked you by claiming they're responsible for your father's death as well."

She held his gaze despite the pity she read in his. "Yes."

"Avery, the woman was trying to pass herself off as your father's daughter. Doesn't that tell you something?"

"I know. I thought the same thing at first but—"

"But you want to believe it."

"No." She shook her head. "That's not it."

"Have you talked to Dad about this?"

"I talked to him about The Seven. He says no such group exists—now or ever."

"But you don't believe him?"

Just considering the question felt like a betrayal. "It's not that, I just...I'm thinking he's out of the loop."

"Dad? Out of the loop in this town?"

"Listen to me, Hunter. The day I drove into Cypress Springs, the first thing I thought was that the town hadn't changed. Like it hadn't been touched by time." She paused, then went on. "Since then, what's struck me is how homogeneous this town is. Look in the phone book. How many names do you recognize? It's all the same families as when we were kids."

"What are you getting at, Avery?"

"What does it take to keep time from marching on, Hunter? What does one have to do?"

For a long moment he said nothing. His expression revealed nothing of his thoughts. When he finally spoke, his tone was measured.

"Avery, listen to me. I want you to think about what I'm about to ask you. What would you get out of this? If it's true."

"I don't understand."

"If your dad was killed by this...Seven, what would you get out of it?"

She began to tell him she would get nothing out of it, then swallowed the words.

If he hadn't taken his own life, she would be absolved from guilt.

Avery fisted her fingers, furious at the thought. At the longing that accompanied it. She pushed both away. "You think I want Dad to have been murdered? You think I want Cypress Springs to be home to some murdering, extremist group?"

His expression said it all and she shook her head. "I don't, okay? How awful, how—"

She bit those words back, searching for others, though whether to convince him or herself she didn't know.

"I was always on the outside, Hunter. I never fit in here, never felt like I really belonged. Now I do. Now Cypress Springs feels like home."

He stood. Crossed to her. Cupped her face in his hands. "Grief twists reality."

"I know, but—"

"Don't do this to yourself, Avery."

"I have to know. For sure. I wish I could trust...I know I should, but I can't."

"Then get your proof. Of innocence or guilt. If that's what you need, get it."

CHAPTER 36

Gwen glanced at her dashboard clock. The amber numbers read 10:45. A knot of fear settled in her belly. She gripped the steering wheel tighter, her palms slippery on the vinyl.

The woman had warned her to come alone. She had promised information about The Seven, past and present.

Information about Tom.

Gwen acknowledged that she was scared shitless. She pressed her lips together. They trembled. Tom had disappeared on just such an errand, on just such a promise. Like hers, his meeting time had been a late hour, his destination a deserted spot off an unnamed country road.

If not for Tom, she wouldn't go. She would simply keep

driving, not stopping until she reached the lights of New Orleans.

She had grown to hate Cypress Springs. The quaint buildings and town square, the people whose welcoming smiles hid judgment and suspicion. The sour smell that inundated the community when the wind shifted from the south. The way people went about their business, pretending it didn't exist.

Gwen realized she was holding her breath and released it. She drew another, deeply, working to calm herself. She was alone. No allies. No one to share her fears with. Avery Chauvin had been her last hope for that.

That hope had been abruptly squashed.

Another dead. Trudy Pruitt.

They had cut out her tongue.

Gwen had heard that this morning, while breakfasting at the Azalea Café. She had been devastated.

The woman had been killed only a matter of hours after having met with Gwen. After having confirmed the past and present existence of The Seven. After confirming all of Gwen's suspicions: that a group of citizens met in secret and passed judgment on others, that they delivered one warning, that if it wasn't heeded, they took action, that they had never really disbanded—simply gone deeper underground. That in the past months they had become more active. And it seemed, more dangerous.

Guilt, a sense of responsibility, speared through her. If she hadn't come to Cypress Springs, if she hadn't tracked Trudy Pruitt down, would the woman be alive today?

Go, Gwen. Run. As fast as you can.

She flexed her fingers on the steering wheel. Other than putting her own life and the lives of others in jeopardy, what was she accomplishing? She couldn't help her brother now. Anyone who might have been willing to talk would be too frightened to do so after Trudy Pruitt.

But if she ran, she would never know what happened to Tom.

And she didn't think she could go on with her life until she did.

So, here she was. Gwen focused her attention on the up-coming meeting. The woman's call had come late this afternoon. She had refused to identify herself. Her voice had been unsteady, thick-sounding. As if she had been crying.

Or was trying to disguise her identity.

She had claimed to have information about The Seven and Gwen's brother. Gwen had tried unsuccessfully to get more out of her.

Quite possibly, tonight's rendezvous would prove a setup. Or an ambush.

Gwen squared her shoulders. She wouldn't go without a fight. She glanced at her windbreaker, lying on the seat beside her. Nestled in the right pocket was a .38-caliber Smith & Wesson revolver. Hammerless, with a two-inch barrel, the salesman had called it the ladies' gun of choice. He had assured her it would be plenty effective against an attacker, particularly, she knew, if she had surprise on her side.

She had taken other precautions as well, sent e-mails to the sheriff's department, her family lawyer and her mother. She had updated each with what she had uncovered so far, where she was going tonight and why. She found it hard to believe that both a brother and sister disappearing from the same small community would fly.

Even if she was killed, she had turned up the heat.

Their rendezvous point, Highway 421 and No Name Road loomed before her. The woman had instructed her to turn onto No Name Road and drive a quarter mile to an unmarked dirt road. She would recognize it by the rusted-out hulk of a tractor at the corner. There, she was to take a right and drive another quarter mile to an abandoned hunting cabin.

Gwen turned onto No Name Road. Her headlights sliced

across the roadway. Heavily wooded on either side, the light bounced off and through the branches of the cypress, pine and oak trees.

Some small creature darted in front of her vehicle. Gwen slammed on the brakes. Her tires screamed; her safety harness yanked tight, preventing her from hitting the steering wheel. The creature, a raccoon, she saw, made the side of the road and scurried into the brush.

Legs shaking, she eased the car forward, the dark seeming to swallow her. She strained to see beyond the scope of the headlights. The woman had warned her not to be late. It was nearly eleven now.

The drive came into view. She turned onto it, gravel crunching under her tires.

The cabin lay ahead, illuminated by her headlights. An Acadian, with a high, sloping roof and covered front porch. It looked a part of the landscape, as if it had been here forever. Rustic. Made of some durable wood, most probably cypress.

She drew her vehicle to a stop, searching the area for other signs of life. She found none. Not a light, vehicle or movement. She lowered her window a crack, shut off her engine and listened. The call of the insects and an owl, chirping frogs. Some creature running through the brush.

Nothing that spoke to the presence of another human.

Show time.

Gwen took a deep breath. Her heart beat hard against the wall of her chest. She struggled for a semblance of calm. She had to keep her head. Her wits about her. How could she hope to outsmart a killer if she couldn't think? If she couldn't accurately aim the gun because her hands shook?

She retrieved her jacket, put it on. She slipped her hand into the right pocket to reassure herself the gun was there. The metal was smooth and cool against her fingertips.

She opened the car door, choosing to leave the keys in the

car's ignition. She wanted them there in case she needed to make a quick escape.

Gwen stepped out. The wind stirred the mostly naked branches of the oak and gum trees. The sound affected her like the scrape of fingernails on a blackboard.

She rubbed her arms, the goose bumps that raced up them. "Hello," she called. An owl returned the greeting. She waited. The minutes ticked past. She shifted her gaze to the cabin.

Her caller could be there. Waiting.

She could be dead. Another Trudy Pruitt.

Gwen didn't know why that thought had filtered into her brain, but it had. And now, planted there, she couldn't shake it.

Minutes passed. Eleven o'clock became eleven-fifteen. Eleven-thirty.

Midnight.

Do it. Check out the cabin.

Or go. And never know.

She turned to the building. She stared at it, knees rubbery with fear. She couldn't not check. What if the woman was there and hurt; she would need help.

Gwen put her hand in her pocket, closed her fingers around the gun's grip and started forward, acknowledging terror. The Lord's Prayer ran through her head, the familiar words comforting.

Our Father who art in heaven

Hallowed be thy name

She reached the porch steps. She saw then that they were in disrepair. She grabbed the handrail, tested it, found it sturdy and began to pick her way up the steps.

She reached the porch. Took a step. The wood groaned beneath her weight. She quickly crossed. Made the door. Hand trembling, she reached out, grasped the knob and twisted.

Thy kingdom come, Thy will be done

On earth as it is in—

The door swung open. Taking a deep breath, she peered inside. Called out, voice barely a whisper. She waited, listening. Letting her eyes adjust to the absolute dark.

As they did, several large forms took shape. Furniture, she realized, taking a tentative step inside. A couple broken-down chairs. A shipping crate serving as a coffee table. Things left behind by previous residents, she decided.

She picked her way inside, blindly, calling herself a dozen different kinds of idiot. What was she trying to prove? Nobody was here. She had been sent on a wild-goose chase. Somebody's idea of a joke. A sick joke.

She turned. A baglike white shape in the doorway up ahead caught her eye. She made her way cautiously toward it. Not a bag, she saw, a white sheet, drawn up and knotted to form a kind of pouch.

She gazed at the package with a sense of inevitability. Of predestination. Whoever had contacted her had predicted her every step. Keeping the rendezvous. Waiting. Coming into the cabin. Finding this package.

And opening it.

She squatted and with trembling fingers untied the knot, peeled away the sheet.

Revealing a cat. Or rather, what had been a cat. A tabby. It had been slit open and gutted. Gwen brought a hand to her mouth; stomach lurching to her throat. The creature's sandy-colored fur was matted with blood, the sheet soaked.

She reached out. And found the blood was tacky.

This had been done recently. Just before she had been scheduled to meet her informant.

The Seven gave one warning. If it wasn't heeded, they took action.

She had gotten her warning.

Something stirred behind her. *Someone.* Gwen sprang backward, whirled around. The cabin door stood open; nothing—or no one—blocked her path. Panicked, she ran forward. Through the main room and onto the porch. Her foot went through a rotten board. She cried out in pain, stumbled and landed on her knees.

Clawing her way to her feet, she darted toward her car. She reached it, yanked open the door and scrambled inside. Sobbing with relief, she started the vehicle, threw it into Reverse and hit the gas. When she reached the main road, she dared a glance back, terrified at what she would see.

The deserted country road seemed to mock her.

CHAPTER 37

Avery parked her car around the corner from The Guest-house. She cut her lights, then the engine as she glanced quickly around. The square appeared deserted, its surrounding businesses dark. Cypress Springs retired early and slept soundly.

Just as she had planned for.

She meant to collect Gwen and head to Trudy Pruitt's trailer to have a look around. If Gwen refused, which was entirely possible, considering how Avery had treated her, she would go alone.

Avery had decided on this course of action after leaving Hunter. He had told her to get her proof and that's just what she meant to do. She had planned carefully. Had assembled everything she and Gwen would need: latex gloves, penlights, plastic Ziploc bags. And finally, her courage.

Now, to convince Gwen they were on the same team. She had tried the cell phone number the woman had given her. She had repeatedly gotten a reply stating the cell number she had called was no longer in service. Contacting the other woman by land line required having The Guesthouse management ring her room or calling the pay phone in the hall. She hadn't wanted to do either.

Nor had she wanted to be seen paying her a visit. Which left a chance encounter or stealth.

During the drive there, she had kept careful watch in her rearview mirror. She had not wanted to be followed. She had not wanted the wrong set of eyes to see her arriving at Gwen's.

The wrong set of eyes? Cloak-and-dagger driving maneuvers? Secret meeting?

She was losing her mind. Spiraling into a kind of paranoid schizophrenia, one in which she suspected her home of being watched, her phone of being bugged. One in which every smiling and familiar face hid a secret agenda.

A nervous laugh flew to her lips. She wanted the truth. No, she needed it. And she would do whatever was necessary to get it.

She thought of Hunter. Of the afternoon spent with him, in his bed. The experience felt surreal to her. As if she had dreamed it.

What had she done? Consummated some ancient passion she hadn't even consciously acknowledged? How could she be with Hunter when Matt was the one she had always wanted? What had she been thinking?

Obviously, she hadn't been thinking. She had acted on emotion. And physical urges.

She closed her eyes, thinking of the past, her relationship with Hunter. With Matt. All those years ago, had she chosen Matt because Hunter took her out of her safety zone? Because he had always pushed her, both emotionally and intellectually?

She had always been comfortable with the outgoing Matt. She had known where she stood all the time. Had never felt out of control. Weren't control and comfort good things? What did she really want?

Avery shook her head, refocusing on this moment. On what she had set out to do. Thoughts of Hunter, Matt and her future would have to wait.

She slipped out of the Blazer. Dressed entirely in black, she hoped to meld with the shadows. She eased the door shut and quickly made her way to the corner, hanging close to the inside edge of the sidewalk, near the shrubs and trees.

Until they had drifted apart their junior year of high school, Laurie Landry had been one of her best friends. Laurie had taught Avery that her parents kept a spare house key tucked inside the covered electrical outlet to the right of the front door. She and Laurie had used it many times over the years to slip in and out at all times of the night.

If it wasn't there, she wasn't certain what she would do.

She needn't have worried. The Landrys kept the key in the same place they had twelve years ago. A testament to how slowly some things changed in Cypress Springs. How safe a place to live it was.

Unless, of course, you were targeted by The Seven for behavior modification.

Permanent behavior modification.

Avery retrieved the key, opened the door and stepped into The Guesthouse's main hall. Turning, she relocked the door, slipped the key into her pocket and started up the stairs. The desk closed at 8:00 p.m.; each guest was given a key to come and go as they pleased.

Neither the Landry family nor a guest would give a second thought to the sound of someone moving about.

Avery quietly climbed the stairs. She reached the top landing and turned left. Gwen occupied the unit at the far end of the hall. Avery reached it and stopped, a dizzying sense of déjà vu settling over her.

Gwen's door stood ajar.

Not again. Please God, not again.

With the tips of her fingers, Avery nudged the door the rest of the way open. She called Gwen's name, her voice a thick whisper.

Gwen didn't reply.

But she hadn't expected her to. She expected the worst.

Avery reached into her pocket and retrieved her penlight. She switched it on and stepped fully into the room, the slim beam of light illuminating the way. The place had been ransacked. Drawers and armoire emptied. Dresser mirror shattered. Lamps toppled.

She moved through the room, sweeping the light back and forth in a jittery arc. No bloody prints. No body. Swallowing hard, she crossed to the made bed. Bending, she lifted the bed skirt, pointed the light and peered underneath.

Nothing. Not even a dust bunny.

She dropped the skirt and straightened. Turned toward the armoire. Its doors hung open, contents emptied onto the floor in front. Avery pivoted toward the bathroom's closed door, then glanced back at the hallway. She shouldn't be handling this alone. She should call Buddy, the CSPD. Get them over here. Let them search for Gwen.

She couldn't do that. How would she explain being here? Latex gloves and penlight in her pocket? Last night at Trudy Pruitt's and tonight at Gwen Lancaster's—

Get the hell out. Call the cops from the car. Or better yet, from a pay phone on the other side of town.

Instead, Avery took a step toward the bathroom. Then another. As she neared it, she heard what sounded like water running.

She grasped the knob, twisted it and pushed. The door eased open. She inched closer, shone her light inside.

The room was small—a pedestal sink, medicine cabinet, claw-footed tub with pink, flowered shower curtain circling it. The floor clear.

The sound she'd heard was the toilet running. She crossed to it, jiggled the handle. It stopped filling.

So far so good.

She returned her gaze to the tub. To that flowered curtain. *She had to look. Just in case.*

She sidled toward it. As if a less direct approach might influence what she found. She stopped within arm's reach of the curtain. Her heart thundered in her chest. Her mouth went dry, her pits and palms were wet.

Do it, Chauvin.

She forced herself to lift her arm, grab a handful of the vinyl and yank it away.

"Don't move a muscle or I'll blow your fucking head off!"

Avery froze. Gwen, she realized. She was alive!

"Hands up!" Gwen snapped. "Then turn around. Slowly."

Avery did. Gwen stood in the doorway, face white as a sheet. She held a gun, had it trained on her.

"It's me, Gwen. Avery."

"I have eyes."

"This isn't how it looks. Your door was open...I found the place like this."

"Sure you did."

"It's true. I needed to reach you...your cell number wasn't working and I couldn't call here because I didn't want anyone to know we were in contact."

The gun wavered. Gwen narrowed her eyes. "You needed to reach me? I seem to remember you telling me you wanted nothing to do with me."

"That was before Trudy Pruitt."

Her already ashen face paled more. "What do you know about Trudy—"

"I was there last night. She called me, set up a meeting. When I got there her door was open, her trailer ransacked. I found her in the kitchen...on the floor. When I saw your door...your place, I...I thought they'd gotten you, too."

For a long moment Gwen simply stared at her. As if evaluating her words, deciding if she was being truthful. Then with the tiniest nod, she lowered the gun.

"Thank you." Avery let out a shaky breath. "That's twice in two days I've found myself staring down the barrel of a gun."

From the hallway came what sounded like someone climbing the stairs. They both swung in that direction. Gwen darted toward her door and shut it. She locked the dead bolt, then looked at Avery. She held a finger to her lips and pointed at the bathroom.

Avery indicated she understood. A moment later Gwen closed them in it, crossed to the tub and started the shower. White noise, Avery realized. To muffle their words, in case someone was listening.

That done, Gwen crossed to the toilet, lowered the lid and sank onto it. She dropped her head to her hands.

After several moments Gwen lifted her head and looked at Avery. "I thought I was dead."

Her voice shook. So, Avery saw, did her hands. She clasped them together.

"A woman called," Gwen continued. "She said she had information about The Seven and about Tom. We were supposed to meet tonight."

"She didn't show."

"No. She was a decoy."

"A decoy? You mean to lure you away from here?"

"To deliver my warning."

"I don't understand."

"I interviewed Trudy Pruitt yesterday. She told me The Seven exist. Past and present. She said they killed Elaine St. Claire. That they always deliver a warning before taking action. A terrible threat."

"Elaine St. Claire was warned?"

"Yes. She and Trudy were friends. They both served drinks down at Hard Eight. One day Elaine just up and disappeared."

"She took the warning seriously and left Cypress Springs?"

"Yes. A couple months later, Trudy got a letter from the woman. Apparently a representative of the group had paid St. Claire a late-night visit. He had made this weapon...a phallus with sharp spines and a knife blade imbedded in its tip.

"The man told her she had been judged and found guilty— of moral corruption. Because she slept around. A lot, apparently. He told her he would give her what she loved—that he would fuck her to death."

Avery pressed her lips together to hold back a sound of horror. She recalled what Hunter had told her about Elaine St. Claire's death. The two stories jibed.

Gwen stood. Avery sensed she was too jumpy to remain seated. "They warned me tonight. A cat...they gutted it, left it for me. At the meeting place. They meant to frighten me."

"And they succeeded."

"Hell, yes. I'm terrified."

"You've got to get out of Cypress Springs. Now. Tonight. I'll keep in touch, let you know what I find out."

"What makes you think you're immune?"

"I don't understand."

"You're not one of them anymore, Avery. If they discover you're onto them, they'll kill you."

"I'll make sure they don't find out."

Gwen laughed, the sound hard, humorless. "It's too late for that. They've seen us talking. You've asked questions around town. They see everything, Avery. *Everything.*"

"I'm not leaving until I know the truth about my dad's death."

Gwen looked at her. Avery understood. Gwen wouldn't leave until she knew what had happened to her brother.

"We're in this together then," Avery said.

"Guess so."

Avery rubbed her arms, chilled. "In the interview, did Trudy Pruitt say anything about me or my father? Did she say anything about Sallie Waguespack?"

Gwen shook her head. "She talked exclusively about The Seven. I've got it all in my... Oh, no."

"What?"

"My notes!"

Gwen leaped toward the door, yanked it open and raced into the bedroom.

Avery followed. Watched as she tore through the debris littering the floor, looked under the bed and in the armoire, expression frantic.

"Gone. Everything is gone. My notes. Interview tapes." She sank to her knees. "They get away with murder."

"No, they don't. We won't let them." Avery crossed to the woman. "I believe you. God help me, but I do. Together, we can beat them."

Gwen shook her head. "We can't beat them. No one can."

"That's what they want us to believe. That's how they've gotten away with this for so long." She held out a hand to help the other woman up. "Tell me exactly what happened tonight, everything you've learned so far. I'll do the same. Together, we'll figure this out. We'll go to the state police or the FBI. We can do it, Gwen. Together."

"Together," Gwen repeated, taking Avery's hand, getting to her feet, returning with her to the bathroom. There, Gwen explained the events of the day, from the woman's call to finding the gutted cat and running for what she assumed was her life.

Avery thought a moment. "And you have no idea who the woman was?"

"None."

"Did she call on the pay phone in the hall?" Gwen shook her head. "So she had to go through the front desk. Did you ask—"

"Yes. They said they didn't know who it was. Said they assumed it was a friend of mine from out of town."

"But you don't believe that?"

"I don't believe anything anymore." She laced her fingers. "What about you?"

Avery began with the first anonymous call. "She said Dad got what he deserved. That I would, too. Before that call I was struggling with the idea of Dad killing himself. After it—"

"You didn't buy it at all."

"Yes. She called a couple more times. She accused Dad of being a liar and a murderer, of helping frame her boys for Sallie Waguespack's murder. She said she had proof."

"Why did you believe her? Everything you've told me about your dad—"

"I found this box of newspaper clippings in Dad's closet. They were all from the summer of 1988. All concerning Sallie Waguespack's murder."

"His having them supports Trudy Pruitt's claim."

"Not necessarily. Her murder was the biggest thing to ever hit this town. It was a shock, a wake-up call. He was civic-minded. He probably followed the story because he—"

"Avery," she interrupted gently, "he clipped all those newspaper articles and kept them for fifteen years. There has to be a reason. Something personal."

Avery knew she was right. She had thought the same all along. But no way had he been an accomplice to murder. No way. She told Gwen so.

The other woman didn't argue. "When did you learn your caller was Trudy Pruitt?"

"The same afternoon she was killed. I goaded her into telling me her name. I promised that if she showed me proof of her claims, I'd make it right. That I'd find a way to exonerate Donny and Dylan. We set up a meeting for that night."

Avery pulled in a deep breath. "She was still alive...she tried to tell me something but died before she could."

Gwen's expression altered. "Didn't you know? They cut out her tongue."

"Are you...that can't..." But it was true, Avery realized, picturing the woman's face, her bloody mouth.

They fell silent. Gwen broke it first. "Seems to me that shoots the whole random-act-of-violence thing to hell."

Avery winced at her sarcasm. Shifted the subject. "Buddy let me look at his records of the Waguespack murder. Everything seemed in order, but I keep coming back to that box of clippings. And my belief that Dad wouldn't take his own life. And now, all the deaths." A lump formed in her throat; she swallowed past it. "Who are these people, Gwen? Who are The Seven?"

"Put it together, Avery." She leaned toward her. "You're a reporter...who fits the profile?"

When Avery didn't respond, Gwen filled in for her. "They're probably all men. Though, obviously, since a woman lured me out tonight, women are part of the group. They're no doubt longtime Cypress Springs residents. Pillars of the community. Men who are looked up to. Ones in influential positions or ones who have influence." She paused. "Like your dad."

"He would never have been party to this. Never, he—"

Gwen held up a hand, stopping her. "It's the only way this would work. I guess them all to be mature, forty and up. Maybe way up, if the members of today's Seven are the same, or partly the same, as the past's.

"And," she finished, "if today's group mirrors the one of the 1980s, they have many accomplices in the community.

Like-minded citizens willing to spy for them. Break the law for them."

Avery frowned. "The past and the present, they're inter-twined. The group from the 1980s, Sallie Waguespack's death. I just don't know how."

"What do you think Trudy Pruitt's proof was?"

"I don't know. But if it was for real, the way I figure it, there's a chance it's still in her trailer."

Gwen moved her gaze over Avery, her expression subtly shifting to one of understanding. "And you're thinking we should go find it?"

"If you're up for it."

"At this point, what do I have to lose?"

They both knew, both were acutely aware of what they could lose.

Their lives.

"Besides," Gwen murmured, smile sassy, "I've got a pair of black jeans I've been dying to wear."

CHAPTER 38

Avery parked the SUV just outside the trailer park and they walked in. Neither spoke. They kept as much as possible to the deepest shadows. Unlike the previous evening, Avery was grateful for the blown-out safety lights.

They reached Trudy Pruitt's trailer. The yellow crime scene tape stretched across the front, sagging in the center, forming an obscene smile. Avery shivered despite the warm night.

"How are we going to get in?"

"You'll see." She quickly crossed to the trailer. Instead of climbing the steps, she stepped into the garden. The frog figurine was just where she had expected it to be. She picked it up, turned it over, opened the hidden compartment and took out a key. "My bet is, this is a key to her front door."

"How did you know that was there?"

"I noticed the figurine, thought it was concrete until I accidentally knocked it off the porch. Why else would someone have a fake concrete frog on the front steps?"

"Good detective work."

Avery lifted a shoulder. "Journalists notice things."

They climbed the steps, let themselves in. Avery retrieved her penlight, switched it on. Gwen did the same. No one had cleaned up the mess. In all likelihood, even when the police gave the okay, there would be no one to clean it up. She averted her gaze from the bloody smear on the back wall.

From her back pocket, she took the two pairs of gloves she had picked up at the paint store that afternoon. She handed a pair to Gwen. "This is still a crime scene. I don't want my prints all over the place."

Gwen slipped them on. "We get caught, we're in deep shit."

"We're already in deep shit. Let's start in the bedroom."

They made their way there, finding it in the same state of chaos as the front room: the bed was unmade, the dresser drawers hung open, clothes spilling out. Beer cans, an overflowing ashtray, newspapers and fashion magazines littered the dresser top and floor.

They exchanged glances. "Wasn't a neat freak, was she?" Gwen murmured.

Avery frowned. She moved her gaze over the room, taking in the mess. "You're right, Gwen. The killer didn't make this mess, Trudy Pruitt was simply a slob."

"Okay. So?"

"Last night I thought the place had been ransacked. Now I realize that wasn't the case. Why search the living room but not the bedroom?"

"What do you think it means?"

"Maybe nothing. Just an observation. Let's get started."

"What are we looking for?"

"I'll know it when I see it. I hope."

They began to search, carefully examining the contents of each drawer, then the closet, finally picking through items on the dresser top. Avery shifted her attention to the floor.

The *Gazette,* she saw. Strewn across the floor. Avery squatted beside it. Not a current issue, she realized. The issue reporting her father's death. Trudy Pruitt had drawn devil horns and a goatee on his picture.

"What?"

Avery indicated the newspaper. Gwen read the headline aloud. "'Beloved Physician Commits Suicide. Community Mourns.'" She met Avery's eyes. "I'm sor—" She stopped, frowning. "Look at this, Avery. Trudy made some sort of notations, here in the margin."

The woman had used a series of marks to count. Four perpendicular hatchet marks with another crosswise through them. Beside it she had written "All but two."

"Five," Gwen murmured. "What do you think she was counting?"

"Don't know for certai—" She swallowed, eyes widening. "My God, five plus two—"

"Equals seven. Holy shit."

"She was counting the dead. Dad was number five. There are, or were, two left."

"But who were they?"

"On the phone she said there weren't many of them left. That they were dropping like flies."

"People who knew the truth."

"Gotta be."

Avery carefully leafed through the remaining pages of the paper. Nothing jumped out at her. She carefully folded the page with her father's photo and Trudy Pruitt's notations, then slipped it into a plastic bag.

They searched the living room next, checking the undersides and linings of the chairs and sofa, behind the few framed photos, inside magazines. They found nothing.

"Kitchen's next," Avery murmured, voice thick.

"That's where...it's going to be bad." Gwen paled. "I've never—" They exchanged glances, and by unspoken agreement, Avery took the lead.

Using tape, the police had marked where Trudy had died. A pool of blood, dried now, circled the shape. Several bloody handprints stood out clearly on the dingy linoleum floor.

Her handprints.

Avery started to shake. She dragged her gaze away, took a deep, fortifying breath. "Let's get this over with."

Avery checked the freezer. It was empty save for a couple unopened Lean Cuisine frozen meals and a half-dozen empty ice trays. The cabinets and pantry also proved mostly bare. They found nothing taped to the underside of shelves, the dining table or trash barrel.

"Either she never had any proof or the killer already picked it up," Avery said, frustrated.

"Maybe her proof was in her head," Gwen offered. "In the form of an argument."

"Maybe."

Gwen frowned. "No answering machine."

Avery glanced at her. "What?"

"Everybody's got an answering machine these days." She pointed at the phone, hanging on the patch of wall beside the refrigerator. "I didn't see one in the bedroom, either. Did you?"

Avery shook her head and crossed to the phone, picked it up. Instead of a dial tone, a series of beeps greeted her. She frowned and handed the receiver to the other woman.

"Memory call," Gwen said. "It's an answering service offered through the phone company. I have it."

"How do you retrieve the messages?"

"You dial the service, then punch in a five-digit password. The beeps mean she has a message waiting."

"What's the number?"

"Mine's local. It'd be different here. Sorry."

Avery glanced around. "My guess is, Trudy wrote that number down, that it's here, near the phone. So she wouldn't have to remember it." She slid open the drawers nearest the phone, shuffled through the mix of papers, flyers and unopened mail.

"Look on the receiver itself," Gwen offered. "Until I learned mine, that's where I taped it."

Avery did. Nothing had been taped to either receiver or cradle. She made a sound of frustration and looked at Gwen. "No good."

"Tom had the service," she murmured. "He programmed it into his—"

"Speed dial," Avery finished for her, glancing at the phone. Sure enough, the phone offered that feature, for up to six numbers. She tried the first and was connected to the Hard Eight.

She gave Gwen a thumbs-up, then tried the second programmed number, awakening someone from a deep sleep. She hung up and tried again.

The third proved the winner. A recording welcomed her to "her memory call service."

"Got it," Avery said, excited. "Take a guess at a password."

"1-2-3-4-5."

Avery punched it in and was politely informed that password was invalid. She tried the same combination, backward. She punched in several random combinations.

All with no luck. She hung up and looked at Gwen. "What now?"

"Most people choose passwords they can easily remember, their anniversary, birthday, kid's birthday. But we don't know any of those."

"Oh yes we do," Avery murmured. The date Trudy Pruitt had never forgotten. The one she might use as a painful, self-mocking reminder. "June 18, 1988. The night Sallie Waguespack was murdered and her sons were killed in a shoot-out with the police."

Avery connected with the answering service again, then punched in 0-6-1-9-8-8. The automated operator announced that she had five new messages waiting and one saved message.

Avery gave Gwen another thumbs-up, then pressed the appropriate buttons to listen to each. The recording announced the day, date and time of call, then played the message. The woman's boss at the bar, pissed that she hadn't shown up for work. Several hang-ups. A woman, crying. Her soft sobs despairing, hopeless. Then Hunter. He said his name, gave his number and hung up.

Avery's knees went weak. She laid her hand on the counter for support. *Hunter had called Trudy Pruitt the last afternoon of her life. Why?*

"What's wrong?"

Avery looked at Gwen. She saw by the other woman's expression that her own must have registered shock. She worked to mask it. "Nothing. A...a woman crying. Just crying. It was weird."

"Replay it."

Avery did, holding the phone to both their ears, disconnecting the moment the call ended.

"The woman who called me sounded as if she had been crying," Gwen told her. "What if they were one and the same?"

"What time did she call you?"

Gwen screwed up her face in thought. "About five in the afternoon."

Avery dialed, called up the messages again. The woman

had called Trudy Pruitt at four forty-five. Avery looked at Gwen. "A coincidence?"

"A weird one." Gwen frowned. "What do you think it means?"

"I don't know. I wonder if the police have listened to the messages."

"They could be retrieving them directly from the service. After all, the calls could be evidence."

"Or the police might have missed them, same way we almost did. Let's get out of here," Avery said.

They left the way they'd come, reaching the SUV without incident. Avery started the engine and they eased off the road's shoulder. She didn't flip on her headlights until they'd gone a couple hundred feet.

She couldn't stop thinking about Hunter having called Trudy Pruitt. Why? What business could he have had with the woman? And on the last day of her life? And why hadn't he mentioned it when they'd discussed the woman's death?

The answers to those questions were damning.

"Something's bothering you."

She glanced at Gwen. She should tell her. They were partners now, in this thing together. If Gwen had been one of her colleagues at the *Post,* she would.

But she couldn't. Not yet. She had to think it through.

"I'm wondering why people like Trudy Pruitt stayed in Cypress Springs? Why not leave?"

"I asked her that. She said some did leave. For others, for most, this was their home. Their friends were here. Their family. So they stayed."

"But to live in fear. To know you're being watched. Judged. It's just so wrong. So...un-American."

Avery realized in that moment how carelessly she took for granted her freedoms, the ones granted by the Bill of Rights. What if one day they were gone? If she woke up to discover she couldn't express her views, see the movies or read the books she chose to. Or if skipping worship Sunday morning or drinking one too many margaritas might land her on a Most Wanted list.

"It's not been until recently that things have gotten really weird," Gwen continued. "For a long time before that it was quiet."

"Recently? What do you mean?"

"In the last eight months to a year. About the time the accidents and suicides began. Trudy said that after Elaine disappeared she thought about going. But she couldn't afford to leave."

Avery hadn't considered that. It cost money to pick up and move. One couldn't simply carry a trailer on their back. Apartments required security deposits, first and last month's rent, utility deposits. Then there was the matter of securing a job.

Not like the moves she had made, ones where she'd lined up a job, and her new employer had covered her moving expenses. She'd had money in the bank to fall back on, a father she could have turned to if need be.

To a degree, people like Trudy Pruitt were trapped.

Now she was dead.

"According to what Trudy told me, most of the citizens fell in like sheep. They were frightened of what Cypress Springs was becoming, only too happy to head back to church, rein in their behavior or spy on their neighbors if it meant being able to leave their house unlocked at night."

"What about her? She didn't fall in line with the rest."

Gwen's expression became grim. "I don't think she knew how to be any different. And...I don't think she felt any motivation to change. She hated this town, the people. Because of her boys."

"But she didn't say anything about them? About their deaths, Sallie Waguespack's murder?"

"Nothing except that they didn't do it. That they were framed."

"How about Tom? Did she say anything about him?"

"I asked. She didn't know anything about him but what she'd read in the paper. She told me she didn't have a doubt The Seven killed him."

"He hadn't interviewed her?"

"Nope. She found me, actually."

Avery pulled to a stop at a red light. She looked at Gwen. "Did she say who The Seven were?"

"No. She said revealing that would get her dead."

She got dead anyway. The light changed; Avery eased forward.

The square came into view up ahead. "Drop me at that corner," Gwen said.

"You're sure? I could park around the corner, give you a hand cleaning up?"

"It's better this way. The less possibility of us being seen together, the better."

Avery agreed. She stopped at the next corner. "Call me tomorrow."

Gwen nodded, grabbed the door handle. "What's next?"

"I'm not sure. I need to think about it. Lay out the facts, decide which direction to go."

Gwen opened her car door and stepped out. Avery leaned across the seat.

"Gwen?" The other woman bent, met her eyes. "Be careful."

She said she would, shut the door and walked quickly off. Avery watched her go, a knot of fear settling in her chest. She glanced over her shoulder, feeling suddenly as if she was being watched, but seeing nothing but the dark, deserted street.

But they were out there. The Seven, their spies. A killer.

Being careful wasn't going to be enough to keep either of them safe, she thought. Not near enough.

CHAPTER 39

The Gavel stood alone in his dark bathroom. Naked. Trembling. He stared at his reflection in the mirror above the sink. The man who stared back at him barely resembled the one he knew himself to be.

He was sweating, he realized. He pushed the hair off his forehead. He leaned closer to the mirror. Were those tears in his eyes?

He stiffened, furious. He wasn't a child. Not some weak-bellied girl who fell apart anytime the going got tough. He was the strong one. The one whose will, whose determination, carried them all.

Without him, Cypress Springs would have been lost. They all would have been lost.

He bent, splashed his face with cold water, then straightened. Rivulets of water ran over his shoulders, down his belly, beyond. He breathed deeply through his nose. His chest expanded; he felt the oxygen feed his blood, the blood his muscles. He swelled in size, stature.

He smiled. Then laughed. They didn't understand. His eyes were everywhere. While his generals scurried pathetically about, he saw everything, knew everything. Did they think he didn't hear them whispering to one another, exchanging furtive, knowing glances? Making their plans?

His enemies, it seemed, were growing in number.

Rage welled up in him. Those he trusted turning on him. Those he had turned to for support—indeed, for love—planning his demise. He had given his life for them. The things he had done, the chances he had taken—that he continued to take—to make their lives, their world, a better place. All he had done for them.

Was absolute loyalty too much to ask for in return?

He narrowed his eyes. Apparently so. And for that, they would pay dearly.

This was his town. He was their leader. Nothing and no one would change that.

Not Gwen Lancaster. Not Avery Chauvin.

Tonight, he had stood in the shadows and watched as the two women formed an unholy alliance. One of Cypress Springs's favored daughters had proved herself an outsider. And traitor.

A spear of sadness pierced his armor, he fought it off. The urge to open his arms again, to forgive. Forget. Such emotions were for the weak. The self-indulgent. The unencumbered.

None of those applied to him.

His every instinct told him to silence Gwen Lancaster, do it quickly, before she caused more damage. But there were rules to be followed, a proven system to be adhered to. To willfully ignore either would be a step toward anarchy.

It only took one, he thought grimly. One spoiled fruit. One self-indulgent individual on a misdirected campaign.

How was it that only he had great resolve? Why had he been cursed with this perfect vision? This absolute knowledge? He had been born to lead. To show others the way.

It was lonely. He longed to turn from his gift, his call, but how could he? He opened his eyes each day and saw the truth.

He didn't enjoy killing. He had hoped, prayed, that each of those found guilty would take his warning to heart. His lips twisted. But they had been stupid. Ignorant and small-minded.

Liar. Killing the last had been a blessing. A pleasure. The woman had left him no other option. Meeting with outsiders, calling insiders. She had forced his hand. She should have been silenced years ago. He had allowed others to sway him.

A mistake. One of several recent mistakes his generals loved to discuss. That they used against him. Who did they plan to replace him with? Blue? Hawk?

Laughable. He would show them. Soon they would see. They would all see.

CHAPTER 40

Hunter sat bolt upright in bed, the sound of children's screams echoing in his head. For a moment he couldn't think. Couldn't separate himself from the nightmare.

With his mind's eye he saw the car careening out of control. The fence going down. The children's terror. The one child standing frozen in the path of his two thousand pounds of steel and glass.

The woman, throwing herself at the child. Saving the boy. Sacrificing herself.

He became aware of the light streaming through the blinds. The soft hum of traffic, of the Monday-morning delivery trucks in the alley. Sarah's puppies whimpering, hungry.

Hunter leaned over the side of the bed and looked at her.

It seemed to him she was doing her best to block out their cries. "You're being paged," he said to her.

She lifted her head, looked at him.

"I'll get up if you will."

She stared at him a moment, then thumped her tail once. "I'll take that as a yes," he said and climbed out of bed.

He pulled on a pair of shorts and headed to the bathroom. Teeth brushed, bladder emptied, he beelined for the kitchen. Sarah beat him there. She stood at the door, anxious but patient. He grabbed her lead off the hook, clipped it onto her collar and then together they stepped out into the bright, warm morning.

He and Sarah had their routine. A quick trip out to the nearest patch of grass to take care of her immediate needs, then back for her to feed her pups and him to guzzle coffee. Later, they would take a longer walk or a run.

Sarah did her business and they started back. They rounded the corner. His steps faltered. The dog whined.

Avery waited at his door.

She turned. Their eyes met. He sent her a sleepy, pleased smile. "No breaking and entering today?"

She didn't blink. "We need to talk."

"Guess not." Hunter crossed to the door, pushed it open. From the corner of his eye, he saw her bend and scratch Sarah behind the ears. "Come on in. I need coffee."

He headed for the coffeemaker. She didn't wait for him to reach it. "You called Trudy Pruitt the day she was killed. Why?"

Son of a bitch. Not good.

"A little intense for this time of the morning, aren't we, Avery? It's not even eight."

"I asked you a question."

He filled the coffeemaker's carafe with water, then poured it into the reservoir. "Yeah, but you didn't ask it very nicely."

"I'm not playing a game here."

He turned, met her eyes. "She called me. I don't know why because she got my machine. I returned her call. That's it."

He measured dark roast into the filter, slid the basket into place and switched on the machine. That done, he crossed to stand directly in front of her. "And where, exactly, did you get that information? From Matt? Was he trying to poison your mind against me?"

"You don't need any help in that department."

"And here I thought you'd still respect me in the morning."

Angry color shot into her cheeks. "We talked about her, Hunter. You and I, we talked about her calls to me...that I was there that night. You never said anything. Do you have any idea how damning that looks?"

"I don't really care how it looks, Avery."

She curled her hands into fists. "You don't care, do you? You wear your indifference like some twisted badge of honor."

The coffeemaker gurgled; the scent of the brew filled the air. "What do you want me to say?"

"I want you to tell me the truth."

"I was writing. She called, left a message. Truthfully, I didn't remember she was Dylan and Donny's mother. Not until later. I assumed she was calling about legal representation. Why else? Other than a vague recollection of the name, I didn't have a clue who she was. That's the truth, believe it if you want."

"Why didn't you mention she called, when we were talking about her? She was murdered, Hunter!"

He laid his hands on her shoulders. "What would it have brought to the equation? I never even spoke to the woman."

She shrugged off his hands. Took a step away. "You told me to get my proof, Hunter. I went there, to her trailer to look for it."

"When?" he asked, her words, the ramifications of them hitting him like a sledgehammer.

"Last night. Late."

He made a sound of disbelief. "Do you know how stupid that was, Avery? A woman was murdered there. What if the killer had come back? Looking for the same thing you were. Or to relive the kill?"

He pressed his point, seeing that it was having its intended effect—scaring her. "The percentage of killers who do just that is high, so high that police manuals suggest staking out a murder scene as an effective investigative strategy."

She looked shaken, but didn't back down. "I found your message. It's on her machine, okay? The woman saved it."

He thought of Matt. His brother was already hot to pin Elaine St. Claire's murder on him. Why not this murder as well?

He looked at the ceiling. "Shit."

"Care how things look now, Hunter?"

He swung away from her, crossed to the cupboard. He selected a mug, then filled it. Took a sip. He glanced over his shoulder at her. "Was there anything else you wanted to grill me about this morning?"

She opened her mouth as if to answer, then shut it, turned and started for the door.

He followed her. "I take it you're not staying for coffee."

"Go to hell."

Careening out of control. Children screaming.

"Been there, done that."

Her steps faltered. She stopped but didn't turn.

He stood directly behind her, so close he could hear her breathing, smell the fruity shampoo she used. He longed to touch her. To coax her back into his arms. Tell her everything, anything that would convince her to stay.

"And that's supposed to make me feel what?" she asked softly, voice vibrating with emotion. "Sorry for you? You think there's anyone alive who hasn't experienced real pain? Personal tragedy?"

"I wasn't asking for your pity. I was being honest."

"Well, bully for you."

She pushed the screen door open. Stepped out into the alley. And ran smack-dab into Matt.

"Avery!" Matt caught her arm, steadying her. "What are you doing here?"

"Ask your brother." She glanced back at Hunter, standing at the door. "Maybe he'll give *you* a straight answer."

"I don't understand."

She shook her head, stood on tiptoe and kissed Matt's cheek. "Call me later, Matt. I've got to go."

CHAPTER 41

Hunter watched Avery go. She had asked Matt to call her later. Why? To make certain he knew about the call on Trudy Pruitt's answering machine? Or because they were sleeping together?

"What was Avery doing here?"

Hunter faced his brother. "Nothing kinky. Unfortunately."

A muscle in his brother's jaw twitched. "Prick."

"So I've been called on more than one occasion." One corner of his mouth lifted. "This seems to be my morning for visitors. Lucky me."

Matt moved his gaze over him, taking in the fact he wore nothing but a pair of shorts, that he had obviously not been out of bed long. "What did she mean, about getting a straight answer out of you?"

Hunter leaned against the door frame, mug cradled between his palms. "I haven't a clue."

"Bullshit."

He lifted the mug to his lips, sipped. "Believe what you will. It's a free country."

"How free?"

"I don't follow."

"Maybe you're one of those Americans who believe your personal freedoms entitle you to trample on the freedoms of others? Maybe even take the law into your own hands? Or take a life?"

Hunter laughed. "I'm a lawyer. I uphold the law."

"Funny, that's what I do, too."

"What can I do for you, Matt?"

"I'm here on official business, Hunter."

"And here I'd thought you might be wanting a brotherly chat. I'm devastated."

Matt ignored his sarcasm. "May I come in?"

Wordlessly, he stepped away from the door. Matt entered the kitchen. He moved his gaze over the room, then brought it back to Hunter. "Where were you night before last? Between nine and ten-thirty?"

The night Trudy Pruitt was murdered.

Hunter folded his arms across his chest. "I was here. Working."

"Alone?"

"With Sarah."

"Sarah?"

Hunter nodded in the direction of the dog. "And her pups."

A look of annoyance passed over his brother's face. "You seem to spend an awful lot of time here, alone."

"I like it that way."

"You hear about Trudy Pruitt?"

"Yeah."

"You know the woman?"

"Nope. Not personally."

"Not personally. What does that mean?"

"I'd heard of her. I knew who she was. Who her kids were."

Hunter waited. This was where Matt would call Hunter a liar, challenge his story, throw up the message on the recorder. *If* he had checked Pruitt's answering machine.

And if he did, this was where Hunter would lawyer-up.

"Mind if I have a look around?"

Hunter laughed, the sound humorless. His brother and his crew of small-town constables had just flunked crime scene investigation 101. "Yeah, I mind. You want a look around, you get a search warrant."

"Expect it."

"Want to tell me why you're so interested in me?"

"You'll know soon enough."

"Right. You don't have dick. Go fish someplace else."

Matt shook his head. "For a lawyer, you're not very smart."

"And for a cop, you're not very observant."

"I don't have time for this." Matt made a sound of disgust and turned toward the door. "I'll see you when I've got that warrant."

"You'd love to pin this on me, wouldn't you, Matt? For a lot of different reasons, all of which have nothing to do with guilt or innocence."

His brother stopped. But didn't turn. "Name one."

"Avery."

The barb hit his mark, Hunter saw. His brother stiffened. Swung to face him. "Stay away from her. She's too good for you."

"At least we agree on something. A miracle."

"You're such an asshole. I can't believe you're my brother."

"Your twin," Hunter corrected. "Your other half."

Matt laughed, the sound tight. "We're nothing alike. I believe in family and community, hard work, loyalty."

"Just that I'm alive pisses you off, doesn't it?"

"Stay away from Avery."

"Why should I? She doesn't belong to you anymore. You let her go."

Matt flexed his fingers, longing, Hunter knew, to take a swing at him. How many times as kids had they argued, then come to blows, determined to beat the other senseless.

Even so, they had been a team then. Now, they were adversaries.

"What do you have to offer her?" Matt challenged. "Nothing. You're a broken-down drunk who—"

"A former drunk. There's a difference, brother." He took a step toward the other man. "Don't you see it? She and I are the same. We never fit in here. We never will."

Matt trembled with fury. This time it was he who took a step forward. "All these years, is this what it's been about, Hunter? Avery? Jealousy? Over what I am and what I had?"

"Had. You said it, Matt. No longer. You chose Cypress Springs over her."

"Shut up! Shut the fuck up!"

Hunter closed the remaining distance between them. They stood nose to nose, his twin's fury, his lust for blood palpable. Hunter recognized it because the same emotion charged through him.

"Make me," Hunter said.

"You'd love that. You'd scream police brutality. Get my badge."

"I'm not built that way. Take a punch. It's on me."

His brother didn't move. Hunter knew exactly where to push, how. They'd grown up together, knew each other's strengths—and weaknesses. Ever so softly, he clucked.

"Afraid?" he taunted. "Chicken? Remember when we were

kids? You wouldn't fight unless you knew you could win. Guess the big tough sheriff's not so tou—"

Matt's fist caught the side of Hunter's nose. Blood spurted. Pain ricocheted through his head, momentarily blinding him.

With a sound of fury, Hunter charged his brother. He caught him square in the chest, sending them both flying backward. Matt slammed into the refrigerator. From inside came the sound of items toppling.

"You son of a bitch!" Matt shoved him backward. "You have nothing to offer her! You threw away everything you ever had. Your family and community. Your career. Reputation. You're pathetic!"

"I'm pathetic? That's the difference between us, bro. The way I look at it, you threw away the only thing that really mattered."

Hunter twisted sideways, destabilizing the other man. They went down, taking the assortment of plates and glasses that had been drying on the rack by the sink with them. They crashed to the floor, the crockery raining down on them.

Hunter reared back, smashed his fist into his brother's face. Sarah barked, the sound high, frenzied. Matt grunted in pain; retaliated, catching Hunter in the side of his head.

Sarah's bark changed, deepened. She growled low in her throat. The sound, what it meant, penetrated; Hunter glanced toward the circling dog. "Sarah!" he ordered. "Heel!"

Matt used the distraction to his advantage, forcing Hunter onto his back. Glass crunched beneath his bare shoulders. A hiss of pain ripped past his lips as the shards pierced his skin. Sarah made her move.

She leaped at Matt, teeth bared. In a quick move, Matt rolled sideways, unsheathed his weapon and aimed at the dog.

"No!" Hunter threw himself at Sarah, plowing into her side, knocking her out of harm's way. They landed in a heap; she whimpered in pain, then scrambled to all fours.

Hunter jumped to his feet, shaking with rage. "You're a maniac."

Matt eased to his feet, holstered his weapon. "It would have been self-defense. The bitch could have torn me apart."

"Get the hell out of here." Hunter wiped his bloody nose with the back of his hand, aware of blood running in rivulets down his back. "You're not worth it, Matt. Not anymore."

Expression impassive, Matt tucked in his shirt, smoothed back his hair. "Two was always too many, wasn't it, Hunter? Two of us, just alike?"

"That's bullshit." He crossed to the sink. Yanked a paper towel off the roll, soaked it in cold water, then looked back at the other man. "You're blind, Matt. You don't have a clue."

"You're the one who's blind. Blinded by jealousy. For me, my relationship with Mom and Dad. Because of Avery."

Hunter's gut tightened at the grain of truth. Matt had always been the leader of the two, the charismatic one, the one everybody gravitated to: girls, the other kids, teachers. Even their parents and Cherry.

"I always loved you," Hunter said softly. "No matter what. I was proud you were my brother."

"Now who's shoveling the shit?"

"You've got to open your eyes, Matt. When it comes to Dad, our family, this town, you don't see anything as it really is."

"Better being a blind man than a dead one."

"Is that a threat, Sheriff Stevens?"

Matt laughed. "I don't have to kill you, Hunter. You're already dead."

CHAPTER 42

Avery decided to spend the morning going through her parents' attic, separating things she wanted to save from those she would donate to charity or toss. If she ever intended to put the house up for sale, it had to be done. Besides, she needed something to occupy her hands while she mentally reviewed the events of the past few days.

The pieces fit together; she just hadn't figured out how. Not yet. This was no different from any story she had ever tackled. A puzzle to be solved, assembled from bits of information gleaned from a variety of sources. The meaning of some of those bits obvious, others obtuse. Some would prove unrelated, some surprisingly key.

In the end, every story required a cognitive leap. That *ah-*

ha moment when the pieces all fell into place—with or without the facts to back them up. That moment when she simply *knew*.

Avery climbed the stairs. When she reached the top, she glanced toward her parents' bedroom. At the unmade bed. She stared at it a moment, then turned quickly away and started toward the end of the hall and the door to the attic stairs. She unlocked and opened the door, then headed up.

It was only March, but the attic was warm, the air heavy. During the summer months it would be unbearable. She moved her gaze over the rows of neatly stacked boxes, the racks of bagged clothes. From hooks hung holiday decorations: wreaths, wind socks and flags, one wall for each season. Evenly spaced aisles between the boxes.

So neatly organized, she thought. Her mother had been like that. Precise. Orderly. Never a hair out of place or social grace forgotten. No wonder the two of them butted heads so often. They'd had almost nothing in common.

Avery began picking through the boxes. She settled first on one filled with books. While she sorted through them, she pondered the newspaper she and Gwen had found in Trudy Pruitt's bedroom, the woman's cryptic notation. The hatchet marks. The words *All but two*. Trudy Pruitt had been counting the dead. Avery felt certain of that.

All but two who knew the truth about the Waguespack murder? It made sense in light of what she had said on the phone, that those who knew were dropping like flies. But, she could also have been counting the passing of people she hated. Or ones she feared. Or people she believed responsible for her sons' deaths.

The last rang true, made sense. Trudy Pruitt had been consumed by that event, that had been obvious to Avery. Had she found the note that had been written on the article about her father's suicide before the woman's murder, she would have considered Trudy Pruitt a suspect in his death as well as that of the others.

But she hadn't. Nor did she believe the woman had been smart or sophisticated enough to have pulled off the murders. Not alone, anyway.

Avery's fingers stilled. An accomplice. That could be. Perhaps the accomplice had decided Trudy Pruitt had outlived her usefulness. Or had become a liability.

Hunter. He'd left a message for her. Had he simply been returning the woman's call, as he claimed?

His explanation was plausible. She wanted it to be true. Wanted it in a way that was anything but uninvolved. Anything but unemotional.

Avery squeezed her eyes shut, struggling to recall exactly what he'd said in the message. His full name and phone number. Not that he was returning her call.

But if they had been accomplices, surely he wouldn't have had to identify himself, the woman would have recognized his voice. And surely he wouldn't have identified himself with his full name, Hunter Stevens. Nor, she supposed, would he have had to give her his number.

She frowned, shifting absently through the box of books, most of them westerns. Her dad had loved the genre. He'd eaten them up, chewing through the paperback novels as fast as publishers could put them out.

Her mother had read, too. Not as voraciously, however. In truth, the book Avery remembered seeing her mother with most had been her journal. She had carried one everywhere, doggedly recording the moments and events of her life.

Her mother had dreamed of being a writer. She had shared that before Avery left for college. They had been arguing about Avery's decision to leave Cypress Springs—and Matt—behind.

At the time, Avery hadn't believed her mother. Now, she wondered.

She recalled the scene clearly. Her mother had shared that tidbit in the context of making choices in life. She had expected her daughter to follow in her footsteps—be the traditional Southern woman, wife and mother, community volunteer. She had expected Avery to acknowledge what was important.

Chasing a dream wasn't. A career wasn't.

She had urged her to marry Matt. Start a family. Look at her, she had said. Where would Avery be if she had chased a career instead of marrying her father?

Perhaps she and her mother had had something in common, after all.

A headache started at the base of Avery's skull. She brought her hand to the back of her neck and rubbed the spot, recalling how their conversation had ended. They'd fought. It had been ugly.

"You took the easy way, Mom. You settled. I'm not going to be like you!"

And then, later, *"You never loved me, Mother. Not for me. You always tried to change me, make me like you. Well, it didn't work."*

Avery cringed, remembering the hateful words, recalling her mother's devastated expression. She had never taken those words back. Had never apologized.

And then it had been too late.

"Shit," Avery muttered, regret so sharp and bitter she tasted it. She thought of what Hunter had said, that her father believed her unresolved issues with her mother had been the reason she'd visited so rarely. Had he been right? Had she been waiting for an apology? Or had she stayed away because she knew how badly she had hurt her mother and hadn't wanted to look her in the—

She had carried a journal everywhere, doggedly recording the moments and events of her life.

Of course, Avery thought. Her mother's journals. She

would have noted Sallie Waguespack's death, its effect on the community and if her husband had somehow been involved.

But where were they? Avery had searched the house, emptied closets and drawers and bookcases. She hadn't seen even one of the journals. So, what had her father done with them?

Up here. Had to be.

Although she had already done a perfunctory search of the attic, she started a more complete one now. She not only checked the notations on each box, she opened each to make certain the contents matched the labels.

By the time she had checked the last carton, she was hot, dirty and disappointed. Could her father have disposed of them? Or her mother, sometime before she died?

Maybe Lilah would know. Checking her watch, Avery headed downstairs to the phone. She dialed the Stevenses number and Lilah answered immediately.

"Hi, Lilah, it's Avery."

"Avery! What a pleasant surprise. What are you up to this morning?"

"I'm working on the house, packing things up, and realized Mother's journals are missing."

"Her journals? My goodness, I'd forgotten she used to do that."

"So had I. Until this morning."

"At one time she was quite committed to it. Remember the Sunday she pulled her journal out during Pastor Dastugue's sermon? We were all sitting right up front, he was so pleased." The woman laughed lightly. "He thought she was taking notes."

"What do you mean, she had been committed to it? Did she give it up?"

"Yes, indeed. Let me think." The woman paused. "About the time you went off to university."

Avery felt the words like a blow. About the time she went

off to L.S.U. After their fight. After her mother had confided in Avery—and been met with disbelief and disdain.

"She never said anything, you understand," Lilah continued. "I just noticed she didn't have one with her. When I asked, she said she had given it up."

"Lilah, would you have any idea where she or Dad might have stored them?"

"Stored them?" The other woman sounded confused. "If they're not at the house, I imagine she got rid of them. Or your father, with the rest of her things."

Avery's stomach fell at the thought. "I just can't imagine either of them—"

"We all thought him so strong, clearing out her things the way he did. The reminders were just all too painful."

The doorbell rang. Avery ended the call and hurried to answer it.

Hunter stood at her door. She gazed at him through the screen, taking in his battered face. "My God, what happened to you?"

"Long story. Can I come in?"

"I don't think that's such a good idea."

He looked away, then back at her. "I've got this problem, Avery. And it has to do with you."

She folded her arms across her chest. "With me?"

"This morning Matt called me a dead man. And I realized it was true." He paused. "Except when I'm with you."

His words crashed over her. She laid her hand against the door frame for support, suddenly unbalanced. Light-headed. One second became two, became many.

"Avery," he said softly. "Please."

Wordlessly, she swung the screen door open. Was she letting in friend or foe? She didn't know, was simply acting on instinct. Or, if she was being honest, on longing. She moved aside as he entered and with shaky hands closed the door, using the moment to break their eye contact as she attempted to regain her equilibrium. She turned the dead bolt, took a deep breath and faced him. "I'll make us an iced tea."

Without waiting for a response, she started for the kitchen.

Avery was acutely aware of him following her, watching her as she poured them both an iced tea, as she added a wedge of lemon. She cleared her throat, turned and handed him the glass.

Their fingers brushed as he took the glass. He brought it to his lips; the ice clinked against its side as he drank.

She dragged her gaze away, heart thundering. "You and Matt got into it this morning."

It wasn't a question. He answered anyway. "Yes. We fought about you."

"I see."

"Do you?"

She shifted her gaze. Wet her lips.

"He wanted to know where I was night before last."

"And did you tell him?"

"Of course. I was home working. Alone." He set his glass on the counter. "I told you the truth this morning, Avery. Trudy Pruitt called me. I don't know why, but I assumed it was for legal counsel. I returned her call. I never even met the woman let alone killed her."

"Is that what Matt thinks, that you killed her?"

"That's what he wants to think."

She defended the other man. "I doubt that, Hunter. You're brothers. He's just doing his job."

"Believe that if it makes you feel better." He glanced away, then back. "He didn't think to check the woman's recorder. Yet, anyway. Are you going to tell him about the message?"

She wasn't, she realized. And not only because doing so would mean admitting to having broken and entered a posted crime scene.

She shook her head. "No."

"I have to ask you something."

"All right."

"Are you sleeping with him?"

She met his gaze. "That's a pretty shitty question, considering."

"He's acting awfully possessive."

"So are you."

He took a step toward her. "But we *are* sleeping together."

Her mouth went dry. "Did," she corrected. "One time. Besides, would it matter to you if we were?"

"Ditto on the pretty shitty question."

"No," she answered. "I'm not."

He brought a hand to the back of her neck and drew her toward him. "Yes," he murmured. "It would."

Heart thundering against the wall of her chest, she trailed her fingers across his bruised jaw. "Who threw the first punch?"

"He did. But I goaded him into it."

She laughed softly. Not because it was funny, but because it was so true to the boys she had known all those years ago. "Well, frankly, you look like he kicked your ass."

"Yeah, but you should see him."

Avery laughed again. "By the way," she murmured, "I believe you. About your call to Trudy Pruitt."

"Thank you." A smile tugged at his mouth. "Does this mean we can revisit the sleeping-together versus the slept-together thing?"

"You're awful."

His smile faded. "Matt accused me of being jealous of him. Of his relationship with you. With our parents. Jealous of his ability to lead. He suggested envy was at the root of everything that's happened between the two of us. That I withdrew from the family because of it."

She rested her hands on his chest, her right palm over his heart. "And what did you tell him?"

"That it was bullshit." He cupped her face in his palms. "I

always wanted you. But you chose Matt. And he was my brother."

The simple honesty inherent in those words rang true. They touched her. They spoke to the man he was. And the relationship he and Matt had shared.

In light of her intense feelings for Hunter, she wondered what would have happened all those years ago if Hunter had made a play for her. She wondered where they would all be today.

"What about now, Avery? I have to know, do you still belong to my brother?"

She answered without words. She stood on tiptoe, pressed her mouth to his, kissing him deeply. She slid her hands to his shoulders. He tensed, wincing.

She drew away. "You're hurt."

"It's nothing. A few cuts."

"Turn around." When he tried to balk, she cut him off. "Now, please."

He did. She lifted his shirt and made a sound of dismay. Cuts riddled his back and shoulders, some of them jagged and ugly. "How did this happen?"

"It's no big deal."

"It is. A very big deal." She lightly touched a particularly nasty cut with her index finger. "Some of these look deep. You need stitches."

"Stitches are for sissies." He looked over his shoulder and scowled at her. "I picked out the pieces. As best I could, anyway."

Frowning, she examined his back. "Most of them, anyway."

"Come on." She led him to the bathroom and ordered him to sit, pointing to the commode. "Take off your shirt."

He did as he was told. From the medicine cabinet she collected bandages of varying sizes, disinfectant and a pair of tweezers.

He eyed the tweezers. "What do you plan to do with those?"

She ignored the question. "This might hurt."

He nearly came off the seat as she began probing with the tweezers. "Might hurt! Take it easy."

She held up the sliver of glass, pinned between the tweezer's prongs. "How did you say this happened?"

"Matt and I were going at each other like a couple of jackasses, broke some gla— Hey! Ow!"

"Big baby." She dropped another sliver into the trash. "So you two broke some glass and rolled around in it."

"Something like that."

"Bright."

"You had to be there."

"No thanks." She examined the rest of his injuries, didn't see any more glass and began carefully cleaning the cuts. Each time she touched him with the disinfectant-soaked cotton, he flinched.

"I don't get it," she murmured, being as gentle as she could. "You can roll on a bed of glass, but a little Betadine and you're ready to tuck tail and run."

"Tuck tail? No way. It's a guy thing."

"And I say, thank God for the female of the species." She fitted a bandage over the last wound. "There, all done."

He grabbed her hand and tumbled her onto his lap. She gazed up at him, surprised, heart racing.

"I agree," he murmured, voice thick. "Thank God."

They made love there, in the bathroom, against the back of the door. It shouldn't have been romantic, but it was. The most romantic and exciting sex she had ever had. She orgasmed loudly, crying out. He caught her cries with his mouth and carried her, their bodies still joined, to the bed. They fell on it, facing one another.

He brought her hand to his chest, laid it over his wildly pumping heart. "I can't catch my breath."

She smiled and stretched, pleased. Satisfied beyond measure. "Mmm...good."

They fell silent. Moments ticked past as they gazed at one another, hearts slowing, bodies cooling.

Everything about him was familiar, she realized. The cut of his strong jaw, the brilliant blue of his eyes, the way his thick dark hair liked to fall across his forehead.

And everything was foreign as well. The boy she had known and liked had grown into a man she desired but didn't know at all.

"I'm sorry," he said softly. "About this morning. I acted like an ass. Another one of my problems."

She trailed a finger over his bottom lip. "What happened, Hunter? In New Orleans? Why'd you come home?"

"Home?" he repeated. "After all these years, you still call Cypress Springs home?"

"Don't you?"

He was silent a moment. "No. It ceased being home the day I walked away."

"But you've returned."

"To write a book."

"But why here?" He didn't reply. After a moment she answered for him. "Maybe because you felt safe here? Or felt you had nowhere else to go? Both could be called definitions of home."

He laughed scornfully. Humorless. "More like returning to the scene of the crime. The place my life began to go wrong."

She propped herself on an elbow and gazed down at him. He met her gaze; the expression in his bleak. "Talk to me," she said quietly. "Make me understand."

He looked as if he might balk again, then began instead. "New Orleans, my time at Jackson, Thompson and Witherspoon, passed in a blur. I was good at what I did. Too good, maybe. I moved up too fast, made too much money. I didn't have to work hard enough."

So he didn't respect it. Or himself.

"I became counsel of choice for New Orleans's young movers and shakers. Not the old guard, but their offspring. Life was a party. Drugs, sex and rock 'n' roll."

Avery cringed at the thought. She certainly wasn't naive. Her years in journalism had been...illuminating. But she had been lucky enough—strong enough—to resist falling into that particular pit.

"The drugs were everywhere, Avery. When you're dealing with the rich and famous, everything's available. Anything. Alcohol remained my drug of choice, though I didn't turn down much of anything."

He rolled onto his back and gazed up at the ceiling. Retreating from her, she knew. And into the past. "At first, the firm looked the other way. I was a hot commodity. Staying on top of my cases and clients despite my after-hours excesses. Substance abuse is not unheard of in lawyers. A by-product of the stresses of the job and the opportunity for abuse.

"Then the line blurred. I started using during the day. Started screwing up at work. A missed court date here and forgotten deadline there. The firm made excuses for me. After all, if word got out that one of their junior partners was a drunk, their exposure would have been huge. When I showed up drunk for a meeting with an important client, they'd had enough. They fired me.

"Of course, I was in denial. It was everybody's problem but mine. I could handle the alcohol. The drugs. I was a god."

Avery hurt for him. If was difficult to reconcile the man he described with the one she had known as a teenager—or the one she lay beside now.

"I went on a binge. My friends deserted me. The woman I was living with left. I had no more restraints, no one and nothing to hold me back."

He fell silent a moment, still deeply in the past. Struggling, Avery suspected, with dark, painful memories.

When he resumed, his voice shook slightly. "One morning I lost control of my vehicle by an elementary school. The kids were at recess. My car windows were open, I heard their laughter, squeals of joy. And then their screams of terror.

"I was speeding. Under the influence, big time. I crashed through the playground fence. There was nothing I could do but watch in horror. The children scattered. But one boy just stood there...I couldn't react."

He covered his eyes with his hands as if wanting to block out the memory. "A teacher threw herself at him, knocking him out of the way.

"I hit her. She bounced onto the hood, then windshield. The thud, it—" He squeezed his eyes shut, expression twisted with pain. "Miraculously, she wasn't killed. Just a couple broken ribs, lacerations...I thank God every day for that.

"The fence and the tree I clipped had slowed my forward momentum. Still, if I'd hit that boy, I would have killed him."

He looked at her then, eyes wet. "She came to see me. *Me,* the man who— She forgave me, she said. She begged me to see the miracle I had been offered. To use it to change my life."

Avery silently studied him. He had, she knew, without his saying so. The novel was part of that change. Coming back to Cypress Springs. Going back to move forward.

"That boy, I wonder if he finds joy in the playground now. I wonder if any of them can. Do they wake up screaming? Do they relive the terror? I do. Not a day goes by I don't remember. That I don't see their faces, hear their screams."

"I'm sorry, Hunter," she said softly. "I'm so sorry."

"So you see, I'm both cliché and a cautionary tale. The drunk driver barreling into a schoolyard full of children, the one lawyers like me argue don't exist."

He said the last with sarcasm, then continued, "I was

charged with driving under the influence and reckless endangerment. The judge ordered me into a court-monitored detox program. Took away my license for two weeks. Slapped me with a ridiculously low fine and ordered me to serve a hundred hours of community service."

If someone had been killed he would have been charged with vehicular homicide. He would have served time.

Hunter was already serving time.

"I haven't had a drink since," he finished. "I pray I never will again."

She found his hand, curled her fingers around his.

Moments ticked past.

"Matt's still in love with you."

She started to deny it, he stopped her. "It's true. He never stopped."

"Why are you telling me this?"

"I goaded him into losing control today, into throwing the first punch. The sick thing is, I took so much pleasure in doing it. In being able to do it. Perverse SOB, aren't I?"

"You're not so bad." Her lips lifted slightly. "Not as bad as you think you are, not by a long shot."

He turned his head, met her eyes. "Run, Avery. Go as fast as you can. I'm no good for you."

"Maybe I should be the judge of that."

His smile didn't reach his eyes. "That'd be risky. We both know you've never been that great a judge of character."

"Is that so?" She sat up, feigning indignation. "Actually, I'm a pretty damn good judge of— You're bleeding again."

"Where?" He sat up, craning to see over his shoulder.

"Here." She twisted to grab a couple of tissues from the box on her bed stand, then dabbed at the trickle of blood seeping from the bandage under his left shoulder blade. She remembered it had been the ugliest of the gashes.

Avery climbed out of bed, dragging the sheet with her. Wrapping it around her, toga style. "I'll bet there are some heavy-duty bandages in Dad's bathroom." She wagged a finger at him. "Stay put."

"Yes, Nurse Chauvin."

Avery padded into the hallway, heading toward her parents' bedroom. The door stood open, giving her a clear view of the bed. She should make it, she thought. Or strip it. Seeing it like that, day after day, reminded her of the last night of her father's life. And in doing so, it reminded her of his death.

The last night of his life.

The unmade bed.

Avery brought a hand to her mouth. Her dad had been in his pajamas. He had taken sleep medication. Obviously, he had either been asleep or had climbed into bed. Why put on his pj's if he meant to kill himself? Why climb into bed, under the covers? Only to get out, step into his slippers and head to the garage to kill himself?

It didn't make sense to her. Even considering her father's state of mind as described by his friends and neighbors.

She closed her eyes, thoughts racing, assembling another scenario. Her father in bed. Sleep aided by medication. Someone at the door. Ringing the bell or pounding.

The coroner had found trace amounts of the drug Halcion in his bloodstream. She had taken a similar medication before, to help her sleep on international flights. She had been easily roused. The medication had simply relaxed her, aided her ability to sleep.

Her dad had been a physician. Had spent his working life on call. Someone pounding on the door would have awakened him, even from a deep, medicated sleep.

So he had climbed out of bed. Stepped into his slippers and headed down to the front door. Or side door. There the enemy had waited. In the guise of a friend, she thought. Someone he had recognized and trusted.

So, he had opened the door.

Avery realized she was shaking. Her heart racing. It hurt, but she kept building the scenario, fitting the pieces together.

He would have been groggy. Easy to surprise and over-power, especially by someone he trusted.

How had they done it? she wondered. She flipped through the possibilities. Neither the coroner nor police had found any indication of foul play. No marks. No fractures. No detectable signs of a struggle, not at the scene or on the body.

She recalled what she had learned about death by fire— that the flesh basically melted but the body didn't incinerate. An autopsy could be performed. A blow to the head with enough force to disable a man would leave evidence for the pathologist.

Could his assailant have subdued him, secured him with ropes and carried him to the garage? She shook her head, eliminating the possibility. According to Ben Mitchell, her dad had crawled a few feet toward the door, impossible if bound.

So, how did one subdue a man without leaving a detectable mark on the body or in the bloodstream?

Then she had it. A friend in D.C. had carried a stun gun in-stead of pepper spray. She had sung its praises and tried to convince Avery to purchase one. What had she told Avery? That it delivered a high-voltage electrical charge that would immobilize an attacker for up to fifteen minutes. With no per-manent damage. And no detectable mark on the body.

It would have paralyzed her father long enough for his mur-derer to carry him out to the garage, douse him with fuel and toss a match.

His slipper had fallen off on the path between the house and garage.

That's why he hadn't stopped to slip it back on. He hadn't been walking. He'd been carried. She pictured the murderer dumping him in the garage. He'd had the fuel there, ready.

Diesel fuel lit on contact. No flashover. The murderer could have tossed the match and walked away.

While her father burned alive. By the time he had been able to respond, it had been too late.

"What's wrong?"

She turned. Hunter had come up behind her. "I know how it happened. With Dad. I know how they killed him."

CHAPTER 43

Hunter awakened to realize he was alone in bed. He glanced at Avery's bedside clock. Just after 5:00 p.m. They had slept the afternoon away.

At least he had.

He sat up. The pillow next to his still bore the imprint of Avery's head. He laid his hand in the indention and found it cold. He shifted his gaze to the window. The light had changed, lost the brilliance of midday and taken on the violet of early evening.

He ran a hand absently across his jaw, rough with a five o'clock shadow, thoughts on Avery. She had shared her theory with him—that her father had been awakened by a trusted friend at the door. That a stun gun had been used to immobilize him. That her father had dragged himself to the door, but that his effort had been too late.

Afterward, Hunter had held her while she cried. Her weeping had broken his heart and he had tried to comfort her by poking holes in her theory. Why would someone have killed her father? he'd asked. What could their motive have been?

Nothing he said had helped, so he had simply held her until her tears stopped. And then he'd led her to the bed and lay with her until they had both drifted off.

Hunter threw the coverlet aside and climbed out of bed. After retrieving his jeans from the floor, he went in search of Avery.

He found her in the kitchen. She stood at the sink, gazing out the window behind it. The portable phone lay on the kitchen table. Beside it a steno-size spiral notebook and a folded newspaper.

She had been up for some time.

He approached silently. She wore a white terry-cloth robe, cinched at the waist. It swallowed her, accentuating her diminutive stature. With her little-boy haircut and pixie features she looked like a child dressed up in her mother's things.

Those who underestimated her because of her petite size made a big mistake. She possessed a keen mind and the kind of determination that sometimes bordered on pigheadedness. He'd always admired her, even when she'd dug in her heels about something that to his mind had made no sense.

He'd admired her character, as well as her sense of fair play. She had stood up to the bullies. Had taken the side of the underdog, befriended the new kids and odd ones, championed the outsiders. It hadn't made her popular, but for the most she hadn't cared about popularity.

Truth was, he had always been in awe of her strength.

He had always been a little bit in love with her.

Was that what was going on now? he wondered. Had she

decided to befriend the underdog? Champion him, the outsider? No matter what others thought?

She became aware of his presence and looked at him. The barest of smiles touched her mouth. "It's going to storm."

He crossed to stand beside her. The wind had begun to blow, he saw. Dark clouds tumbled across the evening sky. "It's spring. We need the rain."

"I suppose."

He touched her cheek lightly. "Are you all right?"

"Hanging in there." She tilted her head into his hand. "Hungry?"

"Starving. We could order out."

She shook her head. "I have eggs. And cheese."

"Sounds like an omelette."

They worked together, playfully arguing over what ingredients to include. Onions were out. Bell peppers in. Mushrooms were a must. Lots of cheese. A bit of cayenne pepper.

"I'll make toast," he offered.

"I have English muffins. In the fridge."

"Even better." He retrieved them along with the orange juice and butter. After splitting two of the muffins and popping them into the toaster, he rummaged around in the cabinets and drawers, collecting flatware, plates, glasses and napkins.

Hunter carried them to the oak table. He moved the phone and newspaper; as he did, he saw it was the issue of the *Gazette* that had reported her dad's death. He frowned, shifting his gaze to the spiral notebook that lay beside it. A column of names with a date beside each ran down the page. *Pat Greene. Sal Mandina. Pete Trimble. Kevin Gallagher. Dolly Farmer.* Her father's name was there. At the bottom, Trudy Pruitt's.

"What's this?"

She didn't look at him. "Something I'm working on."

"Working on?" he repeated. "It looks like a list of people who have died in—"

"The past eight months," she finished for him. "Here in Cypress Springs."

She wouldn't have the list out if she hadn't wanted him to see it. "This is about those things Trudy Pruitt said to you, isn't it? About your dad being involved in Sallie Waguespack's death?"

She turned the omelette. "Yes. And about the clippings I found in his closet. And two murders and two disappearances in the past six weeks. And a group called The Seven."

He frowned. "I'm not going to be able to deter you from this, am I?"

She looked over her shoulder at him. "No."

Determined to the point of pigheaded. She wouldn't let this go until she was satisfied she knew the truth. Beyond-a-shadow-of-a-doubt truth.

No wonder she was such a good investigative reporter.

"Dammit, Avery. You drive me crazy."

She lifted a shoulder. "Forget it then if it'll make you feel better."

"Like hell. You think I'm going to leave you to track down a killer yourself? Two women have already been murdered. I don't want you to be the third."

She smiled and batted her eyelashes at him in exaggerated coquetry. "That's so sweet, Hunter."

"This isn't funny. There's a killer out there."

"That's right. And he may have killed my father."

"Would you like my help?" he asked, resigned.

She thought a moment, then nodded. "I think I would. Eggs are ready."

She slid the omelettes onto plates. He buttered the English muffins and set them on the table. While they ate, Hunter curbed his impatience. This was her party, after all.

When they had finished, she stood, cleared the plates then

sat back down. She met his eyes. "As you know, last night I went to Trudy Pruitt's trailer. The woman had accused my father of being involved in Sallie Waguespack's murder. Of helping the police to frame her sons. She said she had proof, but she was killed before she could give it to me."

"So you went looking for it. Gwen Lancaster was with you."

"How did you—?"

"Good guess."

"What you don't know is that Gwen had interviewed Trudy about The Seven just hours before Trudy's death."

Hunter straightened. "She interviewed Trudy Pruitt?"

"Yes. The woman confirmed the existence of The Seven. She claimed the group was responsible for Elaine St. Claire's murder."

"Avery," Hunter said, frowning, "word is, the woman was an unstable drunk. Because of her boys, she had an ax to grind with this town. I wouldn't put too much stock in what she had to say."

"You sound like Matt. Buddy, too."

"They're right. You should listen."

She looked frustrated. "What about Gwen? Her place was ransacked. All her notes stolen. Someone lured her out to a hunting camp off Highway 421 and No Name Road. They left her a gutted cat."

"Try that again."

"A woman phoned Gwen. She told her she had information about Gwen's brother's disappearance. She arranged a meeting at the hunting camp."

"But she didn't show."

"Right. Instead, Gwen found the cat. It was a warning. To cease and desist. That's the way The Seven works. One warning, then they act."

Hunter listened, his sense of unease growing. "How do you know any of that's true, Avery? She could have ransacked her own place, lied about the cat, the phone call and notes. All in an effort to convince you it was true. To gain your trust."

She shook her head. "I was at The Guesthouse when she returned. She was frightened, Hunter. Terrified."

She slid the piece of newspaper across the table. "Last night Gwen and I found this. On Trudy Pruitt's bedroom floor."

Hunter gazed at the clipping. The woman had drawn devil horns and a goatee on the picture of Avery's father, yet Avery seemed so matter-of-fact about the item it was as if finding such an upsetting thing in a murdered woman's bedroom was an everyday occurrence.

"Look here, in the margin," she continued. "She was tallying something, keeping score."

"'All but two,'" he murmured. "What do you think it means?"

"I believe she was counting the dead so far. My dad was number five."

"Plus two equals seven."

"I noticed that."

"Okay, you have my full attention."

She tapped the page. "The way I figure it, these were either people she believed had been involved in the cover-up of Sallie Waguespack's murder or ones who knew the truth about it."

"Presuming there was a cover-up."

"Yes." She stood and began to pace. "You're a lawyer... Who would have been involved in the investigation?"

"I'm not a criminal attorney, but obviously you've got a murderer and a victim. Person or persons who discovered the body. First officer. Detectives, criminalists. The coroner or his deputy."

"Witnesses, if any."

"Right."

"Your dad let me read the file," she said. "Officer Pat

Greene was out on patrol. He saw the Pruitt boys leaving Sallie Waguespack's. The boys had a history of trouble with the law, so he decides he'd better check it out. He finds the woman dead, then calls Buddy."

She stopped, expression intent, as if working to recall the exact sequence of events. "From Pat's description, Buddy figures it was the Pruitt brothers Pat saw. He and Pat go looking for them. The meeting ends in a shoot-out that left the boys dead."

"They left the murder scene untended?"

She thought a moment. "I can't remember. They may have waited for the coroner, but I don't think so. According to the file, no other officer was called to the scene."

"Go on."

"The murder weapon was found in the ditch behind the Pruitt's trailer. Donny's prints were on it. One of the boys had the victim's blood on his shoe. They opened fire on the police when approached and Pat Greene had already placed them at the scene. Case closed. No need for further investigation, nice and neat."

"Too nice and neat, you're thinking?"

"Maybe"

"What about the autopsy? As I understand it, an autopsy is always requested in a murder case."

"It wasn't in the file. Buddy thought it had been misplaced and promised to locate it for me. I'll give him a call tomorrow."

Silence fell between them. Hunter sensed her doing the same as he, considering the possibilities, doing a mental tally. The numbers didn't add up.

"Let's count who could have been involved," he said. "You've got two officers at the scene, Dad and Pat Greene. You've got the coroner. That's three. Throw in the victim and the Pruitts you've got six. Your dad could be number seven, though how he fit in I'm not certain."

He drummed his fingers against the tabletop. "Maybe she was counting the deaths of The Seven? Maybe she was the one bumping them off? Maybe one of the last two killed her first?"

"Maybe, but I don't think so. Unless she had an accomplice. These deaths were made to look like accidents. There was a level of sophistication I don't believe Trudy Pruitt capable of."

"If she had an accomplice, who would that be? Someone who thought as she did. Someone with an ax to grind against Cypress Springs or a group of her citizens."

Avery thought a moment, then shook her head. "Then who killed Elaine St. Claire? Not Trudy Pruitt, they were friends. She told Gwen that The Seven were responsible for Elaine's death."

"Maybe The Seven are the ones who killed Sallie Waguespack."

"That doesn't work because the way I understand it, the Waguespack murder was the catalyst for the formation of The Seven."

"But you don't know that for sure."

She made a sound of frustration. "No, dammit. All I have is speculation."

"And a growing number of dead." He stood and crossed to her. "Let's back up again. Who could have known the truth about Sallie Waguespack's death?"

"The Pruitt boys. Buddy. Pat Greene. My dad, because Trudy Pruitt implicated him."

"Trudy herself," he offered. "Maybe whoever prepared Sallie for burial."

"Oh my God."

"What?"

She crossed to the counter, to her notebook. She ran a finger down the column of names, mouth moving as she silently read them.

He watched her, a sinking sensation in the pit of his stomach. "What?"

She lifted her gaze to his. "Everyone we named is dead, Hunter. Except your dad."

The words landed heavily between them. Hunter stared at her, his world shifting slightly. "That can't be."

"It is." She held the steno pad out and he saw that her hand trembled. "Take a look."

He shook his head, but didn't reach for the notebook. "Do you realize what you're saying?"

She nodded slowly, face pale.

Either Buddy Stevens was a killer. Or next in line to die.

"Look at the list," she said again. "Pat Greene, Dad, Kevin Gallagher, Trudy Pru—"

"I don't give a damn about your list!" The words exploded from him. "You've gone around the bend with this thing, Avery. Way past rational."

She took a step back, expression hurt. "This doesn't mean your dad's the one. He could be in danger, Hunter. If so, we need to warn him."

It was bullshit. Nothing went on in this town without his dad knowing, never had. Who better than the chief of police to orchestrate a cover-up? Who better than a lawman to arrange deaths to look like accidents?

Hunter tipped his face to the ceiling, thoughts racing. Reviewing the things they had discussed, the key players in the Waguespack investigation.

But why? After all these years? Had someone threatened to blow the whistle on them all?

That didn't make sense. His father killing old friends in an effort to quiet them fifteen years after the fact didn't make sense.

Someone else was the perpetrator.

His dad was in danger.

He looked at Avery. "What about the coroner? Is he on your list?"

"Dr. Harris. No, he's not." She glanced at the steno pad as if to reconfirm her answer, then looked back at him. "Dr. Harris has been the parish coroner on and off for twenty-eight years."

"Was he coroner in 1988?"

"I don't know. If he was—"

"Then Dad's not the last."

CHAPTER 44

Gwen's eyes snapped open. Heart pounding, she scrambled into a sitting position. She had been dreaming about her brother. He had been trying to warn her.

As the effects of the dream began to fade, a chill slid down her spine.

Something was wrong.

Gwen moved her gaze over the dark room, stopping on the window. From outside came the sound of rain. A sudden, blinding flash of light.

She jumped, then laughed softly at herself. At her jitters. The storm had awakened her. She glanced at the bed stand. The clock's face, usually a reassuring glow in the night, was dark.

The power had gone out.

Gwen climbed out of bed, heading for the bathroom.

She stopped as her foot landed in something wet. She looked down at the floor, confused. How—

A breeze stirred against her ankles. She looked back at the window. It was closed. Locked.

The bathroom window. It faced the side yard. The big oak tree.

Lightning illuminated the room. She lowered her gaze. Water, she saw. A trail of it from the bathroom to the bed. She glanced over her shoulder at the half-open bathroom door. The darkness beyond.

Someone, waiting.

A cry spilling past her lips, she bolted forward. He burst from the bathroom. Grabbed her from behind. One strong arm circled her waist; a gloved hand covered her mouth. Tightly. She was dragged backward.

He held her pinned against his chest. She fought as best she could, kicking out, trying to twist free of her assailant's grasp. He was too strong. His grip was so tight over her nose and mouth she couldn't breathe. She grew light-headed. Pinpricks of lights danced before her eyes.

He bent his head close to hers. His labored breath was hot against her ear. He wore a ski mask. The fuzzy knit tickled her cheek.

"You have been judged, Gwen Lancaster. Judged and found guilty."

The Seven. They had come for her.

As they had come for Tom.

Terror exploded inside her. It stole her ability to think. To resist. Was this what it had been like for Tom? In the moments before the end, had he thought of her? Their parents? Or had the fear stolen his ability to do that as well?

Don't give in, Gwen. Keep your head.

It was as if Tom had spoken to her. The sound of his voice

moved over her, calming, steadying. She had to keep her wits about her, not fall apart. Everybody made mistakes. Slipped up. He would, too.

She needed to be able to act at that moment. She forced herself to relax.

"We warned you," he hissed. "Why didn't you go? Why did you have to involve others? Now it's too late for you."

Others.

Avery.

She heard what sounded like regret in his voice. She tried to respond, to apologize, to beg for one last chance. Her words came out in pitiable whimpers against his hand.

"I really am sorry," he murmured, forcing her forward, toward the bathroom. "Sorry for the abominable state of the world that makes this necessary. Sorry you were dragged into something that wasn't your battle. But this is war. In war collateral damage is inevitable."

Collateral damage. The unfortunate but unavoidable loss of life.

Had he said the same to Tom? The others?

They reached the bathroom. He forced her through the door, shutting it behind them. Lightning flashed. What it illuminated sent fear spiraling through her. A black plastic drop cloth laid out in the old-fashioned claw-footed tub. Several lengths of rope. A knife, its jagged edge gleaming against the black plastic.

She dug in her heels, fighting him in earnest. The mistake wasn't coming, she realized. He had thought this through, every detail.

What of Avery, she thought dizzily. Had she been killed already? Had she suffered the knife as well?

She didn't want to die.

Tears flooded her eyes. Her vision blurred. *She didn't want to die this way.*

He made a sound of disappointment. "This isn't about me.

Or you. It's so much bigger than either of us." He forced her closer to the tub. "I know what you're thinking. That Cypress Springs is too small and inconsequential for what happens here to make a difference in the world. You're wrong. Consider what happens when you toss a pebble in the pool, how that little plunk affects the entire pool in ever-widening ripples. So too with us.

"Our influence is spreading. We're branching out into other small communities. Finding others who think as we do. Others who are sick of the filth. The drugs. The moral decay that has spread to every nook and cranny of this country. Others who believe the end justifies the means."

Gwen began to cry. She shook her head, unable to take her eyes off the knife.

"Time for sentencing, Gwen Lancaster."

He turned quickly, dragging her with him, propelling her forward. Before she could grasp what was happening, her head smashed into the doorjamb.

Pain exploded behind her eyes. Her world went black.

CHAPTER 45

Avery gazed out at the rain-soaked morning. Leaves and branches littered the yard; a limb from the neighbor's tree had fallen and partially blocked her driveway.

Hunter had left hours ago, sometime before the storm hit. He'd used Sarah as an excuse. She had known the truth to be otherwise; he had wanted to be alone. To sort through his thoughts, come to grips with them.

Whatever they were. She wasn't certain. He had been shaken, that she knew. But noncommittal. Almost secretive.

They'd gone over the list again. And again. With the possible exception of the coroner, every person involved with the investigation had died recently. And unexpectedly.

She closed her eyes, picturing the notations Trudy Pruitt had made on the newspaper—*All but two.*

Was Buddy Stevens one of those two? Was his life in danger?

Or was he a killer?

Avery turned away from the window. Buddy Stevens was a good man. The very epitome of law and order. To imagine him as otherwise was to ponder the ridiculous.

Then why did she have this heavy feeling of dread in the pit of her stomach?

No. She squeezed her eyes shut. Buddy wasn't a part of this. And she wouldn't lose him to a killer.

Avery made her way to the kitchen. She and Hunter had agreed that she would call Dr. Harris and Buddy this morning. The clock on the microwave revealed that it was not quite eight. She would wait a few more minutes before trying the man.

And before trying Gwen. Again.

Gwen hadn't called yesterday, neither Avery's home line nor her cell. So Avery had tried the woman's cell while Hunter slept. The number had worked, but Gwen hadn't answered. She had tried early this morning with the same result.

Avery sank onto one of the kitchen chairs then returned to her feet, too antsy to sit. She began to pace. Neither time she had left a message; now she wished she had. At least Gwen would know they were still on the same side. And that she was okay.

Where was her friend? Why hadn't she called?

Avery stopped, picked up the phone and brought it to her ear, checking for a dial tone. At the welcoming hum, she hesitated then punched in the woman's cell number. It went straight to her message service, indicating she didn't have the device on.

"Gwen, hi. It's Avery. I have information. Call me."

She replaced the receiver. Now what? Call The Guesthouse, going through the operator? Try the hall pay phone? Or wait?

She decided on the last. In the meantime she would call Dr. Harris.

The coroner answered the phone himself, on the first ring. "Dr Harris. It Avery Chauvin."

"Ms. Chauvin," he said warmly. "How are you?"

"Better," she said. "Thank you for asking."

"Glad to hear it. What can I do for you this morning?"

"I'm working on a story about the Sallie Waguespack murder."

"Did you say Waguespack?"

"I did."

"My, that's an old one."

"Yes—1988. Were you coroner at that time?"

"Nope. That was during one of my hiatuses. Believe Dr. Bill Badeaux was coroner then."

"Would you know how I could contact him?"

"I'm afraid that'd be tough, seeing he passed on."

That left Buddy. He was the last one.

"I'm sorry to hear that," she said, forcing normalcy into her tone. "Did he pass away recently?"

"A year or so ago. Heard through the grapevine. He'd moved away from the parish way back."

A year or so. Maybe he had been the first.

Her legs began to shake. She found a chair and sank onto it.

"Ms. Chauvin? Are you okay?"

"Absolutely." She cleared her throat. She wanted to ask how the man had died, but didn't want to arouse his suspicions, especially in light of what she intended to ask next. "Did Buddy Stevens get in touch with you?"

"Buddy? No, was he supposed to?"

"He couldn't find the Waguespack autopsy report. He was going to give you a call. Probably slipped his mind."

"'Course, the autopsy would have been done in Baton Rouge, but I'd have a copy. I tell you what, I'll pull it and give you a call back."

"Could you do it now, Dr. Harris? I'm sorry to be such a pest, but my editor gave me an unreal deadline on this story."

"I can't." He sounded genuinely sorry. "I was on my way over to the hospital when you called and it's going to take a few minutes to locate the file."

"Oh." She couldn't quite hide her disappointment.

"I tell you what, I should be back in a couple hours. I'll take care of it then. What number should I call?"

To ensure she wouldn't miss him, Avery gave him her cell number. "Thank you, Dr. Harris. You've been a big help."

She hung up, then dialed Hunter. He answered right away.

"It's Avery," she said. "A Dr. Bill Badeaux was West Feliciana Parish coroner in 1988. He died about a year ago."

"Shit. How?"

"I was afraid to come off too nosy. I figured it wouldn't be too hard to find out. One trip over to the *Gazette*—"

"I'll do it."

"But—"

"But nothing. You've already poked around over there. I don't want you drawing any more attention to yourself."

"You think I'm right, don't you? About The Seven?"

She heard a rustling sound from the other end of the phone, then Sarah began to bark. "I'll let you know," he said. "Where are you going to be?"

His voice had changed. Become tight. Angry-sounding. "Are you all right?" she asked.

"Fine."

In the background Sarah was going nuts. A thought occurred to her. "Are you alone?"

"Not completely."

"I don't understand. I—"

"Stay put. I'll call you back."

"But—"

"Promise."

She hesitated, then agreed.

The next instant, the phone went dead.

CHAPTER 46

Avery showered and dressed. Made her bed and separated her laundry before throwing a load of whites in the washer. Then she foraged through the refrigerator and checked her e-mail via her laptop. She responded evasively to her editor's query about progress on her story and figured everyone else could wait.

Time ticked past at an agonizing pace. She glanced at the clock every couple of minutes. After nearly an hour, she acknowledged she couldn't stand another minute of inactivity.

Bringing both the portable and cell phone with her, she headed upstairs. As she reached the top landing, her gaze settled on the framed photographs that lined the long hallway wall. She had always jokingly called it her parents' wall of fame.

How many times had she walked past all these photos without looking at them? Without considering the fact that she was pictured in almost every one? How could she have taken her parents' love so for granted?

She stopped, pivoted to her right. Her gaze landed on a photo of her as a toddler. Her first steps, Avery thought, taking in her mother on her knees on the floor, arms out. Coaxing and encouraging her. Promising she would be there to catch her.

Avery moved her gaze across the wall. Baby pictures, school portraits, pictures from every imaginable holiday and event of her life. And in a great number of them, there stood her mother, looking on with love and pride.

She took in the photograph of her first steps once more, studying her mother's expression. The truth was, she hadn't known her mother at all. What had been her hopes, dreams and aspirations? She had longed to be a writer. Yet Avery knew nothing of her writing.

She had always blamed her mother for their distant relationship, but perhaps the fault had been hers. She'd had her father, and loving him had been so easy.

She, it seemed, was the one who had taken the easy way. The one who had settled—for a loving relationship with one parent instead of two. If only she had her mother's journals. In them resided her mother's heart and soul. Her beliefs and wishes, disappointments and fears. The opportunity to know her mother.

Her father wouldn't have thrown them out. Her mother—the woman pictured in these photographs—would not have destroyed them, even if she had given up on them.

They were here. Somewhere.

Avery started for the attic, a sense of urgency settling over her. A sense that time was running out.

She reached the attic. Scanned the rows and stacks of cartons. In one of these boxes she would find the journals. Stored with other items. Hidden beneath.

She began the search, tearing through the cartons—her mother's clothing, personal items, other books, family memorabilia.

She found them in the box housing Avery's doll collection. The dolls her mother had insisted on buying and lining Avery's bedroom shelves with—despite Avery's disdain for them.

Her mother had packed the volumes neatly, arranging the books in chronological order. The first one was dated 1965. Her mother had been seventeen. The last one dated August 1990—just as Lilah had said, her mother had given up journaling the August when Avery had gone off to university.

Avery trailed a finger over the spines with their perfectly aligned, dated labels. She stopped on the one dated January through June 1988.

All the answers she sought were here, she thought, pulse quickening. About Sallie Waguespack's death and her father's part in it. Perhaps ones about The Seven, their formation.

But other answers were here as well. Ones to personal questions, personal issues that had plagued her all her life.

Sallie Waguespack could wait, she decided, easing the volume dated 1965 from its slot. Her mother could not.

Avery began to read. She learned about a girl raised by strict, traditional parents. About her dreams of writing. She learned that her mother had been a deeply passionate woman, that she had often been afraid, that in her own way she had rebelled against her parents' strict upbringing.

Through her mother's words, Avery relived the day she met Phillip Chauvin, their first date. Their courtship, wedding. The first time they made love. Avery's birth.

Avery struggled to breathe evenly. She realized her cheeks were wet with tears.

Her mother had given up a lot to be a wife and mother.

But what she had gotten in return had been huge.

She had loved being a mother. Had loved being Avery's mother. She had described with pride her daughter's determination. That she was different from the other girls—that she seemed insistent on marching to her own tune.

She baffles me. I put a bow in her hair and when I'm not looking, she rips it out.

Today Avery won first prize in the parish-wide essay contest. She read her essay to the class. I hid my tears. Her talent takes my breath away. Secretly, I smile and think, "She got that from me. My gift to my precious daughter."

Avery wiped tears from her cheeks and read on, this time from the 1986 journal.

She breaks my heart daily. Doesn't she know I want the world for her? Doesn't she know how frightened I am of losing her?

And then later she poured out her heart.

I've lost her. She and I have nothing in common. She turns to her dad, always. They laugh together, share everything. I often think I made a huge mistake. If I'd pursued my writing, we would have had something in common. Maybe then she wouldn't look at me as if she thought I had no purpose in her life. That I had wasted my life.

Avery selected the last volume next—1990, the year she had graduated from high school.

Where did I go wrong? How did she and I grow so far apart? She's leaving Cypress Springs. I begged her to stay. Even as I thought of my own choices, my mistakes and regrets, I pleaded with her. I shared my dreams, but it is too late.

Avery closed the book, hands shaking, fighting not to fall apart. She had accused her mother of not loving her. But her mother had loved her deeply. Avery had accused her of trying to change her, of trying to mold her into someone different, something other than who she was.

But her mother had understood and admired her for the person she was, different from the other girls, the one who had never fit in.

In truth, her mother had never fit in either. Not with her own parents. Not with her community. Not with her daughter.

She and her mother had been just alike.

Avery pressed her lips together, holding back a sound of pain. If only she had read the journals before her mother died. If only she had let go of her pride.

She had wanted to. She'd been sorry for the way she'd acted, the way she had hurt her mother. Instead of acting on the emotion, she had let pride control her. She had been so certain she was right.

So, she had stayed away. Nursed her feeling of self-righteous indignation.

And had missed out on so much. Time with her mother and father. Now it was too late.

To be with them. But not for justice for Sallie Waguespack and the Pruitt brothers.

She located the appropriate volume and flipped through to the entry for June 19, the day after Sallie Waguespack's murder.

That poor woman. And pregnant, too. It's too horrible to contemplate.

Her mother had then gone on to describe other, mundane events.

Avery frowned, her investigative instincts kicking into overdrive. Pregnant? Nothing else she had read had mentioned the woman being pregnant. Avery flipped ahead, looking for another reference.

She didn't find one. Could her mother have been mistaken? That didn't seem likely. Where had she gotten her information?

Maybe from her husband, Avery thought. The local general practitioner. Perhaps Sallie Waguespack's physician. Probably.

So why had that information been kept from the public?

Avery read on, heart racing, realizing that all the answers she sought were here, in her mother's words.

Phillip was quiet today. Something is terribly wrong but he won't speak of it.

And then later,

Phillip and Buddy argued. They aren't speaking and it pains me that such good friends are being torn apart by something like this.

Something like what? Avery wondered. Sallie Waguespack's murder? Had they been on opposite sides of the tide of public opinion?

Avery found no further mention of conflict between the two friends or about the murder or investigation until a passage that caused her heart to skip a beat.

Buddy has involved himself in something...a group. There's seven of them. Something secret. I heard him trying to convince Phillip to join.

Avery stopped, working to collect her thoughts. Buddy a member of the original Seven? Trying to convince her father to join?

She read on.

> Phillip went out tonight; he met with that group, The Seven. He seemed troubled when he returned. I'm concerned... Everything is different now. Everything has...changed.

Avery glanced at her watch, shocked to see that nearly two hours had passed already. There were so many journals yet to read. She needed another pair of eyes.

Hands shaking, she dug in her pocket for the paper she had scrawled Gwen's cell number on. She dialed the number, left a message and stood, a ripple of unease moving over her. Where was Gwen?

To hell with stealth, she decided, hurrying for the attic stairs, stopping when she reached them. Turning, she darted back to the boxes of journals. She bent, collected the ones from 1988 and 1990, then ran for the stairs.

Minutes later, journals stuffed into her handbag, she backed her SUV down the driveway. She reached The Guesthouse in no time at all, parked in front and hurried up the walk. As she made a move to grab the doorknob, the door opened.

Avery jumped backward, making a sound of surprise.

Her old friend Laurie stepped through.

"Avery," she said, looking startled. "This is so weird. I was just thinking about you. I've meant to call or stop by, but it's been nuts around here what with Fall Festival and—"

"Don't worry about it. It's good to see you."

Laurie glanced at her watch. "I'd love to chat, but I'm late."

"Actually, I stopped by to see Gwen Lancaster. Is she in?"

Laurie drew her eyebrows together. "Gwen Lancaster? The woman in 2C?"

"Yes. Is she here?"

"I don't know. I haven't seen her today."

"When's the last time you did see her? It's important."

The other woman frowned. "I don't know...I don't keep tabs on our guests."

Realizing how she sounded, Avery forced a laugh. "Of course you don't. If she's not there, could I leave her a note?"

"Sure, Avery. No law against that." She hitched her purse strap higher on her shoulder, started off, then stopped and looked back at Avery, eyes narrowed. "Gwen Lancaster's not from around here. How do you know her?"

Avery lifted a shoulder in feigned nonchalance. "We met down at the Azalea Café. Hit it off."

"Oh." Laurie frowned slightly. "Her brother's the one who disappeared. Tom. He stayed with us, too."

"I'd heard that."

"A girl can't be too careful, Avery."

Chill bumps raced up her arms. Had that been a warning? A threat?

Or nothing at all but small-town gossip?

"It seems that in this case," Avery murmured, "a guy can't be too careful, either."

The woman hesitated, then laughed, the sound lacking warmth. "I've got to go," she said. "See you around."

Avery watched her walk away, then turned and headed inside. The front desk was empty; she trotted up the stairs, to the end of the hall.

She half expected to find Gwen's door as she had last time—propped open, chaos inside.

It was closed tight. She knocked, waited a moment, then knocked again. "Gwen," she called softly. "It's Avery."

Still no answer. From downstairs came the sound of the front door opening and closing. She glanced over her shoulder, saw she was alone, then tried the door. And found it locked.

Reassured, she took the notepad and pen out of her purse, scrawled a brief note asking Gwen to call her on her cell, ASAP, telling her she had found something important. She wrote the number, bent and slid the note under the door.

She turned and found Laurie standing a dozen feet behind her. Avery laughed nervously. "You surprised me, Laurie. I thought you'd left."

"This is a nice place to live, Avery," the woman said. "You don't know, you've been away."

"Pardon me?"

"Folks around here like things the way they are. I thought you should know that."

Avery stared at her old friend, heart thundering. "You're referring to The Seven, aren't you?"

"I don't know what you're talking about."

"Yes, you do. The Seven. The ones who keep Cypress Springs a nice place to live. By whatever means necessary."

"Gwen Lancaster is a troublemaker. An outsider." Laurie took a step back. "We take care of our own. You should know that. You used to be one of us, too."

CHAPTER 47

"Hunter!" Avery called, rapping on his door. "It's me. Avery."

When he didn't answer after a moment, she called out again, urgency pressing at her. Time was running out. She had found the clues to the past and Sallie Waguespack's murder. She had proof The Seven existed. She had figured out how her father had been killed. She knew from experience that once the pieces of a story began falling into place, anything could happen. And it usually happened fast.

She needed to uncover the killer's identity. Why he had done it.

Before it was too late. Before he killed again.

If he hadn't already.

Sarah whined and pawed at the door. Avery peered through the window at the obviously empty kitchen. Where was Hunter? It had been several hours since they'd spoken; he'd said he would get back to her. Why hadn't he?

She checked her watch, frowning. He could have gone for a run. To the grocery or out for lunch. He could be over at the *Gazette,* researching how Dr. Badeaux had died.

Sure, she reassured herself. That was it. He was fine. He— He'd sounded strange when they spoke. Sarah had been going nuts in the background. Barking. Growling.

Are you alone?

Not completely.

Panicked, she tried the door. She found it unlocked and stumbled inside. "Hunter," she called. "Hunter!"

She moved her gaze over the kitchen. Nothing appeared out of order and she hurried to the living room. Hunter's computer was on, a document on the screen. She swung to the right. The puppies slept in the pen Hunter had constructed for them, a heap of soft, golden fur.

Nothing out of place.

Turning, she crossed to Hunter's bedroom. And found it much as she had the rest of the apartment. Feeling more than a little neurotic, she checked under the bed and in the closet.

Nothing. Thank God.

She laughed to herself and turned. Her gazed landed on Sarah. The dog sat at the closed bathroom door, nose pressed to the crack. She whined, pawed at the door.

The breath hissed past Avery's lips; her knees went weak.

Screwing up her courage, she inched toward the closed door. She reached the dog. Hand visibly trembling, Avery reached for the knob, grasped it and twisted.

The door eased open. Sarah charged through. Avery stumbled in after. Something brushed against her ankles and a scream flew to her throat.

A puppy, Avery realized. One of Sarah's pups had gotten locked in the bathroom.

Avery crossed to the commode, sank onto it. She dropped her head into her hands. She was losing it. Going around the bend at the speed of light.

As if sensing her distress, Sarah laid her head in Avery's lap. Avery stroked the dog's silky head and ears, then patted her side. "I bet I look pretty silly to you."

The dog thumped her tail against the tile floor.

"Where'd he go, girl?"

Sarah lifted her head, expression baleful. Avery pressed her forehead to the dog's. "Right. He didn't take me either. How about we wait together?"

Sarah wagged her tail, collected her wayward pup by the scruff of its neck and carried it back to its brothers and sisters.

Avery followed, thoughts racing. Hunter had left his computer on, document up. She crossed to his desk, sat and closed the document. She saw that he had last saved at 7:37 that morning. Right about the time she had called. Just before. That meant that he hadn't written since they'd spoken. She glanced at her watch. Five hours ago.

She frowned. Computer on. Document up. Door unlocked. Where could he have gone?

A scrap of paper peeking out from the keyboard caught her eye. She inched it out.

Gwen's name. Her room number at The Guesthouse.

Avery gazed at the notation. At Hunter's bold print. A tingling sensation started at her fingertips and spread. Why had he written this? Why would he have needed to know her room number?

Hunter had left before the storm hit. Because of Sarah, he'd said. How did she know he'd even gone home? Maybe he had left her and gone to Gwen's?

She had told him about Gwen. Everything. How they had

met. About her brother. The gutted cat. That she had interviewed Trudy Pruitt.

He had stopped on that, she recalled. He had looked strange, she remembered. Shaken.

Hunter's voice on the answering machine.

Avery brought a hand to her mouth, thoughts tumbling one over another. Hunter had returned to Cypress Springs about ten months ago.

About the time the rash of unexpected deaths had started. *No.* She shook her head. *Not Hunter.*

Cherry's words rang in her head. *He's come home to hurt us. To punish us.*

Someone her father had trusted, someone he would open the door to in the middle of the night.

"Your father and I had become friends. Every time we were together, he talked about you."

Run, Avery. Go as fast as you can.

With a sense of inevitability, Avery reopened the computer document and read:

His thoughts settled on vengeance. On the act he had just carried out. Some thought revenge an ugly, futile endeavor. He fed on it. On thoughts of the pain he could inflict. Punishment deserved—

Avery leaped to her feet. The chair went sailing backward. *Not Hunter! It couldn't be true.*

She took a deep breath, fighting for calm. A clear head. Her gaze settled on the desk once again, its drawers. She tried them. And found them locked.

She had found the paper with Gwen's name on it, maybe she would find something else.

She hoped to God she didn't.

Turning, she headed for the bedroom. She went to the closet, rifled through it, then turned to the dresser. There, underneath some sweaters, she found a plastic storage bag. With trembling fingers she eased it from under the garments and held it up.

Tom Lancaster's Tulane University ID card. A cheap gold crucifix. A man's class ring.

A cry of disbelief slipped past her lips. She dropped the bag, turned and ran blindly for the door. What to do? Where to go? Buddy? Matt?

Gwen. Dear God, let her be all right.

Even as the prayer ran through her head, fear clawed at her. The sense of impending disaster. That it was too late. That the clock had just stopped.

She had been sleeping with the enemy.

She made it to her car. Fighting hysteria, she unlocked it and climbed inside. It took her three tries, but she finally got the keys into the ignition and the vehicle started.

She glanced out her window. Several people on the sidewalk had stopped and were staring at her.

She jerked away from the curb—a kid on a bike appeared before her and she slammed on the brakes. The momentum of the vehicle jerked her against the safety harness, knocking the wind out of her.

The kid whizzed by. She collected herself and merged into traffic, gripping the steering wheel so tightly her fingers went numb. The sound of a siren penetrated her panic. She glanced in the rearview mirror. A sheriff's cruiser, cherry lights flashing.

Matt! She pulled over. Tumbled out of the vehicle and ran to him. He met her halfway. Caught her in his arms.

"Avery, thank God you're safe." He held her tightly to his chest. "When I heard, I was so afraid—"

She clung to him. "How did you know about Hunter? When did you find out?"

"Hunter?" He frowned, searching her gaze, his concerned. "What are you talking about?"

"But I thought...the way you pulled me over..."

Her words trailed off. She went cold with dread. "What's wrong, Matt? What's happened?"

"Your parents' house is on fire. I just got the call."

CHAPTER 48

Avery left her car and rode with Matt. She smelled the fire a block before she saw the flames. Saw the smoke billowing up into the pristine blue spring sky. The two trucks came into view next, the pumper and water truck, lights flashing. Half a dozen guys had turned out, the firefighters in their chartreuse coats and helmets, hoses spewing water at the dancing flames.

Then she caught sight of the house. The fire had completely engulfed the structure. A cry ripped past her lips. Until that moment, she had hoped—prayed—Matt was wrong. That it was a mistake.

Matt stopped the car and she stumbled out. The heat slammed into her, the acrid smell of smoke. Her eyes and throat burned. She brought a hand to her mouth, holding back a cry.

Neighbors clustered around the perimeter of the scene, huddling together, their expressions ranging from fear and disbelief to horrified fascination. They glanced at her, then looked away. As if ashamed. As if in meeting her eyes, her tragedy became theirs. And because they were so very grateful this had happened to her not them.

If they looked away, maybe they could pretend it hadn't happened.

She hugged herself, chilled despite the heat. Lucky them. She wished she could pretend. That her childhood home wasn't in flames. Gone, she thought. All her parents' things. Mementos. The photographs she had looked at that very morning. Gone. Forever.

She had nothing left to remember them by.

"Wait here," Matt said. "I'm going to see if I can help." He hesitated, searching her expression, his concerned. "Are you going to be all right?"

A hysterical-sounding laugh raced to her lips. Oh sure, she thought. Just dandy.

"Fine," she managed to say. "Go."

He squeezed her hand, then disappeared. She watched him, and turned at the sound of her name. Buddy had arrived and was hurrying toward her.

She ran to him. He enfolded her in his arms, holding her tightly. "When the call came in, I was so frightened. No one knew if you were in the house. Thank God you're all right. Thank God."

She clung to him. "What am I going to do, Buddy? I've lost everything."

"Not us, baby girl," he said fiercely. "You haven't lost us."

"Where will I go? Where is home now?"

"You will stay with us as long as you like. We're your family now, Avery. That hasn't changed. It will never change."

"Ms. Chauvin?"

She glanced over her shoulder at John Price, the firefighter she'd met at her father's wake. He took off his helmet. His dark hair was plastered to his head with sweat, his face black with soot. "I'm sorry we couldn't save it, Ms. Chauvin. I'm really...sorry."

She nodded, unable to speak. She shifted her gaze. Ben Mitchell, the arson investigator, had arrived; he was conferring with Matt. They disappeared around the side of the house.

"Do you know how this happened?" she asked.

The fireman shook his head. "Arson takes over from here."

"I don't understand how...I was home this morning. I used my laptop, made some coffee, everything was fine."

The man shifted his helmet from one hand to the other, expression uneasy. "You have to know how odd this is, considering your father's death."

Her dad had burned. Now his house. A small sound passed her lips. Until that moment she hadn't made that connection.

One of his colleagues called him. "I've got to go. Ben's good, he'll figure it out."

Buddy put an arm around her shoulders. "Here comes Matt and Mitchell."

Avery turned. Waited. When they reached her, Matt and his dad exchanged glances, their expressions grim.

"Looks like arson, Avery," Matt said. "Whoever did it left the fuel can."

"Arson," she repeated. "But why...who—"

"Can you account for your whereabouts for the last few hours?" Ben Mitchell asked.

"Yes, I—"

The journals. Going to The Guesthouse, looking for Gwen. Leaving the note.

Hunter. Gwen's name and room number scrawled on paper by his computer.

"Avery?" Matt laid his hands on her shoulders. "Earlier,

you said something about Hunter. You asked me how I had found out. What were you talking about?"

She stared at her friend, mouth working. She fought to think clearly. To focus. Not to panic.

Her mother's journals. Evidence of The Seven. Of something wrong with the Waguespack murder investigation.

All destroyed in the fire. All but...

But she hadn't told anyone about the journals.

"Avery?" Matt shook her lightly. "Avery, what—"

"You have to help me, Matt." She caught his hands. "You have to come with me now."

"Avery," Buddy said softly, "you're in shock. You need to rest. Come home with me and—"

"No!" She shook her head. "A friend. Gwen Lancaster, she's in trouble." Her voice rose. "You have to help me!"

"Okay," Buddy said softly, tone soothing. "I'll help you. We'll go find this friend of yours. Everything will be fine."

"I'll go, Dad." Matt looked from Avery to her father. "You've got your hands full here."

Buddy looked as if he wanted to argue, then nodded. "Okay, but keep me posted. And bring her back to the ranch. Lilah and Cherry will get her fixed up for the night."

Matt agreed and they walked to his cruiser. He helped her into the vehicle, went around and climbed behind the wheel. He looked at her. "Where are we going?"

"The Guesthouse. I think there might have been another murder."

CHAPTER 49

Matt flipped on the vehicle's cherry lights and siren and threw the cruiser into gear. He flew through the streets, handling the vehicle like a professional driver, the only indication of his distress the muscle that jumped in his jaw.

"What the hell's going on, Avery?" He didn't take his eyes from the road. "How do you know Gwen Lancaster?"

"It's a long story." She wrapped her arms around her middle. "Do you know her?"

"Yes, because of her brother. I worked on the investigation." He paused. "I felt real bad for her. She seemed like a nice person."

"And now she's dead, too."

"We don't know that."

"Then where is she?" Her voice rose, hysteria pulling at her. "We were supposed to talk. She didn't call. She wouldn't have left without—"

"Stop it," he said sharply. "We don't know she's dead. Until there's a body, we'll presume she's alive. Okay?"

They arrived at The Guesthouse. He screamed to a stop; they piled out and hurried up the walk. Unlike earlier, Laurie sat at the front desk. She stood as they entered. "Matt, Avery, what—"

"Have you seen Gwen Lancaster today?"

Her gaze moved between them. "No, I—"

"Mind if we go upstairs?" She shook her head. "We may need you to open the door."

It was only the second time Avery had seen Matt acting in an official capacity and she acknowledged being impressed. And a bit taken aback. Gone was the aw-shucks small-town sheriff, replaced by a determined lawman whose tone left no doubt he meant business.

The three hurried up the stairs. Matt rapped on Gwen's door. "Sheriff, Ms. Lancaster." When he repeated the process without answer, he turned to Laurie. "Open it, please."

Laurie nodded, face deathly pale. She took out a master key, unlocked the door and stepped back.

"Wait downstairs for now. But don't leave the premises, I may need to question you." He softened his tone. "Please, Laurie."

The woman hesitated for a fraction of a moment, then backed toward the stairs. Avery watched her, frowning. She looked frightened.

Did she know more than she was telling? Had she played some part in Gwen's disappearance?

Matt unsheathed his service weapon. "Stay put, Avery." He stepped across the threshold, Colt .45 out. "Sheriff!" he called.

He disappeared into the unit, reappearing several moments later, features tight.

"Is she—"

"No."

Avery brought a hand to her chest, relieved. "Thank God. I was so worried."

"I'd like you to look around. You might see something I missed." He paused. "But don't touch anything. Take as few steps as possible."

"I don't understand."

"The fewer people through a crime scene the better."

"But you said she...wasn't dead. You said you didn't find evidence of..."

Her words trailed off. He hadn't said either of those things, she realized.

"Until we find a body, we presume she's alive."

Obviously, he hadn't found a body.

But he had found something else.

She stepped inside. Moved her gaze over the room. "She's cleaned up. The last time I was here, the place had been ransacked."

"Ransacked?" he repeated, scowling at her. "Just how much haven't you told me?"

She met his eyes, feeling like an idiot. "A lot."

His mouth thinned, but he didn't comment. Instead, he motioned to the room. "Anything else?"

She carefully studied the interior. The unmade bed, robe thrown over the foot. Blinds open, Gwen's running shoes on the floor by the bed.

Her gaze stopped at what appeared to be a puddle. "The floor's wet."

"Excuse me?"

"Look."

She pointed. He crossed to the spot, squatted, dipped his middle and index fingers into the liquid and brought his fingers to his nose. "Water."

He shifted his gaze toward the bathroom. "There's another."

In all they found three in what appeared to be a line from the bathroom to the bed.

"What do you think it means?" she asked.

"Don't know yet." He touched her arm. "I need you to take a look at this."

He led her to the bathroom. A circular-shaped bloodstain marred the white wooden door. Splatters radiated from the circle, drips from the bottom of the stain.

Avery stared at the mark, pinpoints of lights dancing in front of her gaze.

"Blood's dry." He leaned close, examining the mark but not touching it. "A few strands of hair," he murmured. "Maybe some tissue."

"I don't feel so good," she said, swaying slightly.

He caught her arm, steadying her. "Are you okay?"

"No."

He led her out of the unit and into the hall. He ordered her to sit.

She did, lowering her head to her knees. She breathed deeply through her nose until she felt steady enough to lift her head.

"My note's gone," she said.

"You left a note?"

"Slid it under her door. Around noon." She realized what that meant and brought a hand to her chest, relieved. "If she picked it up, she's alive."

"*If* she picked it up. Someone else may have."

"But who? The door was locked." She shook her head, refusing to acknowledge he had a point. "No, she got it."

"Avery—" He squatted in front of her, caught her hands, gripping them tightly. "The blood's completely dry. It's been there a while."

"I don't understand what you're..." Her words trailed off as she got it.

"I'm sorry, Avery. I really am."

She brought her head to her knees once more.

"She could have fallen," he said softly. "Have you checked the hospitals?"

She looked up, hopeful. "No."

"I'll do it. I need to make a few calls, including one to Dad. Order an evidence crew over. Talk to Laurie, her family. The other guests. But first, I think we should talk."

"Talk," she repeated weakly. "Now?"

"It's important." He rubbed her hands between his. "I need you to tell me everything. Are you up to it?"

She managed a nod. "I'll try."

"That's my girl. First, how did you become involved with Gwen Lancaster?"

As quickly and as succinctly as she could, Avery filled him in on how she and Gwen had become acquainted. She explained about Gwen coming to her with proof of The Seven's existence. The suicides, the freak accidental deaths. "I didn't believe her until I researched at the *Gazette*. When I saw all the deaths...there...in black and white, I couldn't ignore her. Plus, she believed my father was murdered."

"And that's what you believed?"

She laced her fingers. "I just couldn't accept he had killed himself."

"Go on."

"So we joined forces."

He paused a moment as if mulling over what she had told him, putting the various pieces together, filling in the blanks. "Why did you believe she had been murdered?"

"Because we had arranged to speak by phone and I wasn't able to reach her. And because The Seven knew she was onto them. They had given her a warning."

He frowned. "What kind of warning?"

"A gutted cat. They ransacked her room. Stole her notes and interview tapes." When he simply stared at her, she stiffened her spine. "You think I'm making all this up, don't you? You think I'm losing my mind."

"I wish I did. As unbelievable as this all is, I can't discount it." He pointed. "That bloodstain is stopping me. The fact that she's missing. And that two other women are dead."

He paused. "The note you left, what did it say, Avery?"

"To call me. That I had found some evidence." It seemed a lifetime already since this morning, so much had happened. "Sallie Waguespack was pregnant, Matt."

He looked startled. "Are you certain?"

"It was in my mother's journals. She had...boxes of—" Her voice broke.

All gone. Her parents. Her childhood home. Every memento of growing up, ash now.

"He burned my house down. Because of the journals. He found out somehow. He killed Gwen. And the others. I found evidence. Trophies."

Matt leaned toward her. "Who, Avery? Who did it?"

"Hunter," she said, words sticking in her throat. "I think Hunter did it."

CHAPTER 50

After the sheriff's department criminalists arrived at the scene, Matt drove her out to his parents' house. As they drove across town, she detailed everything that had happened in the past few days—about her and Gwen going to Trudy Pruitt's trailer and finding Hunter's message on the woman's voice mail; discovering Gwen's name and room number scrawled on a paper by his computer; realizing that all the deaths had begun after Hunter's return to Cypress Springs; and then finding the Ziploc bag of personal items that had obviously belonged to the victims.

"It's my fault," she said as he drew the vehicle to a stop in the driveway. "I told him about Gwen. About what we discovered. That she had interviewed Trudy Pruitt." Her voice thickened. "I trusted him, Matt."

He turned and drew her into his arms. Held her tightly. When he released her, she saw that his eyes were bright with unshed tears.

She realized how hard this must be for him. Hunter was his brother. His twin.

His other half.

She brought a hand to his cheek. "Matt, I don't know what to say. I wish—"

"Shh." He brought her hand to his mouth. "We'll have time for this later. I have to go. Are you going to be all right?"

She forced lightness into her tone. "With Lilah and Cherry cooing and clucking over me, are you kidding?"

He glanced toward the doorway where his mother and sister waited. "I'll come by later. Okay?"

She said it was and climbed out of the cruiser. She watched him back out of the driveway, then turned and started toward the two women.

Lilah hugged her. "Avery, honey, I don't know what to say. I'm devastated."

Cherry touched her arm. "Don't worry about a thing, Avery. If I don't have something you need, I'll go out and buy it."

"Buddy called. He said it was arson." Lilah shuddered. "Who would do such a thing?"

Avery didn't want to talk about it. Truth was, she had neither the energy nor heart for it.

There would be time for talking, hashing and rehashing. Time to break it to Lilah what her son had become. She prayed she wasn't around when that happened.

"Would you mind terribly if we didn't talk about it right now? I'm just...overwhelmed."

"Poor baby. Of course I don't mind." The woman's cheeks

turned rosy. "Maybe you should lie down, take a little nap. I know everything is clearer when I'm rested."

"Thank you, Lilah. You're so good to me."

The woman looked at her daughter. "Why don't you take Avery up to the guest room. I'll get some towels and soap for the guest bath."

"Sure." She smiled sympathetically at Avery. "I'll grab you a change of clothes, in case you want to clean up."

"Thanks," Avery said, realizing then that she smelled of smoke.

They started upstairs. Halfway up, Lilah stopped them. Avery glanced back. "I'm fixing baked macaroni and cheese for supper. With blueberry pie for dessert. We'll eat about six."

Avery managed a small smile, though thoughts of eating couldn't be farther from her mind.

Cherry left her at the guest room, then returned moments later with clothes and a basket of toiletries, including a new toothbrush. Cherry held the items out. "If you need anything else, just ask."

Avery saw real concern in her eyes. She experienced a twinge of guilt for her former suspicions about the other woman. "Thank you, Cherry, I...really appreciate this."

"It's the least I—" She took a step backward. "Bathroom's all yours."

"Thanks." Avery hugged the items to her chest. "I think I...a shower will be nice."

"Are you going to be all right?"

"I'll manage. Thanks for worrying about me. It means a lot."

Avery watched Cherry hurry down the hall, then retreated to the silence of her room. As that silence surrounded her, the smell of the fire filled her head.

With it came the image of her family's home being engulfed in flames. And a feeling of despair. Of betrayal.

Hunter, how could you?

Turning, she carried the toiletries and clothes to the guest bath, which was accessible from the bedroom. A Jack and Jill-style bath, consisting of one bath and commode area, flanked on either side by individual sink and dressing areas. She locked the door that led to the other bedroom's dressing area.

A half hour later she stepped out dressed in the pair of light-weight, drawstring cotton pants and white T-shirt Cherry had lent her, the smell of the fire scrubbed from her hair and skin. She towel-dried and combed her hair, then crossed to the bed. Sank onto a corner.

She closed her eyes. Her head filled with images—of fire engulfing her home, of Gwen's name and room number scrawled on a paper by Hunter's manuscript, of blood smeared across the wall of Trudy Pruitt's trailer.

Her cell phone rang.

She jumped, startled, then scrambled across the bed for her purse. She grabbed it, dug inside for the device. She answered before it rang a third time. "Gwen, is that—"

"Ms. Chauvin?"

Her heart sank. "Yes?"

"Dr. Harris. I apologize for it having taken so long for me to get back to you, I had some trouble locating the information you needed."

Avery frowned, confused. *Dr. Harris? Why was he—*

Then she remembered—the autopsy report. Her call to the coroner that morning seemed a light-year ago.

"Ms. Chauvin, are you there?"

"Yes, sorry. It's been a rough day."

"And I'm afraid my news won't make it any better. There was no autopsy performed on Sallie Waguespack."

"No autopsy," she repeated. "Aren't autopsies always performed in the case of a murder?"

"Yes, I'm surprised as well. That said, however, because of the circumstances, the coroner determined an autopsy unnecessary."

"The coroner has that option?"

"Certainly." He paused a moment. "With a typical homicide, the lawyers will require one. The police or victim's family."

"But the Waguespack murder wasn't a typical homicide."

"Far from it. The perpetrators were dead, there would be no trial. No lawyers requiring proof of cause of death. The police had plenty of evidence to support their conclusion, including the murder weapon."

"An open and closed case," she murmured. *Perfect for a setup. Everything tied up nice and neat.*

"Would you have made that call, Dr. Harris?"

"Me? No. But that's my way. When it comes to the cessation of life, I don't take anything for granted." He paused, cleared his throat. "I have one more piece of information that's going to surprise you, Ms. Chauvin. Dr. Badeaux wasn't the coroner on this homicide."

She straightened. "He wasn't. Then who—"

"Your father was, Avery. Dr. Phillip Chauvin."

CHAPTER 51

Avery sat stone still, heart and thoughts racing, cell phone still clutched in her hands. Dr. Harris had explained. Dr. Badeaux had employed two deputy coroners, all West Feliciana Parish physicians, all appointed by him. The coroner or one of his deputies went to the scene of every death, be it from natural causes, the result of accident, suicide or homicide.

The night of the Waguespack murder, Dr. Badeaux had been winging his way to Paris for a second honeymoon. Her dad had been the closest deputy coroner. When Dr. Badeaux had returned, Sallie Waguespack had been in the ground. He had accepted his deputy's call and it had stood for fifteen years.

"My boys didn't kill that Sallie Waguespack. They was framed."

"Your father got what he deserved."

Trudy Pruitt had been telling the truth. Her sons had been framed. And her father had been a part of it.

Betrayal tasted bitter against her tongue. She leaped to her feet, began to pace. She couldn't believe her father would do this. She'd thought him the most honorable man she had ever known. The most moral, upright.

The box of clippings, she realized. That was why he had saved them all these years. As a painful reminder.

What he'd done would have eaten at him. She hadn't a doubt about that. All these years...had he feared exposure? Or had he longed for it?

That was it, she thought. The why. He hadn't been able to live with his guilt any longer. But he hadn't killed himself. He had decided to come clean. Clear the Pruitt boys' names.

And he had been murdered for it.

But why had he done it? For whom had he lied?

His best friend. Sheriff Buddy Stevens.

Avery squeezed her eyes shut. Buddy had lied to her. The day she'd gone to see him, about having found the clippings. She had asked him why her father would have followed this murder so closely, why he would have kept the box of news stories all these years. She had asked if her dad had been involved with the investigation in any way.

Buddy had claimed he hadn't had a clue why her father would have clipped those stories, that her father hadn't been in any way involved in the investigation.

He'd been up to his eyeballs in this. They both had been.

She recalled the words in her mother's journal. That after the murder everything had been different. That her father and Buddy's relationship had been strained. Hunter had claimed that their fathers never even spoke anymore.

What could cause such a serious rift between lifelong friends?

The answer was clear. For a friend, her dad had gone against his principles. Afterward, he had hated both himself and his friend for it.

That poor woman. And pregnant, too.

Pregnant. With whose baby?

Avery didn't like what she was thinking. She glanced toward the doorway. Lilah was in the kitchen, preparing dinner. She would know. Like her mother, she had lived through it. Had watched as best friends grew distant, then to despise one another.

Avery grabbed her handbag, with the two journals tucked inside, and slipped into her shoes. She went to the bedroom door and peeked out. The house was quiet save for sounds coming from the kitchen.

She slipped into the hall and down the stairs. From the study came the sound of Cherry and Buddy, talking softly. Avery tiptoed past the closed door and headed to the kitchen.

Lilah glanced over her shoulder at her and smiled. Avery saw that she was grating cheese. She wore a ruffled, floral apron—a flour smudge decorated her nose and right cheek. The blueberry pie, pretty as a picture from *Bon Appétit,* sat cooling on a rack by the oven.

"You look refreshed," she said brightly.

"At least I don't reek of smoke anymore."

"There's something to the whole comfort-food thing, don't you think?" She turned back to her grating. "Macaroni and cheese, chicken pot pie, tuna casserole. Good, old-fashioned stick-to-your-ribs stuff. Just thinking about it makes one feel better."

If only it was so easy, Avery thought, watching her work. If only life were so simple. Like something out of *Life* magazine in the 1950s. Or an episode of an old TV show.

Life wasn't like that, no matter how much she longed for

it to be. The picture Lilah presented was wrong. She saw that now. A deception. An illusion.

A picture-perfect mask to hide the truth from the world.

But what was the truth?

Avery opened her handbag and drew out the journal from 1988. "Lilah," she said softly, "I need to ask you something. It's important."

The woman glanced at her. Her gaze dropped to Avery's hands. "What's that?"

"One of my mother's journals. I found it in my parents' attic."

"But I thought your father had gotten rid of them."

"No. Mother had packed them away. They were almost all lost in the fire."

Lilah's expression altered slightly. Her gaze skittered from Avery's to the journal. "Not that one."

"No. Or one other."

"Thank God for that."

"Yes." Avery carefully slid it back into her purse. "I discovered something interesting in this journal, Lilah. I wanted to ask you about it."

"Sure, hon." She went to the refrigerator and retrieved a jug of milk. She filled a measuring cup full. "What do you need to know?"

"Whose baby was Sallie Waguespack carrying?"

The measuring cup slipped from her fingers. It hit the countertop and milk spewed across the country-blue Formica. With a small cry, she began mopping up the mess.

"Lilah?"

"I don't know what you're talking about."

"Yes, you do. Whose baby was it?"

Lilah's movements stilled. The kitchen was silent save for the steady drip drip of milk dropping onto the tile floor.

"They're all dead now, Lilah. Everyone connected with the

Waguespack murder investigation. All of them but Buddy. Do you know how damning that is?"

Lilah whimpered. Avery took a step toward her. "What really happened that night? Buddy, my dad, Pat Greene, they were all in on it. All covering up for somebody. Who was it, Lilah? Who?"

Avery grabbed her arm. "Those boys were framed, weren't they? They didn't kill Sallie Waguespack."

Lilah's mouth moved, but no sound emerged. Avery shook her. "Those boys were sacrificial lambs. It's in the journal, Lilah! I discovered it this morning. You were the only person I mentioned the journals to. Who did you tell? That's why my house was torched, to destroy the evidence!"

A sound of pain escaped Lilah's lips. "No. Please, it's not—"

"Stop protecting him, Lilah. You have to come clean. You have to make this right." She lowered her voice, pleading. "Only you can do it, Lilah. Only you can—"

"It was Buddy's baby!" she said, the words exploding from her. "He betrayed me, our children. This town. By day, Mr. Morality. Lecturing about how the citizens needed to take action, restore Cypress Springs to a God-fearing, law-abiding place to live. By night fornicating with that...with that cheap whore!"

Her tears came then, deep wrenching sobs. She doubled over. Her small frame shaking with the force of her despair.

"And she became pregnant."

"Yes." Lilah looked up, expression naked with pain. "That's when Buddy confessed to me what had been going on, that the woman was pregnant. I hadn't...I never—"

She bit the words back but they landed between them— *She hadn't known. She never suspected.*

Avery's heart went out to the other woman. She had always thought the Stevenses had the perfect marriage. Apparently, Lilah had thought so, too.

"She was going to make trouble for him. She wanted to ruin him. Make it public. Shame him...all of us."

Lilah met Avery's gaze, calm seeming to move over her. "I couldn't have that. I couldn't have my family exposed to his filth. I couldn't let that happen."

"What did you do?" Avery asked softly, though she already knew.

"I went to see her. To beg her to keep quiet. To do the right thing." An angry sound escaped her. "The right thing? I was so naive. Sallie Waguespack wouldn't know the right thing if it hit her with a sledgehammer.

"She laughed at me. Called me pathetic. The stupid little *housewife*." Lilah fisted her fingers. "She bragged about how she seduced him, about the...sex they had. She bragged about being pregnant. She promised that before she gave up Chief Raymond 'Buddy' Stevens, she would drag him and his family through the mud.

"We were in the kitchen. I was crying, begging her to shut up. I saw a knife on the counter." Lilah's eyes took on a glazed look. "I didn't do it on purpose. You have to believe me."

"Go on, Lilah. Tell me everything."

"I picked up the knife and I...stabbed her. Again and again. I didn't even realize...until...the blood. It was everywhere."

Avery took a step back, found the counter, leaned on it for support. "So Buddy took care of it for you," Avery whispered.

"Yes. I didn't ask him to. He told me to stay put, that he would take care of everything. But I didn't understand what that meant... didn't know until...the next day."

He framed the Pruitt boys. Manufactured the evidence against them and covered up the evidence against his wife.

He called upon his best friend to help. Pat Greene and Kevin Gallagher, too.

"I've had to live with that all these years. The guilt. The self-hatred. Those boys...what I did—"

She curved her arms around her middle, seeming to fold

Erica Spindler

in on herself. "We were all so close back then. The best of friends. Buddy begged your daddy to lie, to make the medical facts agree with the evidence. To not request an autopsy. It was easy because the Pruitt boys were dead."

"And nothing would have to stand up to the scrutiny of a trial."

"Yes. Phillip couldn't live with the guilt at what he'd done. That's why he did it. Why he killed himself. I wish to God I had the guts to do the same! My children...my friends, I ruined everything!"

The kitchen door flew open. Buddy charged through, Cherry behind him, expression stricken.

"Enough!" he roared, face mottled with angry color.

Lilah cringed. Cherry rushed to her mother's side, drew her protectively into her arms.

Avery turned to the man she had once thought of as a second father. "It's too late, Buddy. How could you?"

"I never wanted you to know, Avery," he said, tone heavy with regret. "Your father didn't want you to know."

Avery trembled with anger. With betrayal. "How do you know what my father wanted? You used your friendship to force him to lie!"

He shook his head. "I only wanted to protect my family. You understand that, don't you, Avery? What happened wasn't Lilah's fault. I couldn't allow her to go to jail for my mistakes. My sins. Your father understood. Sallie's death was a crime of passion, not premeditated murder."

"Pat Greene didn't see the Pruitt boys leaving Sallie Waguespack's that night, did he?"

"No. I told him I did. Confessed to having an affair with her. Asked him to help me out. Because of how it looked."

"And he believed you?"

"He was my friend. He trusted me."

She made a sound of derision. "And the murder weapon in the ditch behind their trailer—"

"I planted it. The prints on the weapon and the blood on Donny's shoe as well. Pat didn't know."

She had looked up to him. Loved him. To know he had done this hurt. Her vision swam. "And Kevin Gallagher?"

"Kevin prepared Sallie for burial. All he knew was she was pregnant. I asked him to keep it quiet. Why exacerbate the situation? Why smear the poor woman's name any further?"

"And my dad?"

He drew a heavy breath. "Your daddy was hard to convince. In the end, he did it not just for me, but for Lilah and the kids."

"Those two boys," she whispered. "They were—"

"Trash. Delinquents. Only nineteen and twenty and had been busted a half-dozen times each. For drugs, attempted rape, drunk and disorderly conduct. They were never going to amount to anything. Never going to contribute anything to society but ills. To sacrifice them to save my family, it wasn't a difficult decision."

"You don't get to play God, Buddy. It's not your job."

His mouth twisted. "Your daddy said the same. I guess that old saying about the apple not falling far from the tree is true."

"What about Sal?" she asked. "Why include him, Buddy? You needed the *Gazette,* but for what? Swaying public opinion?"

"He wasn't included. He thought the crime went down exactly as officially reported. But I was able to use Sal and the *Gazette* as a way to focus the public's attention on the social context of the crime. Whip them into a state of outrage over the crime rate, the immorality of the young, the drug epidemic, and take their attention away from the crime itself."

"You bought into your own spin, didn't you?" Avery all but spat the words at him. "And The Seven was born. You and your buddies all got together to decide what was appropriate behavior and what wasn't. You took the law into your own hands, Buddy. You and your group became judge and jury. And things got out of hand."

"It wasn't like that. We loved this community, all of us did. We had—have—its good at heart. We only want to make life better, to keep things the way they had been. We keep watch on our friends and fellow citizens. Monitor the important things. If need be, we pay a friendly visit. Use a little muscle if necessary."

"Muscle? A palatable euphemism for what? A brick through the window? The threat of broken bones? Financial ruin through boycotts? Or just good old-fashioned cross burnings on the front lawn? What's the criteria for a death penalty in Cypress Springs?"

He looked shocked. "Good God, Avery, it's nothing like that. We're not terrorists. We're not killers. We offer help. Guidance. If that doesn't work, we suggest a change of residence." He lowered his voice. "If we didn't make things a little uncomfortable for them, what would their motivation for change be?"

She made a sound of disgust. "Motivation for change? You make me sick."

"You don't understand. It's all done in the spirit of caring and community concern. Nobody gets hurt."

"Actually, I think I understand too well." Avery glanced at Cherry. She was holding her mother, crying quietly. She returned her gaze to Buddy. "You're such a hypocrite. Making like you're Mr. Morality. Persecuting others for their sins, when all the while you're the biggest sinner of all."

Tears glistened in his eyes. "Do you think I haven't suffered for my sins? A day doesn't go by that I don't wish I could go back, do it all over. I had everything. A beautiful family. The love of a wonderful woman. The respect of my friends and the community. If I could make that choice again, I wouldn't go near Sallie Waguespack. None of this would have happened."

He held out a hand to her. "Don't look at me like that," he pleaded. "Like I'm some sort of monster. I'm still Buddy, you're still my baby girl."

"No." She took a step back. "Not anymore. Never again."

"You have to understand. I was afraid for my family. I did what I had to in order to protect them." He took another step toward her. "I had to do it, don't you see? A man protects his family."

"At all costs, Buddy?" she asked. "What lengths would you go? From covering up a murder to committing one?"

"No, never."

"Everybody involved in the cover-up is dead now, Buddy. Everyone but you. What am I supposed to think?"

"Daddy?" Cherry whispered. "What's she talking about?"

Buddy glanced nervously at his daughter. "It's not true, sweetheart. Don't listen to her. She's had a shock. She's confused."

"I'm not confused. You killed all your old friends. Why? Did they threaten to come clean? Go to the Feds because the guilt had become too much for them to live with? Is that why you killed your best friend, Buddy? Why you immobilized him, doused him in diesel fuel and—"

"No!" Lilah cried out. "No!"

Buddy darted his gaze between the women. "It's not true! I didn't have anything to do with that. I couldn't! I—"

"You went in the middle of the night. He opened the door because he trusted you. You immobilized him with a stun gun. Then you carried him out to the garage, doused him with fuel and set him on fire!"

"No!" His face went white.

"Hunter had nothing to do with any of this. You set up your own son."

"No. You have to believe me!"

"I can't believe anything you say. Not now. Not ever again."

It all made sense now—Lilah's depression and addiction.

Hunter's break with the family. Cherry's dedication to keeping the family together, to making them look happy and normal.

"No one needs to know, Avery." Buddy lowered his voice, tone soothing. "We're a family. We're your family. We love you."

Tears choked her. She shook her head. She had believed that once. Had thought of this family as an extension of her own. "It's over, Buddy."

"We're all you have left, Avery." He took a step toward her, forcing her backward. "Cypress Springs is your home."

He took another step. He had her cornered, she realized. Had backed her into a wall, the only way out through him. She tamped down her rising panic.

"I'll need those journals." He held out a hand. "Laurie called me. Told me you'd been there. That you'd left Lancaster a note."

"One of your many spies."

"She was worried about you."

"Right. Worried about me."

"We love you, Avery," Lilah whispered. "You're one of us."

"Yes," Cherry piped in. "Give Dad the journals and everything will be okay."

Avery moved her gaze between the three, heart racing, struggling to stay calm. To assess her options. Three against one. One of them the size of a tree and packing a gun. Lilah looked on the verge of falling apart. Cherry seemed stunned, her reactions wooden. The little focus she possessed seemed directed toward supporting her mother.

Only Buddy posed a threat to her escape. Immobilize him and she could make it. But how?

Her pepper spray! She hadn't taken it out of her purse.

"Come on, baby girl." He stretched his hand out. "You know we only want the best for you. It's all in the past. We'll be one big, happy family."

"A family," she repeated, voice shaking. "You're right." She reached into her handbag. Her fingers closed around the cylinder of spray. She drew the can out and lunged forward, shooting the spray directly into Buddy's eyes, blinding him.

With a cry, he stumbled backward, clawing at his eyes. Avery darted past him. Out of the kitchen, into the front hall. She heard Lilah and Cherry calling her back.

The front door was locked. She fumbled with the dead bolt; after what seemed a century, it slid back and she raced out onto the porch. She paused there, realizing she didn't have a vehicle.

Behind her she heard the kitchen door fly open, heard the thunder of footfalls.

She leaped forward, hitting the stairs, racing down them. Into the yard. Avery glanced back. Buddy had gained on her, she saw. He called her name.

Headlights sliced across the dark road. Avery changed direction, running toward them, waving her arms wildly.

The white sedan pulled over. She grabbed the passenger door, yanked it open.

"Thank God! Can you giv—"

She bit the words back, a cry springing to her lips.

"Get in, Avery," Matt ordered. "Quickly, before it's too late."

She froze. Behind her, Buddy closed in.

She saw Matt had his gun. He motioned with it. "It wasn't Hunter," he said. "It was Dad. Come on, he's almost here."

She glanced back. Buddy was calling her name, going for his gun. She dived into the vehicle, yanking the door shut as she did.

Matt hit the autolock and floored the accelerator. The vehicle surged forward, fishtailing, tires squealing. Avery swiveled in her seat, craning her neck to see Buddy. He ran into the street, gave chase for a moment, then stopped.

She brought her shaking hands to her face, fighting hysteria. The urge to fall completely apart.

"Are you okay?"

She nodded, dropping her hands. "When did you...how did you find out—"

"About Dad?" He shook his head. "I love my dad. He's got a good heart, but he's weak. A total fuckup, Avery."

She didn't understand. "You're not making excuses for him, are you? He's a murderer, Matt."

Matt smiled. Oddly. Avery frowned, becoming suddenly aware of the closeness of the vehicle, that Matt kept one hand on his weapon, lying on the seat beside him.

The hair on the back of her neck prickled. "Aren't you going to put that away?"

He ignored her. "You were right to trust me, Avery. Dad's overemotional. He means to do the right thing, but emotion gets in the way. It's what makes him weak."

Matt was in cahoots with his dad. One of The Seven. An accomplice to murder.

And she had gotten into the car with him. He had a gun.

She saw a stop sign ahead. She shifted slightly in her seat in an attempt to hide what she was about to do. As he slowed the sedan, she inched her hand toward the door handle, grasped it and yanked.

The door didn't budge. Matt laughed and eased through the intersection without stopping. "Childproof locks, Avery. How stupid do you think I am?"

"I don't know what you're talking about, Matt. I didn't—"

"Say good-night, Avery."

Before she realized his intention, he struck her in the temple with the butt of his gun. Pain jackknifed through her skull; in the next instant, she felt nothing at all.

CHAPTER 52

Avery came to slowly. She ached all over; her head throbbed. Moaning, she opened her eyes.

She lay on a bed, she realized. A bare mattress. She tried to sit up but found she couldn't. Her arms had been anchored above her head, wrists bound tightly. Her legs were tied to opposite bedposts.

Buddy, his confession. Matt picking her up. The gun.

Fear exploded inside her. Blinding, white hot. It stole her ability to think. To reason. With it came panic. She fought her restraints, tugging and twisting, getting nowhere.

She stopped, wrists and ankles burning, breath coming in trembling gasps. Tears choked her. She fought them as well. She would not give in. She would not lie down and die.

They would not get away with this. She wouldn't let them.

In an attempt to center herself, Avery closed her eyes. She drew in as deep a breath as she could and expelled it slowly. Then repeated the process. She needed calm. Fear and panic bled her ability to think. To reason. She needed to be able to do both if she was going to escape.

She opened her eyes, a semblance of calm restored. The only light in the room came from the open doorway to the right of the bed. The air was damp, heavy. It stank, the smell familiar, though she couldn't place it. The single window stood open. From outside came the sounds of insects, more dense than she was accustomed to.

He had taken her outside the city limits. She traveled her gaze over the room, taking in what she could from her prone position. Spare. Rough-hewn. A hunting cabin, she thought. At the edge of woods. Or along the bayou.

The same one Gwen had been lured to? Avery searched her memory. Gwen had said the junction of Highway 421 and No Name Road.

That would put her south of Cypress Springs. Not far from the old canning factory.

The sour smell, she realized. Of course. The same smell that rolled into town when the wind shifted to a northerly direction.

The stench of the burned-out factory.

Matt appeared in the doorway, a dark silhouette against the rectangle of light. "Rise and shine, beautiful."

"Untie me and I will."

She all but spat the words at him and he laughed. "Somebody wake up on the wrong side of the bed?"

"Bastard."

He sauntered across the room, humming the tune from the children's nursery rhyme "The Itsy-Bitsy Spider." He reached the bed, bent and tiptoed his fingers up her thigh in time with the tune. She saw he had his gun tucked into the waistband of his jeans.

His fingers made the juncture of her thighs and stilled—the tune died on his lips. He cocked his head and gazed at her, expression curiously blank. "I'm sorry it's come to this, Avery. I really am."

"Then let me go, you psycho prick."

"Such language. I'm disappointed in you."

He climbed onto the bed and straddled her, placing a hand on either side of her head. The position brought his pelvis into contact with hers. The butt of the gun pressed into her abdomen.

"You betrayed me, Avery. You betrayed us."

"Don't talk to me about betrayal. You killed my father!"

He laughed softly and trailed a finger down the curve of her cheek, then lower, across her collarbone to her breast. "You always were too smart for your own good. Too opinionated."

He bent and kissed her. Lightly at first, then deeply, forcing his tongue into her mouth.

Avery fought the urge to fight and instead lay frozen beneath him. Her lack of response seemed to frustrate him and he broke the contact.

As he did, she spit in his face. He jerked away, face flooding with angry color. Rearing back, he slapped her. Her head snapped to the side; she tasted blood and saw stars.

But she didn't cry out. She wouldn't give him the satisfaction.

"You know what?" He curled his fingers around the neck of the T-shirt Cherry had lent her. "For a smart girl you do some really stupid things."

He yanked the fabric so hard she came off the bed. The T-shirt gave, ripping from neck to belly button, revealing her naked breasts. He covered them with his hands, squeezing tightly. "Like pissing off the guy who holds your life in his hands. And now, your breasts as well."

He tightened his grip, pinching the nipples, twisting. She swallowed the whimper of pain that flew to her lips. He bent forward so that his face hovered just above hers. His stale breath stirred against her cheek.

Avery shuddered. If the eyes were the windows to the soul, he had none.

"You were supposed to be mine. I chose you. Not once, but twice. And you broke my heart. The first time by leaving. The second by giving yourself to my brother."

He laughed. "You look so surprised. How stupid do you think I am? I was suspicious that day at Tiller's Pond. Like a fool, I gave you the benefit of the doubt. After I found you at his place that morning, I knew."

She whimpered, thinking of Hunter. Of what she had gotten him into.

And what she had suspected him of.

Matt's mouth twisted into a thin line. "Did you think of me, Avery? While you fucked my brother? While you betrayed—" He bit the words back, though he shook with a rage so potent the bed quaked with it.

He could kill her now, this moment.

He wanted to.

Avery shrank back against the mattress, losing her grip on her emotions. Fear became terror, rampaging through her.

For the first time, her own death became a stark reality. She pictured it. Matt's hands around her neck, squeezing and squeezing...being unable to fight him except with her frantic thoughts. Her silent screams for help.

Her fear seemed to calm him. He looked pleased. "I like you this way," he said softly, straightening. "Helpless."

He moved his hands over her breasts, his touch changing from punishing to coaxing. He brought his hands to her waist, then curved his fingers around the waistband of her drawstring pants.

"Remember how it used to be between us?" he asked, trailing his fingers across her abdomen, dipping them lower and dragging the fabric down. Revealing her belly button, then abdomen, the top of her panties and pubic mound.

He bent and pressed his face to the vee, breathing deeply, making a sound of pleasure. "When we were together this way?"

Bile rose in her throat. She fought gagging.

"It was so good. Nobody's ever come close to making me feel the way you did. We were meant to be together."

Get smart, Avery. Play along. Give him what he wants.
There was always a chance. Always.

"Yes," she whispered, voice quaking. "I remember."

"How did we come to this?" he whispered. "You left me. Why?"

"I was young. Stupid." She looked up at him in what she hoped he would take as adoration. "I didn't know how strong you were. I didn't see your power."

His mouth thinned in fury. "Don't bullshit me. You left. You fucked my brother. You—"

"I'm not!" she cried, cutting him off, trying another tack, using his own words against him. "I see it now, I understand why I left. I thought you were like...that you were going to be like your dad. I love him but he's not...not strong like you."

Matt stilled. His gaze bored into hers. She pressed on. "You were so brilliant. You sailed through school. Your SAT scores were perfect and yet...you chose to stay in Cypress Springs and go into law enforcement. Like your dad. You see why I thought that, Matt?"

He studied her a moment more, then inclined his head in agreement. "I needed to lead. I had a mission."

"I understand that now."

"Dad's weak. He's been a disappointment."

"Unwilling to do what's necessary," she said, making a guess.

"Exactly." He looked at her as if he was the proud parent she his gifted child. "Too often, his emotions rule. His heart."

He shook his head sadly. "A leader can't be swayed by emotion. A leader must always keep his focus on the big picture."

"The cause. In this case, the good of the community."

"Yes." Matt searched her gaze. "Dad was the leader of the original Seven. Did you know that?"

She shook her head.

"He proved too weak to lead. He bowed to pressure from others in the group. Mostly your father."

"My dad?" She struggled to inject just the right amount of surprise and disappointment into her tone.

"Oh yeah, your dad. The great Dr. Phillip Chauvin." Dislike dripped from each word. "He threatened to go to the Feds. They had crossed the line, he'd claimed."

Matt leaned closer. "There is no line when it comes to war. Do you understand, Avery? Life and death. Black or white. Win or lose."

"No compromise."

"Exactly." He trailed a finger tenderly over the curve of her cheek. "Some are sacrificed for the good of the many. Individual rights lost...but quality of life maintained."

"My father wouldn't go along with that?"

"A do-gooder pussy. He nearly ruined it for everyone."

She bit down on her lip to keep from defending her father. From cheering him aloud.

"Tonight, did Buddy tell you everything? About that night about Sallie Waguespack?" He answered his own question. "Of course he didn't. He wouldn't."

Matt laughed. "That night, Hunter and I had fought about that new kid, Mike Horn. Remember him? His dad was the plant manager over at the canning factory."

He didn't wait for her reply but went on. "I didn't like the way Mike was acting, like he owned the place. Like he was going to take *my* place. I figured we should give him a little lesson in humility, me, Hunter and a couple of the other guys. Hunter refused to back me up. Told me he liked Mike. And that what I wanted to do was wrong."

Matt's face twisted. "He'd been pulling that shit a lot that summer, refusing to go with the program. I called him on that. And on his feelings for you. He wanted to fuck you. I saw that, too. Everybody saw it. I accused him of doing it. We came to blows," he finished simply, "and he left the house. Went over to Karl's."

"Karl Wright's?"

"Yes. I couldn't sleep. I heard the front door. I thought Hunter had changed his mind, come home to apologize."

"But it wasn't Hunter?"

"No. It was Mother. She was sobbing, hysterical. Covered with blood. It was splattered on her hands and face. Her clothes."

"At first I panicked. I thought she was hurt. Then I realized what she was saying. She had killed someone. Dad's girlfriend. His lover. It was an accident, she didn't know what to do."

Avery pictured the scenario. Lilah covered with blood, hysterical. Matt sixteen and terrified. Reeling with all his mother was telling him.

"I didn't either. Dad was out. I didn't know for sure where. I couldn't call the department. So I went.

"It was just as Mom had said. With one exception—the woman wasn't dead. She must have lost consciousness. By the trail of blood, I saw that sometime between when Mom left and I arrived, she had tried to pull herself to the door. She didn't make it, she couldn't pull herself up to get it open.

"At first I meant to help her. To convince her to be quiet, not to tell anyone about the affair or about Mom.

"She laughed at us," Matt continued. "She laughed at me. How was I going to like seeing his father's bastard take his place in their home? Seeing all of them made a laughingstock. She called me stupid, Avery. *Me.* Can you imagine that? And the whole time she's bleeding all over the place. Struggling not to pass out." He made a sound of disgust. "Like she's the one in charge.

"She wouldn't shut up," he went on. "I begged her to. I was crying. She laughed at me...the things she said were so ugly. So...vile.

"So I shut her up. I put my hands over her nose and mouth and pressed and pressed until she didn't say anything anymore."

Avery shuddered, recalling her image of earlier, of Matt choking the life out of her.

"It felt good," he murmured, a small smile tipping the corners of his mouth. "I felt powerful. Unbeatable."

He leaned toward her. "Power, Avery. My hands. I always knew I was special. I saw things, understood things others didn't. Things regular people couldn't. As I watched her die, I knew that I was meant to lead. That I had the power over life and death."

Avery stared at him, mouth dry, heart hammering. Horrified. That summer...they had been together back then. They had seen each other every day—had been physically intimate. She had considered spending her life with him.

She would have sworn she knew everything about him. *She hadn't known him at all.*

She found her voice. It shook. "So my dad knew you—"

"Killed her? No." He shook his head. "Dad found me there. He promised to protect me. To take care of everything. Told me to get out of there, to keep it to myself."

"He never told anyone, did he? Not even Lilah."

He grinned. She found something about the way his lips stretched over his teeth more terrifying than if he had growled

"He was going to save me. That's a hoot, isn't it? He was going to save *me?* But over the years he has served his purpose. In a limited way, he shared my vision."

In a lightning-quick change of mood, his eyes filled with tears. "We could have been a family," he said. "We could have had children together, grown old together."

The thought that she had imagined that very thing, not long ago, made her ill. She hid her true feelings as best she could. "It's not too late, Matt. Let me go. I won't make any trouble, we can be together."

He looked away, then back. "I'm really sorry, Avery. I didn't want this to happen. None of it. But in a conflict one must sacrifice individual wants and needs for the good of the many."

She caught her breath at his meaning. "It's not too late, I can change. I see now. I understand what you're fighting for."

He bent and pressed his mouth to hers in a hard kiss. One that smacked of finality. "It's not about me, Avery. Not about what I feel or what I want. The generals have called for action. They've voted."

"But you're their leader. They'll do what you—"

"I can't take my eyes off the big picture." He cradled her face in his palms. "No matter how much I want to."

"What are you going to do to me? Kill me? The way you killed Elaine St. Claire and Trudy Pruitt?" Her voice quivered. "The way you killed Gwen?"

He didn't deny it. "I don't enjoy the killing. I do it because it's a necessity. Because—"

From the doorway came the soft click of a gun's hammer falling into place. "Off the bed, son."

Matt twisted, hand going to his weapon.

"Try it and you're dead," the older man warned.

"You will be, too." Matt's hand hovered over his weapon. "And poor Avery will lie on this bed and rot."

Buddy's aim didn't waver. "Drop the fucking gun. To the floor. *Now!*"

Matt hesitated, then slid the weapon from his waistband and tossed it to the floor.

"Good boy. Now, off the bed. Hands up." He motioned with the gun. "To the wall."

Matt lifted his hands, climbed off the bed. "Think this through, Dad. Don't make a mistake."

Buddy moved into the room, gun trained on his son. "Hands on the wall." When Matt obeyed, Buddy bent, never talking his gaze from the other man, retrieved the gun and slid it into his waistband.

"It's okay, baby girl," he said, inching toward the bed. "Everything's going to be okay."

He freed Avery's hands, then feet. She saw that his cheeks were wet.

She pulled up her pants, then scrambled into a sitting position. After tying the pieces of T-shirt together, she scrambled off the bed and crossed to stand behind Buddy.

"You have to stop, Matt." Buddy took a step toward his son. "The killing has to stop."

Matt turned, held out a hand to his father, expression pleading. "We're in this together. Everything I've done, I've done for us. The family. The community."

Tears trickled down Buddy's cheeks. "You're ill, son. I should have faced it long ago but I didn't want to see. That night...Sallie Waguespack, I thought I was doing the right thing. But it wasn't right. I've been covering up and making excuses all these years. And these past months, pretending I didn't suspect something was wrong."

"It's not me, Dad. It's her. She won't keep quiet. We have to keep her quiet. To protect the family. She's just like Sallie."

"I didn't know, baby girl," Buddy said, voice heavy with pain. "Not about your daddy. Not about the others.

thought...let myself believe it wasn't happening. That all the deaths were just what they appeared to be."

Matt's expression went soft. "What would you have had me do? Phillip was going to the district attorney. The others were going to back him up. Tell everyone about Sallie and The Seven. I only meant to protect us."

"I know. I'm sorry." He removed his handcuffs from the pouch on his utility belt. "I've got to cuff you."

"Don't do it, Dad." His eyes filled with tears. "Please, don't cuff me."

Avery saw the emotional toll this was taking on the older man. She ached for him—the father having to face the consequences of his mistakes and the terrible truth about his own flesh and blood.

"I've got to son. I'm sorry."

Matt held out his arms. "I'll come quietly then. If you believe this is the right thing, I'll do whatever you say."

"I'll protect you as best I can, Matt. Within the law." Buddy lowered his weapon, crossed to his son.

Matt's gaze flicked to Avery's. In his she saw triumph.

"Buddy!" she cried, seeing the switchblade cupped in Matt's palm. "It's a trick!"

Matt lunged forward, catching his father by surprise. The blade popped out. He buried it in the side of Buddy's neck.

"No!" Avery screamed. A look of surprise crossed the older man's face; he reached up to grab the blade. Matt twisted it, then yanked it out. Blood sprayed.

Buddy looked at his son, mouth working. He took a step. Wobbled, then crashed to the floor.

Avery turned to run. Matt grabbed her around the middle, dragged her to his chest and brought the blade to her throat. She saw that his hand was splattered with blood. His father's blood.

"See, Avery? Weak. Stupid." He gazed down at his father's still-twitching form. "And a traitor as well."

She saw no remorse in his expression. No regret. "You're crazy. A psychotic, murdering son of a bitch!"

"I'm a soldier. I'm fighting for something bigger than you or I or an old man who'd forgotten what was important." He bent and retrieved his father's handcuffs. Wrenching an arm behind her back, Matt cuffed one wrist, then the next.

He turned his emotionless gaze on her. "You have been judged and found guilty, Avery Chauvin. Of crimes against this community. Of attempting to bring an end to a way of life that has existed for a century. The Seven will decide your fate."

CHAPTER 53

Avery fought to keep hysteria at bay as Matt forced her deeper into the bowels of the charred canning factory. The odor, simply unpleasant from the outside, turned foul inside. Overpowering, like the stench of the grave.

Her throat and eyes burned. She saw that parts of the interior, though fire damaged, were still intact. Here and there a wall stood, oddly unmarred. A piece of untouched furniture sat beside a gaping hole in the flooring, as if the flames had been fickle, choosing one but not another.

Matt nudged her forward, gun between her shoulder blades. Obviously, he had spent a good bit of time here. Though the place was as dark as the devil's will, he guided her through the charred landscape without hesitation.

He pressed his mouth to her ear. "We're going up. But watch your step, you wouldn't want to miss your date with my generals."

"Go to hell."

He laughed, the sound delighted. "We're there, don't you think?"

She did, though she wouldn't give him the satisfaction of a response.

They made their way up the fire-ravaged stairs. As they did he murmured directions in her ear, "Step left, skip the next stair, go all the way right."

She stumbled and righted herself, a difficult feat without her arms for balance. He didn't offer a hand and she sensed he enjoyed watching her struggle. That her discomfort amused him.

Finally at the top landing, she could see. A portion of the roof was gone and moonlight spilled through the opening, revealing a rabbit's warren of doors, hallways and half walls.

They stopped in front of a closed door fixed with a padlock. "We're here," he said.

He took his eyes off her as he unlocked the door. She glanced back toward the stairs. She could take her chances, run. But how far would she get before she stumbled, fell through the floor or he shot her in the back? Two steps? A half-dozen?

"Go ahead," he murmured as if reading her thoughts. "Take your chance. As you lay bleeding to death from internal injuries, you'll beg me to finish you off with a bullet."

"Bastard."

"You think so, that's understandable, I suppose." He unfastened the padlock, swung the door open. "But future generations will hold me up as a hero. A visionary."

"Future generations?" she spat. "You'll be reviled, then forgotten as you rot in a cell at Angola. Or the Feliciana Forensic Facility for the Criminally Insane in Jackson."

"Poor Avery," he murmured. "Blind like the others. In you go." He grabbed her arm and shoved her violently through the door. Without her arms to break her fall, she landed on her knees, then pitched forward. Her chin struck the concrete floor.

Matt chuckled as he slammed and locked the door behind her. She managed to get to her feet, ran to the door. She threw herself against it. "Bastard!" she shouted, kicking it. "You won't get away with this!"

"Don't waste your energy, there's no way out."

The whispered advice came from behind her. Avery whirled around. "Gwen?"

"The one and only."

Avery searched the interior, eyes not yet accustomed to the darkness. "Where are you?"

"Here."

She saw her then, on the floor, pressed into the far corner. Avery hurried to her side and knelt beside her. "Thank God, I thought...I thought you—"

"Were dead. I did, too."

Avery saw that she was hurt. The right side of her head was crusted with dried blood, her blond hair matted with it.

Avery pictured the blood on Gwen's bathroom door. He must have knocked her out. "When did he do it?"

"The storm," Gwen whispered. "I awoke, he was there, in my room. I thought he was going to kill me. But he brought me here, instead." Gwen bent and rested her forehead against Avery's. "I prayed you'd come. But not this way."

With the police.

But Matt was the police.

"We're going to get out of this." Avery frowned. "He said

The Seven would decide my fate. I think they're meeting here tonight."

"He's going to kill us, isn't he?"

He or one of his generals. "Let's not think about that now." Avery moved her gaze over the room's walls. Judging by its size and the shelving along one wall, the room had been a storage closet. "Have you looked for a way out?"

"There's none."

"You're sure?"

"Yes." Gwen's voice broke. "I don't want to die, Avery. Not now. Not like this."

"We will if we give up, that's for sure. Can you stand?"

She nodded and, using the wall for leverage, inched to her feet.

"Good," Avery murmured. "Our only shot may be trying to overpower him when he comes for us. One of us can rush him while the other goes for his gun. Or runs."

It sounded lame even to Avery's own ears. Overpower Matt? Her arms were secured behind her back and Gwen was almost too weak to stand. But she refused to give up. Refused to die without a fight.

"All right," Gwen said, though her voice quavered. "You tell me what to do and I'll do it."

A rapping sound caught her attention. Avery stilled, listening. It had come from behind the shelves.

The sound came again and Avery realized what it was. Matt, calling The Seven to order.

"Come on, Gwen. Let's see if we can move these shelves."

The shelves were metal and heavy, though not bolted in place. Together they eased one unit away from the wall, Gwen using her arms, Avery her body as a wedge.

They managed to create a space big enough to slip behind.

Once behind the shelves Avery found herself, absurdly, reassured by the small, tight space. It felt safe. Like a womb.

Like a child's perfect hiding place. The one where nobody could ever find her.

As a kid she'd had several. She'd been good at hide-and-seek, had had the ability to slip into nooks and crannies and remain still and silent for long periods of time. Sometimes so long, the person who was "It" gave up.

Even as she wondered if Matt would give up if she was quiet enough, still enough, she acknowledged the stupidity of the thought.

Gwen followed her in. They both put an ear to the wall.

Matt was talking. He named her and Gwen as defendants, listing their crime as treason. He called for questions and comments from his generals.

Who were they? Avery wondered, straining to hear. Old friends of hers? Neighbors? Someone she had gone to school with? Would they feel any loyalty to her? Any regret?

Gwen met Avery's eyes and shook her head, indicating she couldn't hear what they were saying.

Avery couldn't either and pressed her ear closer, straining. Matt murmured a reply she couldn't make out, then paused as if listening to another question. She heard him mention his father, voice breaking.

Buddy had not been a part of this inner circle, that had become clear to her back at the cabin. That he had not been party to their extremist ideology had also become obvious. But still, she wondered, would they simply sit back and condone his murder?

If their silence was an indication, they accepted their leader's actions without question. Who were they? she wondered again, disbelieving. Who had he convinced to join his insane cause?

Avery jumped as Matt once again called for order. "A vote, then," he said loudly. "Guilty or not?"

Silence ensued. The seconds ticked past. Avery realized

that she was sweating. Holding her breath though she had no real doubt what the outcome would be.

"It's unanimous then," Matt boomed. "The Seven find Gwen Lancaster and Avery Chauvin guilty of treason."

CHAPTER 54

Hunter paced the length of the windowless interrogation room. Two CSPD uniforms had retrieved him from his home that morning. His father had requested they pick him up, they'd said. Bring him in for questioning. Cooperation hadn't been an option.

They had dumped him here, told him Buddy would be in shortly and left. That had been nearly twelve hours ago.

He stopped. Moved his gaze over the room. A single table made out of wood. Three chairs, also made out of wood. They'd been around a while and bore the evidence of each of those years in the form of cigarette burns, chips, scratches and carvings. He continued his inspection. No fire alarm. No phone. Reinforced door, locked from the outside.

This was wrong. He had known it was wrong this morning. Had sensed a setup.

The officers had said it was about Avery. She was in trouble. Buddy had said to tell him that.

So he had come. And left Avery on the outside. Alone.

He pivoted and crossed to the door. "This is bullshit!" he shouted and pounded on it. "Charge me or release me!"

He pressed his ear to the door, swearing at the silence on the other side. He had to get out of here. Avery was in trouble.

He pounded again. "Hey! I gotta take a piss. Unless you want a mess to clean up, you better get your asses to this doo—"

The door swung open. A pimply-faced officer with big ears stood on the other side, Cherry directly behind him.

"Cherry?" Hunter said, surprised. "What are you doing here?"

"Dad needs our help. Inside," she ordered the officer, nudging him forward.

With a gun, Hunter saw. A big gun. A .357 Magnum, long barrel. He returned his gaze to hers. "You really know how to use that?"

"I'm not dignifying *that* with an answer." She grabbed his arm with her free hand. "Come on, we need to get out of here."

She pulled him through the door, slamming and locking it behind him. She pocketed the key. The officer began pounding on the door.

"What the hell's going on?"

"We'll talk in the car." She hurried forward. "Sammy there was manning the station alone, but the patrol guys are going to be checking in soon."

"What time is it?"

"Eight-thirty."

"I've been locked in that room since early this morning, I need to use the john."

"Make it quick."

She was waiting for him when he emerged moments later. Wordlessly, they went to her car and climbed in. His mother sat in the back seat. She had been crying: her eyes were red and swollen, her skin blotchy.

She looked on the verge of falling apart.

He glanced over at Cherry. "Somebody better start talking, fast."

Cherry pulled away from the curb. "Dad said if we didn't hear from him by eight, to come and get you."

"Get me? What was I doing there?"

"He wanted you to be somewhere safe. He figured locked up at the CSPD was about as safe as he could find."

"What the hell are you talking about?"

"Matt's the one," she said. "And he's got Avery."

CHAPTER 55

"The one?" Hunter moved his gaze between the two women. "What do you mean?"

"The one who killed Elaine St. Claire and Trudy Pruitt." Cherry's voice shook. "He killed Avery's dad as well. At least, we think so. Dad told us before he went after them."

"I didn't know," Lilah whispered. "I thought...all these years, I thought I killed Sallie Waguespack. And now—" her voice broke "—and now I wish I had."

"It's not your fault," Cherry murmured. "You didn't know what he had become, neither did I."

Hunter struggled to come to grips with what they were saying. Struggled not to give in to panic. "What's he become? I don't understand. What did you have to do with Sallie Waguespack's death?"

Lilah met his eyes. "I better start at the beginning."

She told him about his father's affair, Buddy's lover's pregnancy. About going there to plead for her husband.

And about what followed.

"Until tonight, I thought I'd killed her. Buddy...he kept that secret from everyone."

"When people began dying, he reasoned the deaths away," Cherry interjected. "He accepted them as accidents and suicides because...the other was unthinkable.

"Avery forced him to reevaluate," his sister continued. "Her questions. Her unshaking belief that her father hadn't killed himself. Then, when Trudy Pruitt was killed—"

"He was forced to admit what was happening," Hunter said. "That everybody involved in the cover-up had croaked. Except him."

"And Matt." She flexed her fingers on the steering wheel. "He knew for certain today, when he learned about Avery's mother's journals. That's why Matt set the house on fire."

"Slow down. Avery's mother journaled—"

"Every day since she was a teenager," Lilah said. "Avery called about them the other day, wondering if I had any idea what happened to her mother's journals. I mentioned the call to Matt."

Cherry took over. "Avery found the journals. Her mother wrote about The Seven. And Sallie Waguespack being pregnant. Somehow Matt found out and torched her house to destroy the evidence. And now, Gwen Lancaster's missing."

Lilah moaned. "That poor girl. I tried to warn her. I called...was going to meet her...try to convince her to go. Buddy overheard me...he kept me from..."

She dissolved into tears. Hunter looked at his sister, who continued. "Dad checked out Gwen's room, found evidence that indicated foul play. He figured Matt...that if he had her, had her cell phone. That he'd retrieved Avery's messages."

And now he had Avery. Hunter went cold with fear.

Silence fell between them. Cherry broke it. "There's one more thing, Hunter. Matt knew about you and Avery. That you had become...romantically involved. He told Dad. He was in a rage. A cold rage. Dad was afraid for your life."

"So he locked me up."

"Yes. Until he could figure out what to do about Matt. How to protect him."

"Protect Matt!" Hunter exploded. "He's a murderer! He should be behind—"

"He's his son!" she returned, cutting him off. "What was he supposed to do?"

"The right thing, dammit! People are dying!"

She fell silent. Lilah sobbed quietly. Hunter fought to get a grip on his emotions.

"What about Tom Lancaster?" he asked. "And McDougal? How do they fit in?"

"Dad didn't know for sure." She turned onto Highway 421. "Matt was obsessed with The Seven, which could explain Lancaster. But McDougal, he didn't see a connection. There might be none."

"What about Avery?" he demanded. "Where is she?"

"Dad thought the old hunting cabin. The one Grandpa used."

"You've called the authorities, right?" They didn't respond and he made a sound of disbelief. "The sheriff? State police?"

"Buddy said we should keep it to ourselves. Keep it in the family."

"Son of a bitch! Cell phone?" They shook their heads. "How many guns do we have?"

"Just the one."

"Shit. Fucking great."

"But Buddy's here," Lilah said. "He'll—"

"He's in trouble. Or he would have called long before now."

The women couldn't argue with that and they rode the rest of the way in silence. They turned onto No Name Road and moments later the access road that led to the cabin.

They reached it. Two cars sat out front—an unmarked sedan with a dome light on the dash and a CSPD cruiser.

"They're here," Cherry said, voice quivering. She looked at Hunter. "What now?"

He thought a moment. "One of us should stay here, stand watch. Keep the car running in case we need to get out fast. Honk if there's trouble."

Hunter and Cherry looked at their mother then at each other, silently acknowledging she was incapable of the responsibility.

"I'll do it," Cherry offered. "Mom can stay with me. You take the gun."

Lilah tried to argue; Hunter cut her off. "If there's gunfire, I don't want to be worrying about you instead of my own hide. Got that?"

"I agree," Cherry said quickly. "Absolutely."

She handed him the gun, butt out. "You know how to use one of these?"

He took it from her. Like his sister and brother, he had grown up handling a gun. It had been a while but some things you never forgot. He checked the chamber, saw that it carried a full round and snapped it shut. "Yeah," he answered. "Point and shoot."

He climbed out of the car. Weapon out, he crossed to the other vehicles and peered inside. They were empty.

He glanced back at Cherry and pointed toward the cabin. She nodded.

He made his way cautiously toward it. A traditional raised cabin, he climbed the three stairs to the front porch. Half-rotted, they creaked under his weight.

The cabin door was unlocked. He eased it open, then slipped through, pausing to listen.

It was silent. Too silent. The hair on his arms stood up. He inched across the main room, toward the kitchen. It proved empty. The small window above the sink stood open; flies buzzed around an overflowing garbage pail. He saw dirty dishes in the sink.

The cabin might be empty now, but it had been occupied recently. He swiveled, crossed to the bathroom. He found it as deserted as the other two rooms.

Only the bedroom remained. He made his way there, heart pounding. The first thing he saw was the bed, the nylon rope attached to the foot posts, the length coiled on the bare mattress.

Someone had been tied to the bed. The blood rushed from his head. He laid a hand on the doorjamb for support.

Not someone. Avery.

He shifted his gaze and froze. Peeking out from the far side of the bed was the toe of a boot. One he recognized—alligator hide, a deep green-hued black.

His father had worn those boots, made from the hide of a gator he'd caught, for twenty years.

Denial rose in him as he made his way into the room. Around the bed. His father lay facedown in a pool of blood, head twisted at an unnatural angle.

Hunter stumbled backward. Pivoting, he ran back through the cabin and onto the porch. His sister sat behind the wheel of the vehicle, door open. "Cherry," he shouted. "Use Dad's radio, get an ambulance. Tell them an officer's down."

She leaped out of the vehicle, alarmed. "An officer? Dad or—"

"Do it, Cherry. Now!"

Without waiting for her to comply, he returned to his father's side. He knelt beside him, felt for a pulse. Found none.

At a sound from behind him, Hunter turned. Lilah stood

in the doorway, eyes on her husband. A cry spilled past her lips, high and terrible.

Cherry came up behind her and stopped dead. "Dad?" The color drained from her face. "No." She shook her head. "No!"

Lilah made a move to go to her husband's side. Hunter jumped to his feet, caught her in his arms, stopping her. She fought him, pummeling him with her fists, cursing him.

He held her until the fight drained out of her. He met his sister's eyes. "Help me get her outside."

Cherry blinked. Her mouth moved. He saw that she trembled. She looked a hairbreadth from falling apart herself.

"Cherry," he said softly, "it's a crime scene. The police—"

"We know who did it." Her voice shook. "Matt killed Dad."

His brother. His twin. A murderer capable of killing his own father.

And he had Avery.

"Where are they?" he demanded. "Where's Matt taken Avery?"

His sister looked startled by his question. Confused. "I don't... know. I don't—"

"Think, Cherry! They're on foot. Where could he have taken her?"

She shook her head, her gaze riveted to their father's still form. "There's nothing out here. Nothing. Just the—"

"Canning factory," he finished for her. "Cherry, help Mom to the car. Then call the sheriff's department and the state police. I'm going after them."

CHAPTER 56

Avery and Gwen waited by the door. Nearly an hour had passed since The Seven had found them guilty. They had made their plan; feeble though it was, it was their only chance.

"What's he waiting for?" Gwen whispered. "Where did he go?"

Avery didn't know. She had expected him to come for them right away. Perhaps he was preparing, setting the rest of his plan in motion, putting the final pieces in place. She shook her head, indicating she didn't know.

"Do you really think this will work?"

Avery heard the note of panic in her friend's voice. The edge of hysteria. *Seven against two. What hope did they have?*

"What do we have to lose by fighting?" Avery countered

softly, more, she realized, to convince herself than Gwen. "They're going to kill us anyway."

From the other side of the door came the sound of footsteps. Avery looked at Gwen. The other woman's face had gone white. Avery nodded and moved to the far right side of the door. She took her place directly in front of it, though far enough back not to get hit when it swung open.

They heard him at the door, unlocking the padlock. Avery tensed, readying herself. The door eased open. She held her breath, waiting for the right moment. Praying it would come.

It did. Avery lunged at him, using her body as a battering ram, aiming for his middle. As she had prayed she would, she caught him by surprise, nailing him square in the chest.

Matt stumbled. The gun flew from his hand. She heard it clatter to the floor.

"Run, Gwen!" she screamed. "Run!"

Her friend did, her feet pounding against flooring as she tried to race for the stairs. Avery expected to hear the others coming to Matt's aid, expected him to call for them; neither occurred. She wondered if they had left the building, had left the dirty work to him.

Avery regained her balance and threw herself at him again, this time knocking him down. He landed with a grunt of pain.

"Bitch!" he screamed, slamming his fist into her face. Her head snapped to the side, the explosion of pain unimaginable. She couldn't catch her breath, realized she was sobbing.

He straddled her, put his hands to her throat and squeezed. She fought as best she could, twisting, turning. Flailing her legs. Her lungs burned. Pinpricks of light danced in front of her eyes.

Let Gwen make it, she prayed. Please, God, let her make it.

From below came the sound of something crashing to the floor. Matt eased his grip, straightening. Twisting as if to listen.

"What's going on?" Matt shouted. "Blue? Hawk? Have you got her?"

Silence answered. He released her, jumped to his feet, listening. Air rushed into her lungs. Avery sucked it greedily in, gasping, coughing.

"Hawk!" he screamed. "Talk to me."

Avery rolled onto her side, caught sight of his gun. A half-dozen feet to her right, just behind where he stood. Tears stung her eyes. Cuffed, what could she do?

A whimper slipped past her lips. Matt turned. Looked down. He saw the weapon, saw her gaze upon it.

He looked at her and smiled. "Is that what you're wanting?" He bent and retrieved it. "It's just not fair, is it?"

She dragged herself to her feet, took a step, stumbled and went down. Still, she didn't give up. She inched herself along the floor like a worm. Unwilling to say die.

He laughed as he followed, taunting her. "Gutsy little Avery," he mocked. "I admire you. I do. Such a shame it didn't work out between us, with my brains and your determination we would have made awesome babies."

He stepped over her, then in front, blocking her path. She lifted her head, met his gaze defiantly.

His teeth gleamed bright white against the dark shadow of his face. He lifted the gun. "End of the road, sweetheart."

CHAPTER 57

Avery came to and found herself bound to a chair. Her head throbbed. Something liquid rolled down her cheek, then splashed onto her collarbone. Blood, she realized as what had happened came rushing back—Matt, the butt of his gun.

She was still alive. Why?

Her eyelids flickered up. Her vision swam. She made out a table, figures grouped around it, sitting in silence.

Seven figures. Matt and his generals.

One of them turned and stood. Matt. He picked up the lantern at his feet. A camping lantern, turned down low.

He lifted the lantern, brought it close to her face. She squinted against the feeble light, right eye burning. Bloody. He smiled. "You've looked better, Avery."

A retort sprang to her lips, it came out a garbled croak.

His smile widened. "In case you're wondering, Gwen didn't make it."

A moan escaped her, one of grief and denial. Of hopelessness.

He turned toward the table. "Gentlemen," he said, holding the lantern high, "I have good news. Ms. Chauvin has returned to the world of the living. For how long is up to her."

The soft glow from the lantern fell across the men sitting closest to her. Avery blinked, vision going in and out of focus. *It couldn't be.* She traveled her gaze, straining to make out the figures at the far side of the table.

Cadavers. In various stages of decomposition.

A scream rose to her throat. She looked at Matt, waiting for the punch line.

It didn't come.

"Avery, I think you know Karl Wright." He indicated a badly decomposed body directly across from her. "General Hawk to us."

Karl Wright. Matt's oldest friend. The man Cherry loved. The man she had planned to marry.

But he'd moved to California. He'd up and left Cypress Springs without a word to anyone but Matt.

Anyone but Matt.

A sound of horror slipped past her lips. *Matt had killed his best friend.*

Avery shifted her gaze to the cadaver to the right of Karl Less decayed than all but one of the others, the corpse appeared to be that of a young man. A Tulane University sweatshirt, logo partially obliterated by blood, hung on the decomposing form.

"Tom Lancaster," Matt offered, seeing the direction of her gaze.

They found his car, abandoned. His body was never recovered.

Avery moved her gaze again, this time to the other nearly intact corpse.

Luke McDougal missing, his car found empty.

That first day, she remembered, down at the CSPD, the missing persons flyers on the bulletin board. There'd been several.

Too many for such a small community.

Avery's teeth began to chatter. She fought falling apart. *Matt inducted members to The Seven through murder.*

She found her voice, though it trembled. "Tell me how it went down, Matt? Did you just happen upon Luke McDougal, broken down by the side of the road and offer him a ride? Is that when you decided to recruit him?"

Matt smiled. "Not on sight, of course, but soon after. One of the generals had recently defected, I needed a replacement. I offered him a lift and discovered we saw eye to eye, General Blue and I."

Defected? How did that happen? she wondered, hysteria rising up in her. When the bodies became so badly decayed, they could no longer stay propped up in a chair? When they disagreed too vocally with their leader?

Matt looked at the corpse that had been Luke McDougal and smiled. He paused as if listening to something the man said, then nodded and chuckled. "I completely agree, Blue."

Avery watched the exchange, the full realization of what was happening hitting her. Matt believed them to be alive. He heard them speak, vote for life or death, offer comment.

He returned his attention to her. "General Lancaster was more difficult to convince. At first, he didn't understand our cause. But I could see that he wanted to. And that he could be a wonderful addition to our number.

"In the end he believed wholeheartedly in our cause. When I explained the group's vision, there were actually tears in his eyes. He begged to be a member. He pledged his total allegiance to us. Gwen would be proud of him, he has become a tremendous asset."

Avery pictured Tom Lancaster begging. Willing to pledge and promise anything to save his own life.

Having no idea that becoming one of The Seven equaled a death sentence.

"And of course, you know Sal." Matt turned, smiled and nodded toward another corpse. "Our member of the old guard."

"Sal?" she repeated. "But he was...shot. Waked and buried—"

In a closed-casket ceremony.

Matt switched the bodies. But with whose?

"General Wings," Matt murmured. "He faked his own death, Avery. He decided to devote his life to our cause." He turned and smiled at the half-decapitated corpse. "I've been grateful for his dedication. His wisdom has proved invaluable to us."

Matt arched his eyebrows, then nodded and turned back to her. "Just so you know, he has been your champion through this whole thing."

"Who's buried in Sal's casket, Matt? Just some poor slob you picked up?"

"A worthless, homeless drunk. A nobody whose life I gave purpose, Avery." He motioned to the final two figures at the table. "Generals Beauregarde and Starr, outsiders who were drawn to our cause."

"So this is it?" she said, voice shaking. "The infamous Seven. A group formed," she paused to rest, "to counter the crime wave in Cypress Springs resorts to murder. Seems to me, the cure is worse than the illness."

"You sound just like your bleeding-heart father. He ruined the original Seven, reduced them to a system of little more than tattletales and whiners. I wasn't about to allow him to ruin us."

"How did you do it?" she asked. "How did you kill him?"

"It was easy. Phillip wanted to believe me a malleable weakling who would bend to his wishes—the way Buddy and the other Seven had all those years ago. So he underestimated me."

"He trusted you. You knew that. You knew he would open the door to you in the middle of the night. Even though he was groggy from the sleep medication he'd taken before going to bed."

She narrowed her eyes, hate rising up in her, nearly choking her. "Medication you knew he was taking. How? He never locked the doors... Did you go through his medicine cabinet?"

Matt laughed, the sound pleased. "It didn't take even that much effort. Heard it from Earl over at Friendly Drugs."

One of The Seven's network of eyes and ears.

Matt glanced at his generals, then back at her, expression disgusted. "I see what you're thinking. That Earl had no right discussing your dad's private business. People like you never understand. Private business is a nice euphemism for immoral self-indulgence. Human weakness. Such self-indulgences corrupt. They spread from citizen to citizen like a disease, until a whole community is infected."

She fought to keep her tone controlled. It wavered slightly and she cursed the telltale show of vulnerability. "And as not only sheriff but son of Cypress Springs's chief of police, you heard everything, didn't you? It was easy. You knew every citizen's every step? You made it your business to know."

He puffed up, proud. "Mail. Medications. Police calls. What they ate and drank, when they had sex."

"And Elaine St. Claire's weakness?"

"Promiscuity."

She died of internal injuries. An artificial phallus had been inserted into her, it had torn her to shreds.

"What about Pete Trimble?"

"Poor old Pete. Chronic D.W.I. He refused to give up the bottle, refused our efforts to get him into a program."

Drunk, he was crushed by his own tractor.

She thought of the kids who had overdosed, the one into auto-eroticism who had hung himself. Of Trudy Pruitt's tongue cut out of her head. Avery understood. "Their mode of death mirrored their crime."

He inclined his head. "They died as they lived, a fitting punishment, we believe."

Bile rose in her throat. She swallowed past it. "And my dad? The others involved in the Waguespack cover-up? What were their crimes? Knowing too much?"

"Treason," he said softly, regretfully. "They began to talk amongst themselves. Began speculating about Sallie Waguespack's death and the way their good friend Chief Stevens told them it went down. They began speculating that someone had retooled The Seven. Before they could be silenced, they went to Phillip."

"Retooled The Seven?"

"We are the elite, Avery. The best, operating in secret, willing to do whatever necessary to protect what we hold dear. What the original group was supposed to be."

"Cypress Springs's very own version of Delta Force?"

"I like that analogy."

"You would. And the group of seven men at Dad's wake and funeral, who were they?"

"Nobody. Nothing but an unfortunate number of men standing together."

She processed that, then went on. "My dad figured out what was going on?"

"To a degree. But he made a mistake, he thought Dad was the one. Behind it all. He had decided to go to the D.A. about Sallie Waguespack. He went to Lilah first, to prepare her."

"And she told you."

"Yes." He smiled. "After his suicide, she assumed that he

hadn't been able to do it and had killed himself instead. She understood guilt, you see. How it ate at a person."

Avery curled her hands into fists, cuffed behind her back. "So you woke him up in the middle of the night. He opened the door and you immobilized him with a stun gun."

A look of surprise, then respect, crossed his features.

"You had everything ready in the garage," she continued. "The diesel fuel, the syphoning hose."

He inclined his head. "It's not easy to get away with murder these days, forensic science being what it is. The tazer leaves no detectable mark but offered me the time I needed to carry out my plan. That he was groggy from the sleep medication helped."

Tears choked her. She struggled to force the image of her father from her mind, force out what she imagined were his last thoughts. The way he had suffered.

"How did you know?" he asked. "What made you so certain?"

"The slipper," she said. "It was wrong."

"It fell off when I carried him to the garage. A detail I shouldn't have ignored."

"Even without the slipper, I wouldn't have bought the story. My father valued life too much to take his own." She paused. "Unlike you, Matt. Someone disagrees with your politics and you kill them. You're no better than a terrorist."

Color flooded his face. She had angered him. His voice took on the tone of a teacher speaking to a rebellious student. "In a war, Avery, there are only two sides. The good guys and the bad guys. For a cause or against it. They were against us. So they were eliminated."

"And who's been watching you, Matt? Who's been keeping tabs on your activities? Making certain your behavior doesn't veer outside the appropriate?"

She had caught him off guard, she saw by his momentary confusion. "My generals, of course," he answered. "I'm not all-powerful, Avery. I don't want to be. Absolute power corrupts absolutely."

"They're dead, Matt. Your generals are rotting corpses. No one is monitoring you, and if they do, you kill them in the name of the cause."

"You're not helping yourself, Avery. We reevaluated and were prepared to make you an offer. Of an opportunity. Join us. You're smart, courageous. Use those qualities to better the world."

The children's story *Peter Pan* popped into her head, the place in the tale when Captain Hook offers to spare Wendy's and the Lost Boys' lives—*if* they join him, become pirates. Avery had always admired Wendy's bravery. The courage of her convictions in the face of certain death.

Wendy hadn't died. Peter had saved her.

There would be no Peter Pan to save her, Avery acknowledged. Only the courage of her own convictions.

"You have three minutes to decide, Avery." He set his watch. "And the clock's ticking."

CHAPTER 58

Hunter crouched behind the partially gutted wall, sweating, listening to Avery and his brother. *Three minutes. Shit.*

He squeezed his eyes shut in an attempt to force out what lay in the adjoining room. Cadavers. Murder victims.

Ones his brother thought were alive.

If he focused on that, he would be defeated. If he focused on what his brother had become, he would be defeated. If he allowed himself to dwell for even a minute on Avery strapped to that chair, he would lose it.

He needed a plan. Reasoning with Matt was out, that had become obvious. What was left? Charge in, guns blazing?

It sucked. It was all he had.

"Time's up, Avery. Are you with us or against us?"

Hunter tensed, waiting for the right moment, praying for it.

"Please, Matt," she begged, "listen to me. You're in the grip of some sort of paranoid delusion. There is no war. Your generals are corpses, victims of murder. You need a doctor, Matt. A psychiatri—"

He cut her off. "So be it."

Hunter launched himself into the doorway, .357 out, aimed at his brother's chest. "Drop the fucking gun, Matt! Now!"

Avery cried out his name. He didn't look at her, didn't take his eyes off his brother.

"The cavalry arrives," Matt said, then laughed, moving neither his gaze nor his aim from Avery. "In a last-ditch effort to save his true love's life."

"Drop the gun."

"And why would I do that?"

"Because it's over, Matt. Because I'll kill you if you don't."

"And I'll kill her. So I guess it comes down to who's the better, faster shot."

"I'll take my chances."

"That's your right, of course. But how are you going to feel watching her die? Always wondering if maybe, just maybe, you could have saved her."

He was right, dammit. Every minute could be the difference between life and death. Avery's life or death.

Hunter's gaze flicked to Avery, then back. Matt saw it and laughed. "Reading you like a book, bro. Always could."

"Cherry and Mom are going for the police."

"Bullshit."

"They know you killed Dad."

"You're grasping at straws." His features tightened. "Let's stop fucking around. Lay down your piece."

"You won't get away with this," Hunter warned. "Too many people have died. After this, you won't be able to cover your tracks."

"I already have, actually. You're crazy, Hunter. On a murder spree. You hate Cypress Springs and your family. Everybody knows that. Tom Lancaster's Tulane student ID will be found in your apartment. As will Luke McDougal's class ring and Elaine St. Claire's crucifix. You discovered Elaine St. Claire's body and McDougal's vehicle. Your voice is on Trudy Pruitt's recorder...thank you, Avery, for alerting me to that. And to the paper with Gwen Lancaster's name and room number on it."

Fury rose up in Hunter. "Everything nice and neat, just like Sallie Waguespack."

"Just like," he agreed.

Hunter tried another tack. "I just realized why you went into law enforcement, Matt. So you can hide behind your gun. The badge."

"If that helps, believe it."

Hunter laughed. "You never fought unless you knew you could win. And you can't win without the gun."

"I could always take you. I still can."

"Prove it, then. You throw yours, I'll throw mine. Just you and me, no hardware. Winner takes all."

Matt narrowed his eyes. "You think you can take me, bro? You think you're that tough?"

Hunter bent, laid his gun on the floor. He took a step toward his brother, hands up. "I'm willing to give it a try. How about you?" When his brother hesitated, Hunter clucked his tongue. "Or when it really counts, are you just a yellow-belly chicken?"

The tension crackled between the two men. Matt glanced at his silent generals as if for their okay, then nodded. "All right." He crossed to the table and laid his gun on top, then faced his brother, a smile tugging at the corners of his mouth. "Come on, let's dance."

They advanced, circled each other, both waiting for the right moment to throw the first punch.

"Don't chicken out now, Matt," Hunter taunted. "Hate to have the cops arrive and see you're both yellow *and* crazy."

Matt lunged. Only then did Hunter see the knife. Avery did, too, and screamed a warning. Hunter threw himself to the right. But not fast enough to avoid contact with the blade. Matt buried it in his shoulder, lost his grip on it and his footing.

A shot rang out. They both went down.

Cherry stood in the doorway, a shotgun to her shoulder. She had it aimed at them, though even at this distance Hunter saw how unsteady she was. That she was crying.

Hunter silently swore. She hadn't gone for the police. Secrets had won again.

Matt's expression went slack with surprise. "Cherry?" he said.

"You killed Dad, Matt." Her voice broke. "How could you do that? You shouldn't have done it."

"Dad turned on us, Cherry. He turned on the family. He sided with an outsider against us. He had to be eliminated."

She shook her head. "Family sticks together. They always stick together."

"That's right," Matt murmured, tone coaxing. "I taught you that." He got to his feet slowly. "You're my baby sister, but you always took care of us, of all of us."

He took a step toward her and she took a step back. "Don't come any closer."

"He's trying to trick you," Hunter said to Cherry, following Matt to his feet. He grabbed the knife and yanked it out of his shoulder. He went momentarily light-headed at the pain, at the whoosh of blood spurting from the wound. "He's out of his mind. Look around—"

"Don't listen to him." Matt's expression became pleading. "He's not one of us. He left us, remember? He broke our hearts."

"I remember," she whispered. "The two of you fought that

night. Something about school. And Avery. It always scared me when you got like that, Matt. When you got like...this."

Her gaze flicked to Hunter. "Dad was working. Mom had been on edge all day, then had gone out. I went to bed but couldn't sleep. I was scared. It felt like...everything was falling apart."

She drew in a broken breath. "That's when I heard Mom. She was crying. I crept out of bed...I saw the blood. Heard everything. About Dad...his girlfriend...that Mom had...hurt her. Matt told her not to worry, that everything would be all right. I saw him get his car keys.

"I sneaked outside, climbed into the bed of his pickup. Pulled the tarp over me. There...I sneaked in after Matt. I saw what he did."

She'd only been ten at the time, Hunter thought. He imagined her terror. Her confusion. If only he had been home, she could have come to him.

It all made sense now. The way they had withdrawn from him, shut him out. They'd all been a part of the same secret club.

It all made sense.

"I kept quiet." She shifted her gaze from Matt to Hunter. "I wanted to tell you, but I was afraid. I didn't know what would happen if I did. They'd split us up. Send Mom and Matt away."

Hunter ached for his little sister, alone with her terrible secret. Frightened and vulnerable. No wonder she had been so angry with him.

"I'm so sorry, Cherry," he said. "I didn't know I didn't know you needed me. If I had, I would have been there for you. I promise."

"But he wasn't," Matt said sharply. "He abandoned you. Abandoned us. While I stayed. What I did was for all of us."

Cherry turned the shotgun on Hunter. "It wasn't his fault, Hunter. Don't be angry with him. I was there, I saw. He was pushed into doing what he—" Her words cracked on a sob. "That woman was awful. A cheap whore who had stolen my daddy.

"When Avery came back, I was so happy. I thought, if she and Matt got back together, if she would just stay and love him, everything would be okay. The way it was before. But now...I wish she'd stayed away. I wish you had both stayed away. You've ruined everything!"

"It's not true," Hunter said quickly. "Nothing's been okay since that night. And nothing could be. You've been living a lie, all of—"

"It's all their fault," Matt cut him off. "They're outsiders. Traitors to the family. To Cypress Springs."

"Ask him about Karl," Avery called out, voice high, desperate-sounding. "He didn't go to California! He's here, in this room. Ask Matt if it's true."

Cherry looked at Matt. "What's she talking about?"

"I need you, sis. You take care of me. Of all of us. Don't abandon me now, not when I need you most."

"He killed him, Cherry!" Avery struggled against her restraints. "Like he's going to kill all of us. Ask him about Karl and the cause."

"Matt?" Cherry whispered, voice shaking.

"He put the cause before love, sis." Matt held a hand out. "You can't hold that against him. The cause is everything."

Matt glanced toward the table as if for verbal confirmation from the other man. Cherry followed his gaze to the circle of the silent, a look of horror crossing her face. She took a step back, her hold on the shotgun slipping.

"No." She shook her head; her voice rose. "No!"

Matt used the moment and leaped forward. Hunter shouted a warning and dived for his own gun. Avery screamed.

A blast shattered the quiet. Hunter turned in time to see the force of the shot propel his twin backward. Matt seemed to hang suspended a moment, standing yet weightless, before he went down.

The shotgun slipped to the floor. Sobbing, Cherry fell to her knees beside their brother.

CHAPTER 59

In the next instant the room filled with the sound of police sirens. Minutes later, a contingent from both the state police and the West Feliciana Parish Sheriff's Department stormed the factory.

Avery had learned that Lilah and Cherry had called the state police; it had taken some convincing, but they had agreed to send a trooper to the cabin. While waiting, Cherry had remembered that her father carried a shotgun in the trunk of his cruiser. She had retrieved it and gone to back up Hunter.

If she hadn't, Avery knew, she and Hunter would be dead. Like Gwen. Buddy. Her father. And so many others.

Avery and Hunter had been transported by ambulance to West Feliciana Parish Hospital in St. Francisville. She'd re quired fifty stitches to her face and head. A CT scan had revealed neither blood nor swelling to her brain, but the doctor had decided to keep her overnight for observation anyway. Considering, she had come through relatively unscathed.

Unscathed. Tears flooded her eyes. She would never be the same. She hurt deep down, in a way no amount of pain medication, no doctor's skill, could relieve.

"Hello, gorgeous."

Avery turned her head toward the doorway. The pillowcase crackled with the movement. Hunter stood there, fully dressed, smiling at her. "What are you doing up?" she asked.

"Been released."

"No fair." She winced, thinking of Matt's knife sinking into Hunter's shoulder. "Are you all right?"

"Just a flesh wound. Real ugly, lots of blood. No real damage."

"That's not what I meant."

"I know."

His gaze held hers. In his she saw reflected the horror of the past hours. Hers, she knew, reflected the same.

"The police talk to you, too?" he asked.

"Yes." She had been questioned by both the state police and sheriff's department. She had answered questions until her words had begun to slur from fatigue and pain medication. The doctor had stepped in then, firmly insisting that the rest of their questions would have to wait until morning.

"You want to go for a ride?"

"A ride? Are you busting me out of here?"

"That's an idea, but no." He disappeared; a moment later reappearing pushing a wheelchair. "I've got a surprise for you."

He rolled the chair to her bedside. After locking the chair's wheels, he lowered the bed rail and helped her into the seat.

"You know I don't need this thing."

"I know no such thing. And quit being so independent. It was hard enough getting the nurse to approve this trip."

She looked up at him, ready to argue. He stopped her by pressing a quick kiss to her mouth.

Hunter rolled her out of the room and down the hall, toward the nurses' station. The night nurse smiled as they went past. They moved by the empty lounge, with its drink and snack machines, then stopped at a patient's room. The door stood ajar.

Hunter nudged it the rest of the way open and wheeled her in. A woman lay in the bed. Dangerously pale, hooked up to monitors and by IV to all manner of bags and drips.

But alive. She was alive.

"Gwen?" Avery said, her voice a husky croak.

The woman's eyelids fluttered up. She looked their way, staring blankly at Avery a moment, then her mouth curved into a weak smile. "Avery? Is that...really—"

"Yes, it is." Tears of joy flooding her eyes, Avery climbed out of the chair and moved slowly to the other woman's side. She caught her hand, curled her fingers tightly around Gwen's. "Matt told me you were dead."

"He thought...I was," she managed to say.

Her voice fading in and out, she recounted being shot, going down, then managing to get to her feet and making it to the road. There, she collapsed.

Gwen's eyes closed and Avery looked up at Hunter. "How did you know she was here?"

"I heard the emergency room nurses talking about the woman brought in with a gunshot wound. Apparently, a motorist found her unconscious by the side of Highway 421 and brought her to the emergency room. They rushed her into surgery."

"A motorist?" Avery questioned Hunter. "Out there, at that time of night?"

"A miracle," Hunter murmured. "The hand of God at work."

Her thoughts exactly. She turned back to the other woman and found Gwen looking at her, eyes wet. "Is Matt, is he—"

"Dead?" She nodded, bent and kissed her forehead. "I'm so glad you're alive."

"That's enough, you two," the nurse said quietly from the doorway behind them. "Ms. Lancaster needs her rest."

"Can't I stay?" Avery asked, not wanting to let go of Gwen's hand, afraid, irrationally, to leave her. "I promise to be quiet."

"You need your rest as well." The woman's expression softened with understanding. "She'll be here in the morning, Ms. Chauvin."

In the morning, Avery thought. No three words had ever sounded so sweet.

EPILOGUE

Monday, March 31, 2003
9:00 a.m.

Avery watched as Hunter shut the U-Haul trailer's door and snapped the padlock. He gave the lock a yank to make certain it was secure and turned toward her. "Ready?"

She nodded and climbed into the Blazer. Gwen had headed back to New Orleans two days ago, anxious to leave Cypress Springs behind as quickly as possible. Avery missed her already. She and Hunter had promised to stop and visit on their way through the city.

They couldn't stay long, though. Her editor expected her at her desk, bright and early the following Monday morning. She had a story to write. A big one.

Sarah whined. She sat in the back; her pups crated in the

cargo area. "It's okay, girl," Avery murmured, scratching her behind the ears. "No worries."

Avery turned forward in her seat. As she did she caught a glimpse of herself in the side mirror and cringed.

"I saw that," Hunter murmured, checking traffic and pulling away from the curb.

"I look like Frankenstein's bride. And my stitches itch."

"I think you look beautiful."

"Haven't you heard? Blind men aren't supposed to drive."

He laughed softly, reached across the console and squeezed her hand. "I'm really glad you're alive."

She curled her fingers around his, a sudden, surprising knot of tears in her throat.

They turned onto Main Street, easing past town square and its startlingly white gazebo. People stopped, looked their way. A few waved, others simply stared.

Everybody had heard the story. One bigger than the Waguespack murder. Reactions had ranged between shock, disbelief, anger. Many had expressed their sorrow, their confusion. How could this have happened? And here? Cypress Springs was such a nice place to live. A number of citizens had been brought in, questioned by the FBI about The Seven, past and present. No arrests had been made as yet.

Cypress Springs was in mourning. For its dead. For a way of life that had been built upon a lie. Change was coming.

Avery caught sight of Rauche's Dry Goods, at the corner of Main and First Streets. "Hunter, pull over."

He did, drawing the SUV to a stop in front of the store. As she had four weeks ago, she climbed out and gazed down Main Street, at the quaint buildings and lovely town square, the unchanged storefronts.

It looked wrong, she thought. An anachronism. Time marched on—life progressed, for better or worse. All else was unnatural. Like an elixir that promised eternal youth.

Hunter came to stand beside her. "You okay?"

She glanced up at him. "Going to be. How about you?"

"I keep waking up at night wondering why him and not me? We were brothers. Twins. It could have just as easily been me."

The police shrinks believed that Matt had suffered from delusional disorder, a psychotic disorder related to paranoid schizophrenia with a major difference: the afflicted person was able to function normally *except* when acting on their delusions.

Complete and accurate diagnosis was difficult, the psychiatrist had explained, because they could now only be privy to the aftermath of Matt's delusions. The shrink had speculated that the incident with Sallie Waguespack had planted the seed that later provided a dramatic outlet for his illness. Ideology that had fed into his delusions had also been reinforced by his family, the community and his chosen profession.

Avery found Hunter's hand, curled her fingers around his. "No," she murmured, "it couldn't have been you."

He met her eyes, his filled with gratitude. "All those years feeling abandoned by my family. Shut out. Nobody said anything, but I felt it. After that night, everything was changed. Now I know why."

She rubbed her cheek against his shoulder, hurting for him. "I'm so sorry, Hunter."

"Me, too. About everything but you." He met her eyes. "I'm going to help Cherry and Mom through this," he said, tone fierce. "I'm going to be there for them."

The district attorney had decided to waive charges against either of them. Because of Cherry's age at the time of the murder, because of the time that had passed, lack of evidence and the fact the real murderer was dead.

Even so, Cherry had acknowledged that she and Lila couldn't stay in Cypress Springs. They'd already put the house up for sale, already seen a Realtor in Baton Rouge. Cherr had decided to open that catering business she and her mother had been talking about for so long.

They were going to emerge intact, Avery thought. Finally free of the secrets that had been slowly killing them.

"I know how my novel ends," Hunter murmured suddenly.

"You do?"

"Not the specifics. Just that my hero's going to be okay. And that's good enough."

She understood. She felt the same. She didn't know for certain what the future held, she only knew she was ready to face it. Starting now.

Standing on tiptoe, she kissed him. "What do you say we get the hell out of here?"

Acknowledgments

I've become a bit of a fixture at a local coffeehouse, sitting in a quiet corner, feverishly tapping away at my laptop keyboard. I share this with you because many of the people who I intend to acknowledge here, I connected with while sitting in that corner. A friendlier bunch you won't find; I think of us as "Cheers" for the caffeine set.

I continue to be humbled and amazed by the enthusiasm and generosity shown me by the various professionals I approach for information, hat in hand. Thank you one and all. Without your generous contribution of time, personal insights and professional expertise, *In Silence* would have been much more difficult to bring to life. I hope you are pleased with the way I used the fruits of your labor.

I begin with my fellow coffee addicts: Renee Plauché and Linda Daley, who blew me away with their generosity toward me, a total stranger. Renee, a University of New Orleans graduate student in counseling, overheard me discussing avenues to research mental illness and offered help. She went so far as to lend me her textbooks, including the DSM IV, (that I now know to be), *the* clinician's guide to diagnosis. Likewise Linda, hearing that I was tackling the subject of suicide, offered to share the story of her own father's suicide. With a master's in psychology and counseling, she was able to give me both professional and personal insights into suicide and its emotional aftermath. Captains Ralph and Patrick Juneau, Jefferson Parish Fire Department, for the crash course on all things fire: from arson to turn-out gear. Stephanie Otto, nursing student, Charity School of Nursing, for on-the-spot medical terminology and procedure information.

From beyond the coffeehouse walls: Michael D. Defatta, chief deputy coroner, St. Tammany Parish Coroner's Office, for taking time out of his busy schedule to meet and answer my questions about the role of the coroner in criminal investigations and forensic pathology, particularly as it applies to burn victims. Frank Jordan, director of Emergency Medical Services, Mandeville Fire District #4, for his explanation of death by fire. Mrs. Barbara Gould, wife of West Feliciana Parish coroner Dr. Alfred Gould, for the long chat and great quote. Pat McLaughlin, friend, fellow author and journalist, for giving me a glimpse into the mind of the investigative reporter. Tom Mincher, owner of America Hunter Gun and Archery Shop, for information about hunting rifles and ammunition.

Thanks to my friends and colleagues who not only make the journey a smooth one, but a heck of a lot of fun as well. The amazing Dianne Moggy and the entire MIRA crew. My assistant, Rajean Schulze. My agent, Evan Marshall. My publicist, Lori Ames.

To my family, without whose love and support the days would be long, indeed.

And last but unquestionably first, thanks to my God, the one responsible for it all.

Turn the page for a thrilling extract from

RED

by
Erica Spindler

*Available soon
from MIRA® Books*

Red
by
Erica Spindler

Bend, Missisippi
1984

No place in the world smelled quite like the Mississippi Delta in July. Overripe, like fruit left too long in the sun. Pungent, like a drunk's breath at the edge of a whiskey binge. Like sweat.

And it smelled of dirt. Sometimes so dry it coated the mouth and throat, but most times so wet it permeated everything, even the skin. Becky Lynn Lee lifted her hair off the back of her neck, sticky with a combination of perspiration and dust from the unpaved road. Most folks around Bend didn't think much about the smell of things, but she did. She fantasized about a place scented of exotic flowers and rare perfumes, a beautiful world populated by people wearing fine, silky fabrics and welcoming smiles.

She knew that place existed; she'd seen it in the magazines she pored over whenever she could, the ones the women at Opal's snickered at her interest in, the ones her father raged at her about.

None of that mattered. She had promised herself that someday, somehow, she would live in that world.

Becky Lynn picked her way across the railroad tracks used not only to ship rice, cotton and soybeans out of Bend, but to divide the good side of town from the bad, the respectable folk from the poor white trash.

She was poor white trash. The label had hurt, way back the first time she'd heard herself referred to by those words; it still hurt, when she thought about it. And she thought about it a lot. That's the kind of town Bend was.

Becky Lynn lifted her face to the flat blue sky, squinting against the harsh light, wishing for cloud cover to temper the heat. *Poor white trash*. Becky Lynn had been three the first time she'd realized she was different, that she and her family were *less than*; she still remembered the moment vividly. It had been a day like this one, hot and blue. She'd been standing in line at the market with her mother and her brother, Randy. Becky Lynn remembered clinging to her brother's hand and looking down at her feet, bare and dirty from their walk into town, then, lifting her gaze to find the other mothers' eyes upon them, their stares filled with a combination of pity and loathing. In that moment, she'd realized that there were others in the world and that they judged. She had felt strange, self-conscious. For the first time in her young life, she'd felt vulnerable. She had wanted to hide behind her mother's legs, had wanted her mother to tell the other women to stop looking at them that way.

Becky Lynn supposed that had been back before her daddy had turned really mean, back when she thought her mother to be an angel with magical, protective powers.

But maybe she had already realized that her

mother wasn't an angel, that her mother didn't have the ability—or the strength—to make everything all right, because she hadn't said anything. And the women had kept staring, and Becky Lynn had kept on feeling as if she had done something wrong, something ugly and bad.

Most times now, the respectable folks, even the customers she shampooed down at Opal's Cut 'n' Curl, looked right through her. Oh, while she shampooed them they talked to her, but mostly because they liked to hear the sound of themselves and because they knew she was paid to listen and agree with them—something their husbands almost never did. But when they came face-to-face with her on the street, they looked right through her. She wasn't sure if they pretended they didn't see her because she was one of Randall Lee's brood or if they truly didn't recognize her 'cause they'd never really looked at her in the first place.

But whichever, she'd decided being invisible suited her just fine. In fact, she preferred it that way. She felt less different when she was invisible. She felt...safer.

Becky Lynn took a deep breath as she cleared the railroad tracks. The air always seemed a bit sweeter this side of the tracks, the breeze a degree or two cooler. She stepped up her pace, hoping to get to the shop early enough to spend a few minutes looking over the *Bazaar* that had come the day before.

Up ahead, Becky Lynn caught sight of a fire-engine red pickup truck barreling past the square, coming in her direction, a cloud of dust in its wake. Tommy Fischer and his jock gang, she thought, her heart beginning to rap against the wall of her chest. Probably on their way to pick up her brother. She darted a glance to either side of the road, to the fields thick with cotton, knowing there was no place to hide but searching for one, anyway. Sighing, she folded her arms across her middle, jerked her chin up and kept on walking.

The group of boys began to howl the moment they saw her. "Hey, Becky Lynn," one of the teenagers called, "how about a date?" In response, the other three boys began to hoot in amusement. "Yeah, looking good, Becky Lynn. My dad's Labrador retriever's been lonely lately."

That brought a fresh burst of amusement from the boys, and she tightened her fingers into fists, but kept walking, never glancing their way. Even if it killed her, she wouldn't give them the satisfaction of knowing how much their comments hurt.

Tommy slowed the truck more, swerving to the road's dusty shoulder. "Hey, baby…check it out." From the corner of her eyes she saw the two boys in the back of the pickup unzip their flies and pull out their penises. "If you weren't so ugly," taunted Ricky, the meanest of the group, "I'd even let you touch it. You'd like that, wouldn't you, baby?"

The urge to run, as fast and far as she could, screamed through her. She fought the urge back, compressing her lips to keep from making a sound of revulsion and fear.

Ricky leaned over the side of the truck and made a lewd grab for her, forcing her to step off the shoulder and into the muddy field. Tommy gunned the engine and tore off, spitting up gravel and dirt, the boys' laughter ringing in her ears.

Becky Lynn ran then, the gravel road biting the bottoms of her feet through her tattered sneakers, the bile of panic nearly choking her. She ran until she reached the safety of Bend's town square.

Drawing in deep, shuddering breaths, Becky Lynn leaned against the outside wall of the Five and Dime, the corner building on the railroad side of the square. She pressed the flat of her hand to her pitching stomach and squeezed her eyes shut. Sweat beaded her upper lip and underarms; it trickled between her shoulder blades. The image of the boys, holding their penises and taunting her, filled her head, and her stomach rolled again. They'd never done anything like that before. She was used to their taunts, their obscene suggestions, but not...this.

Today they'd scared her.

Becky Lynn hugged herself hard. She was safe, she told herself. It was getting toward the end of summer, the boys were bored and got off on seeing her squirm. In a month they would start football practice and wouldn't have the time or energy to seek her out.

Then she would have to face their jeers at school.

She fought against the tears that flooded her eyes, fought against the despair that filled every other part of her. She had nobody. Not one person in Bend she could turn to for help or support. Alone. She was alone.

Even as fatigue and hopelessness clutched at her, Becky Lynn curled her fingers into fists. She wouldn't give up like her mother had. She wouldn't. And someday, she promised herself, she would show Tommy and Ricky and everybody else in this two-bit town. She didn't know how, but someday they would wish they'd been nice to her.

ERICA SPINDLER

Only one man can uncover the secrets and sins
of three generations of Pierron women.
Tempted by the forbidden...

FORBIDDEN FRUIT

ERICA SPINDLER

A killer who will stop at nothing until...

ALL FALL DOWN